Liars

A Licking Thicket Novel

Lucy Lennox

May Archer

Cover Photo: Wander Aguiar
Editing: One Love Editing
Beta Reading: Leslie Copeland, Shay Haude, Chad Williams
Proofreading: Lori Parks and Victoria Rothenberg

Liars

Parrish Partridge's True Facts:

There's nothing hotter than a tall, gruff, bewildered, tattooed mountain of a man cuddling a sweet, orphaned baby, so you can tell yourself that you'll resist him...

But that's a lie.

And when that man asks you to do him a favor and pretend to be his very temporary, very fake fiance to help him get custody of that adorable baby, you can pretend you know better than to say yes...

But that's a lie, too.

And when you actually get to know your kind, strong, pullet-loving prince of a fiance, and all his crazy, lovable, meddling neighbors, you can tell yourself you're not really falling for Diesel Church and the town of Licking Thicket...

But that might be the biggest lie of all.

Chapter One

Parrish

Mid-August

"THERE YOU GO, handsome. One license for the new Partridge Pit flagship store." Brandi, the pretty, forty-something redhead in the planning office at the county courthouse gave me a flirty wink as she handed over my manila folder. "Can't believe you came all the way out here again, all by yourself, all dressed up in your fancy shirt and tie." She bit her lip. "I'd think y'all have other folks who can do this sort of thing?"

"Er." I glanced down at my plain gray shirt and black tie and wondered when they'd become fancy. "Yes, ma'am. I suppose. But my uncle Beau says if you're gonna do a thing, you should do it right, and he taught me everything I know about business." I smiled politely. "You might say the flagship store is kind of my baby."

This was not a lie. My uncle, General Beauregard T. Partridge, the founder and CEO of Partridge Pit BBQ, with its one hundred restaurants and a bestselling line of sauces, really did say that all the time. And he really had put me in charge of the new flagship location we planned to open too, which was why I'd moved my few belongings out of my furnished studio in Nashville and into the Jackson King Bed and Breakfast in tiny Licking Thicket.

But Uncle Beau also said things like, "For the love of Larry, Parrish Partridge, get you an assistant!" and "Work won't love you back, son," and "Barbecued chicken won't keep a man warm at night, Parrish," and more recently, "Heaven's sakes, boy, if you don't find yourself a fella, your aunt Marnie's gonna do it for you, and then Lord help you both," so maybe it was sort of dishonest to blame him for my need to dive headfirst into this project. Truth was, Uncle Beau and I had been thinking about this store for months, but I hadn't been a hundred percent committed until I'd gotten a stupid Facebook message a couple of weeks back and immediately decided my life would be simpler if I left Nashville temporarily—or permanently—and begged Beau to send me down here.

Leaving the state would have been preferable, or possibly signing up for one of those one-way Mars expedition things, but I couldn't do that to Beau and Marnie.

"And here I thought maybe you were coming out here especially to see me." Brandi pouted and leaned toward me over the counter. "I was hoping you'd invite me to the new restaurant. I was hoping you'd *buy me some tater tots*." She wiggled her eyebrows.

I blinked. Buy her tater tots? Was that some sort of straight-person euphemism for something?

I decided I didn't want to know.

"Er... No." I said it gently but also firmly, because honesty was always the best policy. "I mean, I do like you, Brandi. Very much. You've been a huge help in getting all this done. But, um..."

"Oh, Parrish." She laughed merrily and waved a dismissive hand. "You're a sweetheart. But you need a wife to take care of you, honey, and that's the truth."

I shook my head. I didn't bother addressing the large gay elephant between us, but I did dart a look at the calendar on the counter to confirm that I hadn't somehow traveled back in time. "No, ma'am. Truth of the matter is, I'm not the type who'll ever get married. To anyone."

Not anymore.

And if she didn't believe me, she could ask my ex-fiancé. Or his new girlfriend.

Brandi set a hand on her hip, instantly morphing from pouty seductress to fond older sister. "That's what they all say! You're young yet. Wait and see."

"Sure," I agreed, letting her pat my hand as we said goodbye, "I'll wait and see." But I knew in my heart there were some mistakes I'd never be tempted to make twice, not when I was totally content with my life the way it was. I had a great job, a supportive family, and a kick-ass vintage red Mustang. What more could I want?

There was a line at the elevator, so I trotted down the back staircase clutching my folder. Four o'clock on a Friday wasn't the best time to organize a meeting, but if I talked to the contractors tonight, I could—

A bloodcurdling wail echoed through the little stairwell, and I froze for a second, then rushed headlong down the steps two at a time, skidding to a halt halfway down the staircase when I found the source of the sound—a wriggling baby in a fuzzy pink sweater who was literally crying herself purple, possibly because the giant, tattooed mountain of a man holding her was growling down at her with a ferocious scowl on his face.

I gripped my folder tightly and opened my mouth to

protest even though the guy was twice my size, when the baby's cries quieted for half a second and I caught that the man wasn't growling. He was... singing?

"Something... sunshine. Only sunshine. You make me happy. Something gray? Christ." He heaved a frustrated sigh. "Marigold, you've got to stop now. You've made your point. Be reasonable, baby girl."

Oh. Oh, good gravy. That changed everything.

I caught my breath and stared. The man looked like he'd been torn off the stage at a rock concert, transported to Nowhere, Tennessee, and stuffed into the outfit I once wore to a middle school dance. There was no other explanation for a guy with overlong brown-blond hair, graceful black inked scrolls emerging from the collar of his wrinkled, blue button-down shirt, shiny Dockers that clung to his tree-trunk thighs, and black steel-toed boots to have appeared in this stairwell. I sure as heck hadn't seen any other guys in this neck of the woods who were so unapologetically themselves.

And if that weren't enough to pierce my heart, the kidlet in his arms was gorgeous, despite her tears and wiggling. She had a head full of dark curls, way more than should have been possible for a baby her age, which I'd peg at somewhere around nine months—somewhere past the shriveled-potato stage of early infancy but not nearly at the terrifying walking age.

The baby wailed again, and the giant looked genuinely panicked. He held her flat across his outstretched forearms, like he was carrying a box of pizza or helping her learn the backstroke, and he bent his knees in a kind of next-level Oompa Loompa jig in time to his stammered singing. A pink-and-white striped tote bag sat on the floor next to the wall.

"Work with me, Marigold, okay? You're not hungry, 'cause you just drank ten gallons of formula. You're not stinky..." He lifted the kid gingerly. "Not stinky," he confirmed in a deep, raspy voice that did things to me. "Are you having an existential crisis? Is that a thing kids do? Do you need alone time? Are your lips chapped? Do you hate my cologne?"

The baby fussed harder, flailing her tiny feet. The man groaned, and I belatedly noticed one of those pacifier stuffed animal things lying on the floor by the giant's boot.

I scurried down the stairs and picked it up. "I think she might be looking for this," I said, holding it aloft. It was a gray-and-white polka-dotted chicken with a green sucker on the end.

The guy shut his eyes and shook his head. "Ah, *shit.*"

His eyes popped open in shock as he realized what he'd said, and he looked from me to the kid guiltily. "Fuck, forget I said that," he muttered.

His eyes widened further. "Goddamn it all."

I snickered. "Maybe quit while you're ahead?"

"Yeah." He sighed again and reached for the pacifier, only to do an awkward shuffle when he realized he couldn't hold it and the baby simultaneously.

"You could hold her up," I suggested. "Babies that age like to see stuff, and it'll help her digest if she's just eaten. Also maybe chill out on the squats." I motioned toward his knees. "Your thighs are plenty shapely already."

He lifted one eyebrow but ignored my comment—thank the stars, since I couldn't think of a single logical reason why I'd said that aloud. "You need to support the baby's head," he recited. "That's, like, the one thing I know."

"She's old enough to be held up," I promised. "Try."

He tilted her upright, clasping her to his chest with two

hands, and the baby's cries calmed to hiccups almost immediately.

"Ha! Sweet." His eyes met mine over the baby's head. "Worked."

I smiled back because his smile was so infectious I couldn't help it. "It did."

"Thanks, man. Could you, uh, pop that thing back in her mouth? Then we'll be good to go, I think."

"This?" I stared down at the pacifier in horror. "It was on the floor. Don't you have another?"

"What? No! She only came with the one!" He looked sideways at the pink tote bag like it had betrayed him.

"Ah. Well, the trouble with kids is that some accessories are sold separately," I said sympathetically.

The guy was back to panicked again, and the baby reacted, fussing more loudly.

"Okay, here's what we're going to do," I soothed. "We'll go into the washroom and I'll clean this off for you. Alright?"

"Yeah. Yes. That would be amazing. Thank you. Then we'll be..."

The baby coughed once, hardly any warning at all, then erupted like a volcano spewing ten gallons of formula right down the center of the man's shirt.

"...all set," the guy finished weakly.

I didn't bother asking if he had a change of shirt. "Bathroom," I instructed, grabbing the tote bag and taking charge of the situation. "Now."

We emerged from the stairwell into the lobby by the courtrooms, and a red-faced guy with a beer gut and a too-tight suit rushed over. "Took you long enough. It's almost time for... oh, sweet Fanny Adams." His eyes widened. "What'd you do to your shirt?"

The giant rolled his eyes and kept walking. "I'll be right back, Stewie."

"Hurry up," he called.

I marched our little parade across the lobby and into the bathroom. I set the pacifier and my papers on the hand dryer, wet a paper towel for the guy, and turned to take the baby. "I'll hold her while you mop up."

I sort of expected him to hand the baby over gladly, but instead he shook his head. "Nah, man. *She's* perfectly clean. And she just conked out." He was right. The baby was snuggled up with her head pillowed on his pec—lucky her— and one chubby fist clutching his shirt pocket.

Gah. I steeled myself against the melty feeling in my stomach and did what any concerned citizen would do.

"Fine, then. I'll just, um... I'll clean you off." I motioned toward him with the towel.

I wasn't sure which was more surprising, that I said those words out loud, or that the man actually stood silently and let me approach him, but I reminded myself it was definitely only because this was an emergency-type situation, not for any other reason. I definitely did not notice how hard and warm his chest was under the shirt, or the musky sandalwood scent of his cologne. He very definitely did not stare down at me and hold his breath the entire time I touched him. There was one hundred percent not any kind of weird humming vibration between the two of us, and I was definitely not thinking thoughts about how far down his tattoos went, or whether he'd like it if I traced them with my tongue—

And Jesus, maybe Aunt Marnie was right about me finding a fella, 'cause if I was finding myself getting hot by *any* situation that involved baby puke, it had been entirely too long since I got laid.

I cleared my throat and took a step back to assess him. "Pretty good," I croaked.

"Yeah?" His voice was so hopeful. His smile was so sweet.

"No," I said truthfully. "It's still a mess." I loosened my tie, pulled the loop off my head, and motioned for him to bend down. "This will cover the worst of it, I think. Come on," I coaxed when he hesitated. "I've been told it's fancy."

The guy looked at me like I was crazy, but he bent so I could put the tie over his head and tighten it into place around his neck anyway. His breath was warm on my face.

I straightened his collar and gave him an approving pat, then snatched my hand away before I did something really stupid like fondle the man.

"You'll do." I grabbed the pacifier and brought it to the sink to wash it under hot water. "Crisis averted, friend."

"Thanks to you." His deep voice was pitched whisper-low for the sake of the baby. "So, how d'you know so much about kids?"

I paused in my cleaning and clenched my hands into fists. Direct hit, and the guy hadn't even known he was aiming. But I forced my voice to be easy as I replied, "Just things I've picked up here and there."

He snorted. "Your here and there must be different than mine."

"Maybe so," I conceded with a chuckle. I met his eyes in the mirror. "She's adorable."

He nodded down at the baby in his arms. "Like her mama," he said ruefully. "Temperament like her mama too."

Her mama. The baby's mother. Right. As in, the third leg of this family trio.

Somehow, this seemed a painfully important reminder. I'd been way too close to asking the tattooed giant out for *tater tots* like a big, broody, gay Brandi who didn't know better, when I did.

I. Knew. Better.

The giant was probably straight, almost definitely involved with someone, and I was not in the market for anything he was selling anyway, as I'd explained to Brandi minutes before.

"But her mama was cut out for this parenting gig," the giant continued in a pitiful sigh-grumble. "I'm clearly not."

"Oh, please," I scoffed, annoyed at myself and, therefore, annoyed at him. I cleaned the pacifier with such vicious thoroughness, germs would be afraid to land on this thing for the rest of eternity. "No one's cut out for it. You just *do* it."

"Pardon?" The man sounded genuinely bewildered by this concept, and I felt sorry for his baby mama, I really did, because the guy might be very nice to look at... and talk to... and, okay, *smell*... but he was clearly clueless about his parental responsibilities if he wanted a shiny gold star for doing basic childcare.

For *ineptly* doing basic childcare, at that.

"I said, nobody is born to parent," I repeated clearly. "There's no degree you're meant to have or some qualification you weren't born with. You just have to be a decent, responsible human who cares more about the kid than about your own whims, or stupid social-climbing ambitions, or..." I cut myself off and swallowed hard. "You just have to decide your kid deserves the best of everything, and not be too proud to try, even if you mess up. End of."

Wow. Could I sound more like a self-righteous, lecturing asshole? The poor father was having a hard time, and here I was, implying he was selfish, mostly because I was cranky. Way to go, Parrish.

The giant blinked at me in the mirror, stunned. "That—"

The bathroom door pushed open with a squeak, and the red-faced man from the hallway poked his head in. "It's time, dude. Now." He slipped back out.

The giant stared at me in the mirror another second, then grabbed the pink striped bag off the floor and bolted out.

I closed my eyes, dropped my chin to my chest, and took a deep breath.

Ah, well. Not the first time I'd been a little *too* forthright with someone, and it wouldn't be the last. I shut off the water and grabbed a paper towel to dry off the pacifier. I felt bad, but really this was a sign that I needed to stay focused on...

The pacifier? *Crap.*

I grabbed my folder and ran out into the hall in time to see the giant disappear into a courtroom. I charged after him, only to be pulled up short when a bailiff with a clipboard stepped in front of me, blocking the door.

"Sorry, sir," the bailiff said. "This is family court. Proceedings are closed to the public. Unless you're representing one of the parties seeking custody of the child?"

Seeking custody?

"What?" I whispered.

"Are you one of the parties seeking custody of the orphaned child, Marigold Church?" he repeated impatiently. "Are you representing the grandparents or the uncle?"

I shook my head mutely.

No, I was the poor sap who'd misjudged the situation completely. I hadn't just been a trifle rude back in the bathroom. I'd been incredibly insensitive to a guy seeking custody of an orphan.

———

"Beau wants to open a restaurant with a market area," Brooks Johnson, the guy who handled all of Partridge Pit's marketing, explained to his boyfriend, Mal. "Where local artisans can show their craft."

"That's amazing," Mal said. "What a cool idea."

I blinked out of my daze for about the eleventy billionth time in two days and forced myself to pay attention to my surroundings. I was standing in Malachi Forrester's display tent at Licking Thicket's annual Lickin'—a festival devoted to all things bovine, because why not?—surrounded by my uncle Beau and aunt Marnie, Brooks, Mal, and Brooks's business partner, Paul Siegel, watching Uncle Beau make faces at baby Beau, Paul's infant son. I was fairly confident I hadn't contributed anything to the conversation in quite some time, which was probably why Uncle Beau was giving me not-so-subtle looks of concern. It wasn't like me to be so distracted, but I couldn't seem to help it. I was pretty sure less than 50 percent of my brain had been present and accounted for at any time over the weekend.

I'd trudged out of the courthouse Friday, so consumed by planning my epic apology—should I send the guy flowers? A singing telegram? A new car?—that I'd gotten halfway home before it dawned on me how tricky apologizing would be when I didn't know the man's name or even where he lived in the county. What little information I did have either wasn't helpful—"I'm looking for a tall guy with light brown hair and tattoos. Two eyes. One nose with a mouth just below. Have you seen him?"—or, like the baby's name, seemed creepy and wrong to google.

But, because I was me, of course I couldn't let the incident go either. The man had seen me at my know-it-all worst, and I couldn't say why it bothered me so much that he'd have a negative opinion of me, but it did. The desire to find him and explain myself had swelled all out of proportion, and I couldn't seem to focus on real stuff—important stuff, like my job—until I did it.

So, I'd spent the last couple of days looking for the tattooed man's face in every store and coffee shop to no avail. I'd even debated asking my friendly landlady at the bed-and-breakfast if she knew him, since she seemed to be acquainted with everyone between here and Nashville, but I'd held back because I didn't want to confess *why* I wanted to find the guy.

It was starting to get ridiculous.

I cleared my throat and turned toward Mal.

"I hadn't seen much of your work before today other than the tables at the restaurants, but I love it," I offered kinda lamely, "I could use a piece like this for my office." I picked up a random cow sculpture from the table of artwork for sale, but when I actually looked at it, I grinned. It *was* kind of adorable. It was even wearing a tiny football jersey.

Mal's eyes widened, and he rushed toward me with his hands outstretched.

"Oh, no, wait! Not that one!"

I instinctively took a step back and collided with something behind me—something so huge, that for a second I thought the tent had come down on me. It wasn't until it started talking that I realized I'd knocked over a person.

Jeez. *Definitely* less than half my brain present and accounted for.

"Shit," the guy said. "Sorry, man." He pushed to his feet and held out a hand.

"Nah, don't even worry," I said, letting him help me up and brush halfheartedly at the dust on the back of my shirt. "It was totally my—"

I broke off the second I saw the guy's face and stared at him in shock. It was the man from the courthouse—same golden-brown hair, same gorgeous tattoos, same stunning eyes—and he looked almost as horrified as I felt.

"I—" I began, ready to launch into my apology right then and there, but before I could utter another syllable, the man turned on his heel and left. Clearly, he didn't want to hear another word out of my mouth, and I couldn't really blame him.

The next few minutes were kind of a blur—I knocked over a bunch of shit at Mal's table, I kept replaying the look on the man's face, and I very definitely didn't make eye contact with anyone, 'cause I knew they'd all ask me what was wrong. Instead, I waited as long as I could, then made my escape from the booth and started looking for a particular head bobbing a foot above the crowd.

Of course, as soon as I started looking for him again, the guy had disappeared. I plowed through the throng of people anyway.

"Parrish, son, are you alright?" Uncle Beau hurried to catch up to me, his cane hitting the ground with every other step.

"Yes. Sure. Perfectly perfect. Why do you ask?" I said brightly, like I hadn't acted like a total idiot. "Just give me a minute to check something out, alright? Then we'll get some biscuits and we can talk about staffing for the store!"

Beau grabbed my elbow and yanked me to a stop. "We already went over the staffing, remember? When you picked Marnie 'n' me up in Nashville this morning? Your aunt asked if you'd heard the news about Payne, and you said yes, and I asked how you were feelin' about that, and you said you were perfectly perfect. And then you launched into a whole spiel about staffing, followed by you recounting all the new thingamajibbers you installed on that jalopy you've got parked out in the lot, and somehow that explanation took *exactly* as long as the ride to the Thicket, so I couldn't ask you any more questions about your reaction to Payne being a giant, enormous jerk."

"Convenient how that worked out."

"Wasn't it, though?" He looped his arm through mine. "A little too convenient. So, help your old uncle around for just a minute, why don't you, since Marnie's off looking at the craft stalls. I ain't as young and spry as I used to be."

I snorted and relented, though I kept my eye out for tattooed mountains. "You? The man who was jogging after me a minute ago and dandling Paul's baby on his lap a few minutes before that?"

"I'm just plain worn out by it all," he claimed, but the twinkle in his eyes said differently.

We walked among the stalls for a minute in silence, watching the crowd of giggling children and coffee-sipping parents—of note, none of the children were adorable, dark-curled babies, and all of the parents were of average size.

"Parrish," Beau complained. "This is the part where you're supposed to spill all your sad secrets to your favorite uncle, boy. You're missing your cue."

I laughed. "Me? Secrets? You've got the wrong nephew. I'm an open book, Uncle Beau. And I'm happy as a clam. Never been better."

"I believe you believe that," he said wryly. "Alright, then. If you won't come clean, our stroll's gonna become an inquisition, and just you remember you brought this on yourself." He cleared his throat. "What's been going on with you the last couple days, Parrish? You've been jumpy and distracted."

"What? No. I'm—"

"My knees might be frail, but my eyes aren't."

I winced. I hadn't thought my distraction was interfering with my work, but apparently I was wrong. "I'm sorry, Uncle Beau. I'll work harder. Promise."

"Parrish," he sighed. "If Licking Thicket were the point I was trying to make, you'd be in Outer Mongolia right now, missing it entirely."

"Huh?"

He sighed. "What happened back in Malachi's tent?"

"Oh, that." I cleared my throat. "I was super clumsy and knocked into—"

"Into Diesel Church, who looked at you like you were the ghost of Christmas past, present, and future all rolled into one? Yep, I saw. What I don't know is why he looked at you like that, or why you turned red and looked like someone had kicked your puppy."

I stopped dead in the path. "Wait, you know that man? The tall one with the tattoos?"

"Diesel," he repeated. "'Course I know him. He's a friend of Malachi's. Helped him source some of the pieces for the restaurants."

My heart beat faster. "And his... his child?"

"Child?" Beau frowned. "Nah. You're barking up the wrong tree. Diesel lives alone. Been to his place over at the junkyard a time or two, and it's not real child-friendly—"

"You've been to his house?" I screeched. I'd low-key considered hiring a private detective to find the guy, and all along Uncle Beau knew him?

"The question is, Parrish, how do *you* know him?"

"I don't!" I insisted. "Didn't even know his name. But I ran into him once before, and I was... I was rude," I admitted.

"You were?" Beau shook his head, as astonished as if I'd told him I could fly. "But you're never rude."

I laughed. "I think you have too much faith in me, Uncle Beau."

"I think I have just the right amount of faith in you, son." He patted my arm comfortingly. "That's how I know that whatever misunderstanding you and Diesel might've had, you'll set it right."

I chewed my lip and nodded. "I'll have to apologize."

"Sure enough, and do him a favor to make up for it, if you can. And maybe bring him a casserole."

"A casserole?" I eyed him skeptically. Not a car? Not a telegram? "Really? For Diesel?"

"Trust me, Parrish." Beau nodded sagely. "No one's ever gone wrong with an apology casserole."

Chapter Two

Diesel

It wasn't so much that Stewie wasn't a good person. He was. The guy had agreed to help me out for not much more than a promise of free parts for his broken-down washer and dryer. But when the guy advertised his legal practice on the back of a bathroom stall door at the tractor supply store, it didn't necessarily mean he was all that great a lawyer either.

"I'm just sayin', Diesel, that this doesn't look good, man. You know," Stewie said, flapping his hand around to encompass the old house, the salvage yard, and my old beat-up truck. A few of the chickens had gotten past the fence and were wandering around looking for treats. "All this won't exactly impress the caseworker as much as the Kensingtons' mansion and racing stables will, and Judge Merriman didn't seem too enthusiastic about the results of your initial home visit from last week. If the Kensingtons' attorney hadn't made that comment about being a Vols fan, and if Merriman hadn't been a proud Alabama alum—*Roll Tide!*— we might be having a very different conversation right now. If you don't ace the next inspection—and I'm talking A-plus-plus, where the caseworker puts a shiny gold star *and* a smiley face at the top of the paper—there's not gonna be much we can do. I've looked at the court schedule for your hearing date next month, and you're not getting Merriman again."

I ran a hand through my hair in frustration. You might think it was weird to put my faith in a man who measured success based on smiley faces at the top of a paper, and you'd be right. But beggars couldn't be choosers.

Besides, it wasn't like he was telling me anything I didn't already know. "The caseworker who came out before was barely here ten minutes. She took one look at the yard and at me"—I motioned to my very visible tattoos—"and made up her mind before she stepped inside the door. I can't help how I live, Stewie. It's not like I have millions of dollars like the Kensingtons. But I will love this baby more than they ever could, and we both know it."

He held up a hand. "Now, that remains to be seen. Brenda and Hunt seem enamored with her, same as you. But they don't have the blood connection, and that's what we're going to emphasize. It ain't gonna be easy, though. The next caseworker they send will be somebody new, so you're gonna have a clean slate. We need to use that to our advantage. I made a punch list of things you need to work on to make yourself the best candidate possible."

I nodded. "Alright."

He reached into a faded red backpack that looked like he'd probably dragged it through Licking Thicket High a decade ago and was still using it to this day. When he pulled out a crumpled-up piece of notebook paper with handwritten notes on it, I started to really worry.

"You sure you have an actual law degree?" I asked for the third time.

Stewie sighed. "Yes. I told you I did. But I also told you

that I do real estate closings, not this family shit, alright? However… you really did us a solid last year when you took Phil's spot on the mound at the championship game, and that's the kind of loyalty the Nine Inch Males don't forget."

"You really need a new team name," I muttered, remembering the softball game where the only redeeming part of the day had been all the beer Stewie and his friends had bought me after I'd pitched a no-hitter. The day had brought back memories of Aunt Birdie teaching me how to throw snowballs at a makeshift target she'd painted on the side of the tractor shed the first winter I was in the Thicket. She'd said I was such a natural, I should try out for the baseball team at Licking Thicket High. I hadn't, but it had been nice to know she cared.

I shook off the memory and focused on the task at hand. "Show me this list." I took the paper and perused it. "Get a new job? What for? I make okay money."

Business had actually been booming since our local found-objects artist, Mal Forrester, had made it well-known where he sourced most of his materials. With the town sign made almost exclusively from parts found at my salvage yard, my place had become a revolving door. In fact, I needed to put added lot security on whatever this to-do list was if I wanted to keep my girl safe.

Stewie looked around awkwardly. "Well… I mean… selling junk for cash means you don't really have a decent employment history on paper. We kind of need you to have a steady job, with things like insurance."

"I have insurance," I grumbled, skimming down the list. "Paint the house and fix up the front yard—yeah, figured those would be on here. Get rid of the—" I looked up at Stewie. "Get rid of the chickens?"

Stewie smiled nervously. "I mean, they're not exactly classing up the joint, are they?"

I set my jaw. "I'm not getting rid of my chickens." Then, thinking of Marigold, I added, "Unless the home inspection person specifically tells me they're a problem."

"Fine, fine." Stewie shrugged. "Your call."

Yes. It was. I nodded firmly and went back to the list. "Wait... Get a wife? Are you serious?"

Stewie didn't even look embarrassed about this one. "C'mon, man, you have to know how much better this would go if you had the whole picture-perfect family going on. Get you one of them church wives. There's like a million ladies down there who would love to—"

I held up a hand. "I'm going to stop you right there. I'm gay. And I'm not about to change that for anyone."

Stewie lifted an eyebrow. "Not even for Marigold?"

It was a gut punch, but he was right. "Do I need to be straight to get custody? Are things still that backwards around here?" God, I hoped not. Or else I needed to move and raise Marigold somewhere more accepting.

"Naw. Not really. But it is family oriented. A stable marriage is considered a much better place for a child than a single person living alone. Besides, what if something happens to you? Who's going to look after the baby?"

I opened my mouth to remind him about my adoptive aunts, Birdie and Dot Johnson, but then I remembered they'd recently left on a four-week retirement trip to Europe. They'd come back in a skinny minute if I needed them to, but there was no way I could ask them to give up any more of their lives for me than they already had. And I wasn't quite sure putting two octogenarians down as my back-up custody arrangement was going to fly.

Stewie kept going on and on about what a difference a

stable marriage would make in gaining custody of my niece. "Plus, if your husband had a stable income and benefits, we could claim you as the stay-at-home parent, and problem solved, right? You need the appearance of respectability. This list is going to get you as close to it as possible, but..." He sighed. "I'm not sure it's going to get you there without something big, you know?"

Just then an old red Mustang came crunching down the drive. It wasn't the *good* kind of old Mustang, but the 1980s kind that didn't look much different from a Toyota Corolla from the same era. The owner probably needed to search my lot for engine parts. I wondered idly what I might have to direct him to.

But when the driver's door opened and a slender man stepped out in a prim button-down shirt and khaki pants... I recognized the narrow set of his shoulders right away.

It was the cutie from the courthouse who'd helped me calm Marigold down and loaned me his tie while I'd blithered on like an idiot—the one I'd never thought I'd see again, until I'd literally mowed him down outside Mal's tent the other day, which had been like adding insult to injury. I'd gotten Parrish's name and pertinent info from Malachi, and I'd sort of debated hunting him up to thank him for all his help, especially since his pep talk had inspired me, but I'd figured I'd probably only find a new way to embarrass myself.

I stared at him. What was he doing here? From what Mal had said, this guy's family owned a hundred or so barbecue restaurants all across the South and were Brooks and Paul's biggest client. Surely this clean-cut corporate type didn't know his ass from an alternator, so he couldn't possibly be here searching for parts.

I watched as he went around to the passenger-side door,

and I swear he was talking to himself in a low voice about forgetting to write down the reheating instructions. He leaned over, showcasing the most delicious little tight ass on earth, and stood back up with some kind of baking pan in his arms covered in tinfoil.

When he turned and found Stewie and me staring at him, he squeaked. "Oh, oh, sorry. I didn't even see you there. I'm sorry to interrupt." He looked between the two of us and finally settled on me, blinking his eyes rapidly and flushing pink. "I, um... I came to apologize. And, um..." He looked like he was about to faint from discomfort or something. "Do you like chicken? Never mind, of course you do. Everyone likes chicken. Don't be ridiculous, Parrish. Lord."

He was goddamned adorable.

And I wanted him to come closer. In fact, I wanted him full stop. He was easy on the eyes, perfectly put together, gainfully employed, and great with babies. It was like Jesus had looked down on me and sent me the answer to Stewie's punch list.

And desperate times called for desperate measures.

"Of course I like chicken," I lied, stepping closer to the flustered man. "Honeybunch. Now come on over here and meet our lawyer, Stewie." I slid my arm over Parrish's shoulders and beamed at Stewie. "This here's my fiancé, Parrish Partridge. Parrish, this is Stewie, the lawyer helping me with Marigold's custody case."

I knew the poor barbecue man didn't have a clue what I was talking about, but I at least hoped I'd confused him long enough to stay shocked into silence. Besides, he'd mentioned wanting to apologize, so maybe he'd go along with it as a favor to me, even though Lord only knew what he'd needed to apologize for.

Parrish's mouth opened, but nothing came out. Good.

"Fiancé?" Stewie looked poleaxed. "But you never mentioned a fiancé! Diesel, this changes everything. We gotta—"

I ushered Stewie toward the door with a firm hand on his shoulder. "What we gotta do is to get to work on this list! I'll give you a call in a couple of days. Alright, Stewie? Great. See ya!"

After making a big show of waving him off, I hustled Parrish into the house and shut the door behind me. "Fuck," I muttered. What had I done?

"Um..." Parrish said, shrugging out from under my arms. "Hi? I'm Parrish Partridge and... have we actually met?"

I ran my hands through my hair and looked around, suddenly wondering if the house was even fit for company at the moment, much less whatever the hell groveling session I was getting ready to host. I'd only had Marigold at the house for a week now, and it already looked like a tornado had whipped up all the contents of the house and spilled them back down in no particular order, hence the terrible initial home visit.

"I'm Diesel Church. Sorry about all this."

"The sudden marriage proposal or the dirty diaper on the floor?" Parrish asked with a raised eyebrow.

"Oh shit," I said, spotting the offending item. I lurched forward to dispose of it, taking it to the small kitchen and shoving it in the lidded trash can before washing my hands at the sink.

Parrish followed me and set the baking pan on the counter. "This is really pretty, actually."

I followed his gaze as he looked around at the honeyed wood paneling I'd installed on the walls and ceiling in the kitchen and the living area just beyond it. Despite baby crap everywhere, my home was clean and bright. It may have been small and really run-down on the outside, but I'd been working hard to fix up the inside myself, and I was proud of it.

"Thank you," I said gruffly, turning away to look for enough space in the fridge to fit his chicken dish. I didn't have much in the way of food right now, so it was mostly an excuse not to have to meet his eyes after throwing him under the bus like I had.

"So... this is chicken pot pie with bacon-and-cheddar biscuits. I forgot to write down the reheating instructions. Do you have a pen and piece of paper?"

I glanced up at him from the door of the fridge. That was it? He wasn't going to ask me what kind of crack I was smoking and why I'd claimed him as mine before we'd even officially met?

"Uh, sure. Lemme see..." I rooted around in the nearby junk drawer until I found a sticky-note pad and half-chewed pencil. "Sorry," I muttered.

He took it delicately between two fingers and began to write the instructions in tidy penmanship before placing the sticky note onto the tinfoil.

"There. I hope you like it. I know it's not much, but... I wanted to apologize for the way I snapped at you the other day, and Uncle Beau says no one's ever gone wrong with an apology casserole." He blinked rapidly and began looking everywhere but at me. "Which is probably not true. I kind of wonder if anyone's accidentally poisoned someone with one, you know? Like, God forbid, at a funeral or a wake? What if they'd accidentally used old mayo or bad eggs or..." He blinked up at me and blushed as red as his old beater car out front. "Maybe that's inappropriate. I promise I used all fresh ingredients in yours."

He was adorably flustered, and I wanted to kiss his fool face off right there in the middle of my kitchen.

"It's alright. I'm sure it'll be fine," I managed. I wasn't about to tell him I was a vegetarian. I didn't tell most people anyway, but I for damned sure wasn't telling a man who'd gone out of his way to bring me a bacon-and-chicken casserole thing.

We stared at each other for a beat before he pulled the dish off the counter and shoved it at me. "Fridge is best. And, um... I probably have to go now."

I took the dish and turned to throw it in the fridge, but when I turned back around, he was already halfway across the room waving goodbye over his shoulder and thanking me for my generosity in supplying him with writing implements. He reached the door and pulled it open, only to realize it was the coat closet. "Oh."

I slapped my hand over my mouth as he turned in a few confused circles and tried a different door. That one was to my bedroom. He let out a little squeaky noise of alarm and slammed the door closed again. The sound shot like a crack through the small house, waking the baby he probably hadn't noticed asleep in the portable crib on the far side of my bed. Suddenly, Marigold's angry shrieks rang out around us.

The look of horror on Parrish's face was almost comical. "Oh my God, my apology casserole visit is going to need an apology casserole," he whispered in shock. "This is unprecedented."

For once, I didn't feel the same fear and horror at the sudden baby cry that had become my usual response over the past few days. Instead, I felt a laugh bubble up.

"She was probably going to wake up around now anyway," I tried assuring him. "But I'll let you give me an apology diaper change instead of another casserole. How about that?"

He glanced at me as my words sank in.

"Give her an apology diaper change," I amended. "Not me. *Her*."

Parrish's frown softened slightly into the barest hint of a smile. "Okay. I can do that while you fix a bottle."

Bottle. *Right.* I nodded at him and told him where to find the supplies while I headed back to the kitchen for the formula. Within seconds, the baby's cries quieted, and I heard the low mumble of Parrish's soothing baby talk through the open bedroom door.

Hearing him with Marigold brought back all the reasons I'd blurted out the thing about him being my fiancé. He was good with her. For some reason, he knew how to handle a screaming baby, and I definitely didn't. But more than that, the little barbecue king had an air of utter *competence* about him. He was like what Stewie's punch list would look like if someone fed it into a robot generator. Not that Parrish was like a robot or anything. He wasn't.

I wandered into the bedroom to see what was taking so long and saw Parrish sitting on the end of my unmade bed, smiling and making faces at Marigold while bouncing her on his knee and singing some song about the way the farmers ride.

No, he was the furthest thing from a robot. Mal said Parrish was a nice guy with a good reputation, and I could already tell from being around him a few minutes he was gentle and kind, steady and put together. Dependable.

And I needed him to help me get custody of my niece.

I cleared my throat and held out the bottle. "Did you want to feed her, or do you want me to?"

Parrish startled and shot wide eyes at me. "Oh, sorry. I

guess I got distracted by this sweet girl. She sure is lovely." His face softened again as he looked at her. "Aren't you? Aren't you the sweetest thing ever?"

He stood up and put Marigold on his hip. She looked up at him like he was the second coming of Christ even though I was the one holding her bottle. Typical.

"I'd love to give her the bottle if that's okay?" Parrish asked, suddenly looking unsure.

I nodded and gestured out of the bedroom to the big comfortable chair in the living room. "It rocks," I said stupidly, realizing I'd made it sound like it was a cool chair instead of one that had a rocking motion. "The chair. It's kind of like a rocking chair even though it looks like a recliner. It's a recliner too. But it also rocks."

What the fuck was happening? Had I lost the ability to form proper sentences?

Parrish looked at me with a shy smile. "Okay if I sit there to feed her?"

"Of course," I huffed. "That's what I..." I noticed the twinkle in his eye and grunted my frustration.

Parrish chuckled softly and sat down, cradling my adorably chubby niece in his arms like a natural and putting the nipple into her mouth. "Your uncle is a silly billy," he cooed. "Isn't he?"

I sat down on the edge of the sofa closest to him and clasped my hands between my knees. Wait.

"How did you know she was my niece?"

Parrish's face flushed an attractive pink again. His creamy skin showed everything.

"I didn't mean to. It's just that you left her chicken passie and I tried to follow you with it and the bailiff told me it was a custody case between an uncle and grandparents and I thought, 'No way that beautiful man is a grand-parent,' which, I mean, look at you. Ha. Oh."

He seemed to realize he'd called me beautiful right about the time Marigold let rip a massive burp. She'd unknowingly saved us from an awkward moment.

"Oh," he said again, glancing down at the offender. "I'm sure you feel better after that, right, Miss Priss? Of course you do. Anyway, like I said, I didn't mean to pry or anything. And I wanted to apologize for getting... judgy in the men's room. That certainly wasn't my intention. I'm sure you don't need a nosy busybody butting in where he doesn't belong and passing judgment on you when you're—"

I couldn't take another minute of his apologies. "Stop. Please stop." Parrish looked up at me like a rabbit frozen in fear. "I just... you keep apologizing, and I don't understand why. You were incredibly helpful that day, and I should be the one bringing you a casserole. In fact, I have your tie. I need to dry-clean it, though. Or whatever takes baby puke residue out of polyester."

"Silk," he said faintly. "But it's fine. Keep it. If I could help in any way at all..."

"Actually," I said, clenching my hands together even tighter. "There is something you can help me with." How the hell could I ask this of a complete stranger?

Marigold burped again, and I sighed. That was why. I would do anything to keep my sweet girl from being raised by nannies in a cold house full of the worst kind of snobs who probably wouldn't even let the girl burp when she wanted. The Kensingtons had taken my sister in after our parents died, but they'd never made her feel loved. Hell, even their own daughter, Stella, hadn't grown up feeling loved and accepted. Instead, she'd bolted from their stringent rules at the first opportunity, marrying a man she'd met on vacation in Australia during college and never coming back.

I couldn't let those assholes raise my sister's baby. I'd do whatever it took to win full custody of her the way my sister had wanted.

I swallowed my pride and forged ahead. Parrish looked at me with an innocently eager expression on his face, like he'd be willing to change another diaper or warm up the casserole if I'd needed.

This wasn't quite as simple.

"Um, so... you know I'm trying to get custody of her, and..." I closed my eyes and tightened my jaw. I hated telling people my personal business. No one in town really knew what was going on. Hell, I didn't think anyone other than Birdie and Dot even knew I'd had a sister once upon a time.

"And, what?" Parrish encouraged softly.

"And I'm not a good enough candidate. Stewie thinks I'm going to lose even though my sister stipulated me as Marigold's guardian in her will."

"How is that possible?" Parrish asked, seemingly disgusted on my behalf. Then his face fell. "Do you have a record or something? Is that why?"

I narrowed my eyes at him. It wasn't the first time someone had made a snap judgment about me, but it stung more coming from him for some reason. "I do not have a record."

He at least looked a little embarrassed. "Sorry," he muttered, focusing back on Marigold. "I... sorry."

"Anyway, the reason is because the people who adopted my sister, the ones claiming to be Marigold's grandparents, are rich and perfect on paper in a way I could never be. So, by comparison I look like gutter trash. I have temporary custody of the baby while the hearings are ongoing, and the Kensingtons only have visitation, but that could all change if the judge decides to overrule my sister's wishes."

Parrish's chin firmed up. "You're not gutter trash. You're..." He looked around, glancing outside the window where a stack of rusting vehicles glowed in the afternoon sun. "A businessman," he finished lamely.

I appreciated the effort.

"Yeah, well, they aren't very impressed with my business since most of my transactions are in cash and trade. On paper I look like an unemployed loser as well as some kind of single man playboy."

"You're a playboy? What does that mean, exactly? You sleep around or something?" Parrish looked like he didn't want to appear curious, but I could see right through him. "How would they even know that about you? Did they hire a private detective?"

As if I needed one more thing to worry about. The Kensingtons were totally the kind of people who would hire a PI to dig up dirt on me. Thankfully, there wasn't much to find that the Kensingtons didn't already know.

"No, I... no. I don't sleep around. I mean, I..." I sighed and shook my head. I couldn't help but laugh. "I get around fine, but no, I'm not a playboy."

"Why are we even talking about this?" Parrish asked a little snappishly. "Whoever you choose to sleep with is your business. It's certainly no business of mine. I only came with the apology chicken. And now I should go." He stood up and plunked Marigold in my lap before putting the bottle in the kitchen sink and heading for the door.

"Wait!" I called out. I hadn't even gotten to the favor yet.

He turned around and snapped his fingers. "Of course. The chicken passie. Here." He pulled something out of his pocket and handed it to me. It was one of Marigold's toys from the courthouse.

"I need you to pretend to be my fiancé to help me get custody of Marigold," I blurted.

Parrish blinked at me before turning on his heel and marching out of the house. This time, unfortunately, he picked the correct door. By the time I raced after him, he was skidding his way out of my driveway in his dusty red Mustang.

"Well, fuck, baby girl," I muttered into Marigold's dark curls. "That didn't exactly go the way I'd planned."

Chapter Three

Parrish

"AND THEN. *Then!* The idiot says, 'Hey there, Parrish, could you do me a favor and pretend to be my fiancé real quick, to help me get custody of the baby?'" I lowered my voice to mimic Diesel Church's deep, throaty rumble but couldn't quite get there because I wasn't built like a freakin' grizzly bear. "You know who says things like that, Miss Sara?"

Sarabeth Kelly, the sixtysomething owner of the Jackson King Bed and Breakfast, glanced up from the butter cake she was frosting at the center island, and her long, dangling bell earrings tinkled.

"Insane people, that's who!" I answered myself as I paced to the end of the wide pine floors where the giant refrigerator sat. I turned on my heel to pace back, and grudgingly I admitted, "Granted, he doesn't *look* insane."

I paused by the large island as my mind unhelpfully conjured a picture of Diesel from earlier in the day, tall and muscled, cradling baby Marigold in his massive, tattooed paws, staring at her with his beautiful eyes full of undisguised affection.

"Insanely *hot* maybe," I muttered, resuming my pacing until I reached the door to the yard, where I pivoted again. "Insanely, adorably, ridiculously hot. And funny. And he felt…" I swallowed, remembering the warm solidity of his arm over my shoulder as he'd pulled me against his side and claimed me. "Really good." Too good. Too comfortable. "Which is all the more reason why his idea is a one-way ticket to crazytown! Don't you think?"

I reached the edge of the island again, and Miss Sara glanced up from her frosting once more. She blew a strand of chin-length platinum-blonde hair out of her eyes.

"Parrish, sweetie, you're making me dizzy." She grabbed a spoon from the stoneware jug on the counter, scooped up a big dollop of buttercream, and motioned me toward one of the wooden stools. "Take a load off and eat some frosting, alright?"

I took the spoon, heaved a sigh, and sat. Immediately, Miss Sara's basset hound, Elvis, came and plonked his bulk down on top of my foot, so I bent down to scratch his floppy ears.

Golden late-afternoon sunlight poured through the windows from the backyard, glinting off the copper pots that hung over the island and giving a warm glow to the floors and the reclaimed wood ceiling. It was a tidy, homey place, way smaller than my aunt Marnie's big kitchen up in Nashville, but with the same sort of vibe. The kind of place I'd always wanted for my own but was starting to think I'd never have.

Miss Sara worked some kind of stressful day job to make a living, but the B&B had been a passion project for her and her late husband, and she said she found it incredibly fulfilling. She was the sort of woman who wore tailored jeans but bare feet, and perfectly styled hair but no makeup. She spent hours listening to romance novel audiobooks and made a new dessert for us every night, even though all the other guests had checked out right after the Lickin'. She also wore a bright yellow apron with the name of the Cherryville Butterfly Conservatory at the top and a picture of a pipevine swallowtail with iridescent blue wings underneath, and you could tell a lot about a person by their favorite species of butterfly. It was impossible not to like her or to feel at home in her house, which was probably why I'd driven here immediately after leaving Diesel's place, with my head still whirling over the idea he'd proposed.

"I abhor lying. I've been lied to, and I do *not* recommend it. I couldn't live with myself if I participated in some sort of sham engagement. Besides, there's no guarantee that Diesel would get custody even if I did." I licked the spoon experimentally, and comforting vanilla sweetness flooded my mouth. "So I can't get involved in this mad scheme. Obviously."

"Obviously," Miss Sara echoed. She set a second layer of cake on top of the first. "Which is why you told him no."

"I couldn't tell him no! Diesel is a good person. I'd bet my bottom dollar on it. He clearly loves the baby, and he's trying to do his best for her. Plus the baby is gorgeous, and she has this look in her eyes where you can tell she's going to be a genius mathematician philanthropist or invent a new kind of poetry or something. You know the look I mean? So, I can't just abandon the two of them in their hour of need, Miss Sara. It's not about what's convenient for me. It's about something bigger."

"Ah." She nodded. "So you told him yes."

"God, no! No-ho-ho-no. I couldn't say yes! That would kill me." I took a new spoon from the crock and leaned over to scoop another gob of frosting from the bowl. "I've been down this road before. I was engaged once." I shoved the entire blob of frosting in my mouth at once and barely managed to garble out, "To Payne."

Miss Sara blinked confusedly. "In the ass?"

"What? No. I mean, *yes*, ultimately, I suppose he was. But his name was Payne." I paused. "*Is* Payne. He's not dead, just dead to me."

"Parrish, honey, are you drunk?" Miss Sara paused with her frosting spatula in the air.

"No, ma'am." I stretched my arm out for another spoon of frosting. "Just a little high on sugar and anxiety."

"Right." Her lips twitched, and she resumed frosting. "Proceed."

"Where was I?"

"Payne."

"Yeah. Payne was married before me, and he has two boys. Ethan was two when we first met, and Zane was just four months."

"Four months. That's..." She broke off with a whistle.

"A lot of work?" I gave her a small smile. "Yeah. But I was happy to help. I always wanted kids, so it was perfect." My shoulders slumped. "Until it wasn't. And when I said goodbye to Payne a year later, I said goodbye to the boys too." I licked the spoon and tried not to think too hard about the weeks after the breakup, where every box of Cheerios I found in the pantry, or sippy cup lid I spotted in my junk drawer, or single tiny sock caught in the lint trap of my dryer would trigger a fresh round of tears.

Truth to tell, I'd missed the boys way more than I'd missed their father, which told me I'd probably stuck with Payne for way too long and for all the wrong reasons.

"I can't believe I've found myself in this situation again. I mean, more or less."

Miss Sara moved the frosting bowl directly in front of me and leaned her elbows on the countertop to watch me eat. "So what *did* you tell Diesel?"

"Er. Well. Technically... nothing."

She lifted an eyebrow.

"I maybe ran out of his house and burned rubber down his driveway?" I said in a rush. I rubbed my forehead. "It's all sort of a blur. And I know! I know what you're thinking. You're thinking I need to tell him no to protect my heart."

"Well..."

"You're not wrong." I shook my head sadly and dug into the frosting again. "But how? If I say no, the kidlet goes to her rich, stuck-up relatives. And I know you're gonna tell me there are worse things than growing up rich." I waved the spoon in the air. "You're right, of course. Just 'cause people are wealthy doesn't mean they're evil. I always had plenty of money, thanks to Uncle Beau, and I like to think I'm a decent person."

"Yes, but—"

"But how could I sleep at night, knowing Marigold isn't with the person who loves her best, the person her mama chose to be her guardian? Bingo." I pointed the spoon at her. "You hit the nail on the head. That's exactly the question I'm wrestling with. Because money doesn't solve everything either. In fact," I added ruefully, "sometimes it causes a whole other set of problems."

"Maybe—"

"Maybe Diesel could find someone else to be his partner? Yes, but..." The very idea made me wince... and then wince again because I'd winced the first time. I was already way too into Diesel Church for my own good. "No. Seems like everyone in the Thicket knows what everyone else ate for dinner last night. The only way to sell a relationship like this is for Diesel's new fiancé to be someone who conveniently lived out of town until recently. Otherwise, the judge or the caseworker or the lawyer person, Stewie, or whoever will know we're a pair of liars from the first minute."

"Parrish, I really think—"

"It's not my place to make those decisions? I hear where you're coming from, Miss Sara, and you're wise to mention it. Love is crucial, but Marigold needs stability and consistency too. Maybe it's best to let the caseworkers and the courts weigh those things and make a decision." I sighed and pushed the frosting bowl away, suddenly nauseous. "But I don't know this judge from Adam, and neither does Diesel, I'm sure. What if they pick wrong? Could I live with the guilt of knowing I could have done something to stop it?"

"You really—"

"Can only control as much as I can control?" I sighed again. "Yeah. I know. And if I get in too deep and got my heart stomped, I'd have to live with that too. There are no easy answers."

"Could you—?"

"Sleep on it? See how I feel in the morning after a good night's rest?" I nodded appreciatively. "Good call. You know, I do feel sort of weirdly exhausted after our conversation, come to think of it."

"I can't think why," she said faintly.

I hopped off the stool, went around the counter, and bent to kiss her cheek. "I can't thank you enough for talking through this with me. I really value your advice."

"Oh." Miss Sara clapped a hand to her cheek over the spot where I'd kissed her and snickered as I walked out. "Anytime, honey."

———

Colin, the flagship store's interior designer, knocked on my open office door and stuck his head in. "Morning, Parrish. Beau said you're not picking up your cell, so he asked me to tell you he's having dinner at the Tavern Friday night with Mal and Brooks, and he'd like you to put it on your calendar. Seven o'clock."

"Huh?" I blinked up from my contemplation of my laptop screen like I was waking up from a dream. "Oh, sure." I picked up my phone and flipped the switch on the side. "Shoot. I had it on silent, I guess. Sorry about that, Colin. Uncle Beau doesn't do voicemail."

"No worries!" Colin glanced at my computer and did a double take at the images on my screen. He grinned broadly. "You have anything you wanna share, boss?"

"What? No!" I slammed the lid firmly like he'd caught me watching porn and not shopping for replacement baby bottle tops. "I just happened to run into a-a-a friend with a baby yesterday, and the poor thing had gas. I sort of thought it might be her bottle. Too much air." I cleared my throat. "Thanks for the message."

Instead of looking at me like I was crazy—which was probably what I deserved because seriously, what twentysomething gay man picked out *nipples* for a friend?—Colin nodded enthusiastically.

"Oh, sure. When Sadie had colic, my husband and I probably tried every kind of nipple on the market. Is your friend feeding his baby a sensitive formula? That's what pinged for us in the end."

"Er. I don't know." Nor should I, I reminded myself, since nothing about this situation was any of my business. And furthermore, after my conversation with Miss Sara, I'd decided once and for all last night—at approximately 3:00 a.m., which was when I made all my best decisions—that it *couldn't* be my business. That way lay madness and heartbreak and disaster. "But I'll pass the info along."

"Sure." Colin tapped the doorframe lightly with his wedding ring. "You know, you might also want to check out Kinder-potamus, the baby store over on Francis Street. They have one of everything, and they're super helpful."

I nodded and filed away this knowledge to pass on to Diesel when I called him up and very politely declined his fake-marriage proposal, which I'd sort of been putting off all morning. I rolled my chair back and paced the little office whose front window looked out on Walnut Street.

Calling him was totally appropriate, right? Probably best to just rip off the Band-Aid? No need to see the man again and make things all... feelsy and complicated. No need to see that sweet baby again, either, and wonder what her future was going to look like if she was taken away from her uncle. I couldn't imagine the look in Diesel's eyes when he realized I wasn't going to help him.

I pressed a hand to my stomach, which somehow felt as sick as when I'd eaten all that frosting.

A phone call was the answer. Definitely.

I chewed my lip. But then again... I would imagine if Uncle Beau were here, he'd say a phone call wasn't nearly good enough. If I was going to say no, I really should do it face-to-face... and probably bring him a present. Something even better than an apology casserole.

My eyes fell on my closed laptop, and then I grabbed my phone and ran out the door.

"Hey, Colin? Where'd you say that baby store was?"

Kinder-potamus was a pastel kaleidoscope that smelled like strawberry candy and sounded like a tinny music box lullaby. It was equal parts delightful and horrifying. It was also, conveniently enough, nearly empty.

"Excuse me, ma'am," I said to the cool blonde behind the counter. "I need your help. I—"

She turned around and blasted me with a high-octane smile. "Welcome to Kinder-potamus! I'm Kelsey. Expectant father or baby shower guest?"

"Uh." I opened and closed my mouth like a fish. "Neither? The baby's already born."

"Ah. So you'll be needing a gift, then. How old is the precious bundle? Newborn? First birthday? Second birthday?"

"Er." I shook my head. "I don't need a gift, exactly. More like—"

"Something for your own little one, then! How old?"

"Around nine months," I said, bewildered. "I think. But—"

"You think?" Kelsey pursed her lips. "Shouldn't you know, if you're the father?"

Wow. It was incredibly annoying when people tried to answer their own questions.

"I'm afraid you've got the wrong idea, Kelsey. You see..." I hesitated. "I'm looking for something in the way of an apology baby basket."

It was Kelsey's turn to look at me in confusion. "An apology... baby basket."

"Yes! Mmhmm. Sort of like an apology casserole, but on a larger scale. Something that says 'I'm sorry things won't work out, but I still want to support you and the baby.' I'm thinking something with, like, a soft toy? And maybe also some of the bottles with the good nipples that prevent gas?"

Kelsey's perkiness evaporated. "You're breaking up with someone by sending them a baby basket? Seriously?"

"What? Lord, no. Not breaking up! More like..." I coughed lightly. "Saying the relationship will never happen? But with high-quality nipples, to soften the blow? And I'm going to deliver it. In person."

She tilted her head to study me. "Sir, have you thought this through?"

I sighed. "I promise you, Kelsey, I have thought of hardly anything else in the past day. Can you help me with my nipples? And..." I remembered the day at the courthouse and Diesel saying the baby had only come with one of each accessory. "Do you have a chicken pacifier or two?"

"Sir, we only sell pacifiers for babies," Kelsey said faintly.

I ignored her. "And one of those nondescript black diaper bags for dads? Oh, and maybe some board books? And some teethers? Some butterfly pajamas?"

By the time we were done, my order rang in at just under eight hundred dollars, and Kelsey had to haul it all to the back room so she could find a basket big enough to contain it. But unlike when I'd borrowed Miss Sara's kitchen to make my apology casserole, buying the apology baby basket only made me feel worse; every squeeze pouch of organic baby food I'd selected had been a reminder that I was telling Diesel "no."

Which was possibly why apology baby baskets were not a *thing*.

The bell over the front door chimed, and I recognized the voices of the people coming in before I could see them over the display of gift cards near the door.

"Stop trying to steal my son's affections, Malachi Forrester!"

"Steal," Mal scoffed. "Like I don't already have them locked down. Your mom's so silly, Beau. Isn't she? Yes, she is. Say 'Mal,' buddy. Come on. Say *'Mal Mal Mal.'*"

The baby made a noise that sounded like "Ma ma ma," and both Mal and Ava crowed in triumph.

"He said 'Mama,'" Ava sniffed. "Clear as a bell."

"Delusions. He spoke the name of his favorite uncle."

"Nonsense. He didn't say anything *close* to 'Brooks.'"

Mal laughed out loud as they came fully into the store, Ava pushing an empty baby carriage and Mal cuddling Ava's infant son to his chest. They both looked up in surprise when they spotted me.

"Well, hey, Parrish!" Ava Siegel's blonde curls bounced as she came forward to give me a hug. She looked summertime perfect in a sundress printed with yellow flowers. "Fancy meeting you here."

"Morning, Ava." I returned her hug and nodded at Mal, who had his hands full. "Mal." Then I grinned at the drooly baby in Mal's arms. "Beau! Cuttin' some teeth, there, little man? How are y'all doin'?"

I'd spent plenty of time with Mal and his boyfriend, Brooks, since Uncle Beau had first gotten to know them a year ago. I knew Ava and her husband, Paul, who was Brooks's business partner, slightly less well. But Uncle Beau adored all of them and had more or less adopted them all into our extended family... so much so that Paul and Ava had named their baby after him.

"Oh, nothing new to report for me." Ava waved a hand airily. "But word on the street is that *someone* just got engaged." She gave me a mischievous smile that made my heart beat double time.

Had she heard about Diesel's crazy fake proposal?

What had she heard? *How* had she heard?

Was it that Stewie person? Wasn't that a breach of attorney-client privilege?

Oh, God, or what if Diesel assumed my leaving meant I'd agreed, in some ass-backward way? What if he was telling everyone we were engaged? What if someone told Uncle Beau?

"I don't know what folks are saying, but it's absolutely untrue," I said vehemently. "I'm not engaged. Not even a little engaged. I'm single as a Pringle. Single as a dollar bill. Single as single can be!"

Ava's gaze narrowed on me, and I could almost see the Terminator computer working behind her big blue eyes as she no doubt came to some kind of crazy conclusions.

Though, to be fair, nothing she came up with could be crazier than the truth.

I pulled at my collar. "Gracious gravy, it's warm in here, huh?"

"Uh. Ava meant me, Parrish," Mal volunteered. Over Beau's head, he looked down at the hand splayed across the baby's back and flexed his fingers to show off the simple gold and black band there. He smiled with a kind of quiet pride and bit his lip like he couldn't quite believe it was real. "Me and Brooks got engaged. That's what the ring was about at the Lickin' the other day, remember?"

"Oh. Wow. That's..." I swallowed against the wave of pure *want* that nearly towed me under. "Excellent. So happy for you. Congratulations."

"Thanks," Mal said. "I sort of figured everyone knew, otherwise I would have told you."

I shook my head. "Probably my fault I didn't put two and two together. It's been a weird week. I've been... distracted."

"Hmm," Ava said, like a detective who'd gotten a break

in a case. "So. Who are you shopping for today?" She glanced around the little boutique.

"Oh, just buying some things for a...a friend."

"Oooh! Someone local?" Her eyes widened with genuine excitement. "I love getting to meet the new parents in town. We've got a great group that meets over at the splash park on Tuesdays through September. It's fun to see the littlest ones interacting with their future best friends." She ran a fond hand over her son's head.

I looked at baby Beau, and it struck me like a physical blow that he was the same age as Marigold. That, if Marigold stayed in the Thicket, she could be his bestie someday. That, if she didn't stay in town, she wouldn't just miss out on having Diesel for a dad, she'd miss out on *this*. The community. The whole zany, close-knit bunch of them.

Which was not my concern, really. It *wasn't*. It couldn't be.

But my palms started to sweat anyway.

I wasn't sure whether Diesel wanted anyone in town to know about the baby, especially since things were still so uncertain. But if he did, it was up to him to tell folks.

"Er, no one local," I said, a little shocked that the lie came to my lips so darn easily. Apparently, it was easy enough to lie when you were protecting someone.

Not just someone. Diesel and Marigold.

Of course, that was the exact moment Kelsey came from the back, hauling a pink basket the size of Ava's baby carriage.

"Here you are, sir." Kelsey set the basket on the ground at my feet, only panting slightly. "Your apology baby basket for you to hand deliver in person." She dusted her hands and said disapprovingly, "Best of luck with it."

"Thanks." I cleared my throat and hefted the basket. "So! It was great to see you guys, but I've gotta run—"

"You're coming to the Tavern with us on Friday, right?" Mal said. "Since you're super single? It'll be fun."

Oh, right. Dinner with Uncle Beau, Mal, and Brooks.

"Yeah, I'll be there." Even though fun was the last thing I wanted to think about when I had to break this news to Diesel.

I was so, so screwed.

Mal's eyes had a mischievous glint way too similar to Ava's. "I'm looking forward to it."

I was glad at least one of us was.

Chapter Four

Diesel

I had approximately seventeen and a half minutes at most before the ticking time bomb that was my sweet girl went off and stopped my productivity for the rest of the afternoon. I'd already mowed the dirt patch that pretended to be a lawn out front and picked the aggressive weed colony from the flower bed by the mailbox. Up next was finishing the tall wooden privacy fence that would block the view of the salvage yard from the street and allow the caseworker to ignore the giant lot full of sharp, rusty parts just lying in wait to attack my niece at any moment.

I'd set the fence posts last night after putting Marigold to sleep. After the frustrating visit from Stewie and the horribly embarrassing desperation I'd shown to poor Parrish Partridge, I'd been full up on angry energy.

How the hell could I have ever asked a perfect stranger to pretend to be married to me? I was a no-good salvage dealer who didn't even have a proper high school diploma. And Parrish... Parrish was the very opposite. He was smart and successful, tidy and poised. The man was a breath of fresh air that shouldn't ever even be near all my stink.

I sighed and kicked the empty weed bucket across the gravel parking pad, accidentally scaring the chickens who'd snuck out of the yard since I'd pulled down the old chain-link fence. Even though I had the baby monitor clipped to my belt, I'd still had to rush into the house every ten minutes to make sure it wasn't accidentally broken. Being a parent was no joke. My chore list was taking forever to get through, and at this rate I thought I might get in good enough shape to win custody of her right around the time she became a legal adult.

"Stop bitching and get back to work," I told myself. "Parrish Partridge isn't for the likes of you."

As I began nailing fence pickets to the rails, I couldn't help but slide back into thoughts of the pretty little man. He was adorably flustered and prim, and something about him made me want to pull him into my arms and protect him from the world.

As if I needed someone else to protect right now.

"You just want to fuck him," I grumbled out loud. "It's your lonely dick talking."

One of the chickens squawked in response and tried to get in my face. I shooed her away from the box of nails she mistook for feed. "Get away, Brenda, this isn't for you," I muttered. She tossed her plume of white head feathers and strutted off in a snit.

My brain unhelpfully provided the memory of Parrish's gentle touch with Marigold, the sweet sound of his singing to her, and the way he'd blushed to the tips of his ears when I'd caught him checking out my ink.

Memories of him helping me in the courthouse were quickly overridden by memories of the rich boys in high school calling me Reverend Rust and Deacon Dirt. They'd thought they were so fucking funny after they'd learned where I'd come from, that I'd stowed away on a wrecker that had brought me to the salvage yard, before Stix Yancey had found me and pulled me out of an old Chrysler chassis by my ear and turned me over to the aunts next door for safe-keeping.

But this place had become my own version of home. Even after the aunts had cleaned me up and presented me to the courts to foster me, I'd escaped time and time again back to the salvage yard until Aunt Birdie, Aunt Dot, and Stix had come to some kind of agreement. I'd started working for Stix on the up-and-up, hauling shit and sorting parts, cataloging inventory until I suddenly understood how to run the whole damned place. Which, I guess, had been their point all along since Stix was gone not two years later from lung fucking cancer.

This was never going to work. Any judge in the world would be stupid to award me custody of a baby. I was uneducated, unsuccessful, unpopular, unpolished, and probably lots of other un's too. Case in point: Parrish didn't even stop to decline my request before getting the hell out of Dodge. Hell, I'd probably scared him with all of my grunting, and... had I told the man I slept around? Did that actually happen?

I whacked my hammer into my thumb and bit back a shout. Even though Marigold was far away from me, tucked inside the house, I wasn't taking any damned chances. I needed her to sleep or I was never going to make this place presentable for the caseworker's inspection.

Add uncoordinated to the list of un's.

This time, I tried again to focus on the task at hand. After three more pickets, I heard the familiar crunch of gravel indicating someone turning into my driveway. I stopped hammering and turned to see who it was. When I spotted the dusty Mustang from yesterday, my heart did a little stutter. Maybe this would be my chance to apologize to Parrish for being a raving lunatic yesterday.

I tossed the hammer at the toolbox and stood up, trying to smack the dirt and dust off my work pants as if that would make me more presentable. Putting me next to someone like Parrish was like setting a homegrown turnip on a plate next to sushi.

My insecurities all reared their ugly heads at once, and I found myself crossing my arms in front of my chest and tightening my jaw against the desire to start apologizing for being dirty and sweaty.

When Parrish stepped out of the car, I noticed he looked nervous and flustered which seemed to be his default state when he was around me. I was used to people being nervous around me with my tall, muscular frame and heavily inked skin, but seeing Parrish nervous around me was a kick in the teeth. For some reason, I wanted him to like me, as ridiculous and immature as that sounded.

"H-hi, uh, Diesel," he stammered. He kept his eyes on mine as he shuffled around the car to the passenger side. "I'm just... I just brought over a... um..." He opened the door and leaned in before coming out with a giant basket covered in pink ribbons.

The basket could host a party for a collection of miniature horses, it was so big.

"What's that?" I asked.

The ribbons all trembled as he approached me, indicating his nerves were even greater than I'd thought.

"More apology stuff," he said, suddenly looking up, down, over toward the forest, and back toward the house. Anywhere except at the man he was getting closer to.

"I don't want your apology stuff," I grunted, thinking

about the chicken casserole I'd taken over to my next-door neighbor's house the night before.

Parrish flushed red and looked down at the basket before turning his chatter speed up to manic. "Oh. Well, sure. It's just that... there's a special nipple that might help Marigold with her gas problem and I also found a book about uncles and nieces and there was this little elephant stuffy that needed to come home with me—with her, I mean —and also, Kelsey said everyone needs the Gentria hip carrier for babies this age which is... actually a lie. I'm the one who said it, but you really should trust me on this because I know what I'm talking about. Also, no one should go into the crazy cakes crawling stage without some outlet covers which is just good safety practice, so those had to get chucked in the basket too. And if you're going to go all out on outlet covers, then how in the world can you forget to get cabinet and drawer locks as well as a few of those handle spinners? You can't. Obviously. And since I couldn't remember if you had round doorknobs or the push-down kind, I had to get covers for both, you know? Right?"

He looked up at me as if expecting an answer, but he didn't wait for one. "Right," he said, seemingly to himself. "So, I'm going to go. Except... except, I guess I forgot to actually apologize which would mean this was just a gift basket instead of an apology basket which, ha! Of course it's not. That would be ridiculous and completely..." He started panting a little bit. "Completely unprecedented," he finished faintly.

He blinked up at me, and I swear to fucking God I almost lurched forward and smashed my mouth on his. He was drop-dead beautiful and the most adorable man I'd ever had the good fortune to lay eyes on.

"I'm sorry," he whispered. "For not marrying you."

He placed the basket into my hands and turned to go. In that moment, I was sorry for the same damned thing. Nothing sounded more tempting to me than marrying a sweetheart like Parrish Partridge. But that wasn't what this was about.

"You wouldn't have to actually do it," I called out. "Just pretend for a little while. Please, Parrish. I'm... I'm desperate. I wouldn't ask if..." I hated this. I hated begging. I especially hated asking someone good and pure to get caught up in a giant, illegal lie like this. But I'd meant what I'd said. I was desperate. And I'd do anything to make sure my Marigold grew up loved and protected, even if it meant using this beautiful sweetheart in my nefarious plans to make sure it happened. "Please," I said again.

He stopped, his narrow shoulders tense and his hands knotted into fists. I tried not to gawk at his sexy ass packaged perfectly in today's suit pants. I expected him to turn around and give me what for—to tell me off with his unending manners and stammering apologies—but Marigold's shriek through the monitor at my hip split through the space between us and called me away before I could do any more damage to the man than I already had.

"'Scuse me," I mumbled, stepping past him toward the house. Diaper and bottle duty called, and I wouldn't let my princess down just to fight for something that clearly wasn't ever gonna happen.

Before I knew what was happening, Parrish had bolted ahead of me at top speed and slammed his way into the house, leaving me in the dust. When I caught up to him, I saw why he'd reacted so strongly.

Marigold had somehow managed to stand up in her portable crib and reach the coffee mug I'd left on my bedside table, pulling it into the crib with her and dousing her in, thankfully cold, coffee.

"Shhhh," Parrish cooed, reaching in to pick her up. "Shh, sweet girl. 'S'alright. You're okay. Just a little caffeine to wake you right up, hmm? Not quite the way it was intended, but sometimes that's life."

Without a single care for the white button-down shirt he wore, he pulled her into his chest to soothe her.

I was horrified.

"I didn't know she could stand up," I said in a panic, thinking of all the ways she could have gotten really hurt. "I've never seen her stand up before." My voice sounded weird to me as the blood rushed in my ears. "I didn't know. How could she reach that far when she can't even walk?"

"Take a breath," he said, looking at me over Marigold's head. He said it with the same soothing tone he spoke to Marigold with. "You clean up the crib while I clean up the girl, okay?"

I nodded frantically, trying to do anything to push back the panic threatening to completely take over.

Do not freak out. Do not freak out.

"I almost killed her," I blurted, grabbing at my hair and yanking. "I... I can't be trusted with her. They're right. I'll make a terrible father. I'm unfit. This is never going to work. What was I thinking?"

Dark spots blinked at the edges of my vision, and my lungs seized up. I could have killed her. What if it had been a knife I'd left on the table? I didn't own a gun, but I did have a hunting knife I usually kept tucked in a drawer in my bedside table in case of intruders. What if she'd been able to open the drawer and get to it?

"Hey, hey," he said in that same sweet voice, softer now with a hint of worry. His cool hand reached up and clasped my face to get me to look at him. "It's okay. Every parent on earth has stuff like this happen. I promise. The key is to do the best you can and then learn from your mistakes."

"I can't do this," I whispered. "I'm not good enough for her."

It was something I'd never admitted out loud even though I'd thought it a million times since getting the call that my sister was gone and Marigold had been left in my care.

Parrish's hand smoothed across my forehead and my cheek while his other held Marigold tight to his chest. She was sucking on her thumb while staring at me, and I suddenly realized I didn't want her to see me this way. I reached out and cradled her dark curls in my palm.

"I love her so much," I admitted softly. "If I love her this much, shouldn't I let her go?"

It was agony to ask him that, but if there was one thing I could guess about Parrish Partridge, it was that he had a much better head on his shoulders than I did. Clearly he knew more about kids, and maybe he could do me the favor of at least telling me if my attempt to keep Marigold was a fool's errand.

His eyes narrowed and he practically spat out the words. "Absolutely not, and I don't want to hear you say that ever again. It's because you love her this much that she needs to stay right where she is. With you. With the person who loves her the most."

Our eyes met over her head, and I wondered when was the last time someone had fiercely defended me like that? Maybe when one of my classmates had called me trailer trash and Aunt Dot had lit into them with a nasty string of hellfire and damnation under the guise of what she referred to as a "concerned Christian woman." Which was something she called herself whenever the title suited her despite the fact she hadn't set foot in a church since deciding staying in bed naked with her woman was preferable on a Sunday morning.

And now Parrish Partridge was telling me I was good enough, that not only was I an acceptable choice to raise Marigold, but that I was the only choice.

"Thank you," I said. "I guess I didn't realize how bad I needed to hear it."

His hand trailed down from my face to my chest, but before I could get too excited about his touch, he patted my chest and cleared his throat. "Well, what are fiancés for, if not to support their man. Now... let's get to work. This coffee isn't going to clean itself."

He turned and busied himself at the makeshift changing station on my dresser while I stared after him in shock. Had he just...?

"Stop staring at my ass and get to work," he said over his shoulder before wincing. "Um, I mean... stop staring at my back and get to work. Not that you would ever stare at my ass. Don't be ridiculous, Parrish."

I couldn't hold back a laugh. It wasn't a giddy giggle at all, and I didn't feel high with the possibility he'd actually agreed to my nutty scheme. "Do you always talk to yourself like this?" I asked, leaning over to strip the soiled bedding from the portable crib.

"You're teasing me," he said petulantly. "After I just agreed to be your pretend fiancé, now you're teasing me."

So he did agree. The confirmation sent my heart into the stratosphere. "I think it's cute."

"Mpfh," he muttered.

"And I might have been staring at your ass," I said as I

exited the room to toss the dirty stuff in the washing machine. "It's an award-winning ass."

When I got back to the bedroom, I noticed deep pink stains on his cheeks and ears. "No flirting," he said. "That's a rule."

I reached over him to the shelf above the dresser to get another fitted sheet. When my mouth was right by his ear, I said in a low voice, "I reject that rule."

Parrish's entire body shuddered, and he made a little whimper sound deep in his throat. "You," he said with a squeak before trying again. "You can't reject the rule. It's a rule. Rules are... rules."

I moved over to put the sheet in the crib. "If I can't flirt with my own fiancé, how am I going to convince anyone I'm in love with you?"

Parrish whipped around and flashed me wide eyes. I noticed he kept a hand on Marigold to keep her from squirming off the changing pad. "In love with me? What?" It took his brain a minute to catch up. "Oh. Oh, you mean pretend love. Fake love. Right. Well... you'll just have to... um..."

"Flirt?" I suggested.

"Oh dear God on a golf ball," he said faintly, turning back to finish dressing Marigold in fresh clothes. "I didn't exactly think this through, did I, baby girl?"

I stepped up behind him, feeling more in control of the situation since they'd put Marigold into my arms ten days ago. With Parrish's help, I might just be able to do this.

Instead of leaning in and inhaling the back of his neck like I really wanted to, I put my hand on his shoulder and squeezed. "I don't know why you agreed to help me, Parrish, but thank you. From the bottom of my heart."

"No need to thank me," he said quickly, as if trying to shove off the emotion that sparked in the room around us. "I'm only doing this because you obviously need a lot, and I mean a *lot*, of help. And, um, also, it's super temporary. Like *super* temporary. I'll stay to help because you have a lot to learn."

"Duly noted," I said with a laugh. "A lot."

I moved back out to the main room to fix a bottle for Marigold, but I still heard his whispered words to my niece.

"What the heck have I just gotten myself into? I'm an idiot who can't say no to a big, beautiful teddy bear, isn't that right, sweet girl? Parrish is an idiot, and Parrish doesn't know how to guard his freaking heart, does he? No he doesn't."

I stopped and let the words sink in. I wanted desperately to know which one of us he thought he might lose his heart to in all of this—me or Marigold. And what happened if he'd gotten it all wrong and it ended up being me who lost everything?

Chapter Five

Parrish

LATER THAT WEEK, it became pretty clear that what I had gotten myself into was what my aunt Marnie would call a hell of a pickle, and guarding my heart was going to be even trickier than I'd thought. I'd known from our first meeting that I found Diesel Church attractive. What I hadn't realized was that I'd also find him comforting and fascinating and more addictive than Miss Sara's frosting.

But life was all about discovery, right? As it happened, just that week I'd discovered that the sight of a big man sprinkling organic feed for his chickens—all of whom were *named*, mind you, and all of whom had distinct personalities—was a huge turn-on, and suddenly, "Brenda, girl, you need to get your beak in there and don't be shy" and "Lloyd, do not attempt to establish a pecking order with me. I *am* the pecking order" had become phrases that triggered my arousal.

Similarly, I'd discovered that the only thing more heartwarming than a tattooed badass cuddling a tiny baby was when said badass put on a pair of reading glasses so he could double-check the instructions on her new formula and then continued to wear them while he discussed your day at the restaurant, his day at the junkyard, the intricacies of baby digestion, and how to get his sweet girl to sleep through the night.

Additionally, I'd discovered that standing next to that big, tattooed, chicken-loving, far-sighted, not-flirtatious man while he gave a vegetable-puree-covered infant a bath in the kitchen sink was more dangerous to my well-being than a game of Russian roulette, which was why I was right now on my hands and knees, scrubbing Diesel's kitchen floor, while he handled tubby time alone.

"Who loves her bubble bath?" Diesel's deep, soothing voice set off little earthquakes in my stomach. "Would you look at that smile? Parrish, come look!"

Marigold's happy shrieks and the sound of violent splashing filled the kitchen.

I squeezed my eyes shut, glad Diesel couldn't see me from where he stood at the sink. "Can't. Busy."

Possibly the most important discovery of the last few days was that Diesel's whole "I reject that rule" confident flirtation had lasted about as long as Marigold's diaper change.

Which was a *good* thing. A really good thing. Obviously.

I mean, the similarities of this situation to the whole clusterfuck with Payne were undeniable, but at least Diesel wasn't pretending he was interested in sexing me up anymore, which would only muddy the already-murky fake-fiancé waters. We were doing this for Marigold, after all. I was spending most of my free time at his place for the next week and a half so we could cement our happy-family façade and impress the caseworker for *her* sake. The fact that Diesel seemed perfectly content to forget about my award-winning ass was all for the best, when looked at through that lens, and I would absolutely not ruin this situation by wanting more.

Which was why I would remain on this floor until every particle of baby food that had wedged itself in the cracks was clean, or until Diesel Church ceased being so goddamn irresistible.

I was planning to be here a while.

Diesel sighed impatiently. "I told you I'd wash the floor myself. I don't want you to—"

"I know." I scrubbed at the floor as hard as I could with both hands, my whole body getting into the act. "It's fine. I want to." Or, okay, if we were being honest, it was more like I'd needed an excuse to step away from Diesel for a minute, but honesty and I were no longer on speaking terms, so I wasn't gonna say that out loud. "The apple-carrot squeezey was my idea after all."

"And it was a great one! I swear, I feed her the same stuff already, but the squeeze pouch makes it cooler or something. Your gift basket was a hit, bab—uh, Parrish."

I stifled a sigh. Yeah, so no flirtation... but there'd been this. Diesel looking at me with weird intensity every once in a while. Diesel calling me a pet name and correcting himself, which only drew attention to it. Diesel teasing me or flicking me with a kitchen towel, like he'd breathed a giant sigh of relief and become more relaxed, more comfortable in his skin, since I'd agreed to this plan. Diesel smelling like clean sandalwood soap, which was some kind of unresearched aphrodisiac and scientists needed to get on that.

I was pretty sure most of it was unintentional—I was not crazy enough to think he had ulterior motives for his soap or whatever—but it didn't matter. The way we'd connected in such a short time was messing with my brain, making me want things I knew better than to want. And while I loved knowing something I'd done had contributed to his comfort and happiness, I also hated thinking he didn't feel like he could do this on his own.

It wasn't like I was anyone special. It wasn't like my presence alone was going to magically fix this for him. It wasn't like I was gonna be a permanent fixture in his life... or Marigold's.

But then again, I knew from experience that I ticked a lot of the right boxes on paper when it came to getting custody of a baby. I was the responsible, upstanding, good influence you wanted as a prospective co-parent. I was the ace in the hole. So maybe those pet names were Diesel's way of practicing for the home inspection that would be coming, or his way of keeping me turned up sweet for the duration. Either way, this didn't mean I was the guy Diesel wanted warming his bed.

Which, again, was a *good* thing. And if I just kept telling myself that, at some point I'd believe it.

Objectively speaking, I knew I wasn't bad-looking. I was, you know, average. Average height and average build, average intelligence and average ambitions, a little more high-strung than most and blessed with a higher bank balance, but too wholesome and white-bread to ever be considered sexy, let alone hot. Payne used to jokingly call me "basic," and it had taken me a long time to realize it wasn't a joke and even longer for the sting of it to go away, but once we'd broken up, I'd embraced the fuck out of it. I *liked* chinos and listening to NPR. I genuinely *enjoyed* dinners with my elderly relatives. I read *Birds and Butter-flies* magazine and daydreamed about the pollinator garden I would someday grow, once I had a home of my own. I was who I was, and I wasn't going to pretend to be more or less than that.

It was no one's fault that Diesel Church existed at the opposite end of the "basic" spectrum—that his body should be sculpted by artists; that his golden-brown hair was a little long and a little wild and almost insisted you run your fingers through it; that his skin was covered in these gorgeous, swirling, cryptic tattoos—I'd picked out a hummingbird at his collar-bone, but I didn't know what the others were, or what they stood for, and I wanted to, rather desperately; that his night-stand was stacked with books on everything from studying French to building a chicken coop to something called *Husbandry of the American Wyandotte*, which was straight-up mystifying; that he was smart and funny and kind and could do anything, but seemed to enjoy running a salvage yard.

Diesel Church was only forced into chinos under duress, like that day at the courthouse. He probably understood "basic" about as well as I understood French, which was to say not at all. And while I wanted to ask the man endless questions, and wanted to hear him explain every facet of himself in his deep, comforting voice, and wanted to look at him forever, I couldn't imagine he'd have any interest in me beyond being a fake fiancé.

Which, I believed, perfectly explained why I was on the floor and not watching Marigold take her bath.

I was backing up before I started to believe this fake relationship was real.

Fool me twice and all that.

"Who knew that stuff could go airborne the way it did, though, huh?" Diesel continued ruefully. "Or that she'd decide to rub it into her hair while we were busy figuring out how to clean the walls?"

"It was very Jackson Pollock," I defended. "Her artistic genius cannot be contained by walls. Or, um, the ceiling." I glanced up at the peachy-pink stain over my head that looked vaguely like a sunflower. "I could grab some stain killer at the hardware store, if you want. Should take that right out."

"Or you could just keep buying her squeezy pouches." Diesel grinned. "And then on rainy winter days, we can lie on the floor and pick out shapes, like they're clouds."

Marigold crowed like she endorsed this plan, but me? I sighed with helpless longing. Really, how the heck was I supposed to remain strong against the combined pull of this man and this baby, when all I wanted was to imagine I'd still be in their lives come winter?

Masochist that I was, I stood and let their smiles reel me closer to the half-filled sink where Marigold pounded the surface of the water with her chubby fists and blinked against the splash with eyelashes that had gone thick and spiky.

"You need more bubbles," I pronounced, reaching for the bottle of lavender bubble bath that had also been part of the basket. "Just a teeny bit more, okay, sweetie, okay? Lavender is supposed to be relaxing, and it's almost bedtime."

"Baba," she said happily as I turned on the water and poured a capful of the liquid under the stream.

"That's right! *Bubbles*! Did you hear her repeat that perfectly?" I grinned and turned to Diesel to find him staring at me with one of those weird, intense looks I couldn't interpret. I focused on Marigold and cleared my throat. "So, you never told me... how was the casserole?"

"The what?"

"The chicken casserole I brought over the other day."

"Oh! *That* casserole. Um. It was… delectable?" He nodded vehemently. "Yup. Best ever."

"Yeah?" I smiled, relieved. I hadn't realized I was anxious about what he'd think of my cooking skills until that moment. "The recipe called for mushrooms, but I wasn't sure if you'd like them, so—"

"Are you kidding? I love mushrooms. Adore them. They were the best part of the dish!"

"—so I left them out," I finished. I cocked my head. "Did it taste like mushrooms?"

"Er." Diesel rubbed the back of his neck. "Only in the sense that mushrooms are delicious and so was the casserole?"

"Oh." I frowned. "Well, good, then. I figured you'd have that for a couple days anyway. Want me to heat you up some?"

"You can't! It's… gone." He shrugged and patted his flat stomach. "It was just too good."

"Wait, you mean you ate it all? That fast?" I laughed slightly. "No way! The whole casserole and all fifteen biscuits?"

"Maybe?" He looked a little sheepish, and I hoped I wasn't making him uncomfortable. Lord knew it probably took a lot to keep a guy of his bulk running.

"Well, grab me the dish and I'll make you more!" I offered. "Miss Sara at the bed-and-breakfast probably wants her pan back anyway."

Diesel looked momentarily panicked. "Oh, I uh… couldn't return it empty. That's bad manners."

"Of course you can!"

"No," Diesel insisted. He looked deeply uncomfortable, which was both cute and weird. "I'll get it back to you later."

"If you're sure—"

I broke off as Marigold sent up another splash, this one big enough to drench the whole front of me.

"Oh, sh... ugar," I said, looking down at my dress shirt. I'd avoided the worst of the coffee stains from holding Marigold earlier, but this splash had been a full-frontal assault because the water level in the sink was so high. "Gah! Pro tip: don't leave the tap running when you add more bubbles."

Diesel snorted. "Noted." He grabbed a clean towel from the drawer by the sink and started to mop the bubble-water off my chest with slow strokes that felt so good I made myself grab the towel and turn away.

"It's good to make the bath part of her nighttime routine," I babbled nervously. "A bath, then some of that lavender lotion, then jammie time, then read her a book. Even if she doesn't pay attention, it's good to get her in the habit. Then hopefully she'll be ready to conk out."

Diesel blew out a breath that hit the side of my neck and sent shivers down my back. "You're like the Baby Whisperer."

"Me? Nah—"

"You don't even know how amazing you are, hon—er, Parrish. Sometimes I feel like I'll never learn it all. Like, the other day when you came over, and she started crying after her nap. She cries *every* time she wakes up and I'm not there, so I usually walk in, stop in the kitchen to wash my hands, then go get her. But you somehow knew to go running." He shook his head. "It's like you're psychic."

I frowned, thinking back. "Well, that was a panicked cry, as opposed to her lonely cry, as opposed to her hungry cry. And pretty soon, if she hasn't already, she'll add in a pissed-off cry when you take away the shiny, pretty dangerous objects she wants to play with. It's not magic. You'll learn which cries are real," I assured him.

"You know, I always figured I wasn't cut out for kids, that it was a lifelong commitment to stress and worry. I never bought into the idea before." He brushed back one of Marigold's curls.

Chalk up another way Diesel and I were wholly and dramatically incompatible. I was the king of commitment.

"What about you? You ever thought about having kids of your own?"

"Me?" I shrugged. I'd always known I wanted children, even back when I'd thought being gay meant I wouldn't be able to have them, but it felt weird to admit that. Like it might make Diesel realize just how desperately I wished this fake relationship were real.

"Parrish, if we're gonna pull this off, we need to know more about each other, don't you think?" he prompted.

I looked up at him again. "To make things convincing?" I asked softly. "Like with the flirting?"

"No! Or... that too, I guess." He shrugged. "I just find you interesting."

I shook my head. "I already agreed to do this, Diesel." There was no need for him to butter me up by feeding me lines, especially unbelievable ones like that. I was in this for the long haul.

"I'm not asking for deep secrets," he wheedled. "Just simple stuff, in case someone asks. Like, what's your middle name?"

I frowned. I couldn't imagine anyone quizzing us on these things, but what did I know? "Flynn. It was my mother's maiden name."

"Parrish Flynn Partridge," Diesel said with satisfaction. "I like it."

That should not have felt like a compliment since I hadn't exactly picked it myself, but it felt good anyway. "What's yours, then?"

"Mine?" He frowned and double-blinked, like he hadn't thought forward to the part where he'd have to reciprocate and answer silly questions too. "Montgomery."

"Really? Diesel Montgomery Church?" Okay, that was adorable. "Is that a family name too?"

"Oh. Uh. No. It was where my mom was waiting tables when my dad came along and knocked her up?" He swallowed so loud I could hear it. "And my first name isn't Diesel, it's actually Edwin. And... you know what? You're right. Maybe sharing info was a stupid idea."

Ah, shit. The only thing more irresistible than teasing, flirty Diesel Church was Diesel Church with that uncertain look in his eyes and that pucker on his forehead that made me want to kiss it away. I'd never felt this much this fast about any guy, not even Payne, and it scared me almost enough to make me wish I could back out, but I wouldn't. It wasn't Diesel's fault that when I met a great guy, my brain bypassed "good time" and made a beeline for "future husband."

"We do need to get our act together. I agree with that part." I darted a glance at the clock over the microwave and winced. "But not tonight. I, um... have plans."

I didn't lie and say I had a date, but it was pretty clear that's what Diesel thought, and I didn't correct him. I *could* have had a date, after all.

If I were smart, I would have had one.

In fact, maybe I should get one.

"Oh." He nodded, but disappointment was clear in his eyes. "Right. Sure. You need to go and... do that, then."

"And you'll be fine without me?"

Diesel rolled his eyes. "Been surviving thirty years without you. I'll last another night."

My cheeks went hot, and I concentrated very hard on drying my hands with the towel. "Okay, then. Good luck with the bedtime routine thing. I think it'll help her sleep through the night better, and I'll... I'll see you soon."

But maybe not too soon.

I bent to place a kiss on Marigold's wet curls. "Be good for your uncle, sweetie pie," I murmured, then turned to flee... at a very calm and composed pace.

"Parrish, wait!" Diesel said before I'd taken my first step. His voice was like a rumble of thunder—exciting and a little scary, but somehow cozy too. "I can't let you leave—"

I turned back in surprise, and he lifted a hand to cup my jaw, his eyes warm and intent on mine.

Oh, shit. He was going to kiss me. Holy shit, Diesel Church was going to *kiss me*.

My eyes widened, my lips parted, my breath came in tiny pants. He swiped his thumb over my cheekbone... and then suddenly, he backed away.

Wait, what?

"—with bubbles on your face," he finished with a sheepish grin, holding up the evidence on his thumb. "Enjoy your evening."

I swallowed hard and left without a word... neither calmly nor composedly.

———

I was late getting to the Tavern, of course. I hadn't paid attention to the time, and it was ten after seven by the time I made it to the center of town. Running to the B&B to get a change of clothes would have made me even later—or, let's be honest, I would have found a reason not to go at all—so I decided Beau, Mal, and Brooks would have to enjoy my company damp. I hadn't counted on the Tavern being as crowded as it was, but that was my own fault. It was a Friday in the Thicket, and this was where the action was.

I spotted Mal and Brooks taking up one side of a table in the back of the restaurant, chatting with a vaguely familiar guy standing nearby, and I steeled myself to be social when all I wanted to do was crawl into bed and stew over what an idiot I'd been.

Diesel Church, actually kissing me? I'd be more likely to be struck by lightning during a shark attack right here in middle Tennessee. Our relationship was fake. Fake, fake, fake. And the sooner I actually convinced myself of that, the better off I'd be.

I summoned a smile and superglued it to my face. "Hey, guys!" I shook hands with Brooks and Mal as I slid into the booth across from them. "Beau not here yet?"

Mal and Brooks exchanged a look.

"No," Mal said. "Actually, he called Brooks a little while ago and said he couldn't make it." He shrugged. "Just us chickens tonight."

The word chickens should not have made me think of Diesel and his pets, so I pretended it didn't.

I frowned and glanced from Mal to Brooks to the guy standing by the table. "Is Beau sick? Maybe I should call him and see if he's okay."

"N-no!" Brooks said. "You can't! He specifically said to tell you not to call him. At all. Because he's doing *great*."

"What?" I shook my head. "If he's great, why would he—?"

Mal rolled his eyes and jabbed Brooks in the side. "Brooks, my one true love, you're being rude."

"Huh? Oh, yeah." Brooks rubbed his side and smiled broadly. "Parrish Partridge, meet Tucker Wright."

Mal leaned over the table slightly. "*Doctor* Tucker Wright."

"Hey." Tucker Wright had russet-colored hair, freckles, and a sweet, slow smile that emerged when I extended my hand to shake his. "Good to meet you."

"Same."

"So, Brooks and Tuck were just explaining the concept of the Lickin' Pickin' to me," Mal said with a kind of enthusiasm I'd honestly rarely seen from him. "It's a fall fun fair for charity, and Brooks and I missed it last year because we were out of town, which is so sad because it sounds like literally the most fun a person could ever have in their life."

I blinked. "Uh. Is it much different from the Lickin' Festival?"

Licking Thicket had recently had its big annual festival... or so I'd thought. How many football throws and ice-cream-eating contests and milk-based relay races could one town handle?

"Like night and day," Tucker said with no trace of irony. "Whole different thing."

"No dairy products, for one thing," Brooks agreed. "And it's not an entire week long."

"No," Tucker said with a chuckle. "Can you imagine? Shutting down the town for seven whole days again, right after the Lickin'?"

Brooks shook his head at the very idea. "That would be crazy."

"Crazy," I echoed. "So how long is it?"

"Four days," Brooks said solemnly. "Two weekends in a row."

"'Course, it's a little more intense since it's shorter,"

Tucker said, leaning his hands against the table. "We shut down the streets through the center of town."

"You shut the streets?" Mal and I said at the same time.

"Well, yeah. We've got a hard apple cider tasting this weekend," Brooks explained. "And the Licking Thicket Appl-icious Cocktail and Mocktail Marathon, in which vendors show off their apple-based cocktails and mocktails all night long, the following weekend. Driving can become a problem."

Mal and I exchanged a wide-eyed look. Brooks had said this like it was totally understood and expected and *reasonable*.

"You have never been sexier to me than you are at this moment," Mal said earnestly, cuddling closer to Brooks's arm.

"Baby." Brooks peered down at Mal. "You've only had one beer—"

"Irrelevant. You know it drives me wild when you talk about this ridiculous town like it's normal. Keep seducing me with your talk of apple antics. *Please.*"

Brooks blushed and cleared his throat. "Well, there's an apple-picking contest out at the orchard this weekend."

"Uh-huh," Mal breathed.

"And an apple-bobbing contest too."

"*Hngh.* Aw, yeah there is."

"And an apple-pie-eating contest, and a cider-donut-eating contest for the kids—"

"Do we need to give you two a minute?" I demanded a trifle bitterly as Mal's eyes crossed.

Tucker chuckled. "Every year I get at least half a dozen kids in the office who've got a mysterious stomach ailment the day after those contests." He grinned. "That's the dark side of the Pickin'."

"Ah, so you're a pediatrician?"

Tucker nodded. "Guilty. And I should probably add that when I was younger, I was the kid eating too much pie, so I'm sympathetic to the kids."

I laughed. "You grew up around here, then?"

"Thicket born and raised, yep. My dad owns Pete's Pork Pavillion out on Rosewood."

"Oooh, a Partridge Pit competitor," I joked. "Should we even be talking?"

Tucker leaned closer so he could stage-whisper, "I won't tell if you won't."

I smiled and mimed zipping my lips and throwing away the key.

"Anyway, the Thicket's special," Tucker said. "I went away for school, of course, but I came back a couple years ago once my residency was done. It's home. The place I wanna raise my family someday. In fact, I help run one of the charities that the Lickin' Pickin' helps support—Rainbows over Tennessee, our local LGBTQ organization."

"No way! I didn't even know that existed. Are you looking for volunteers?"

Tucker smiled again and it was warmer this time. More... flirtatious. Definitely interested.

I squirmed a little in my seat and told myself this was great. Perfect, even. Tucker Wright was cute but not the kind of insanely hot where I'd get distracted and overwhelmed every time I thought of him. When he whispered in my ear, it was pleasant but didn't make me tremble like a leaf in a damn EF-4 twister. He was interesting but not mysterious. He wore slacks. He wanted a family.

"Sure thing!" Tucker said. "In fact, I'd—"

"Hey, hey! Look who's here." Brooks's brother, Dunn, strolled up to the table and wrapped a friendly arm around

Tucker's shoulder while using the other to poke Tucker's ribs. "Malachi, my favorite brother! Always nice to see you! Brooks, I suppose it's nice to see you too." Mal chuckled and Brooks rolled his eyes. "And Parrish Partridge, lookin' good. What's new in the world of barbecue, my man?"

I grinned. "Not much. Hot and spicy. Same old, same old."

Dunn laughed. "I'll just bet. So what were y'all talking about?" He shook Tucker's shoulder gently.

The table went weirdly quiet, so I piped up, "Tucker was just telling me about his LGBTQ organization. I think I'm gonna volunteer."

"Ah." Dunn's smile faded, but he nodded enthusiastically anyway. "Sure. Yeah. You, uh... you'd be qualified for that?"

"Oh." I exchanged a look with Tucker. "I sort of assumed every organization can use admin help, but if not—"

"That was Dunn Johnson's super-smooth way of asking if you were gay," Brooks interjected wryly. "Dunn, buddy, I keep telling you, it's not subtle if no one gets what you're asking."

"Ha frickity ha," Dunn mumbled. He shot his brother a smug smile. "FYI, I just came from the Johnson family homestead, and Mom told me to tell you she expects both of her darling boys for dinner tomorrow night. Which is to say, you two schlubs." He pointed between Mal and Brooks. "Since I already told her I'm busy."

Brooks groaned.

"She has a book of color swatches for your wedding," Dunn said, twisting the knife. "And she was telling Dad how hard it is to decide whether periwinkle or cornflower goes best with navy accents."

"What did Dad say?" Brooks looked vaguely horrified.

"Not a thing. ESPN was on, and they were discussing NASCAR at Talladega this week. Mom could have been talking about an alien spaceship landing in Amos Nutter's pasture and Dad wouldn't have noticed. She's gonna present you with all her accumulated data and check her fabric samples against your *eyes*." He laughed evilly. "I'm almost sad I'll miss it."

"We've only been engaged a minute," Brooks whined. He buried his face in Mal's shoulder. "Mal, I'm sorry to tell you this, but we need to elope, possibly tomorrow. Name your price."

Mal lifted a hand to stroke Brooks's head. "Hush! Don't fear the swatches, my cornflower princess. Besides, if we eloped now, we'd miss the Lickin' Apple-tini Slosh Fest."

"That's not until next weekend," Brooks said hopefully. "Wouldn't you like to go to the Pickin' as *my husband*?"

"Oh." Mal opened his mouth, then shut it again and narrowed his eyes. "That was low, Brooks Johnson. How dare you use my weaknesses against me." He folded his arms over his chest. "Just for that, I'm letting her plan the biggest wedding in Thicket history. Also, I'm wearing navy, and you're wearing cornflower for *real*." He sniffed. "Remember, Cindy Ann denies me *nothing*."

"I remember." Brooks nodded remorsefully and ducked his head, but he didn't look remotely put out by this. In fact, he looked so deeply contented and in love that I sighed. So did Tucker. He gave me a tight little smile that I returned.

Dunn grabbed an empty chair from another table and pulled Tucker into it, before dropping onto the booth seat beside me. "I know how much you like a little extra leg room, Doc. So, are we getting wings? Beer? Parrish, what are you in the mood..." He paused and sniffed at me, then wrinkled his nose and sniffed again. "Dude, you smell like lavender and coffee. What kind of fabric softener are you using?"

My cheeks went red. "I, um…"

Brooks snorted. "Since when do you know what lavender smells like, Dunn Johnson? That's what I'd like to know."

"Since I got a scented candle that's lavender, Brooks Johnson. *Duh.*"

"You? Burn scented candles in your bachelor hovel?" Brooks lifted an eyebrow, and Dunn rolled his eyes.

"It's not a hovel. And that's prejudiced," Dunn retorted smartly. "Gay men aren't the only ones who appreciate a little lavender vanilla to brighten up the sitting room. Right, Tuck?" He leaned over to slap Tucker's chest with the back of his hand and then shake him gently by the shoulder. "You tell him."

Dunn and Tucker were clearly close friends, given the way Dunn acted so familiar around him and the fact that Tucker didn't seem to mind.

"Scented candles don't make you gay," Tucker recited, like they'd had this discussion before, possibly more than once.

Dunn nodded. "*Thank* you."

"So, let me guess. You two were best friends growing up?" I asked Tucker.

Dunn hooted. "Us? No way. Tucker's like, a bajillion years older than me."

"Eight," Tucker corrected a bit sourly. "Just *slightly* less than a bajillion. In fact," he added to me, "Dunn was friends with my brother Thom once upon a time. But since I came back to town, I guess you could say we've… hit it off."

"Tucker tries to keep up with me. Right?" Dunn nearly leaned out of his seat to grab Tucker by the back of the neck. "Hey, speaking of, you wanna go fishing this weekend? I know you've gotta do your Rainbows thing at the Pickin', but I figure we can head up to the cabin tomorrow night after you're done, fish Sunday morning at dawn, and you'll be back in time for the festivities Sunday afternoon? Been a long week, and I'd love to sneak away with my best friend to unwind for a bit."

"Oh." Tucker flushed a little. "Well, I guess I..."

"Excellent!" Dunn said. He leaned back in his seat, satisfied. "See, I told my mom I wanted to take Jenn Shipley out and that's why I couldn't make it to dinner, so if you don't come to the cabin with me, I'll probably have to actually ask her. But I've already been out with her twice! Three dates and it'll become, like, a whole *thing*." He rolled his eyes. "And Lord save me from whole things, am I right? But if I tell my mom I had plans with you and forgot, that'll be that. Easy peasy. Mom loves you."

"Easy peasy." Tucker huffed out a half laugh. "You know what? Actually, I can't go fishing, Dunn. Because before you arrived and rudely interrupted, I was about to make plans of my own." He looked at me. "Would you like to come to the Pickin' with me Sunday, Parrish?"

———

"And I said yes," I told Miss Sara, who was sitting in an overstuffed floral-print armchair in her living room with her feet up on a hassock and Elvis curled up on the floor beneath. "I mean, there was nothing else *to* say. He's the perfect man for me, right?"

Miss Sara watched me pacing the carpet and took a

delicate sip of her tea to let me know she agreed whole-heartedly.

"And I like him! I do. He's good-looking. Straight teeth. Kind eyes. He's a pediatrician who does volunteer work, so he's basically a saint. I like his freckles. He wants a family. Heck, if I custom-ordered a guy, it would be this guy. There is literally not a single thing wrong with him! There's no spark, or whatever, but sparks are way overrated. And dangerous," I added.

I grabbed a random book off one of the dark wood shelves that lined the room, flipped through it, and put it back immediately.

"You know what happens with sparks, Miss Sara? Forest fires," I answered so she wouldn't have to. "Exactly. And responsible adults don't go around creating forest fires, nor letting forest fires be created around them. What Tucker and I have could be a slow burn, which is infinitely superior."

Miss Sara uncrossed her ankles, then crossed them again in the other direction.

"I knew you'd agree!" I cried. "Slow burn, steady burn, right? That's what they taught us in Camper Scouts, and I think it applies to basically all of...of everything... in the world. So much better than constantly putting your foot in your mouth and acting like a jerk, or misinterpreting the things he says and does, and feeling like you're on a thrilling roller coaster but knowing in your heart of hearts that the track ends somewhere around the bend."

I humphed, and Elvis thumped his tail in a commiserating sort of way.

"I'm gonna tell Diesel, if he wants to keep this pretense going, there'll be no pet names or touching or... or... or looking at me with those *eyes*." I nodded firmly.

"Sounds logical," Miss Sara agreed. "No looking. What could go wrong?"

"And furthermore—" I broke off as my phone chimed with an incoming text, and I extracted it from my pocket.

It was a picture of Marigold sound asleep in her temporary crib, all sleep flushed and dark-curled, dressed in the footie butterfly pajamas I'd bought her, with her chicken pacifier clutched in her hand. My heart skipped and my brain fizzed as I read the text that came next.

Diesel: *She's been good as gold, just like you said, Baby Whisperer. Hope your plans went okay. Sweet dreams. - D.*

Well, fuck.

"Whatcha got there?" Miss Sara asked.

I handed over the phone without a word, and she grinned as she handed it back.

"Maybe you can start the not looking tomorrow," she suggested, and I sighed.

There was not a darn thing wrong with Tucker Wright. Except, annoyingly, that he wasn't Diesel Church.

Chapter Six

Diesel

I WAS FEEDING THE CHICKENS, trying not to think about the feel of Parrish's smooth face under my fingers or the sight of his sweet ass poking up from the kitchen floor, when Marigold giggled at something and almost lurched out of my arms.

I scrambled to keep a hold of her and settle her back on one hip. "Scared me, girl," I muttered. "Not sure I know what to do if you go headfirst into the dirt. Maybe I should try that sling thing Uncle Parrish got you."

I could have sworn she smiled when she heard me say Parrish's name, but then again, it could have been a reaction to my own smile. Whenever I thought about the man, I couldn't help but feel happier, and not just because he'd agreed to help me get custody. All the time that we were spending together to get to know each other in preparation for next week's home visit, all the things I'd learned about him made me like him that much more. It was hard not to like a man who muttered to himself constantly, clearly adored his elderly uncle, and who'd talk to me for hours on end about politics, or chickens, or Marvel movies, like he really valued my opinions on the subjects.

But that was also why I'd tried not to push him too hard by being overly flirtatious. He was doing enough for me, and I didn't want to make him feel awkward by ogling his ass or going overboard with pet names, even if it felt weirdly natural.

Marigold gurgled happily at the chickens surrounding us, so I introduced her. "This here zebra-looking one is a Plymouth Rock variety named Helga. She was named Helen until the great pecking incident of 2018, but we try not to talk about that time. Now this one…" I pointed to the maroon lady at my feet who was trying to nudge her way into my pockets. "This one is a Rhode Island Red. Her name is Samantha, but everyone calls her Nosy. I think you can imagine why. And this sweet girl," I said, reaching down to run a finger down the long neck of one of my favorite chickens, "is Henry, but only because I got a little confused early on, and by the time I figured it out, she was just… Henry. I tried shortening it to Hen, but that was a bit too on the nose."

I loved watching Marigold chatter happily to the chickens. These ladies were like pets to me, and seeing how happy they made my girl was like the best thing ever. One of the roosters strutted over to see what was going on.

"And that's Lloyd. Don't pay much attention to him. He's a grouch. Thinks he owns the place. But that other rooster over there"—I pointed to my favorite of the two roosters—"is much nicer even though he's noisy as all heck. We call him Uncle. Again, it was a little bit of confusion on my part because of the type of rooster he is, but we don't need to get into that. Aren't his toe feathers pretty?"

I moved around to grab the hose to rinse out the

watering system I'd built. The girls seemed to love it, and it had significantly lowered my stress about keeping them supplied with clean water. My gushing email of thanks to the people at BeakTime had gone unanswered, but their system design had been such a game-changer, I'd considered sending another one.

Before I could turn on the spigot, I heard a woman's voice call out. "Yoo-hoo, Diesel, is that you?"

I'd finished installing the fence pickets to hide the chicken enclosure and salvage yard from the street, but it was only six feet tall. That meant four inches of my face and head poked over the top like a nosy neighbor.

I turned to see who was calling me and saw Ava Siegel's signature blonde curls. She was pushing a stroller with her baby in it and seemed not to notice how out of place her brightly colored sundress looked in my weed-encrusted forecourt.

"Oh, uh, yeah? Hi. It's me," I stammered, tossing the hose back toward its coil and shifting Marigold on my hip again. "Be right with you."

I quickly hustled all the chickens away from the gate before slipping through and slamming it closed again. Hopefully I didn't smell like chicken poop or have feathers sticking to my clothes here and there.

I tried brushing myself off, but it wasn't easy with an armful of curious baby. She leaned this way and that trying to get a look at our visitors.

"Oh my goodness gracious," Ava squealed. "Is this... who is this little one? She is so precious!"

The chubby baby in her stroller was dead asleep. Little blond wisps of hair stuck to his temples with sweat even though the stroller's sunshade was pulled over him. I gestured her over to the shaded area under the big oak tree where the air was much cooler. There was a wooden picnic table there, and I asked if she wanted a lemonade or something.

"No, thanks. I have a bottle of water here. But you didn't answer my question. Is this little one yours?"

I didn't know Ava that well, but I knew her well enough to know she was a smart woman who knew everyone and everything. I wondered what I was willing to reveal about my situation.

"Well, not exactly," I said, scrambling to come up with an explanation that didn't include a scary custody battle. "Marigold's my niece, but I'm taking care of her."

I slid onto the bench opposite Ava and shifted Marigold until she was standing on my lap pounding the table with her little palms. Ava's face softened as she reached across the table to slide an index finger into one of Marigold's hands for a handshake.

"How do you do, princess?" she asked softly. "Aren't you beautiful? And I can already tell your uncle Diesel adores you, doesn't he?"

"Pretty hard not to," I admitted with a laugh. "Even though the dirty diapers are enough to make me question my sanity."

Ava's laugh filled the shaded area around us, relaxing me almost instantly. I'd begun to figure out that when another baby person was around, I could let go of some of my crazy vigilance. I seemed to carry around this kind of debilitating stress that I was going to fuck up without even realizing it. But when another parent was around—or Parrish—then I felt less alone. Like I had proper supervision to make sure I didn't do something awful like tip the baby into the dirt while feeding chickens.

I cleared my throat and tried to be normal. "How old is your baby? I'm sorry, I forgot his name."

She was a beautiful woman, and her smile was contagious. I could see why the advertising guy had fallen in love with her. "His name is Beau, and he's eight months. What about Marigold? How old is she?"

"Almost ten months," I said, pulling out a little baggie of Cheerios to keep Marigold busy while we talked. She liked mashing them between her teeth, and I liked watching her try to pick them up with her bizarrely intense concentration. Cheerio time was one of our favorites. "My friend Parrish says I should start teaching her sign language. Do you... I mean... is that something you do with your baby?"

Her smile softened. "I tried to teach him the sign for help, but he kept signing poop instead. I gave up after I wasted about a thousand diapers, and Paul started trying to talk me into switching to cloth. I'm as environmentally conscious as the next person, but sometimes you have to draw a line, Diesel. You know?"

I laughed and nodded. "Pretty sure I have enough on my plate without all that. 'Course, I'd probably get kicked out of all the playgroups if anyone found out how many disposables I've been through already in just one week."

"Oh!" she said, clapping her hands together and startling Marigold and me. "Speaking of playgroup, you should come to Splash Park Tuesdays! All the moms and dads gather there with babies under two. It's a day set aside for the littlest ones so they don't get trampled. I'll swing by and pick you up. Be sure to bring plenty of sunscreen and a hat. My heart would break if that perfect skin got a sunburn."

Surely her mom group didn't want me tagging along. I could only imagine the hushed gasps when the big hairy tattooed guy walked up.

"Uh... I'll think about it."

She shot me a look that said there was no thinking necessary. "You're coming with me. Deal with it."

My eyes shot wide in surprise. She kind of reminded me of my sister. Beautiful and a little frail-looking from the outside but tough as nails on the inside.

"Yes, sir," I mumbled, leaning down to brush an ant off the table near Marigold's hand.

"Good. Now that's settled, let me tell you why I stopped by today."

I blinked up at her just as Lloyd crowed at top volume from the chicken pen. "Ignore him," I said. "He gets pissy if he hears me talking to someone for too long. I'd say it's jealousy, but he hates my guts. Parrish says Lloyd is jealous of any attention I give to someone else, which... I'm not sure I agree since Lloyd doesn't mind it when I give affection to the hens." I stopped and realized I was giving a near stranger way too much information. "Sorry. Go ahead. Are you looking for spare parts?"

Her forehead crinkled. "What? Oh, no. Not at all. I was at a Beautification Corps meeting this morning where it was decided that the jun... *salvage* yard could use our help."

I tilted my head. "I don't understand."

"You see, since Mal's sign made such a big splash last year, and his work has been bringing in all kinds of new interest in found-object art, we—that is, the Licking Thicket Beautification Corps—recognize that your... salvage yard has become somewhat of a destination for tourists."

I nodded. It was true. Business was booming for me, and much of it could be traced back to Mal and that sign. I owed him big-time and had made it clear that he could pretty much take whatever he wanted for free at this point as long as he kept spreading the word about my place.

Ava continued. "So, we have a budget allotment to help spruce up the place."

"What place?" I asked, feeling stupid. "This place?" My voice sounded a little high. I tried again. "You want to spruce up the salvage yard?"

She nodded happily. "Exactly. Fresh paint on the... house, some new planters with colorful flowers spilling out..." She cooed at my niece. "Maybe some *marigolds*, even. And an all-new sign. We want to make this place aesthetically pleasing and representative of the new and improved Licking Thicket."

"Did you come here from the Tavern?" I asked carefully. It wasn't polite to accuse a lady of being day drunk, but all signs pointed in that direction. "Do you want me to call Paul to come get you?"

She furrowed her brows again. "Well... it is hot out here, and I have walked a long way today already. This baby weight is a total bitch."

I stood up and put Marigold on my hip. "Why don't we go inside and I'll fix us an iced coffee?"

Ava was busy finger-typing into her phone. "Hang on. I'm going to see if Mal will make the new sign for us, and I think Brooks's brother, Dunn, will build us the planters. He's handy like that."

"You're serious?" I asked.

"Sarabeth Kelly was the one who came up with the idea, but then it was a unanimous vote. I think it's because you're so close to town and they saw you'd already been working on it yourself by putting up this nice new fence. Ooh! Maybe we could find someone to paint a mural on the fence. A pastoral scene representative of the area."

"No cows," I said, remembering the hallway of horrors I'd seen at Brooks's parents' house when I'd delivered a condenser coil for their fridge. "Maybe chickens, though. My friend Parrish says..."

I stopped when I realized I'd mentioned Parrish three times too many.

Ava narrowed her eyes at me and then focused on the cute butterfly romper Marigold was wearing. I could almost see the little cogs snapping into place.

Oh hell.

"Parrish, hm?" She tapped her chin with the pad of her pointer finger. "Did he give her that outfit? Did it come from Kinder-potamus?"

I felt my heart rate kick up. "How about that iced coffee? I have low-fat milk and Splenda."

I turned to head toward the house. The telltale crunch of her stroller wheels on gravel followed me. "How do you know Parrish?" she asked.

I swallowed. I didn't want to ruin things for sweet Parrish. If Ava thought for one minute that Parrish and I had anything going between us—which of course we did not. *Not.*—then it would ruin any chances he'd have at meeting a nice man in town. But at the same time, I didn't want to lie and say I didn't know him. Chances were, someone might see us together at any number of meetings or hearings. Plus... I kind of wanted him to come to Splash Park Tuesdays with me. If he wanted to, that was.

"Doesn't everyone know Parrish?" I asked, pulling the door to the house open.

As soon as I entered the house, I came to an abrupt stop. I'd forgotten the giant Kinder-potamus gift basket was still front and center on the living room floor. Marigold had been using it to throw her new toys into. It was overflowing with all of the adorable baby things Parrish had picked out for her. I swallowed around a nervous lump in my throat.

"Hm," she said, stepping around me and patting little Beau's back where she'd tossed him against her shoulder. The boy was still dead asleep and drooling. Of course his nosy mother's eyes went straight to the basket of evidence on the floor. Before I had a chance to stammer out an explanation, Ava turned to me with a big, sunny smile.

"You're coming to the Lickin' Pickin' with us tomorrow. I insist."

I had whiplash from the subject change, but then again, I was relieved as all hell she hadn't mentioned Parrish again.

"I can't," I tried. "I have plans."

She poked me gently on the nose like I was a child. "Of course you do, big guy. Plans with Paul, Beau, and me to pick some apples. Don't you think Marigold deserves to be shown off amongst the Thicketeers? Don't you think she needs to bond with the town who's going to love and support her during her formative years?"

I studied the manipulative, conniving beauty in front of me and then finally let out a sigh of defeat. "You're good. I haven't had a guilt trip like that in a very long time."

She flounced toward the kitchen. "Honey, you don't even know the half of it yet."

Chapter Seven

Parrish

"And you shoulda seen the way Dunn Johnson ripped that crankbait through the coontail!"

Tucker Wright's laughter rang through the grassy, tree-ringed picnic area where he'd laid out our checkered blanket, and mingled with the excited chatter of dozens of other folks hanging out in this section of the English Family Apple Orchard. "There he was, right? Standing on the riverbank, bracing himself like he's gonna pull in the motherlode, like he's caught the granddaddy bass that's gonna be in his Facebook profile picture for all the rest of his born days..."

Tucker doubled over for a second, laughing so hard he wheezed. "And he's yellin' at me, 'Tuck, wade on in with the net! Tuck, this is the one. Tuck, we're gonna need more batter to fry this puppy! Tuck, get in there!'" Tucker broke off with a chuckling sigh and a fond head shake. "Turned out the idiot had hooked himself a plastic Kroger bag and about half a ton of coontail, and we ate ham sandwiches for dinner." He wiped his eyes and sniffled a little. "But if you hear him tell the story, that was exactly what he meant to do all along. That's Dunn Johnson for you."

"Yeah, he really sounds great," I agreed, leaning back on my hands so I could stretch my legs out in front of me and tip my face toward the sun. "If I didn't believe it after the story where Dunn caught the runaway heifer, or the time he made a Pride flag crop circle for you in his back pasture, these fishing stories would've really sealed the deal!"

Tucker shot me a side-eyed look, and his mouth curved up on one side. He pushed the ice in his soda cup around with his straw. "I don't know why I'm rattling on. I invited you here today so we could get to know one another, not to talk about my friend Dunn, of all people."

"Nonsense! It's fine," I assured him. "It's a beautiful day, and it's nice sitting here, listening to your stories."

Tucker's eyes were warm on my face. "You're kind of a glass-half-full person, aren't you? I like that about you." He reached out a hand to cover mine on the blanket. "I like a lot of things about you, Parrish."

I immediately sat up and reached for my own soda cup. "Sweet Methuselah on buttered toast, that sun is tryna *fry* us, huh?" I slurped at what was now only melting ice. "I should go get us another drink. Hydration is important. Be right back!" I jumped up without waiting for him to reply.

When I'd agreed to spend Sunday afternoon with Tucker at the Pickin', it was safe to say I hadn't understood what I was getting myself into on many levels.

For one thing, even though Tucker had said the Pickin' was way different from the Lickin', I hadn't really believed it until I'd pulled my Mustang into the bumpy, grass-covered field out by the road and found out I'd have to take a hayride to get to the official entry area at the back of the orchard.

When I'd crowded into the back of the horse-drawn wagon with a dozen children and six frazzled but friendly parents, including Gracie Johnson Mawbry, Brooks's sister, I should've kinda read the writing on the wall... but I hadn't.

I'd met Tucker at the entry table as we'd planned, since Rainbows over Tennessee was sponsoring the day's events, and he'd greeted me with an enthusiastic hug and an awkward half kiss that landed somewhere between my cheek and my lips. He'd also introduced me to the three middle-aged women at the table, all of whom had winked at me and told Tucker to, "Enjoy your sweet self, Tucker, honey, but remember to keep it G-rated for the young ones," which should've been a huge red flag... but I'd ignored it.

Then Tucker had grabbed a big backpack from behind the table and draped an arm over my shoulders as we walked away. I'd stiffened a little at the feeling of his arm around me but tried to hide it by asking where they'd set up the area with the vendor stalls. I needed some fried fair food and, please baby Jesus, some moonshine, to help get me over this first awkward part of the date.

"There's no alcohol here today." Tucker looked bewildered. "The cider tasting was last night in town, and the cocktail things are next Saturday. Oh, shoot. Did you not know that? Both Sundays at the Pickin' are more like family fun days." His face had fallen into a nearly comical frown. "Which means I should have invited you for last night, shouldn't I? I was just thinking I'd be manning the table earlier today and maybe it'd be fun to have a picnic and talk, but... Damn it. This is going to be the most awkward, boring first date in history, isn't it? God, I suck at this."

"Nonsense," I'd assured him. "Low-key is fine with me."

Except... Tucker had kinda been right. It *had* been

awkward, just the two of us walking among a sea of little families. Or maybe it was just that *I'd* felt awkward, like I'd forgotten something... or someone.

Possibly two someones.

I'd spotted a monarch fluttering among the grasses, and I'd wanted to point it out to Marigold. I'd seen a cloud that looked kind of like the splotch of carrot gunk on Diesel's ceiling, but there was no one to laugh about it with. Dozens of kids laughing, but none of them were mine.

Still, I'd tried to make the best of things. It was a gorgeous September day in Tennessee—which was to say, it was maybe three degrees cooler than it had been in July—bees were buzzing through the grass, and there was a beautiful, apple-scented breeze blowing through the trees. Tucker and I had gotten ourselves sodas and some crepes smeared with local apple blossom honey and sat down on Tucker's blanket in the shade-dappled orchard to talk. As it turned out, we had a *ton* in common.

He'd gone to UT like I did, though he was a few years ahead of me, and we'd even lived in the same residence hall our freshman years, so we'd compared notes for a bit. He'd helped his brother restore a Mustang—a Shelby—which was awesome, and we'd talked about that too. We'd even talked about how neither of us liked sweet tea very much, but both of us pretended to, because while some hidebound traditions were made to be broken, some would continue until the end of the world, amen. All in all, we could not have had more in common if we'd been cut from the same cloth and stitched together like one of Aunt Marnie's quilt patterns.

And yet...

Here I was, walking away from Tucker, and it didn't

occur to me to look over my shoulder to see if he was watching, or to smile goodbye the way I did every time I left Diesel's place. It hadn't occurred to me to ask Tucker to come along to the refreshment booth so we could keep talking either. I didn't want to hold his hand, let alone push him up against a tree and kiss him. It wasn't *his* head I kept searching for above the crowd or his face I kept hoping to see. And though he seemed determined to push through it, I was pretty sure Tucker felt the same about me. While Diesel made my stomach swoop and dive like a roller coaster every time he twitched, Tucker made me feel nothing at all, except sort of vaguely *wrong* whenever he tried to touch me.

In short, though Tucker Wright was a perfectly nice guy, I was afraid I had a one-track mind, and that track led directly to Diesel Church. But if dating other guys wouldn't work to help me guard my heart, what the heck was I gonna do to stop myself from falling for my fake fiancé?

Fortunately for me, Miss Sara was running the refreshment counter. Maybe she'd have some advice.

I got in line behind old Amos Nutter as a loud cheer went up from the far side of the field, along with delighted kiddie screams.

"Ah, that'll be the apple bobbing done," Amos remarked, his gray-and-white mustache twitching. "D'you know, Parrish, there was a time I couldn't be beat in that contest?"

"Is that so, sir?" I asked politely, still distracted.

"Yep. All Nutters love bobbing. It's kind of our thing."

I blinked, my attention caught. "Pardon?"

"Now everyone knows Johnsons are big fans of the Lickin.'" Amos rolled his eyes. "That ain't no secret. Big

Red Johnson goes crazy at Lickin' time. And don't get me wrong, Nutters like the Lickin' too. But you might say bobbing is what Nutters do best."

"That's... real good to know, sir."

"It's all in the stance, you see, Parrish. You gotta get in there and not be afraid to get wet. Legs spread, mouth open wide. Gotta use a steady up-and-down motion and not go too far, too fast. It's more about the lips than the teeth." He attempted to demonstrate, right there in the refreshment line, but he ended up grabbing my forearm when his legs shook and he had to clap a hand to his mouth to push his dentures back into place. "'Fraid my knees aren't up to much anymore. Not like the good old days. But once upon a time, men would tremble when they heard I'd be bobbing."

I tilted my head to one side and blinked, sure I'd heard him wrong. Had he actually said...

"He's right," the white-haired lady who'd gotten into line behind me confirmed, like maybe I wasn't taking Amos at his word. "And no Nutter in the Thicket's ever bobbed as beautifully as Amos here."

I turned in time to see her duck her curled-and-shellacked head to hide her blush.

"Why, Emmaline Proud," Amos declared, leaning around me. "I had no idea you'd ever seen me bob."

"It was a while back," she whispered. Then Emmaline, Lord help us all, scratched the toe of her sensible shoe in the dirt, bit her lip, and darted a flirtatious glance back at him.

I was becoming extremely uncomfortable, and I was still at least six people back from Miss Sara.

"Must've been! It's been many a year since I bobbed in public," Amos agreed. "Though I do keep my hand in the game privately, of course."

Really? *Really?*

"I remember your last bobbing perfectly," Emmaline insisted. "It was 1958. You were moist but *majestic*."

"Oh. Well now." Amos turned a violent shade of puce and stroked his white mustache like it was an emotional support animal. "That might be the nicest thing anyone ever said about me. You couldn't've been more than a tiny slip of a girl back then, young as you are—"

Young was a relative term, apparently.

"Yes, but some things just stick with you," she said fervently, raising her gaze to his. "No man's ever bobbed the way you do."

Amos looked poleaxed. "Why, Emmaline. All these years, and you've never said…"

"Ms. Emmaline, why don't you go ahead of me?" I interrupted, stepping back to swap spots with her. "I insist."

"Yeah, come stand by me, Emmaline. I'd love to buy you a pop." Amos took her arm and threaded it through his. I wasn't sure who'd be holding who up, but maybe it didn't matter.

"Grandpa!" A redheaded boy of maybe seven or eight with a soaking wet shirt ran up and threw his arms around Amos's waist. "I won!" The boy pulled back and showed him a little medallion and a half-eaten apple.

"'Atta boy, Jackie," Amos praised, wrapping his arms around the boy's slim shoulders. "I never doubted you."

"Bobbing's what Nutters do," the boy said modestly.

"Jack Nutter, you are a chip off the old block," Emmaline tittered, and the boy preened when she ruffled his carrot hair and nudged him ahead of her to the counter.

Wait. Someone had named the poor child—?

"You get used to it, Parrish," a wry voice said.

I turned to find Brooks behind me with Mal tucked up against his arm. Their hands were intertwined.

"Used to what?" I asked.

Mal was the one who answered. "To this town being crazy. Perfectly crazy. And, conversely, crazy-perfect." He grinned and looked around expectantly. "So, where's Tucker?" He looked about as invested as the ladies at the entry table had, though probably less likely to remind me to be G-rated. "How're things going with you two?"

"I... um..." I hesitated.

Dunn Johnson strolled up to stand beside his brother in line. "Dear God. Remind me not to judge the apple bobbing again next year. Those ankle-biters are violent." He glanced right and left before lowering his voice. "The Nutter kid made apple bobbing into a full-contact sport. He was soaked to the gills. But damn if he didn't get the biggest apple on the first try." He sounded admiring.

"Moist but majestic?" I offered.

Dunn gaped at me for a minute, then frowned and nodded. "Huh. You know, it actually kinda was."

"Amos would be glad to hear it."

"Back to the point," Mal interrupted impatiently. "Parrish. Tucker. Picnic. Lurve?"

"Well." I gnawed on my lip. I hated to disappoint him. "It's been a real nice afternoon. Tucker and I never lacked for anything to talk about, that's for sure."

Dunn smiled warmly. "Yep, that's Tuck, alright. He gets so passionate—"

"Hush, Dunn," Mal said. "No one cares what *you* think about Tucker. I wanna hear what Parrish, his potential love match, thinks."

Brooks ran a hand over his face and seemed to stifle a groan.

"Well, I think..." I looked at Mal's eager face and

faltered. "Er. That is to say..." Dunn seemed to hold his breath. "I like Tucker a lot," I finished lamely.

"Yep." Whatever Brooks saw on my face had him nodding resignedly. "Gotcha. Figured as much."

"Gotcha?" Mal repeated, confused. "What've you got? What did you figure?" Without waiting for an answer, he barreled on, "Parrish, you and Tucker have so much in common." He waggled his eyebrows. "Don't you?"

"So much," I echoed faintly. Except any chemistry whatsoever.

"Ha! Hear that?" Mal demanded of no one in particular. "I've basically stolen the Thicket matchmaking crown from Cindy Ann. I'm calling it right now." He paused, considered, then waved a hand. "Admittedly, she wanted Brooks to hook up with Ava, so her crown's a bit tarnished, but I'll restore it to glory once you and Tuck get together."

Brooks wrapped an arm around his fiancé's shoulder. "Mal, baby, maybe let's not get ahead of ourselves. It's early days yet for Parrish and Tucker. Right, Parrish?"

"Early, schm-early! It took us ten seconds to fall for each other and, like, a week to admit it. Love doesn't wear a wristwatch, Brooks," Mal said ardently. "Right, Parrish?"

"I'm with Mal," Dunn agreed. "Parrish knows what's what, and he obviously recognizes there's nobody in the world better than Tucker. He's loyal, and funny, and smart, and he's not ugly. Right, Parrish?"

"Well, I..." I swallowed and darted a glance down the crowded gravel path toward the entry gate which seemed really far away—too far to make a fast exit—then did a double take because I could almost swear I saw a familiar golden-brown head towering above the other Thicketeers. When I glanced back, he was gone.

Or, more likely, he'd never been there in the first place. I was pretty sure he hadn't socialized at all since he got temporary custody of the baby, so it was really unlikely he was here now.

And wasn't that just great? It wasn't enough that my dreams were haunted by Diesel's tattooed gorgeousness, now my waking hours were going to be haunted too? I was literally losing my mind, and I was pretty sure it was Diesel's fault. I kicked at a rock on the ground and wished the line would move faster.

"Yes," I said staunchly, because I wished it were true, "Tucker Wright is an amazing guy, and I like him a lot. A *lot*. I'm so glad we've gotten to know each other better."

"Oh, wow." I whirled to find Tucker standing there, a picnic blanket in his hand, a stupefied expression on his face and hearts in his eyes. "Parrish," he whispered. Then tentatively, he added, "Honey?"

"Oh, wow," Mal breathed, excited.

"Oh, wow." Brooks winced.

"Oh." Dunn looked taken aback. "Wow."

Oh, wow.

I lifted both palms like I was stopping traffic in front of a horrible accident. "No, see, I just..."

But before I could figure out what I wanted to say, let alone force myself to spit it out, Tucker had grabbed my hand, yanked me toward him, and molded his lips to mine.

Here's the God's honest truth: Tucker Wright knew how to kiss. His free hand landed on my hip and held there. His lips pressed against mine, pillowy soft and with just the right firmness. He smelled like apple blossom honey. And when he swiped his tongue over my lips once before pulling away, it was very pleasant. Tingle-inducing, even. Like, seriously good, high-quality kissing that earned two thumbs up from me and for a half second there made me wonder if maybe I'd misjudged things. If maybe I should try harder.

"Good. Lord. Good frickity freakin' Lord. What am I witnessing right now? Paul, cover baby Beau's eyes. Diesel, cover Marigold's eyes. Somebody, cover *my* eyes, or else make Tucker stop giving Parrish the world's worst example of mouth-to-mouth resuscitation!"

At the sound of Ava's voice, I jumped away from Tucker like I was spring-loaded and pressed a shaking hand to my mouth. My eyes found Diesel's immediately—head and shoulders above everyone, as always—and I watched emotions skitter across his face. Surprise. Sadness. Resignation. Utter blankness. Then he stared down at Marigold, who was strapped to his chest in the front carrier I'd bought him, fast asleep.

My stomach plummeted hard, even before I registered the guy standing by Diesel's elbow.

Stewie, the greasy little lawyer who was supposed to be helping Diesel get custody of Marigold, stood between Diesel and Paul Siegel. He stared at me and then behind me at Tucker, then up at Diesel, like he expected some kind of reality TV throwdown.

I swallowed. Stewie worked for Diesel, right? I was pretty sure Diesel had said Stewie was the best he could afford. But was Stewie required to go report what he'd seen? If he had doubts about the stability of my relationship with Diesel, would he report them to the caseworker who was coming next week or to the judge who'd make the final custody decision?

Would I really trust Marigold's future to a man who'd wear a polyester suit to an orchard?

And why, oh why, hadn't I thought about any of this before agreeing to this stupid date?

Because I was an idiot and a coward who was afraid of getting his heart bruised, that was why, and so it was my responsibility to fix this shit.

"It's not what you think," I blurted. "It's a... a town tradition."

Stewie glanced up at Diesel, who still wore that terrible, blank expression on his face, and raised a skeptical eyebrow. "Kissin' other guys? If you say so, kid."

"It's the Lickin' Kissin'," I lied desperately. "It's a... a traditional way of greeting your close friends. Only observed here in the Thicket. On select Sundays. In September. In this orchard." I swallowed. "It's fallen out of fashion in recent years, but I say we bring it back."

There was a moment of stunned silence where eight pairs of eyes stared at me and at each other, and a lone voice in the crowd called out, "I thought the Lickin' Kissin' was in December?" then...

"He speaks the truth!" Ava proclaimed from Diesel's other side. She turned toward Mal so fast her blonde ponytail swung out behind her, clasped his face in her two hands, and pulled him down to press an enthusiastic kiss to his lips.

Mal made a startled *mmmph* noise.

"Joyous Pickin' Tidings, Malachi!" she said as she released him.

"Uh. Okay?" he mumbled. "Joyous Pickin' Tidings?"

"Good God," Brooks muttered, shaking his head and hauling his fiancé back against his side.

"Brooks," Ava prompted insistently. "Don't *you* have a closest friend to kiss?"

He stared wide-eyed across the group of us at Ava's husband, Paul, who smiled a big, cheesy grin.

"Come on, Brooks," he said, making a gimme gesture

with both hands. "It's been a year since the last time you laid one on me in a field."

"It was *you* who laid one on me, and—" Brooks broke off as Ava's glare grew more insistent. "I have no idea what's happening here, but fine. Fine." He brought both hands to his mouth, kissed them, and blew them toward Paul. "Joyous Pickin'..." He looked at Ava expectantly.

"Tidings," she supplied.

"Right. Yes. Of course. Silly me. Joyous Pickin' Tidings," he recited.

Paul jumped in the air exuberantly, catching the kisses. "Back atcha, Big Daddy."

"You solemnly swore you'd never use that name again," Brooks sighed.

Ava Siegel winked at me and tilted her head toward Diesel significantly. "Go on," she mouthed.

I stared at Diesel and swallowed as I took a cautious step toward him. Diesel stared back, and the whole world outside the two of us went fuzzy around the edges like it had completely ceased to matter, 'cause it kinda had, at least to me.

I lifted a hand to touch the golden-brown hair I'd been wanting to touch since I saw him at the courthouse that day, and I almost expected him to pull back at the last second, but he didn't. And when my fingertips slid into the silky strands, his eyes half shut in pleasure.

My heart rate galloped a mile a minute as I pushed myself up on my tiptoes, my free hand braced on his shoulder for balance so I wouldn't squish Marigold. He leaned down the rest of the way and wrapped one arm around me to splay at the small of my back, and then Diesel Church kissed me.

Holy shitballs of fire. Within the first second, my hand

was clutching his hair like it was the only stable thing in the universe and I'd forgotten how to breathe. His tongue licked into my mouth like it owned the place, and his teeth clacked against mine a little. There was no finesse in this kiss, simply raw power and hunger that made me want to sob with relief. I'd wanted this and hadn't thought I could have it. I hadn't known he wanted it too.

And it occurred to me that other guys might know how to kiss just fine, but Diesel Church knew how to kiss *me*.

Marigold made a soft little noise, an indication she was awake, and I forced myself to step back.

"Joyous Pickin' Tidings," I whispered.

Diesel ran one huge hand over my head to clasp the back of my neck and hauled me against his side. "Yeah," he said gruffly. "Those were some damn joyous Pickin' tidings, alright."

I felt my cheeks flame, so I buried my nose in the soapy sandalwood smell of his T-shirt and nodded.

"Hey! Why the heck are we letting the young people have all the fun?" Amos Nutter demanded of the entire assembled crowd. "Whaddya say, Emmaline?"

"Oh!" Ms. Emmaline flushed pink. "Well... alright!"

He bent down and pecked her cheek. "Joyous Pickin' Tidings!"

She clutched a hand to her cheek and giggled, "Joyous Pickin' Tidings!"

Then suddenly literally everyone was doing it—Red and Cindy Ann Johnson, Latonya and Maureen from the grocery store, Miss Sara and a lady from the Thicket Beautification Corps, Ollie and Kendra Nutter, Mario from the vegetarian place and Chad from the library. Cries of "Joyous Pickin' Tidings" and laughter filled the air.

"Ah, what the hell," Dunn said.

He slung his arm around Tucker's shoulder and pulled him in close. I saw Tucker's eyes flare wide half a second before Dunn pressed a kiss to his lips.

And then another, smaller one.

And then one more.

"Dunn Johnson." A curly-haired lady in a pink T-shirt stepped up to our little group and folded her arms over her chest. "What in tarnation are you doing?"

Dunn straightened. "Kissing Tucker. Duh."

"But... you're straight."

"Well, yeah, but he's my best friend."

"But you can't just..."

"It's tradition, Jenn." He rolled his eyes. "Go find your own best friend."

The woman turned on her heel and stomped off.

Dunn kissed Tucker one final time, then cleared his throat. "Joyous Pickin' Tidings, Tuck," he said solemnly.

"Yeah. Uh. Joyous Pickin' Tidings to you too." Tucker's face was nearly as pink as Ms. Emmaline's. His eyes met mine across the little space between us. He looked up at Diesel, then back to me, and he smiled. "Joyous Pickin' Tidings, Parrish."

"Okay, all y'all are insane in the membrane," Stewie pronounced, throwing his hands up. "Clearly you and your fiancé fit in perfectly here," he told Diesel.

"Aww. You feeling left out?" Diesel asked without cracking a smile. "'Cause you're not my *close* friend, but I could—"

"Do not complete that sentence." He rolled his eyes. "Parrish, I came all the way out here 'cause I need you to sign a couple forms for me so I can file 'em first thing tomorrow. Diesel already did his."

"Oh. Yeah, of course," I agreed, glad I hadn't totally

fucked up my chance at helping Diesel and Marigold. "Whatever you need."

Stewie nodded his head toward the entrance. "They're back in my car. Just a hop, skip, and a wagon ride that way," he said dryly.

"Sure. I'll go with you—"

"*We'll* go with you," Diesel corrected in his grumbly voice, and I couldn't lie, entire colonies of bright-winged butterflies swirled and swooped in my stomach. I was totally screwed where this guy was concerned, and maybe it was crazy not to run as far as I could in the other direction, but that hadn't worked real well so far, so maybe I should just let myself enjoy it while it lasted.

"We'll go," I confirmed.

"But you'll come back," Mal said. "Right? You'll come back to hang with me and Brooks and *Tucker*? Huh? *Huh?*"

"Malachi, let it go," Ava said firmly.

"But no! Remember we agreed that it would be so cute if—"

"Mal, honey, you remember the time we went to Coachella? Remember the guy who came with us?"

Mal rolled his eyes. "Your salon manager's one gay cousin she wanted you to set me up with. Boris. Benny. Barney?"

"Jason. And remember the guy you met there? The one who explained piercings to you?"

"Pablo," he supplied with no hesitation. "Oh." He looked from me to Tucker, then to me and Diesel. "*Ohhhh.*"

"Uh-huh." Ava patted his arm consolingly.

"But my matchmaking crown!" Mal complained.

"Maybe set your sights higher," Brooks suggested with a sideways glance at Tucker. "I have some ideas." He pulled Mal away from the group. "Come stroll with me and I'll tell you all about it, and you can tell *me* about Pablo with the piercings. I feel like I have a lot to thank him for."

"Literally crazy," Stewie grumbled as he led us back toward the entrance.

But with Diesel's arm wrapped around me, even temporarily, I was pretty sure Mal had it right earlier. For this one moment, it felt kinda crazy-perfect, and I just wished I could keep it.

Chapter Eight

Diesel

MY BRAIN and heart were fighting WWE style. On the one hand, my heart was mooning stupidly over kissing Parrish's sweet mouth. Feeling his slender body under my hand and his soft lips against mine was one of the single best moments of my life. It was a dream come true.

On the other, my brain kept replaying those same lips on Tucker Wright's mouth. I'd wanted to punch something, namely, Tucker Wright. But the look of horror on Parrish's face when he saw me calmed me a little, enough, at least, to keep from getting arrested for assault right there at the Pickin'.

Marigold made a little sighing noise and shifted in the sling. Parrish scrambled to catch up with me in the parking lot.

"Is she okay? Is she upset? Did I squish her back there?" he asked worriedly.

I slowed down a little, not realizing how long my strides had become in my haste to get away from the awkward Tucker situation. "She's fine. Still asleep."

He walked next to me for a few more steps before clenching his fists by his side. "I shouldn't have done that."

I knew what he was talking about, but I played stupid anyway. "Done what?"

"Just... just... lurched at you like that. Attacked your face like some kind of... some kind of face attacker... thing."

I took a chance and slid my arm around his shoulders, hoping like hell he didn't shrug it off in disgust. "Well, you are my fiancé. So it kind of seems appropriate that I would be the one you'd kiss for Joyous Pickin' Tidings."

He groaned and turned into my side, burying his face in my shoulder. "I can't believe I did that. I'm so embarrassed."

I laughed and rubbed my hand up and down his arm. "Everyone loved it. Besides, how often does one get to claim the origination story for a new Thicket tradition as epic as that?"

His easy laughter was enough to release the final bands of stress from my shoulders.

"Come home with me? With us, I mean? We, uh..." I tried to come up with an excuse. "We have a lot more stuff to go over, in case the caseworker questions us."

He pulled his face out of my shirt and smiled up at me shyly. "I'd like that. Maybe I can fix us dinner?"

I thought of the chicken dish he'd brought me. "You know what? This time let me cook for you. I have a little veggie patch behind the chicken coop, and I've just harvested a ton of fresh tomatoes and basil. I could make us a homemade marinara for spaghetti."

"That sounds perfect," he said. "I didn't know you had a garden."

While I tried transferring my sleeping girl to the car seat, I told him about Aunt Dot and Aunt Birdie forcing me to weed their vegetable garden every time I used a curse word when I was a teenager.

"And the funny thing was," I continued, "those two curse worse than any Navy sailor you'd ever meet. But their point was teaching me control. I was so angry during those years, and I took it out on them with a pissy attitude."

I finished clipping the straps and dropped a kiss on Marigold's sweaty head before climbing into the driver's seat and starting the engine. "Anyway, I kind of ended up loving it. It was peaceful, and it gave me a chance to spend time outside by myself. I did a lot of thinking in that garden over the years, so the first thing I did when Stix left me the salvage yard—well, besides scrubbing the place down with bleach—was put in a garden."

"Did your aunts keep chickens too?"

I laughed and scratched the back of my neck. It was kind of an embarrassing story. "No, that was an accident, really. I had a guy come to the yard looking for a new taillight casing for his truck. He didn't have enough cash, so he wrote me a bad check. When I called him up to ask him to stop by with some cash, he brought the cash and a hen. He was obviously embarrassed about the bounced check, so he sort of shoved the bird at me and grumbled something about it being his best layer."

After slowing down to take the turn onto my street, I continued. "I tried to refuse it, telling him I didn't keep chickens, but he just kept insisting. Finally he blurted out something about not being able to afford to keep her. He lit out of there too fast for me to offer to help. That's how I ended up with Talia. And, of course, it would have been cruel not to get her some company."

Parrish's smile was adorably toothy. "Of course. How many do you have now?"

"That's not important," I said quickly, pulling into my driveway. "What's important is how much money I save on eggs. Besides, I sell them to people who come for salvage items too. Sometimes I have to give them away since the girls are such good layers, but I drop them off at the soup kitchen too, so that helps."

Parrish's eyes twinkled which made my face heat. "Do you think you save more on eggs than you spend on supplies for your girls?"

I threw the truck into park and hopped out, mumbling under my breath about hens having needs. The sound of his laughter was so sweet and unexpected, I blinked across the truck at him. The sunlight hit Parrish's brown hair, lighting up some strands of honey in it I hadn't noticed before. He was the opposite of me: clean-cut and put-together, but it only made me want to mess him up that much more.

"Will you show me the coop?" he asked with a giant grin. "Ava told me that Brooks told her that Mal mentioned it's something special."

Marigold started to fuss when I pulled her out of the car seat. Saved by the baby. "Later, I guess. This one needs a change and a snack."

But later came sooner than I expected when Parrish helped make quick work of changing and feeding Marigold.

After he finished wiping off her hands with a wet wipe, he pulled her out of the high chair. "Want to go see the chickens?" he cooed to her as he sat her on one hip. "Huh? Let's go see Daddy's girls."

I opened my mouth to correct him, to tell him I wasn't her dad, but I couldn't bring myself to say it. She'd never had a dad in her entire short life. Beth's pregnancy had been the result of a random hookup. If anyone was going to claim the title of this girl's father, it was going to be me.

I swallowed around the lump in my throat and begrudgingly followed the two of them outside.

"The fence looks amazing," Parrish said. "Better than that heavy orange gate." He seemed to realize how that had sounded because he started stammering an apology. "Not that there's anything wrong with orange, of course! It's the color of safety. Of caution. Why... it's the color of... of... Um, did you know that orange actually stimulates the appetite? We thought about using it in some of our branding at the Pit, but Brooks nixed it. I can't remember why now..."

I wanted to kiss the concerned frown off his forehead and inhale the clean smell of his hair I'd noticed earlier when he'd leaned his head against my shoulder.

"Well," I said teasingly, "if it stimulates the purchase of salvage parts, we're in trouble. I didn't take down the honk sign, though, because that's too practical. Doesn't look all that great. Maybe I can paint up a new one."

I thought about adding it to Stewie's chore chart that already seemed as long as Santa's nice list. The caseworker's visit was coming this week, and it felt like everything was miles away from being done. Maybe Parrish could help me watch Marigold while I did some painting to the outside of the house. Thankfully, the little clapboard home was so small, I could get to it all myself with a simple stepladder, but it would still take a pressure washing followed by a couple of coats in the bad spots. And I couldn't even really start on that until I patched the problem areas.

Parrish stopped me with a hand on my arm. "Hey, hey. We don't have to do this if it stresses you out. I just thought... I mean... you talk about the girls a lot, and I know they're important to you. I wanted to share that with you." He swallowed and looked away for a second. "You know, like a fiancé would do. In... in case they ask, like... what you're into."

I could tell he only added that last part to cover up for being interested in something I liked, and I had to admit to it making me feel ten feet tall and bulletproof.

"Thank you for wanting to share it with me, whatever the reason," I said roughly. "It's real nice of you, and you're right. They are important to me."

It hadn't been easy to admit out loud. I was used to keeping personal info close to the vest, but with Parrish, I didn't want to hold back. I didn't want him to be doing this huge favor for me and getting jack squat in return.

I opened the gate and held it for him while we slipped through. As soon as it was closed behind us, I gestured to the left. "That's the pen and the coop."

My jaw was tight. Old habits meant I was bracing myself for judgment. It was embarrassing that someone like me went all out on something as silly as chickens.

"Oh. My. God." Parrish said before clapping his hands to his mouth. His eyes widened, and he looked between me and the coop and back again. "Did you make this?"

He sounded hushed and reverent, and I could tell from his expression he wasn't simply pretending to be impressed. My chest swelled.

"Yeah. I mean... I bought the plans online..." I ran my hand through my hair. "I made a few modifications, but it's mostly from the plans."

"Sweet Moses on a graham cracker, Diesel, this thing is amazing. This is..."

"Nicer than my house?" I asked with a nervous laugh. "It's called the Pullet Palace even though I obviously have more than just pullets here."

"Obviously," he said faintly, wandering around the

outside of the enclosure. The girls preened for him, strutting along the fence line clucking at him. Lloyd shot Parrish the evil eye and then glared at me for a beat before turning and wandering off. Meanwhile, Uncle thrust his chest out and began squawking to get everyone's attention.

"Aren't you a pretty boy?" Parrish said to the little rooster.

"That's Uncle. He has a bit of a Napoleon complex," I explained. "Ignore him."

Marigold giggled when Brenda shook her plume of head feathers and scared Trixie, causing her to jump and flap her wings. One of the flapping wings knocked over one of my newest pullets, and I let out a growl of warning.

"Simmer down, all of you." I opened the hatch so I could go in and check on the little pullet. She was okay, but a little shaky. "Shh."

"What's that one's name?" Parrish asked.

"Actually, I haven't named her yet. Maybe you can name her?" I turned to hold the slender bird out to him and realized he was staring past me. I followed his eyes to see Rhonda on one of the swings.

I cleared my throat and placed the pullet back on the ground. "We've probably had enough chicken fun for now. Why don't we head on back insi—"

Parrish's voice was soft with awe as he continued looking around at all of the chickens and taking everything in—all the hard work I'd done to make them happy and healthy, all the time and care I put into keeping them productive and safe. "You really love them, don't you, Diesel?"

I must have swallowed some dust or something. I coughed again. "They keep me busy. I'm getting a little hungry. Why don't I get started on dinner? Marigold is infatuated with the stacking cups you got her, so maybe she'll let you build a tower she can Hulk smash. I swear we spent hours doing that last night before bed."

With a hand on his lower back, I angled him out of the pen and back toward the house. Once we entered the living room, Parrish turned and pressed a kiss against my cheek. His lips stayed against my skin for several long beats before he pulled away and pretended to fuss over Marigold's basket of toys.

"What..." My voice broke so I tried again. "What was that for?"

He didn't turn to look at me. "Oh, you know. Just... we should probably, um, act like fiancés more. Get used to it so it doesn't seem awkward."

"That definitely didn't feel awkward," I said, holding a hand up to my cheek as if I could keep the ghost of his lips pressed there forever.

"Besides, I think the way you take care of those chickens is really nice, Diesel."

I couldn't see his face, but I could see the crimson edges of his ears, and they were damned adorable. "Thank you," I said gruffly. "I'm going to get started on dinner."

Jesus.

It was ridiculous how awkward I acted around him sometimes. I looked back on my effortless flirtation with him the first day he was here and wondered where I'd taken a wrong turn. But the truth was, the more time I spent with him, the more I purely liked him. And while he was maybe the easiest man I'd ever met to be myself with... I also didn't want to do anything that might inadvertently send him packing precisely *because* I liked him so much. More than I'd ever liked anyone in my life, besides my aunts.

In short, I'd caught myself in a neat little trap.

I turned on some music at a low volume and pulled out the old dutch oven pot, pouring some olive oil in it before moving over to chop an onion and some garlic. Parrish sat on the rag rug nearby and played with Marigold. Suddenly, I was in the middle of the kind of domestic scene I'd never in a million years envisioned for myself.

It was better than I'd ever imagined, and I couldn't decide which part of it was hurting my heart. Was it the fact that Marigold wouldn't grow up in a two-parent household like this or the fact that I hadn't? I felt a tightness in the back of my throat and tried to stop thinking about it.

"Tell me about work," I said, hoping to get my mind away from going in this dangerous direction. "How are things going with the new restaurant?"

Parrish's face lit up. "Great! You should come by and see all the work Mal has done on the furnishings. It looks amazing. And the manager we hired is already doing a great job pre-screening employees. The contractor—do you know Gil Hammersmith?—he's been amazing."

As he continued to tell me about the progress they'd made, I pictured the handsome, successful contractor. I'd seen his ass on Grindr—literally—and knew that he would love nothing more than to get sweet Parrish naked.

"Be careful with Gil," I grunted, taking out my frustration on the tomatoes with my cleaver.

Parrish's eyes blinked up at me. "Really? Why?"

"He's gay," I said, as if that explained everything.

Parrish bit his bottom lip against a smile. Dammit, the man was irresistible.

"Diesel?" he asked, standing up and moving Marigold into the stand-up exerciser thingy Ava had suggested I pick up. She'd been right. The thing had been a lifesaver already.

I could haul it outside and jail the little troublemaker in it while I did some of my chores. Marigold loved every minute of it too. The tray had all kinds of bits and pieces to keep her entertained.

"Huh?" I tossed the tomato chunks into the pot after the onions looked ready enough to share the pot.

I felt the heat of Parrish's body behind mine. The man was sneaky. I closed my eyes and reminded myself this wasn't real.

"I know Gil is gay," he said softly. "Because he hasn't stopped flirting with me since the day we met."

I whipped around, almost knocking the poor man over. "That's unprofessional! He should know better. That's... that's considered a hostile working environment!"

He bit his lip again, and I wanted to reach out and pluck it back to safety. With my mouth.

Parrish's hands came up to my chest and brushed a piece of papery garlic skin off my shirt. I had to hold back a groan of disappointment that he wasn't reaching out to caress me for any other reason. He was standing so close, I couldn't think straight.

"You know what? Two days ago I was able to tell him that my giant, hot, tattooed fiancé—you know, the one who could probably get his hands on a car crusher and eats rusty nails for breakfast—wouldn't like hearing about me flirting with other men."

I stared at him, my chest pounding with a strange combination of relief and happiness. "Yeah?"

The idea of him doing that publicly, claiming me for any reason, really, filled me with satisfaction... and made it that much easier to forget the whole Tucker incident.

He nodded. "I hope that's okay. I didn't want to cause

you any problems in town, but... I kind of wanted to put him in his place about it too."

"It's okay," I growled. "Very, very okay. I should come over there and pick you up for lunch one day. I could give him the hairy eyeball or something."

Parrish's eyes danced. "Can you practice your hairy eyeball right now? I'd really like to see it."

"You're a menace," I muttered, turning back around to check the tomatoes. "But that guy is going to feel the full power of the fiancé effect come Monday morning. Just you wait."

"I was thinking," Parrish said. "About the fiancé thing..."

My heart sped up for a different reason. I worried maybe he was going to call it quits for some reason. "Okay?"

"Stewie didn't seem convinced today that we were really together. Maybe... maybe we should practice, um, being together. Like, in the sense of knowing more than each other's middle names."

I gripped the center of my chest and glanced over my shoulder at him. "You mean like, making our kisses more convincing?"

Was that even possible? That kiss had been the best, most amazing kiss in kissing history.

He blushed and looked down. "Well, I meant like learning each other's hopes and dreams, but um... kissing would be okay too."

Marigold let out a happy screech. Before Parrish headed over to check on her, he said, "Maybe tonight, after we put Marigold to sleep?"

I nodded and reached for my phone while he was distracted with the baby. Was it appropriate to do a Google search asking how early was too early to put a baby to bed?

Before I could type in the words, there was a knock on the door.

"I'll get it," Parrish said, moving over to look through the peephole. "It's a bunch of scary dudes."

I bolted past him and moved him behind me. "Probably looking for parts. Stay here, okay?"

When I opened the door, I recognized several guys from the Devoted Dogs MC. They were a motorcycle club who used my yard as their go-to for parts. Crow stepped forward to shake my hand.

"Hey, man," I said. "What're you guys looking for tonight?"

His wide grin split the messy red beard on his face. "Lookin' for a house to paint. That beauty committee hired us to do the house and to ask you if you wanted us to stain or paint the new fence too."

I stared at him while Parrish let out a soft laugh behind me.

"The what? What?" I remembered Ava mentioning the Beautification Corps allocating some money to help me look a little less embarrassing in front of the town, but I hadn't expected to have guys show up to paint my damned house.

Crow let out a boisterous chuckle. "Surprise, man! Guess today's your lucky day. See, Ryder back there—" He dipped his head toward a good-looking dark-haired guy in a T-shirt and ripped jeans, who raised his hand in a wave. "He's an honorary Dog who runs Richards Renovations here in town. Ava Siegel told him you had work what needed done—"

"And I wanted to help," Ryder finished in a voice nearly as deep as my own. He looked past me to Parrish and up-nodded. "Think you know my husband, Colin."

I looked over my shoulder in time to see Parrish do a double take. "Colin?" he squeaked. "As in, Partridge Pit's interior designer Colin? Sadie's dad Colin?"

"One of Sadie's dads, yeah." Ryder winked and folded his arms over his leather vest. "Col says he really enjoys working with you, and I appreciate that. Good work-life balance is crucial when you're raising a family."

The other Dogs nodded amongst themselves, pursed their lips, and murmured in agreement.

"Anyway," Ryder said. "My usual crew's scheduled out on some other projects, but the Dogs here are looking for some extra cash to fix up their clubhouse, so Jackknife, the Sims brothers, Grover, and Hatch volunteered. And Crow's here to supervise, of course, since he's the Pres." He clapped a hand on Crow's shoulder. "So here we are. Cool with you if we do the pressure wash tonight so we can start painting in the morning? Sooner we get started the better, since I promised I'd be home by tubby time."

I nodded. I vaguely recognized the name Richards Renovations from around town, so I was pretty sure I could trust them. Besides, with the caseworker's home visit happening in a few days, I couldn't exactly be choosy. If they were here to help, I'd take it and be grateful.

"What do you need from me?" I asked.

Crow smacked his hands together. "Point me to the nearest spigot and flick on those big lot lights if we're still at it when the sun goes down. That's it."

I hustled out to help them and was surprised to find Parrish already feeding Marigold her dinner when I came back inside. "Find everything okay?" I asked stupidly. My kitchen was probably the size of Parrish's bathroom wherever it was he lived when he wasn't in Licking Thicket.

"Yeah. Just sitting here thinking there's probably an

interesting story about how Ryder and Colin met because you could not imagine two more different people."

"Even more than us?"

"Yeah." Parrish swallowed. "I think. Anyway... I figured Marigold might get upset at the noise, so if we feed her now, we can distract her with a bath when the pressure washing starts."

God, he was good at this. I wouldn't have even thought about something like that. "Thanks," I said, wanting so badly to lean in and drop a kiss on his forehead before returning to the stove.

But I didn't. I got to work on our own dinner so the sauce could simmer while we wrangled Marigold into a bath.

It turned out to be a wasted worry. She made ten times more noise in the bath than any MC crew of pressure washers ever could. Then Parrish found a lullaby station on the music app, and Marigold fell in love with it. We brought my portable speaker into the bedroom and let her fall asleep chatting lazily with the music.

We moved back out to the kitchen and finally sat down for our own meal. I'd made sure to close all of the window blinds for our privacy, and it felt a little bit like being safely tucked inside during a thunderstorm.

When Parrish took his first bite of the pasta, he moaned in pleasure. The sound went straight to my dick and made me shift awkwardly in my seat. "This is amazing. I can't believe how good this is. Is it because everything is so fresh, or is it the recipe?"

I shrugged. "A little of both, probably. I usually make a bunch of this sauce when the tomatoes come in and then freeze it to use during the winter. I have a deep freeze out in one of the sheds."

He took another bite and closed his eyes to savor it. After he swallowed, he told me about learning how to cook from his grandmother.

"Beau's wife?" I asked.

"Oh, heck no. Aunt Marnie is really good at arranging for catering and even takeout. Give her a party to plan and she will be in seventh heaven. But the woman is allergic to her own kitchen. She says she's had more than her fair share of cooking after decades of being around a restaurant business. My maternal grandmother, though, she was a farmer's daughter in Kentucky. Her mom taught her how to make all the traditional American dishes and how to preserve and put up stuff for winter. Actually, I have a pepper jelly recipe from her that's to die for if you end up with peppers left over."

"I'd love that," I said. "Thank you. Maybe you could come over and help with it. Make sure I do it right and all."

He flushed and studied his pasta. "I'd like that."

"Tell me about your parents. Where did you grow up? Nashville?"

He nodded. "Yeah. In the burbs. I went to Brentwood Academy and had a pretty easy childhood. Private school, music lessons, volunteering. I was an only child, but that mostly meant I got a ton of attention. It was a little lonely sometimes, but Uncle Beau always seemed to understand. He went out of his way to make me feel special. By the time I went to college, I knew I wanted to work for the family business and learn from him. I respected him so much. And I can't say I have regrets either. What about you?"

He looked a little unsure of himself, like he knew how different our stories were and couldn't tell if he should feel bad about the disparity or not. I reached across and squeezed his hand. "I'm real happy you had such a happy and safe childhood, Parrish. You deserved it. You deserve the best of everything. They're lucky to have you—your parents and uncle, I mean."

He squeezed my hand back. "Thank you. Every kid deserves it. You deserved it too." He'd said that last part with a soft voice, as if he knew where this story was probably going.

I let go of him and sat back, nudging my empty plate out of the way. "I had it good for a while too. I mean, my parents weren't super rich or anything, but Dad worked as a manager of a distribution center, and my mom had an in-home daycare. My sister, Beth, and I were close. She was only two years younger than me and popular as hell. Everyone loved her. She'd made best friends early on with a girl named Stella Kensington. They were wealthy horse breeders. Well, they still are, I guess."

I took a sip of my ice water to steady myself. Parrish was listening carefully without pressuring me at all. I took a breath and continued. "Our parents died in a house fire that destroyed my grandparents' house with my parents and grandparents in it." My voice cracked, and Parrish jumped out of his seat to come over and hug me.

"You don't have to tell me," he whispered. "I'm so sorry. I'm so, so sorry."

"Beth and I had stayed home because we hated my grandmother's pot pie. We both threw such a fit, our parents finally gave up trying to get us to go with them. We should have been there."

"No. No, sweet man. Your parents would have never wanted you there. They would have wanted you to live your life, a long, full life."

I inhaled the sweet scent of him before forcing myself to pull away. "Thank you," I said. "I was over it, you know? I mean, as much as you can be. But then Beth died and... we weren't even that close anymore, but it still brought back all of it."

"So the two of you came to live with your aunts?"

I let out a humorless laugh. "No. They're not really my aunts. Not by blood. We didn't have any living relatives. Beth had the Kensingtons. They agreed to take her in rather than let her go into the system. But they didn't want me. Beth didn't want us to split up, but I knew growing up with Stella and the Kensingtons' money would mean a big world of opportunity for her. So I ran away before she could turn them down."

I could tell Parrish wanted to come back over to my side of the table to comfort me again, but I'd start crying like a baby if he did.

"I hitched a ride on a truck full of old wrecked cars. The truck came here to the salvage yard. Stix Yancey discovered my skinny ass and ripped me a new one. Turned me in to the police right off the bat. They didn't have anyone who could take in a kid that weekend except Dot and Birdie Johnson, who were already approved as fosters. I guess they decided not to give me back," I said with a laugh.

Parrish smiled. "I guess Mr. Yancey ended up coming around?"

I nodded. "It wasn't easy, but yeah. He ended up letting me work here until suddenly I was managing the place. He died a couple years later. It was around that time I reached out to Beth on Facebook. We reconnected and talked on the phone, but things were weird. I knew her life hadn't ended up as easy as I'd hoped, but she was still grateful for the Kensingtons. When she passed, I was surprised to find out she'd had a baby, let alone that she'd left Marigold to me." I frowned.

"How did Beth die, Diesel?" he asked gently.

"A stroke? At least that's what they said. I'd never heard of that happening to women so young, but they said it can have something to do with childbirth. I don't really know. It's been a month and I still feel like I can't get my brain around it. I guess it doesn't really matter, though, does it? She's gone, and now it's just me and Marigold. Well... unless the Kensingtons get her, that is."

Parrish stood to clear our plates. He looked back over his shoulder and asked, "What claim can they possibly have on her?"

"They adopted Beth when she was fourteen. They're her parents as far as the law is concerned. They say they can provide her a steady, two-parent household with everything she could ever need."

I stood up and joined him at the sink to help with the dishes.

"Bullshit!" Parrish snapped. "That's complete... *malarkey,* and you know it. Don't play that game with me, Diesel Church. You can't possibly think that."

I leaned in and kissed him quickly, pulling back almost as fast as if it hadn't happened. "Thank you," I said gruffly. "You're a good... friend."

He blushed and turned back to the sink. "You deserve a good... friend, so that's... good."

As we began to clean up the dinner mess, I could hear the guys outside turning off their equipment and crunching their way off the property.

The two of us washed up in awkward silence— awkward only because I kept trying to figure out how to get from dirty dishes to kissing him again and then how to get from kissing him again to letting him leave here without first getting him naked beneath me in my bed.

Parrish seemed almost more awkward than I felt. "So, um, time to talk hopes and dreams? Or..." He sighed and reached to put the final plate away. "Maybe I should just go."

I leaned over and kissed him again without warning, pressing my lips against his firmly enough to make sure he knew that him leaving was the very last thing I wanted.

He made a little *mph* sound and then clutched the front of my shirt in his hands. Even though my hands were still wet, I reached up to cup his face so I could hold on to him and taste every bit of his kiss.

For that moment, none of this was pretend. It was him and me in a life-changing moment right there in the middle of my kitchen. I wanted him for real, not pretend. And I wanted him with a passion and desperation I'd never felt for anything else in my life. My feelings for him were so sudden and so strong, it damned near terrified me.

"You're shaking," he whispered against my mouth.

"No," I said, lying straight through my teeth.

Parrish pulled back and looked up at me. His honeyed brown eyes were so warm and soft, I wanted to lose myself in them. "Is it... was it okay?"

I barked out a laugh so sudden and so loud, poor Parrish jumped and widened his eyes.

I held his face and met his eyes. "Darlin', okay doesn't begin to describe what that was. But just to be on the safe side, I think we should for sure practice some more."

Parrish's grin was a little shy but also relieved. "That's probably smart. Do you think maybe we could move to the sofa?"

So that's how we ended up making out on my sofa for the next hour and a half. I'd never "practiced" so hard for anything in my life. We were both hard and aching, humping each other through our clothes but acting like it was all simply preparation for fooling the caseworker.

It would fool them alright. If they came here looking for a man moony-eyed and half in love, they were gonna find him, no problem.

Chapter Nine

Parrish

"So we kissed last night. Again. That makes three nights in a row. Not that anyone's counting," I told Miss Sara from my usual stool in the kitchen bright and early Wednesday morning. "Except me. I'm totally counting. And I suppose, by default, you've been counting too, since I keep telling you about it." I stuffed a piece of Miss Sara's candied apple bacon in my mouth and mumbled, "I totally shouldn't've told you about it, should I?"

Miss Sara smiled as she pulled a tray of pumpkin muffins from the oven. "You haven't shocked me senseless yet, Parrish, honey. It's been a couple years since Garvey died, but I've had a kiss or three in my time. Go on."

"Well, there's not much else to say." I shrugged. "It really was just kissing. A lot of kissing. Did I tell you Colin at work asked if I'd had lip fillers the other day?" I smiled and touched my mouth with my fingertips.

Miss Sara chuckled and started arranging some sunflowers in a big blue pitcher.

"I guess maybe they looked a little swollen, but when I asked Diesel, he said..." I hesitated. "He said they looked fine." He'd actually said I looked fucking gorgeous, but it felt funny admitting that out loud. Like Miss Sara might get the wrong idea and start to think he'd meant it. Or worse, start to worry I'd believed him, which I totally hadn't, even though I'd really wanted to. "What do you think?"

"Oh, I think—"

"He was fibbing so I wouldn't stop practicing? Yeah." I forced a smile. "Exactly my conclusion. But I'll tell you what, we got good at it. Sometimes he kissed me and I couldn't remember my name or what I came for."

Miss Sara sighed a little wistfully, which basically expressed my own feelings on the subject, and started transferring the still-warm muffins to a lined basket.

"And we talked lots too. Which was almost as nice as the kissing." I shoved another piece of bacon in my mouth and chewed pensively. "Okay, that's a lie, but it was a very close second."

Miss Sara's lips twitched.

"And he came and took me out to lunch Monday and yesterday. And then Tuesday I walked down to the splash park off Tater Creek Road to meet him and Marigold after their parent group thing, and we chatted with Ava and her friend Ginger, and Maureen from the grocery store—did you know she and LaTonya are trying for their second?— and a guy named Ward, who's a work-from-home single dad and seemed super excited that Diesel was around, since he's usually the only guy there. But Ward's straight," I added. "Pretty sure."

I winced, remembering how I'd interrogated him like a graduate of the Dunn Johnson school of interrogation. I wasn't proud of it.

"And?" Miss Sara prompted. "What else?"

I shook my head and shrugged.

There was more. So much more. A week's worth of the best experiences of my life. Little acorns of truth I was squirreling away for the long winter after the lie of our relationship was over.

Like, when I'd caught Diesel counseling his hens one morning and he'd given me his sweet, sheepish grin in response, the way my soul had wanted to stretch out like a cat in the sunshine was very, very real. And the way my breath had caught when I'd walked into the kitchen after putting Marigold to bed the other night and found him sitting at the kitchen table, the warm overhead light burnishing his brown-gold hair and glinting off those sexy glasses as he fussed over receipts from the salvage yard? That was real too.

The way his deep voice had rumbled through me when I'd snuck up behind him, nipped at his earlobe, and asked him if he felt like "practicing" some more, and he'd replied, "Anytime you like, baby," was real. And the feeling of his big hand splayed against my back when he'd pushed to his feet, turned on a song called "I Do Not Love You," which turned out to be the most romantic song ever, and swayed me around the hardwood floor? That was the most real thing I'd ever felt in my life.

But those moments were private.

Special.

Mine.

"And it's been a great week!" I forced myself to shrug like I didn't care much so she wouldn't see I cared *too* much. "The best ever. I've enjoyed every second."

"Then why're you talking like it's over?" Miss Sara tucked a strand of white-blonde hair behind her ear, leaned her elbows on the counter, and regarded me steadily. "Why not just continue as you have been?"

"Well, 'cause it'll all be over in a couple hours. Remember, this was all so we could convince the caseworker doing the home interview this morning that our relationship is real and stable." I wasn't sure if I was reminding her or myself. "It was fun, but it was all for a purpose. And it can't go on beyond this without making things strange. And real. And complicated." I flailed my hands. "And really strangely complicated. That's why we've stuck to just kissing."

Or at least this was the reason I'd *told* myself that Diesel hadn't tried to take things further than kissing, even though I was pretty sure I'd been giving out a really strong vibe of Fuck Me Please. I'd been way too embarrassed to actually ask him about it.

I checked the clock beyond Miss Sara's head. "It's eight thirty now. The inspection starts in an hour and a half, and we have got this in the bag. Ava Siegel got a whole crew to come out and beautify the place—bikers doing the painting, and little old ladies hauling big pots of sedum to put by the front door. Heck, even the Camper Scout troop came by to hang a fall wreath on the front door *and* the front door of the chicken coop. The place is cleaner than clean. There's not an unhealthy snack in the fridge. Every outlet has a cover. It's still small as heck, but we've got ideas for that too. I mean... I mean *Diesel* has ideas."

I blew out a breath, thinking of the renovation plans Diesel and I had tried to hash out the night before. Diesel recognized that he needed more room to house Marigold permanently. I'd suggested he try talking to the owner of the huge Victorian that abutted his property from the back, on the far side of a thick tree break, to see if they were interested in selling since the house was gorgeous and perfect for a family; Diesel had said no way.

"It's a beautiful house, but even if they're interested, I

can't afford it, Parrish. And I'll be damned if I mortgage any part of the salvage yard to get a fancy house. I'm handy. I'll build out on this place myself. Add a bedroom and maybe a bathroom. That's the best I can do, and it's better than most people have."

So I'd nodded and agreed. And if I maybe had some private concerns about how that would stack up against Marigold's rich grandparents, I kept them to myself, along with an offer to lend him the money. The last thing Diesel needed was to be any more nervous about this visit.

"By noontime it'll be over," I continued to Miss Sara. "Marigold'll be going to visit her grandparents for the night on an unsupervised visit, which is a little nerve-racking, not gonna lie, 'cause she is smack in the throes of the 'stranger danger' stage, and tears are probably gonna happen. But then the caseworker will bring her back tomorrow afternoon, and everything will go back to normal for the two of them, building their little family. Together. Which will be great!"

Miss Sara raised a skeptical eyebrow.

"Seriously! If it were any peachier, it'd be pie!"

"Uh-huh. But what about—?"

"The actual court appearance next month?" I hopped off my stool, suddenly too filled with energy to sit still. "Yeah, there's that too. I'll definitely have to be there when the judge makes his decision. And I'll keep stopping by to see Marigold regularly, too, so she stays comfortable around me. You shoulda seen how she shrieked when Jackknife and the Devoted Dogs boys came to wash and paint the house this week. But by last night, she was waving back when they said goodbye." I couldn't help but smile as I did a little impression of her fingers opening and closing in a wave. "So it's not like I'm moving away. I'll still see them. As a friend.

As Uncle Parrish, maybe. I just mean I won't be going there every night after work anymore, like I did this week."

I stifled a sigh, remembering how it had felt to sit by Mari's high chair feeding her soft fruits and chatting with Diesel while he chopped vegetables for pad thai. It was funny how fast you could get used to something like that, how comfortable you could be borrowing a life that wasn't meant for you.

"But that means I'll be around here for dinner more, Miss Sara. Maybe I could cook for you," I offered.

Miss Sara nodded thoughtfully. "That'd be nice, honey. I enjoy your company."

"I already decided, no more trying to find a date in Licking Thicket." I stopped in front of the refrigerator and turned on my heel to continue pacing. "I don't want anything getting back to anyone involved in the case. Marigold's grandparents are all the way up in Nashville now, but I wouldn't put it past them to hire an investigator to get dirt and go behind our backs to the judge."

I figured it was safe enough talking to Miss Sara, since I'd blurted out the whole plan to her on day one anyway. Keeping quiet about it now seemed like locking the barn door after the entire barn had burned down. Besides, I trusted Miss Sara's judgment, and Lord knew I needed *someone* to talk to, otherwise I'd have to talk to myself, and wouldn't *that* be crazy?

"You just never know about these things," I continued darkly. "Thanks to my aunt Marnie, I've probably watched at least part of every episode of *Law & Order, and Law & Order SVU, and Matlock* before—only part, though, 'cause I tend to fall asleep partway through. Anyway, I've learned that judges can be bought and blackmailed and connived. I'm taking no chances."

Miss Sara managed to smile and whistle at the same time. "I s'pose it's for the best, now that you explain it. It's not that you've got your heart set on anyone, of course, or that you don't *want* to date..."

"Exactly." I spread both hands in emphasis. "Besides, if I started dating someone, I'd wanna be open and honest with them, and I'd have to explain how I was lying about being engaged and lying about Diesel being in love with me." I shook my head and paced faster. "Not a good look."

"And lying about you being in love with Diesel."

I blinked. "Yes, ma'am, that's what I said."

"Right. Silly me." She made a motion toward her ear. "My hearing, you know."

"Anyway, once the store is up and running, I'll be going back to Nashville, anyway! And yes, I know that's not the dark side of the moon," I added quickly when it seemed like she was going to speak. "But the business keeps expanding, and who knows where Beau might send me next?" Especially if I asked him to send me somewhere far, far from here. "Best not to get involved with anyone in the Thicket."

At least not more than I already was.

"Parrish, honey, I think you're—"

My phone rang, the trilling sharp in the otherwise quiet house, and I frowned as I stepped to the island and saw Diesel's name on the display.

"Hey," I answered. "I'm leaving in two minutes so I can be there to help you get Marigold dressed. Are you almost—"

"He's *here*," Diesel hissed over the sound of Marigold crying. "I was only wearing underwear when he knocked on the door and started peeking in the sidelight, Parrish. Jesus Christ. And then Miss Thing woke up with a runny nose, and her diaper is a hazardous waste situation. And I told him he could have a seat on the sofa, but he said he'd wait outside, but I swear to God he's down looking at the chickens, and writing things in his notebook, and *where are you?*"

I took a deep breath and projected a calmness I legitimately only felt when I was talking to Diesel. "Babe, it's *fine*. We've got this. Change her diaper and get her into that pretty dress you got her. Get her a bib too, because you know how drooly she is when she's stuffy. I'll be there in five minutes." I snatched my keys off the counter.

Miss Sara shoved the entire muffin basket in my direction, and I grabbed it with a grateful smile.

"And I'm bringing muffins."

———

"You're pretty far away from town out here," Terry, a little man in too-baggy pants, said, leaning forward in his rocking chair and adjusting his glasses for the seventeenth time in five minutes.

A breeze blew across Diesel's freshly painted front porch, spreading the mouthwatering scent of Miss Sara's muffins and the coffee Diesel had brewed, and I noticed that Terry relaxed slightly as he inhaled a big lungful. There was a crispness in the air, like fall might actually come eventually, and the entire scene felt homey and comfortable, with the baby jumping up and down in her little exercise dish, and Terry, Diesel, and I sitting in brand-new rocking chairs I maybe happened to haul home from World Market yesterday.

By which I meant hauled to *their* home. Here at Diesel's house. Which was not my home.

Obviously.

"We like to think of it as being far away from dangerous car traffic." I gave a delicate shudder. "Right, honey?"

"Yep," Diesel agreed. "Plus, we've got a huge, fenced-in yard for her to roam."

"And the elementary school is just a quarter-mile walk through the tree farm next door, which will be so convenient in a few years! Have another muffin, Terry? And maybe some more coffee?"

"I really shouldn't." He glanced down at the wreckage of the pumpkin muffin currently on his plate.

"Miss Sara's baking is famous in town. No one would blame you for indulging," I said with a wide smile.

"Oh, go on, then." He held out his plate for another muffin from the basket, and I obligingly refilled his coffee cup.

I made sure Diesel got a second muffin too, because the poor man needed it.

By the time I'd gotten here earlier, he'd had Marigold completely clean and tidy and drinking her bottle. He'd also managed to locate himself some pants and a shirt. But he'd looked more frazzled than I'd ever seen him. Not to mention, the way he was glaring at Terry like he wanted to challenge the man to a duel for invading his home was both hot as fuck and also not winning us any friends.

"So, Mr. Partridge, you're new to town." Terry took a big bite of the muffin, closed his eyes, and contorted his face into such a profoundly orgasmic expression, I couldn't help but glance at Diesel, who was already looking at me in horror. I could tell by the look in his eye that he was fighting laughter as hard as I was.

Diesel busied himself checking on Marigold, and I turned my attention to Terry. Fortunately, we'd practiced the answer to this question.

"I suppose so, officially," I said confidently. "But Diesel and I met last year when I came to town with my uncle Beau. We've been dating since November."

"Dating?" Terry asked sharply. "I thought you were engaged."

I blinked. "Well, yes. I-I-I mean, we've been together since November. We've been engaged since July." I could feel my cheeks going hot.

"Sure," Terry agreed, but his eyes narrowed. Was he suspicious? I thought he looked suspicious. "And what did y'all do for Valentine's Day?"

Valentine's Day? It had never even occurred to me to plan for this question. My heart started beating too fast, and I felt myself getting flustered.

I frowned and looked at Diesel, who answered easily. "I went up to Nashville to surprise him. We ate at a little restaurant... what was the name of it, baby?"

"Uh... Starbucks?" I blurted.

My eyes widened. What the hell was wrong with me?

"Yep, that's the one," Diesel agreed. Somehow, miraculously, his eyes twinkled with laughter, like his re-found confidence was a raft big enough to save both of us from drowning. "My baby loves a caramel Frappuccino with extra whip."

"I... I really do," I agreed faintly, and that was not a lie, but I couldn't imagine how he'd guessed.

"Quaint. Forgive me, but I notice you don't wear engagement rings." Terry cast a side-eyed glance at Diesel. "Was that by choice?"

Was this guy serious? What did this have to do with Marigold?

"Yes," I lied staunchly. "It was very much my choice. I don't need a ring to know I love Diesel."

"Wasn't my choice," Diesel piped up, and both of us turned to stare at him. He shrugged. "I always figured if I got engaged, I'd want the whole world to know my man was taken, but then, I'm kind of a caveman that way. Parrish has been a civilizing influence on me." He winked.

"Not too civilizing, clearly," I said breathlessly, and then I shook my head, my mind caught on the idea of Diesel staking a claim on someone someday.

Lucky them.

"Interesting. So how did you propose?" Terry asked Diesel.

Shit. Another question we really should have thought of.

"I didn't," Diesel lied easily. "Parrish did."

"He did?" Terry asked.

I did?

"He did," Diesel repeated. "And it was perfect." His gaze found mine, and I swear, it was so hypnotizing, I couldn't look away if I wanted to. But I really didn't want to. "It was a random Tuesday, and we were walking down Walnut Street over by the new Partridge Pit store, talking about Parrish's favorite subject..."

"B-butterflies," I supplied, like the answer was being pulled out of me. "I'm an amateur lepidopterist."

"That's right," Diesel agreed smoothly. "And I said how I'd love to build you a pollinator garden to bring in butterflies, and you said..."

My eyes went misty. How did he know I desperately wanted a garden like that?

I cleared my throat. "I, um... I said, 'Diesel Church, you are so damn thoughtful and kind. No one in the world's ever made me feel as special and safe as you do. Will you marry me?' I tried to make it direct and sincere," I told Terry, "Just like Diesel."

There was some kind of emotion working behind Diesel's eyes too, like maybe he was getting caught up in the moment as well. "Greatest day of my life," he said, "When Parrish chose me."

I had to swallow hard against the emotion choking my throat. "I still can't believe you said yes."

Diesel laughed lightly. "To *you?* Baby, who could say no?"

I made a sound that was halfway between a sob and a laugh, and even Terry looked strangely moved.

Suddenly, Marigold laughed one of her deep, full-belly chuckles that never failed to make Diesel and I laugh too, and it broke the strange mood.

Unfortunately, when we all turned to see what had made her laugh, we were just in time to watch Uncle, Diesel's rooster, climb atop the fence post surrounding the chicken coop and perch there to watch as, one by one, his harem jumped the fence and started pecking the yard.

Terry frowned.

Damn it all.

Diesel sighed, and I put a comforting hand on his arm.

"Look, I can't lie," Terry said abruptly. "I like you both. You seem like really good guys, and it's clear you love Marigold and each other."

I bit my lip and had to forcibly restrain my eyes from seeking Diesel's.

"Your house is safe," he continued. "The baby's well cared for, and I'm sure she'd do well here." He hesitated.

"I feel like there's a 'but' coming," Diesel said. He grabbed my hand in his and threaded our fingers together. I held on tight.

Terry nodded. "You've gotta understand, Hunt and Brenda Kensington are not only wealthy, they're well connected. They can provide her everything you can and more besides. A college education, a trust fund, private tutors, summer camp."

"And a sterile McMansion where she's constantly reminded of how much she owes them and not allowed to step a toe out of line." Diesel sounded disgusted. He rubbed a hand over his forehead. "It's like watching what happened to Beth all over again."

"I'm sorry," Terry said sincerely. "Look, I'm not saying that's the way it's gonna shake out for sure. I'm writing up my notes impartially, and the judge will make the final call. I just wanted to... to warn you, I guess. The Kensingtons have a lot of money, and they're really motivated. They're not gonna let this drop. Maybe consider working out a custody agreement that gives you visitation, Mr. Church. I think right now you'd be in a position to get that." The implication was that if he pushed the issue, he might not be in that position later.

Diesel's face crumpled, but he nodded once. "I can't say I'm surprised. This isn't too far off from what Stewie's said in the past. I'm not giving up, though. I love her. She's my flesh and blood, and taking care of her was the last thing Beth asked of me. I have to at least try."

"But consider Marigold," Terry encouraged. "Consider what having that stable environment sooner than later would mean for her future."

Diesel's eyes burned and he turned to look at Marigold, who was babbling happily, completely unaware that her wonderful, selfless uncle was about to slice his heart into pieces because Terry the Tool was suggesting that might be best for her.

"Screw that!" I cried. "There is no one more capable of taking care of this baby than you, Diesel. And Terry, if you look at this man and see a 'nice enough' guy, I encourage you to open your eyes. He's not 'nice enough,' he's the best person I've ever met. Every person who's ever met him loves him. Bikers, church ladies, famous sculptors, you name it. And we don't love him because he's 'nice enough.' *Pfft*. We love him because deep at the core of his being beats the pure heart of a man who strives to do right even when it causes him all kinds of trouble."

I clasped a hand to my chest passionately. "This is a man who doesn't give up on people or let them down when they need him. And you came here today to give him a choice like freakin' Solomon? You're telling him that if he loves the baby, he'll give her into the care of people he truly believes will break her spirit, even as they pad her trust fund? Why? Because he runs a salvage yard? Because he's chosen to adorn himself with these beautiful tattoos?"

I shook my head vehemently. "No. No, Terry. Absolutely not. He will not take that deal. *We* will not take that deal. Because I am not going to give up on *him* or let *him* down when he needs me. You know who I am, right? Who my uncle is? Diesel didn't want me to use my money to help him get a good lawyer. He likes to believe that he can win this fight on his own because other people are as good and trustworthy as he is. But hear me now: I am not going to let him lose custody of Marigold. No matter how long it takes, no how much money it costs. So you tell the Kensingtons that if they want to fight, they can bring it on. And tell them Partridges fight *dirty*."

I stood and stared down at him, channeling every bit of my uncle Beau's fiery temperament. I was shocked to find that I'd actually gotten to my feet at some point in my tirade, but I threw my shoulders back and pretended I'd meant to do it.

Terry got to his feet slowly. His mouth quirked a little to one side as he nodded at me. "Well. I'll make a note of that too, Mr. Partridge. Now. It might be best if we get going while Marigold's still so content, I think?"

Diesel stood too. His fists clenched and unclenched at his sides, like he very badly didn't want to let Terry take Marigold away, even for the one planned night. "You'll bring her back, right?"

"Legally, they cannot keep her," Terry assured him—assured *us*, given the way he darted a glance in my direction too. "I'll bring her back myself by five o'clock tomorrow evening."

Diesel swallowed and nodded. "I'll get her things. I packed 'em up last night. Please tell the Kensingtons that she needs her chicken pacifier to sleep with, and she prefers lavender bubble bath, and..." He broke off. "I guess they'll figure the rest out."

I took Marigold out of the exerciser, kissed her dark curls, and murmured a bunch of nonsense in her ear as I carried her to the car. "You're gonna have an adventure, baby. And then you'll be home with us tomorrow, okay? I'll be waiting right here when you get back, and we'll have fruit squeezes. As many as you like. And then a tubby with untold quantities of lavender bubbles, because I do not trust them to use the right kind, oh no I do not."

Hilarious how I'd just told Miss Sara hours ago that I was going to extricate myself from Marigold's life, beginning today, huh? I was clearly doing really well with that.

Diesel came with her bag and helped strap her into the car. He said his own goodbye, and then before either of us was ready, Terry drove her away.

We stood for a minute in the sunshine, watching until the car was a speck at the end of the road. My throat worked, but I wasn't sure what to say.

"I'm sorry," I began. "I fucked this whole thing up. I couldn't remember my lines. And I got all aggressive at the end there."

Diesel turned to look at me, his eyes hot on my face, but I couldn't read the expression in them.

"Say something," I pleaded. "Yell at me if you have to."

"Get in the house. Now."

I swallowed hard. Fuck. He must be really mad if he didn't want to yell at me outside. But I deserved it.

I scurried up the porch stairs and into the house. Diesel came in a second later and slammed the door shut.

"Really, I'm *very* sorry," I began again. "I—"

Diesel grabbed my arm firmly and spun me around so my back was to the door. He braced his arms on either side of my head and leaned into me so I could feel his warm breath on my face.

This did not feel like practice. This felt like something else entirely.

"Shut up. Don't you *dare* apologize," he said, the words coming out rough and raspy. "Not when I'm about to kiss the shit out of you for everything you said out on that porch."

"Kiss me?" I breathed. "B-but Terry's gone. That part of this is over. You don't have to pretend anymore."

He cradled my face in both his hands and smiled in a way that was gorgeous and wild and perfectly Diesel.

"Oh, Parrish. Baby, there will be no pretending about this."

Chapter Ten

Diesel

I'D GONE into the caseworker visit feeling stressed and frazzled. Even on my best day, I didn't deal with unexpected changes of plans in the most graceful way. Today was not my best day.

Until Parrish Partridge breezed onto the scene and went full Papa Bear on the caseworker's ass.

I'd never felt so supported in my life. He'd stood there with his little fists clenched and skin mottled pink while he told the caseworker that I was *worthy*.

I'd never wanted anyone more, and I was finally ready to take what I'd wanted so badly to be mine.

When I pressed my lips to his, it was just as exciting as the first time I'd kissed him. Despite hours and hours of making out with him this week on my sofa, I felt like I would never get enough—couldn't *possibly* get enough—of his mouth on mine.

"Tell me this is okay," I breathed into the skin of his cheek. "Please, please tell me you want this."

He made a little squeaking noise before nodding comically. I smiled and pressed our foreheads together. "I don't want to scare you, but I want to take you to my bed, sweetheart."

"Oh God," he breathed. "Yes, please. I want that too."

I kissed him again, just a quick one to tide us over until I could get him into the bedroom, but then I couldn't stop. I finally grabbed his thighs and pulled him up until his legs were wrapped around me so I could get us there without having to leave his kiss.

Parrish's arms were around my neck, and his hands were in my hair. I loved seeing him lose his composure when we made out. His skin flushed and his eyes turned a little glassy. Sometimes he even started mumbling nonsense under his breath like funny little reminders to himself about not accidentally biting me or self-deprecating remarks about how he was probably doing it wrong but he wasn't sure if he really cared since it was so good. I wasn't sure he even realized he was saying those things out loud, but I hoped he never stopped. It was part of what made Parrish, Parrish.

I stumbled us across the room, barely missing the sofa and stubbing my toe on the coffee table. I bumped my shoulder into the edge of the doorframe, nearly tripping over my own feet in my haste to get Parrish in my bed so I could strip him down.

"Don't hurt your big, gorgeous body," he muttered between kisses to my neck. "I have plans for it."

I placed him in the center of my big bed like the treasure he was and then began undoing his shirt buttons one at a time, dropping a little licking kiss on his throat and chest as I moved down toward his belt.

"Oh. Oh, that's... okay. Yes." His breathing was full of fits and starts which made my dick hard as fuck. His hands fluttered tentatively by his side as if he wasn't quite sure what to do with them.

I reached out and grabbed his wrists, moving his hands to my hair. Parrish let out a sigh of relief. "I like touching you."

I glanced up at him through my lashes. "Parrish. Touch me. Please touch me. You have permission to touch me anytime anywhere in whatever way you want." My voice sounded rough and slow. Maybe I just wanted to make sure he got the message, because I didn't ever want him to experience one ounce of hesitation in bed with me.

He bit his lip on a smile and tightened his fingers in my hair. "I like that."

As I moved lower, yanking his shirttails out of his pants, he crossed his ankles behind my back and arched up into me. I moved my hands around, under his shirt to his lower back, and felt the smooth, warm skin there. "God, you're fucking gorgeous. You make me want to lose control. You make me want to do things to you I've never even thought about before," I said, licking along his dark happy trail.

As I spoke, Parrish's eyes widened and his lips parted. They were already swollen and pink from our kissing.

"Like what?" he whispered.

I couldn't help but laugh. "Like things you're not ready for, baby. Things we're not ready for."

"What... um..." He cleared his throat. "What are we ready for?"

I moved back up to kiss his mouth because it had been too many seconds since I'd tasted his mouth. "What do you want, sweetheart? What will make you feel good?"

He looked surprised by my question, as if no one had ever asked him what he liked in bed. I hoped like hell that wasn't true.

He scraped his bottom teeth along his upper lip while

he thought. This time, I was able to rescue the poor lip with a kiss.

Parrish pushed me away with a laugh. "I was trying to think!"

"You were thinking too sexily," I growled before leaning back in and nipping the edge of his jaw. "Think faster."

Pink splotches appeared on his cheeks. "Um, I've been wanting to suck you off. Can I... can I do that?"

Now it was my turn to bite back a smile. "No, baby. I'm afraid I don't like oral sex. Pick again."

His forehead crinkled in confusion. "Really?"

I leaned in to kiss him again. "No. Not really." I sat back on my knees and began yanking off his shoes and socks. "Let me get you out of these clothes first, though. I want all the eye candy while you're sucking me off."

He looked down at his clothes that were all askew. "Maybe it's better if I keep them on though. I'm..." He glanced at me, my biceps, and then my thighs before glancing back up at me. "I'm kind of skinny and pale."

Instead of arguing with him, I nodded. "Skinny and pale is my favorite."

"No, but—"

I cut him off. "Do you want to keep your clothes on for you or for me?"

"I don't understand."

I shot him a knowing smile. "If you were alone in here and you were going to jack off in my bed, would you keep your clothes on or would you strip naked?"

"I would never... do that in your bed."

I stopped and met his eyes so he would hear what I said. "I would give anything to walk in on you touching yourself in my bed. And it would be a thousand times better if you were completely bare."

His breath stuttered. "N-naked, then."

While I busied myself undressing him, he reached out and touched me, tentatively at first. His fingers ghosted over the hair on my arm, passed across one of my pecs, and skimmed across my shoulders to the back of my neck and into my hair.

I pulled off his shirt, unfastened his belt, and reached for the button on his pants. His hard cock pressed obscenely against the material, making my mouth water. I wondered how he'd feel if I sucked him off first.

When I peeled his pants open, I noticed hot pink briefs with a darker pink spot centered over the tip of his dick. A growling noise came out of me when I noticed the wet patch of precum on his sexy underwear. I yanked down the pants and buried my face in the front of his briefs to inhale the scent of him.

"Ah, fuck," I groaned. "I'm sorry, but I can't wait." I fished him out and sucked his fat crown into my mouth, using my tongue to explore him.

He let out a yelp and yanked on my hair as he jerked in surprise. "Oh! Oh, but that... I was... *oh please don't stop.*"

I sucked him down and teased him, yanking his underwear off without taking my mouth off him for a second. His slim, muscle-curved legs jerked as I tried my best to make him lose his mind. I kept my eyes on him while I reached up to roll his nuts in my hand and stroke the spot behind his sac with one of my fingers. I wanted to touch his hole, to finger him and rim him until he was babbling incoherently the way I knew he would. But I didn't want to scare him off, and part of me felt like that was a real possibility with Parrish.

He'd been keeping himself a little closed off from me in a way that made me wonder who or what had caused him to put up those walls. Every time I'd tried to ask him about relationships or even kids, he closed up like a stubborn clam and merrily changed the subject, so I'd held back, even though I'd wanted him under me days ago. It wasn't until Parrish had said what he'd said to Terry that I realized things might be getting a little real for him too, and now there'd be no holding back.

I wanted his walls down. I wanted them down so badly, I was willing to scale them brick by brick and dismantle them by hand if he'd let me. But I had to be sneaky about it. If I came on too strong, I had a feeling I'd see a Parrish-shaped hole in the side of the house and a little puff of smoke in his wake.

He moaned and begged, alternately arching up into my mouth and squirming below me on the bed. "Diesel, Diesel... oh God. Oh, gonna come. Please..."

I doubled down on the sucking and licking, taking him into my throat and swallowing around him and pressing harder between his balls and his hole until he froze for a split second and began releasing into my mouth. His eyes rolled back, and his mouth fell open. His abs contracted, and his fingers tightened reflexively in my hair.

I held on to his hips as I swallowed his cum. Once he stopped shaking, I moved back up and lay next to him, pulling his head onto my chest and wrapping an arm around him.

"God, you're beautiful when you come," I said softly. "I want to do that again." And again, and again, and again.

Parrish buried his face in my chest. "Shut up, am not."

I laughed and ruffled his hair. "Are too. Next time I'll set up a camera and show you."

His body stiffened, so I immediately backpedaled.

"Hey, hey. I was just kidding. I would never do something like that, especially without your consent."

"No, sorry. It wasn't that." He lifted his head and looked at me. "Do you really want there to be a next time? With, me, I mean?" He winced. "Of course you mean me," he muttered. "C'mon, Parrish."

I stroked the backs of my fingers along his pink cheek. "I would be honored if there was a next time. Every minute I spend with you is a gift I feel like I don't deserve. I don't know why you stayed today, but... damn. I'm sure grateful."

Parrish flung a leg over me and straddled my hips. His ass brushed my still-rock-hard dick, and his eyes widened when I sucked in a breath. Then they narrowed into a teasing glint.

"What do we have here, Mr. Chicken Man?"

"That... isn't the term of endearment I would have picked," I said, biting my tongue against a laugh. I didn't want him to think I was making fun of him; it was just that I was so damned happy to be here in this moment with him.

Parrish winced. "It sounded better in my head, to be honest."

"It's fine. As long as I can call you Butterfly Boy."

He tilted his head as if thinking about it for a second but then shook his head. "Let's... put a pin in that for now. Meanwhile, I think you need to be taught a lesson."

I leaned up to yank off my shirt since his hands were already wandering underneath it to my chest.

"In the South, it's considered impolite when someone asks you for a certain food at the dinner table and you take a helping before passing them the dish."

I wasn't following. "Are you hungry, cutie?"

"I asked for a taste, and then instead of giving me a taste, you took one for yourself first. Rude."

I loved it when he got that certain playful look in his eyes. "Punish me, Butterfly Boy."

He dissolved into a fit of laughter and collapsed on my chest. I held him tightly to me with my arms across his back. Had I ever been this happy, this relaxed and free? Parrish had the ability to make me feel completely and utterly... *me.*

"Thank you for staying," I whispered in his ear.

"Diesel?"

"Mm?"

He sat back up and looked at me with his hands propped on my chest. "You know when you asked me what I wanted?"

I ran a hand down his chest and held it over his heart. "Baby, pretty sure I'll never, ever forget it as long as I live."

He flashed a sweet, shy smile at me. "That's not all. I... I want you to hold me down and fuck me."

My heart stopped and my lungs ceased to function. Could I have possibly heard him right?

"Hard," he added.

And then bit that fucking lip again.

I blinked at him in too-good-to-be shock.

He frowned. "Is that too much? Did I ruin—"

I didn't let him finish, I grabbed his face and yanked his mouth to mine while simultaneously flipping his naked body underneath me with my legs. Since meeting this sexy man, I'd been on a hair trigger around him. I'd wanted to get to know his quirky self, sure, but I'd also wanted to throw his lithe body up against the nearest flat surface and pound my hard dick into him until he screamed.

He yelped, but then it quickly morphed into a moan of pleasure. His legs wrapped around me again once he was on his back, and I could feel his heartbeat fluttering wildly in his neck.

"Tell me again," I growled into his neck before biting down gently on the skin there.

"Oh God, please. Please fuck me, Diesel. I want to feel you. Want to make you feel good too. I want..." He didn't finish because I ground my cock into his and made him moan again.

"Can't hold back," I warned.

He shuddered and his pupils doubled in size. He reached down to touch himself, but I made a noise to stop him.

I hurried out of the rest of my clothes and paused only for a second when I noticed his eyes roaming over my naked body.

"Holy crap," he breathed, reaching out to run his long fingers over some of my ink. His touch brought up goose bumps all over my skin. "Are you... Is this real?"

I looked down at my colorful skin. Plenty of men had drooled over the ink in the past, but no one had looked at me quite like Parrish did right now. It was enough to make me feel half-drunk.

"You can look later," I grumbled.

He blinked up at me. "Can I lick it later?"

I crashed my lips into his for the millionth time, lying between his legs and grinding my dick against his thigh. His own had already hardened again and was pressing into my belly. After finally pulling myself away, I leaned over to rustle through my bedside table for the lube and a condom.

"You okay?" I asked again. I couldn't bear the idea of him ending up with regrets, and this was not at all what he'd originally signed up for. Not that he'd originally agreed much to any of it.

Parrish reached up and held my cheeks until I focused

on his eyes. "Diesel, don't treat me like a fragile virgin. I've had sex before. I've had rough sex before. I've even—"

"Stop. Talking," I said between my teeth.

Parrish's eyes twinkled and he mimed zipping his lips and throwing away the key. It made me wonder if he'd antagonized me on purpose to fire me up even more. If he wanted rough, I could give him rough. I'd been imaging pounding him into every surface of my house for days now.

I flipped him onto his stomach and yanked his hips toward me until his delicious creamy ass cheeks were level with my chest. Then I leaned down and pressed a gentle kiss to each cheek before parting them and staring at his tight hole.

Fuck.

I leaned in to take a taste, and I wasn't gentle. I didn't treat him like a delicate flower. I treated him like a man whose ass I wanted to devour before using it to get as deep inside of him as possible.

I licked and sucked and probed until he was making sobbing pleas to just fuck him already.

"Deese," he begged. "Can't. Gonna... can't..."

I finally smacked another kiss on his plump butt cheek and moved up to kiss along his spine to the back of his neck. I whispered in his ear about what I wanted to do to him as I lubed up my fingers and slid them into his already wet hole.

He whimpered. "You're a tease. You... you hate me. You... oh God. Oh... oh fuck, right there."

He was so tight around my fingers, I wasn't sure how much longer my own balls would keep from exploding. I sped up the process until I felt like he was prepped enough. After a quick tussle with the condom packet, I suited and slicked up.

"Turn around, baby," I said into his ear. "Want to watch you."

He rolled underneath me. Parrish's eyelashes were wet and spiky, and his eyes were dazed. His lips were red and dented from biting, and his hair was a messy nest.

"You're so fucking beautiful," I told him. "I want you. I want you more than anything."

I wasn't sure I'd ever been so brazen in asking for what I wanted before. Maybe. Maybe when I admitted to wanting to keep Marigold or maybe when I begged Stix for a job at the yard. But this... this was different. This was something I didn't feel like I had a right to ask for, a right to stake a claim on.

"Take me," he said in a voice half-sex-drunk.

I watched his face as I pressed into him. As soon as his eyes tightened, I slowed down or stopped until finally he let out a little huff of breath and relaxed around me.

Parrish's hands reached around to grab my ass and squeeze, encouraging me to start thrusting. Every pull and push was like sweet torture. The squeeze of his body was intense, and the look on his face was even more exquisite. He was consumed by what was happening between us just like I was.

I wasn't so naive that I thought it meant anything more to him than hot sex, but damn. If the sex between us was this good? There was no telling how it could be if I had the chance to learn his body better.

The pull of his channel was too much. I thrust into him hard until we both grunted every time my hips slammed into his ass. He screamed for more and stretched his arm back over his head to hold on to the headboard.

As soon as I felt my balls draw up, I reached down to stroke him off. It only took one pull before we were both crying out and coming. His release covered my hand and his belly while I pressed even deeper inside of him and groaned against the side of his head.

When my body finally stopped jerking with after-shocks, I pulled back enough to glance down at Parrish.

He looked like he'd just smoked weed and had a two-hour massage. He grinned at me like a happy drunk.

"Feeling good?" I teased softly.

"'S fine."

I snorted and pulled away as carefully as I could. "Good to know. I'll mark you down for a 'fine' and see if we can't work up to a 'slightly improved' next time."

He giggled. I looked back over my shoulder after dropping the condom in the trash can. "Why are you laughing?"

"You said next time again. That means it's kind of like a promise. I don't think you meant to do that."

I stepped into the bathroom and wet a cloth to clean him up with. When I returned to see him starfished out in the center of my bed, my chest tightened. I realized I was going to have to find some way of keeping him there. I wanted him to sleep next to me in that big bed for the fore-seeable future.

"Baby, I most certainly did mean to do that." I began wiping him gently with the cloth. "If you think I'm letting you go when I finally got you into my bed, you've got another think coming."

His smile dropped. "Did you really want this? Did you think about me... before? I mean, when we were... pretending?"

I tossed the cloth on the floor and climbed onto the bed to pull him into my side before kissing his hair. "If you really thought I needed that much kissing practice, we need to have a conversation," I mused.

He groaned and covered his face with his hands. "Oh my God, I'm so embarrassed." He looked up at me with a frown. "But wait. The kissing was your idea."

I grinned at him. "Yeah, but a good one. Right?"

He groaned again, but this time it was peppered with a laugh. I rolled him over and started kissing him again, everywhere.

Only this time, it wasn't practice. It was the real thing. He just might not have known it yet.

Chapter Eleven

Parrish

"Mmm. You taste like cinnamon." Diesel licked his lips like he was savoring the flavor, which meant he also licked my lips since my mouth was mere millimeters from his.

"No, I think *you* taste like cinnamon," I corrected, leaning in that last bit so I could kiss him. I loved the way he moaned and his breathing hitched, despite the hours and hours we'd spent wrapped up in each other over the past two days. I pulled back far enough to say, "Yep. Definitely you."

Diesel grinned and shifted a bit on his big sofa, pulling me more fully on top of him and twitching a soft fleece blanket into place over my shoulders. He reached over to the coffee table and broke another sweet morsel off the cinnamon cake I'd baked the day before.

"You might be right," he agreed, popping the cake in his mouth, and I huffed a laugh into his collarbone.

I felt drunk. Not drunk drunk; I hadn't had an alcoholic beverage in ages. But I was starting to see how maybe sex drunk was a thing. Or cum drunk. Or lov—I mean, *lust* drunk. I was no blushing virgin, but I'd never felt so well used. I'd also never felt so wanted.

On the one hand, I was absolutely exhausted. I was sore and scratched up, and I didn't want to move from this spot for a hundred years, or at least until the baby dozing in her crib in the bedroom woke up for the second time that morning, which could happen at any minute. My brain felt fuzzy too, like all my thoughts were floating high above me, just out of reach.

But at the same time, I felt satisfied in a way I hadn't for a long time, or maybe ever. Like having every inch of my skin touching every inch of Diesel's flawless, tattooed skin was exactly where I was meant to be. Like the two of us cuddling and watching the sky lighten from purple to rose to peach was the most important work I'd ever do. Which reminded me...

"I have to get up and go to work," I muttered to his chest.

"You definitely do," Diesel agreed, though his arms tightened around me for a second, giving lie to his words.

"But I don't wanna."

"Uh-huh." I felt Diesel's smile against my hair as his fingers skimmed below the waistband of my underwear beneath the blanket. "That's what you said yesterday morning when you called in."

"Yesterday was a Thursday," I protested. "Hardly anything happens on Thursdays. They didn't need me at all." Which was a true and actual fact—more or less—though I'd had to repeat myself to Colin three times when I'd told him I wasn't coming in, and even then he'd seemed to worry that I was trying to subtly alert him that I'd been kidnapped without letting the bad guys know.

Parrish Partridge did not take unplanned days off as a

rule, but then again, Parrish Partridge didn't have sex eight times in forty-four hours either—a number I would not be sharing with Miss Sara—so maybe I needed to revise my rules about what I did and didn't do.

"I don't want to be a bad influence on you." Diesel ducked his head and ran his nose along my jaw, while his hand slid down my thigh. He hitched my knee up, setting our cocks into perfect alignment with only two very thin pairs of underwear separating us. Unsurprisingly, my dick perked up like it was a divining rod and Diesel was the great, wide ocean, but the wanting didn't feel frantic anymore. It felt peaceful. Satisfying. Delightful.

"Too late," I said, and my voice came out hoarse. "You've already taught me all kinds of questionable skills." I braced my forearms on his broad chest and grinned down at him.

He rolled his eyes and traced a finger over the shell of one ear. "Be serious."

"I'm totally serious! So serious. For example, I know how to make you moan like a porn star."

Diesel snorted. "Please. That's ridicu—*ohhhhhhhhfuck-kkkkyeahhhhhh!*" he groaned as I simultaneously ground our cocks together and sucked one nipple while I rolled the other between my thumb and finger.

"You were saying?" I asked sweetly.

He blinked slowly like he was coming out of a daze. "I think I was saying, please show me more of these sexy skills you've learned."

I smiled and scraped my teeth over his chin, all thought of work forgotten. "Well," I said huskily, "I could show you how I—" I broke off with a wince as Marigold's deep, hiccuping cries emerged from the bedroom. I cleared my throat. "I could show you how I prepare a baby bottle while you go fetch Her Majesty and change her?"

"You've never been sexier to me," Diesel said drily.

I laughed as I pushed myself off him, then reached out a hand to help him up. He kissed my forehead briefly before he sauntered off, and I sighed as I turned to watch his ass sway as he disappeared into the bedroom. It was a particularly fine ass. The man it was attached to was even finer. And after two days of playing house with Diesel Church, two days of seeing his sweet smile when I opened my eyes and watching his gaze flare hot as he fucked me, I wanted him more than ever.

I was also more convinced than ever that Diesel, amazing Diesel, could have any man on the planet, so I couldn't see why he'd want to keep me any longer than necessary.

By the time I'd prepped the bottle, I'd managed to work myself into a little bit of a state where I was half-convinced that as soon as either of us left the property, the bubble around us would burst and I'd wake up back at the Jackson King B&B all alone. I needed to pace.

Diesel appeared in the kitchen with a sleepy Marigold nestled in one arm, and I handed her the bottle just as his phone alarm began blaring.

"Ah, sugar. Time to feed the chickens," Diesel sighed. "Parrish, you wanna stick around for ten minutes and feed Marigold? Or should I put her in the front carrier?"

"Neither!" I said brightly. "I'll take care of the chickens."

"You will?" He raised an eyebrow. "Really?"

"Sure. I've seen you do it enough, right?" I walked back to the bedroom so I could pull on my clothes and an old sweatshirt Diesel had lent me since the last couple of mornings had been unseasonably cool. Naturally, the thing fell to my knees. "Fill the feeders, fill the water-ers, spread out the kitchen scraps. Have a little chat with the girls, catch up on the gossip. No problem."

Diesel grinned and grabbed me as I came through the kitchen so he could press a kiss to my mouth. "I lied before."

I blinked. "You did?"

"Uh-huh. *Now* you've never been sexier to me." He winked.

I sighed as I let myself out the back door and down to the chicken run.

I got out the hose first and cleaned out Diesel's watering system, which was easy enough. Henry pecked the ground nearby, but Nosy got right up in my business and even tried to jump up into it while I cleaned it.

"Excuse me, missy, but it's cold this morning. I'm not looking to take a shower out here," I informed her, and she jumped down obediently, almost like she could understand me.

I snorted. Diesel wasn't wrong. They were kinda sorta cute.

"Alright, food next. Jeez, Louise, I'm coming, ladies. Brenda, do *not* fling that feed all over the place." I nudged her out of the way with my toe. "I'm getting good at this, huh? Maybe I should feed you all the time. For as long as I'm here."

The unnamed pullet pecked her way up to me, twitching her black-and-white feathers sympathetically.

"Oh, I know I'm being ridiculous... at least partly. Diesel's attracted to me, right? I mean, *eight times*." I snorted. "And yesterday morning, I wondered if maybe he was using sex as a distraction so he wouldn't stew over Marigold being with the Kensingtons, but that didn't turn out to be the case, 'cause things didn't slow down any. But... I dunno, ladies. If being with Payne taught me anything, it was that if something seems too good to be true, there's probably a lie in there."

I sighed as I dumped the kitchen scraps out. "It wasn't even about the sex, or not just that. Last night, we went out to wait for Marigold on the front porch as soon as Terry called to say he was getting off the highway, right? And she spotted us as soon as he pulled up to the house. She was fussing like crazy—you know how she can get. So Terry takes her out of her seat and brings her over to me and plops her in my arms, and she gives this little shudder—" I demonstrated for the ladies. "And then she settled right down. Like she trusted me. I just... I don't know how to protect myself from that, you know? How do I build up walls against this guy who looks at me like I'm his favorite kind of candy bar, and a precious baby girl who already trusts me?"

I poured out the rest of the scraps in a little pile in front of the nameless pullet, who watched me steadily with her head tilted to one side, not even distracted by the food.

"I know what you're thinking: Why am I even bothering? I know! I keep coming to the same conclusion," I told her. "'Here I go,' I tell myself. 'I'm gonna enjoy this ride while it lasts.' But then I feel myself sliding, and it's instinctive for me to try to stop it. You go on and eat, no need to be polite." I motioned toward the food, then leaned back against the fence post and watched No-Name peck at it.

"See, when Payne broke up with me and took the boys away, I wasn't just sad, I was mad at myself. I should've seen it coming, right? I should've guarded against it. If I hadn't been such a needy person, maybe I wouldn't have fallen for it. What does it mean that I'm finding myself in the same spot again? Fool me twice, shame on *me*, you know?"

No-Name stopped pecking and looked at me. She did a shuffle dance and settled her feathers once more, like she was trying to tell me something.

"Or maybe... maybe there's no shame in it?" I guessed. "Huh. You know... I hadn't thought about it that way, but maybe you're onto something. I mean, sure I could be hard-hearted and protect myself, but is that really the kind of life I want to live? No! No, it is not. I want to be the sort of person who's open to love, even if it's temporary! Shit." I shook my head. "You have just exploded my mind with this advice. This is amazing."

I toed Wynette away when she tried to come over and snag a broccoli crown, which was my way of thanking the nameless pullet for her free therapy.

"You know, Diesel said I could name you." I tapped my lips thoughtfully. "And I think it's only right to name you for the other great advice-giver in my life! From now on, I'm calling you *Miss Sara*."

I breathed a deep, cleansing breath and left Miss Sara and the other girls to their business as I made my way back inside, but the only signs of Diesel and Marigold in the kitchen were her abandoned high chair and the pot of coffee in the machine. I followed the sound of her high-pitched babbling out to the little bedroom and found her lying on the bed, tickling her own feet, while Diesel prepped a clean diaper.

"We couldn't quite make it through breakfast," Diesel said.

I snorted. "I'm gonna grab a shower, if that's okay. Then I'll head out. Gotta stop at the B&B for some fresh clothes."

"You coming back tonight?"

"Yeah," I said calmly. "For sure. Also, the new pullet is named Sara."

"M'kay." Diesel frowned. "Hey, if you're coming back tonight, maybe bring a change of clothes? That way you'll have 'em for tomorrow."

"Do we have plans tomorrow?"

"Not yet." He shrugged. "But we can make some."

I grinned. That sounded just about perfect. But before I could say so, someone rang the doorbell.

Diesel scowled. "Who the heck could that be?"

"Ava's crew again, maybe? Thicket Beautification Corps Part Deux: Revenge of the Corps?"

"Awesome." He rolled his eyes. "You wanna...?"

"I'll defend us from them," I vowed, giving him an easy smile. "They won't get past me."

But when I threw open the front door, it wasn't Ava.

"Uncle Beau?" I demanded, horrified.

"Morning, Parrish!" He smiled broadly. "What a fine Friday!"

I looked beyond him, to where his Cadillac was parked in Diesel's driveway. "What are you doing here? How... how did you know where to find me?"

"Oh, son." Beau thumped his cane on the porch once and shook his head. "I know I like to say you can do anything you set your mind to, but never try being sneaky. Y'ain't suited to it. Suffice it to say, I have my ways." He pursed his lips, and it made his mustache twitch. "Mind if I come in?"

"I... But I..." I sighed. What the heck was I going to say? "Yes. Of course."

Uncle Beau stepped over the threshold and looked around the relatively tidy living room. "So I heard from Colin that you called in sick yesterday," he said. "I made the mistake of mentioning that to your aunt Marnie, and she texted you, but you didn't reply."

I winced. "Oh. Uh. Shoot." In my defense, that had occurred sometime between rounds five and six, but I felt like Uncle Beau wouldn't be impressed by this excuse. "Sorry?"

"Uh-huh. So, of course this morning she tasked me with finding out whether you were alive or dead. 'But who'll take care of him down there in Licking Thicket, Beau?' she asked."

I rubbed a hand over my forehead. My aunt Marnie was a sweet, caring woman, who loved the heck out of me, but she was not the hover-er of the two of them. I knew exactly who'd wanted to make sure I was alive, and he was right now taking a seat in Diesel's easy chair.

"I stopped by to the B&B, but you weren't there. Imagine my shock when your sweet landlady explained she hadn't seen you since Wednesday."

I winced again. Damn it all, Beau *did* have his ways.

"So then I asked Brooks, and he had the craziest story to tell me—" Beau broke off with a frown and lifted his leg to remove the chicken pacifier that must have been tossed on the chair. "Hmm."

"I, um..." I wasn't sure what the hell I was planning to say, but then Diesel came out of the bedroom carrying Marigold, and what I blurted was, "This is not what it looks like!"

"Really?" Beau chuckled. "'Cause it looks an awful lot like a baby to me."

"Well, yes, she is, but..." I cleared my throat. "Uncle Beau, this is Diesel Church and his niece. I mean, his ward. I mean." I scrubbed a hand through my hair. "This is his daughter. Marigold."

Beau smiled warmly. "Pleased to meet you, Miss Marigold." His smile dimmed a fraction. "And Diesel."

Marigold held out her arms for me and babbled, but I pretended I couldn't see. It wasn't that I was ashamed of anything I was doing here, but I hadn't quite followed my lie through to its natural conclusion: I might not only have to lie to the caseworker and Stewie and Gil Hammersmith about who Diesel and I were to each other, I might have to lie to my aunt and uncle too.

The baby fussed more loudly, not used to me ignoring her *ever*, so I gave in and took her from Diesel. Without hesitation, she cuddled into my neck, just as she had the night before, and I sighed because *she* was the most important person in the room, and I needed to remember that.

"Mr. Partridge," Diesel began. "How about some coffee and some cake Parrish made yesterday?"

"I'd love some," Beau said genially. But after Diesel left the room, he narrowed his gaze on me. "As I was saying, maybe Malachi and Brooks weren't so crazy. In particular, I heard about a kissing incident at the Pickin' the other day?"

"It was a tradition," I whispered helplessly.

Beau's eyes twinkled. "A new tradition you created, according to Brooks," Beau said. "He said you were real convincing, son. I believe his exact words were 'Why don't you have Parrish on your marketing team, Beau? That boy could sell water to a drowning man and make him say thank you.'"

I laughed slightly, but my cheeks burned and, weirdly, my eyes filled up.

Only because I was tired, obviously.

I turned to put the baby in her exercise dish so Beau wouldn't see. "Wow. That's quite a compliment coming from him."

"Parrish," Beau said seriously. "What's going on here?"

"Well, Diesel and I..." I faltered. I couldn't lie to this man, so after a quick look at the doorway to make sure Diesel couldn't hear, I told the truth. "I fell for Diesel the minute I saw him. It was just—" I snapped my fingers. "There's just something about him, Uncle Beau. You'll see it if you get to know him." I smiled, just a little. "He's not just good-looking, he's smart and funny and so kind. He's good to me." I cleared my throat. "Anyway, a little while after that"—as in, minutes —"I learned that Diesel's sister had passed away and left him her daughter to raise, but the baby's grandparents are contesting it. So Diesel's fighting for custody."

Beau's eyes widened in concern. "Oh, no. Oh, Parrish, not again—"

"No, no! I know what you're thinking, but it's not like with Payne," I said in a low voice. "Really! Diesel hasn't asked me to do anything." Except marry him. I hurried on. "I mean, Diesel won't let me spend a dime on him, except for the rocking chairs out on the porch." I couldn't help but smile down at Marigold. "And some chicken pacifiers for this princess. And I can see now that when I was with Payne, he wanted me to be home taking care of the boys like a glorified babysitter while he went out and spent my money. Diesel's... different."

Unlike Payne, Diesel had never lied to me or led me to believe we were more than we were. He genuinely liked me, I knew he did. And he wanted me too, at least for right now. The engagement was a lie, but not everything was. I believed that. I did.

Diesel came in carrying a tray of coffee in mismatched mugs, looking nearly as nervous as he'd been when Terry was here. "I realized too late, I don't really have decent mugs," he apologized. "My aunts like to buy me these for

Christmas and birthday presents, but I'm not totally sure they're appropriate."

I looked down at the mug Diesel handed me, which had a picture of two chickens that looked an awful lot like Brenda and Henry, and read "I'm Just A Guy Who Loves Peckers." Meanwhile, Beau looked down at his and burst out laughing.

"Rise and shine, Mother Clucker?" he wheezed, turning a concerning shade of red. "Oh my God."

He laughed so hard, even Marigold got excited and started laughing, which only made Beau laugh harder.

When he finally subsided with a sigh, he turned to Diesel and looked much more friendly. "So, Diesel, Parrish was starting to tell me about your custody troubles."

Diesel cut a look at me, and I gave him a reassuring smile. "Yes, sir," he replied.

"And you and Parrish are tackling them... together?"

"We are." I nodded firmly. "We're together."

"We're engaged," Diesel blurted.

Shit.

"Engaged?" Beau goggled. "Parrish? And you haven't told us?"

My mouth opened and closed like a fish. Marigold fussed and reached out her arms for me, so I took her out of the exercise dish to buy myself time to formulate a response, but in the end I didn't have to.

"Don't be mad at Parrish," Diesel said, sitting on the edge of the sofa closest to Beau. "The engagement only happened recently, and it was my idea to keep it quiet for a bit." He pushed a hand through his hair. "Let me be honest with you, sir, my life is a hot mess right now. I'm nobody's idea of a good bet. Every bit of my money and time are going to taking care of this little girl and fighting for the right to keep doing it. Meeting Parrish—heck, meeting any man who'd want to take all this on with me, but especially someone as loving and nurturing and encouraging and smart as your nephew—was the furthest thing from my mind, 'cause I'd sorta figured I'd start dating when she was eighteen or so. But then... there he was. Like a rainbow after a storm. Like finding the promised land after wandering around alone in the desert."

He gave me a sheepish grin, like he knew he was being overly sentimental but couldn't help it. I'd never wanted anything more than to believe his words were real.

"I couldn't let a miracle like Parrish pass me by, just because the timing was terrible. I'm no kinda man for your nephew, sir, and that's the truth. I don't deserve him, and I haven't done a thing to earn him. But somehow, I got him. So, I'm gonna try my hardest to keep him." He looked over at me and Marigold, and his gaze softened. "To keep both of them."

"Well, now." Beau pulled a ginormous hankie from his pocket and sniffled into it. He mopped his eyes and cleared his throat. "Well, now," he repeated. "Then I guess I should welcome you to the family, Diesel Church."

Diesel, who'd just relaxed enough to take a sip of his coffee, choked and his coffee went spewing. His eyes flew to me, and I smiled as I sat next to him and thumped him on the back to help get his breathing under control.

"Thank you, sir," he said gruffly, his eyes full of gratitude and maybe just a little bit of shame.

Uncle Beau waved this away. "No thanks necessary. You have no idea how it warms my heart to see Parrish with a baby in his arms again."

Diesel frowned a little in confusion and looked at me, but I looked away. At some point, I was gonna have to tell

Diesel about Payne and the boys. Probably. Maybe. Or not. Honestly, with so many lies floating around, this lie by omission was small potatoes, and I didn't want Diesel to pity me for all the months my idiot self had been deluded into thinking Payne loved me.

I also very much didn't want him to see how close I was to letting history repeat itself.

"Alrighty, then, what we need is a plan." Beau brought his hands down to slap his knees. "Because there's no way am I gonna sit by and watch you three take your chances when I've got the means to make things happen. Isn't that right, Miss Marigold?"

Marigold, who was sitting on my lap blissfully unaware that adults were deciding her future, slapped her own chubby knees in response, and Diesel and I couldn't help but chuckle.

"Would you look at that? She's taking after her uncle Beau already!" Beau crowed delightedly. "So, what's the deal with her grandparents?"

"The Kensingtons," Diesel volunteered. "They took my sister in after our parents died. They live in Nashville now, and they're big in horse breeding, I guess—"

"Brenda and Hunt Kensington?" Uncle Beau snorted. "Oh, I'm familiar. Your aunt Marnie's had run-ins with Brenda in the past. You got a lawyer?"

Diesel and I exchanged a glance.

"Sort of," I said. "Stewie is..." I couldn't think of a word that meant generally harmless, but completely unmotivated and not quite competent. "He's Stewie."

"He's fine," Diesel cut in. "He's qualified. And affordable. Which is exactly what I need."

"No, sir." Uncle Beau shook his head. "No, sir, it is not. I've been where you are, son. I grew up so poor, if a trip around the world cost a dollar I wouldn't've made it to Virginia. I know what it's like to have your pride be the only thing you haven't sold or bartered. But there comes a time when a man realizes he can't do it alone, and if you can't trust family to help you out, then you've got bigger problems than a lack of money." He nodded his head once, like this decided things.

Diesel hesitated, but he looked at Marigold, then at me, and said nothing. Beau took this silence for assent.

"So, as I was saying, this Stewie character can watch and learn, because I'm gonna get my attorneys involved. Deadliest buncha sharks Nashville's got to offer. Only the best for my Parrish's little girl."

I shook my head instinctively. "You mean Diesel's girl."

Beau lifted an eyebrow. "But Parrish, honey, if you two are getting married, she'll be yours too, won't she?"

"Oh." I swallowed hard. "Well, in a manner of speaking, yes. But—"

"Baby doll, tell your Papa Parrish he's nuttier'n a squirrel," Beau instructed Marigold in a singsong voice. "Tell your Papa he's all sauce and no wings. That's right," he approved as she burbled and cooed along with him. To me, he added, "I'm gonna get you in to see Merchant, Greene, and Chandler next week, and they're gonna send all three partners to meet you if they know what's good for 'em. We gotta jump on this like grease on a hot skillet, son. No time to mess around. Trust me, I'm gonna get everything locked up right and tight."

I nodded mutely, but my mind was still stuck on "Papa."

Good Lord. Good *Lord*, I wanted that. Almost, but not quite, as much as I wanted to make sure Diesel got Marigold forever.

"Well, I expect you two need to get on with your day."

Beau pushed himself to his feet with the help of his cane. "You can expect to hear from your aunt Marnie about thirty seconds after I remember how to make a phone call on the car speakers. She's gonna wanna send out a press release to all your cousins, so you'll probably wanna call your parents, if you haven't already. Marnie'll know better'n to try to throw y'all a party, not while there's all this uncertainty, but she'll wanna plan the gala to end all galas when the custody verdict comes through." He slapped Diesel on the arm. "All the wings you can eat, eh?"

Diesel nodded halfheartedly. He looked a trifle nauseous, and I understood why. Beauregard Partridge was a force of nature even when you were used to him like I was.

Beau pressed a kiss to Marigold's dark curls, ruffled my hair like I was twelve, and clomped out the door.

"Are you really okay with this?" I asked Diesel as we waved Beau off from the porch. "Because if you're not, you just have to tell me. Beau means well, but I don't want you to feel forced into anything."

"Nah. 'Course not." Diesel ran a hand over his jaw. His whole body radiated tension, and his eyes didn't meet mine. "I'm grateful to your uncle. And to you."

"Okay. If you're sure," I asked, biting my lip uncertainly.

Diesel looked at me, and his shoulders dropped. "I'm positive, Parrish. It's fine. Honestly." He drew me in and pressed a lingering kiss to the side of my mouth. When he pulled back and smiled, it looked nearly like his usual sweet smile. "Are *you* okay? I don't know why I blurted out our engagement in the first place. Now that Beau knows, he's gonna tell Mal, and you know Mal's gonna tell Ava Siegel, and by tomorrow evening, Ava and the Beautification Corps will make sure every Tibetan yak herder knows."

He didn't sound upset, only wry and maybe resigned. He liked Ava a lot, especially after all the Beautification Corps had done to get his house fixed up, and I knew he liked Mal already.

I gave him a half-smile. "I told you before, I already informed Gil that I had a hot fiancé." I shrugged. "And I'm pretty sure Tucker already knew there wasn't gonna be a repeat of last weekend, but now he'll know for sure."

Diesel's arm tightened around me slightly. "That'll be handy, at least," he grumbled.

"Pardon?"

"Nothing, baby." He reached for Marigold, and I handed her over. "But I'm thinking we should both get to work while we can, because once the Thicket knows about our engagement, it's gonna be..."

"Madness," we said together, and Marigold clapped her hands in agreement.

Chapter Twelve

Diesel

Running the salvage yard wasn't quite as easy with Marigold strapped to my chest as it had been before, but it was definitely more fun in some ways. I'd never seen so many hardened men turn to complete mush when they caught sight of her dark curls.

"Oh, who's this?" they'd ask in unusually high-pitched voices. There was something about a fat-cheeked, smiling baby that brought out the sweetness in almost everyone.

But not Chuck Stanley. He was a Grade A asshole, but he was a Grade A asshole with a very successful mechanic shop the next town over and came to me fairly frequently looking for parts. Stanley's garage helped keep me in business, and I wasn't about to fuck up my relationship just because I was in a bad mood.

"What the fuck is taking so long?" he snapped while I tried to drive the forklift without Marigold getting a good grip on the wheel.

"Earmuffs, baby," I whispered to her. As if she could cover her ears against the man's bad language. "Almost got it," I said louder to the man flinging cigarette ash into a nearby Chevy sedan chassis.

When I finally got the engine block loaded onto the back of his truck and had the cash in hand, I grunted a thanks and made my way back into the house to put the money in my safe. It was time for Marigold's bottle and afternoon nap anyway, so hopefully no one else would stop by needing anything until I could get her down.

My head had been spinning all day with thoughts of Parrish and the situation we now found ourselves in. Watching him lie to his uncle was very uncomfortable because I knew that his family meant everything to him. And now he was possibly alienating them. For me.

I fumbled the baby bottle and accidentally punted it across the kitchen floor. Cursing under my breath, I reached down to grab it and threw the whole thing in the sink in order to start over with a clean bottle. When we finally, finally settled into my favorite chair with the bottle, I was pretty sure we both heaved a sigh of relief.

Two seconds later the doorbell rang, startling us both.

"Dammit," I said under my breath. Marigold was half-asleep in my arms, so I stood up carefully in hopes of keeping her that way.

I answered the door to see Mal and Brooks standing on the porch with a casserole pan. Mal's grin was mischievous enough to scare me a little.

"We heard congratulations are in order," he said in a singsong voice. "Cindy Ann couldn't wait to tell Brooks what she heard up at the Jazzercise studio from Becky Lynn, who heard it from Winter Munsen, who ran into Beau at the coffee shop a little while ago. And you know Brooks's mama when she hears big news... casserole city.

Pretty sure she makes up a pallet of these suckers in advance just in case."

Brooks nodded absently and tried to peer around me into the house. "You got any beer in there? I could stand a drink or three after the visit from my mom."

I closed my eyes and prayed to Snow White and the Seven Dwarves. "Come in. Let me put this one down in her crib. Kitchen's over there. Help yourself."

After settling the milk-drunk girl into the crib and double-checking the baby monitor settings, I made my way back out to the living room and tried to ignore Mal looking through all of my shit. Instead, I threw myself down onto the sofa and kicked my feet up onto the coffee table. "Gimme one of those," I grunted at Brooks.

He set the bottle on a tidy little square of folded paper towel. Our eyes met for a brief moment of WTF before I took a glug of the cold brew and let out a sigh.

"What's going on?" I asked once Mal stopped being nosy and took a seat on the arm of the chair where Brooks sat.

"You and Partridge. Spill." Mal rubbed his hands together in glee before swiping the beer from Brooks's hand and taking a sip.

"What about him. Us. Him. What about him?" *Way to stay cool, Ace.*

Brooks lifted an eyebrow but remained quiet. Mal wasn't so polite. "You're *engaged*? To be *married*? To *Parrish*?" His voice kicked ever higher with each question until I was sure the coyotes in the forest a few miles away were probably twitching their ears in annoyance. Brooks took a sip of beer like this was just Mal being Mal. I kinda felt sorry for the guy and wondered if I should recommend the brand of ear protectors I used with my chainsaw.

"Yeah. So?" I said with a shrug before taking another sip.

Brooks spewed beer all over his shirt. "Wait, what? What?" He turned to Mal. "What?"

Mal looked at Brooks like he was daft. "What did you think your mom meant when she said she heard Diesel and Parrish were getting married?"

Brooks set his beer down and used his own paper towel square to dab at his wet shirt. "I thought it was the Thicket rumor mill getting a little overcranked as it tends to do. I didn't think the rumors were true."

I squinted one eye against the headache nudging its way up the back of my neck. Maybe a few more sips of beer would help.

Mal studied me. "That's a little sudden. Don't you think?"

I met his eyes. "Pot, this is kettle..."

Brooks burst out laughing, accidentally knocking Mal off the arm of the chair. "He got you there, babe."

Mal moved over to the end of the sofa opposite me. "We've been together for like a year. They've only known each other..." He paused and looked at me. "Wait. When did you two meet?"

"A while ago," I said. Which was completely true if you had the life span of a mosquito.

Brooks leaned forward and grabbed his beer again before sitting back with a dangerously smug smile. "Great. Then you can come with us to the Cocktail Marathon tomorrow night. We'll make it a double date. Triple, if we can convince Ava and Paul to come too."

I opened my mouth to explain about the babysitting problem before I remembered that Marigold might be with the Kensingtons again tomorrow night. I was fighting a second overnight visit since Parrish had told me babies this age didn't do well away from home in unfamiliar places.

"I'm not sure. We'll probably have Marigold with us, and something like that would be past her bedtime."

Brooks frowned before his face lit up again. "I know. We'll do the happy hour live music thing in the park tomorrow evening. It's a family event. Starts at five, and Parrish can hook us up with some barbecue. I'll bring picnic blankets and stuff. The baby will love it. Ava's taken little Beau before, and he crawls around all over the place. Sometimes lightning bugs come out by the time they finish up with the music. It's all over by like seven thirty or something."

Mal's eyes met mine, challenging me to decline another heartfelt invitation by his man. I blew out a breath. "Fine. We'll do the damned picnic. But right now, you two need to get the hell out of here because my head's killing me, and Little Miss is going to be up in an hour wanting all my attention again."

The two of them stood up and took their bottles to the kitchen. I mumbled an apology about kicking them out, but they waved me off like it was no big deal. It felt kind of nice to have friends who didn't mind getting the old heave-ho. It reminded me of how I'd felt the first time I'd met them over a year ago. And that reminded me of how Brooks had responded when I'd flirted with Mal. I couldn't exactly pass up an opportunity to get a rise out of him again. Not after he'd roped me into some Licking Thicket family night.

"Hey, Mal," I said as they headed toward the front door. "Lookin' good in those shorts. They from some kind of special tailor? The fit is just... *hngh*."

Brooks sputtered and gaped at me. "Did you..." He looked at Mal. "Did he just..."

Mal laughed and grabbed the front of Brooks's shirt, yanking him through the front door. "Stop looking at my ass, Church. You're practically a married man now," he called out before mumbling reassurances to Brooks.

I heard Brooks ask him if he'd been sneaking off to a tailor while Brooks wasn't looking.

Mal's words echoed in my memory like a wish gone unfulfilled.

You're practically a married man now.

If only.

After closing the door and flipping the bolt, I turned back toward the living room and threw myself down on the sofa for a cat nap, making sure the baby monitor was right next to my ear and had the volume turned up.

I fell asleep to the daydream of bringing Parrish home as my real husband, but it morphed into a dark, twisted nightmare. General Partridge laughed at me with a wicked sound, and his mustache twirled itself. A group of gospel singers swayed behind him in maroon robes and happily sang the words *he lies* over and over while the congregation was made up of chickens and roosters and the collection plates were heaped full of chicken wings. Parrish patted me on the hand and tried to tell me everything would be okay, but then I caught Chuck Stanley—my asshole mechanic client—asking if he could use Parrish as his pretend fiancé next. He said it would be good for business since Parrish was from the right kind of family. By then the gospel singers had changed into prep school uniforms and started repeating *right kind of family* over and over until I woke up to the sound of Marigold screaming through the monitor and Parrish hollering through the front door.

I grabbed the front door first before turning and racing

to get Mari out of the crib. Parrish came up behind me and circled my waist with his arms.

"Bad day?" His voice was so soothing, so calm, I suddenly felt a strange combination of comfort and exhaustion.

Marigold let out a surprised sound of excitement when she heard his voice, and she lurched for him. Parrish laughed and took her from me, turning to lay her down on the changing table. He fell into a newly familiar rhythm of babbling happily to Mari while telling me about his day at work, but I couldn't shake the funk I'd fallen into. The dream had only represented the stress I'd already been feeling.

I was asking too much of Parrish. I'd roped him into this without his consent, and now he was crossing lines he never would have crossed before. It was like a cheesy movie where the good kid was lured into a life of crime by the kid from the wrong side of the tracks. Those stories never ended well for the good kid.

"Diesel?"

I blinked at him, trying desperately to shake off the direction my thoughts were going. Regardless of how I felt, we were in it now. I couldn't afford to lose him before the judge's final decision.

I ground my teeth together in frustration. The truth of the matter was... I couldn't afford to lose him at all. He was one of the purest things that had ever happened to me, and I selfishly wanted to keep him forever. Regardless of what was best for Parrish, I knew *my* life would be immeasurably better with him in it.

"Yeah," I said in a sleep-roughened voice. "Sorry. Dozed on the sofa, and I guess I'm still shaking off the cobwebs."

His eyebrows knitted together. "You sure that's all? You seem... I don't know."

I stepped forward and cupped his neck before leaning down and kissing him softly. He made a soft sound of submission that immediately sent the blood zinging through my body at light speed.

"Missed you is all," I mumbled against his mouth.

He held Marigold on his hip, and I felt her little fist grabbing at my shirt. I moved my hand down from his neck to her messy curls and tried not to think about how everything important to me—everything I held on to in this moment—could be ripped away from me within a matter of days or weeks.

I was living on borrowed time. Because if either of these people were taken from me, I wasn't sure I could keep on going.

"Snap out of it," Parrish said with a nip to my lower lip. "Oh, by the way, Sara made a casserole for us."

I tried to make sense of his words. "The new pullet made us a casserole?"

He laughed and moved out to the living room. "Don't be silly. I mean Miss Sara from the B&B. I had to stop over and pick up some more of my stuff after work."

"Why does everyone keep making us casseroles? It's kind of weird. Brooks and Mal brought one today too."

He set Mari on the rug next to her basket of toys. "It's a small town's love language, I guess. I think it's kind of sweet. Even though you aren't recovering from childbirth and dealing with a newborn, they're still honoring you and your new baby with the same traditions."

That stopped me in my tracks. I'd tried my best to lie low here in the Thicket and not take up too much space or draw any undue attention. I'd never been good enough for a town this quaint and picture-perfect.

"It's probably because you're giving me respectability," I said. "So I'm finally on their radar."

Parrish frowned again and then looked at Marigold. "I think your daddy needs a walk in the park and some fresh air. Let's get your stroller, big girl."

He was right. By the time we finished a big loop through town and the park, I was feeling much better. It was hard to stay down when Parrish's sweet voice was laughing and spinning tales of the unique job applicants who'd shown up for interviews with his store manager today. When we got home, I even discovered the casserole from Miss Sara was a vegetarian pasta dish with tons of fresh veggies in it.

Everything was going to be okay.

———

"This is not fucking okay," I hissed at Parrish the following late afternoon as we walked to the park again to meet Brooks and Mal for the music picnic or whatever it was. "You told me to pull Stewie off the case because of Beau's big Nashville lawyers, and now the Nashville firm can't see us till Monday. I needed someone today, and they didn't fucking show! The Kensingtons are taking her for an overnight visit and—"

Parrish interrupted me with a hip check. "Cut it out. And stop using that language in front of Marigold. I already told you, the man's wife went into early labor, and he had to turn back to meet her at the hospital. It was too late to get anyone else there. Would you have wanted him to miss his own child's birth just so Mari didn't have to spend one night with the Kensingtons?"

Before I could snap, "Maybe," like I wanted to, a chorus of voices shouted, "Surprise!"

I glanced up and saw half the town staring at us with expectant smiles on their faces. Parrish and I froze like hunted rabbits.

"What's happening?" Parrish whispered out of the corner of his mouth.

"Fuck," I said.

"Language," he muttered before pasting on a big fake smile. "What's all this?"

Ava came to the front of the crowd with Parrish's uncle. "We wanted to throw you an engagement party! We're so excited for you two. Paul's opening the champagne so we can all drink a toast to the happy couple."

Beau's eyes sparkled as he reached down to the stroller for Marigold. "Come here, sweet angel. Let me show you off to your great-aunt Marnie."

Before I knew it, the baby was gone, a plastic flute of champagne had been thrust into my hand, and everyone was bombarding us with their well wishes.

Parrish took to the attention as if he'd been born to it, which I suddenly realized he had. He chatted and tittered and smiled and mingled like a champion while I stood next to him like some kind of creepy sidekick who thought a canapé shaded people from the sun.

I felt uncomfortable in my skin. I felt like I was a bug under a microscope. And I felt, more than anything, that I was finally seeing Parrish in his natural environment. Everyone loved him. He was engaging, entertaining, and attentive. Somehow he knew all the right words to say when someone asked about wedding venues and themes, and when his aunt Marnie asked him whether we were going to go with tuxedos, morning suits, or white tie and tails for the wedding, Parrish seemed to know the difference between the three.

I was out of my element, and it showed. Parrish was right at home in society like this, and here he was having to pretend he was marrying the runaway dropout junk dealer whose most prized possession was his chicken collection.

This was so wrong.

As the party continued, my happy bubble of enjoying Parrish while I had him began to thin and tear. Was enjoying this man's company causing him more harm than good? What would his friends and family say when he ended up jilted before the month was out?

"Hey, I grabbed you some of these little drummettes," Parrish said, handing me a plate with two tiny chicken legs on them. "They're teriyaki flavored with fresh pineapple."

My stomach churned as I stared down at yet another example of my string of lies. I glanced up to meet Parrish's eyes. He must have seen something in my expression because he took the plate back and tossed it in a nearby trash can before grabbing my face and pulling it close to his.

"Talk to me," he said softly. "What's going on? You've been in a funk since I got to your house."

I cared about him so much. I wanted him with me forever. It was as clear as the crisp Tennessee sky on a glorious day in September, but I couldn't tell him that.

"Sorry," I breathed instead. "Dunno, I guess."

He pressed a kiss against the side of my cheek. "I don't believe you. Do you want to go home?"

I shook my head. "No, you're having fun, and I like watching you talk to everyone."

"What would make you happy right now?" He searched

my eyes for the answer as if he wasn't going to believe the words themselves. So I vowed to be honest with him.

"You. I just want to be with you." For as long as I could get, even if it was only days.

Parrish's face softened. "Then let's get our girl and go home."

It was a fairy tale. But for the time being, it was mine.

Chapter Thirteen

Parrish

"Thanks a bunch, Terry," I said as I finished stirring up a big pan of fried rice on the stove. "'Preciate you taking the time to work this out on a weekend."

"Not exactly my choice, Parrish," Terry said wryly. His voice sounded tinny and faraway through the phone. "The combined powers of Merchant, Greene, and Chandler, even when Chandler is calling from the labor and delivery ward, are more than my boss or I can resist. At least not if we wanna keep our jobs, which I do."

I winced. This was maybe the dark side of having Uncle Beau's sharky attorneys on the case, but I honestly couldn't bring myself to feel that bad. I looked out the window over the sink at Marigold and Diesel, sitting on a blanket in the scrub grass, watching the chickens peck. Or more like Mari was sitting, while Diesel lay flat on his back staring up at the sky, one arm wrapped protectively around the baby's waist. They'd been sitting out there for nearly an hour, ever since we got back from the impromptu engagement party.

He looked worried and maybe a little lost, and I felt immediately protective.

"It's really in the baby's best interest not to be taken away for another visit so soon," I informed Terry. I tucked the phone between my ear and shoulder and searched Diesel's cabinets for a serving bowl. I happened to find Miss Sara's casserole dish, so I rolled my eyes and picked that. "Marigold hardly knows the Kensingtons, and the whole visit was traumatic. She hasn't slept more than three hours at a stretch since she's been home with us, and she'd been going for eight hours regularly before that."

"I know, I read the reports. I'm glad it worked out." Terry hesitated. "And for what it's worth, I think the Kensingtons are mostly okay with it. As I understand it, she had a pretty rough night over there. I think they're willing to wait until things are permanently decided."

"Yeah? That's great news." I scraped the rice into the dish and put the pan in the sink. "I'm really relieved, and I know Diesel will be too." I was pretty sure Diesel hadn't been sleeping at night the last couple of days either, even when Mari was sleeping.

I covered the dish of rice with foil and set it in the oven to keep warm as Terry and I said our goodbyes. Then I stood and looked at the homey little kitchen with its small table and chairs.

I wanted to do something special for Diesel, something to make him feel appreciated, especially after the week we'd had. Unfortunately, the contents of his fridge hadn't lent themselves to much of anything besides a vegetable fried rice, but I'd found an old tablecloth while poking around in the cabinets, so I spread that out, along with matching cloth napkins, to liven up the usual plates and cutlery. There were a couple of unscented candles in jars tucked in a cabinet too, and I got as far as picking it up before firmly putting it back.

Candles on the tables were too romantic, and the last thing I wanted was to make Diesel uncomfortable by pushing too hard or making him worry that I had expectations. He had enough people who expected things from him; I just wanted to give him something back.

I made my way out into the yard, and Marigold started babbling at me as soon as I got close to the blanket. Diesel sat up and gave me a lopsided smile that made my heartbeat stutter.

"Guess she missed you," he said with a wink. "She's catching you up on the chickens' antics."

"And I wanna hear every detail, Miss Thing," I assured her.

I knelt down behind Diesel and hugged his back. He hummed contentedly as I rested my chin on his shoulder and listened to the baby talk for a minute.

The evening was coming on really quickly, and a giant gust of wind slammed through the yard, setting the wind chimes on the back porch to jingle.

"Looks like rain," I said, watching the clouds gather at the edge of the sky, just beyond the roofline.

"Mmhmm. Big thunderstorms coming, according to the forecast. Gotta batten the hatches."

"Yeah?" I shifted position so I was sitting on the blanket next to him. "Cool!"

Diesel shot me a sideways glance. "I take it you're not scared, huh?"

"Of storms? No way! At least, not unless they think there's a tornado risk, but that's pretty rare over here. When I was a kid, I'd open all the windows in my room so I could feel the breeze and hear the thunder. Made me feel like I was right in the middle of it."

"Wouldn't have been so fun if you'd actually *been* out in

the middle of it," he said, like it was something he'd lived, and my heart squeezed. I was painfully aware that I knew only the briefest facts about his life, but I wanted to know more.

"Definitely not," I agreed. "Part of what made it fun was experiencing all that wildness while knowing I was warm and dry at home. Oh, and speaking of which…" I recounted my whole conversation with Terry. "He thinks the Kensingtons might not push for another overnight. Isn't that amazing?"

Diesel grunted and bent his knee up to his chest, like a wall between us. "Your uncle must be paying top dollar for attorneys who'll work on a weekend evening."

I blinked. "Well, maybe. I mean, probably, yeah." After a beat I asked softly, "Would it be better if I told Beau I'd pay for everything myself? 'Cause I have the money."

"No!" He shook his head impatiently. "Jesus, Parrish."

I found myself wanting to apologize, but I wasn't sure what for. "I thought you'd be happy," I ventured. "Didn't you want her to be able to stay home?"

"Yeah. Yes! Of course I'm happy," he said grudgingly, squeezing Marigold tighter. "Better than anything Stewie could have done."

I decided not to touch this remark. Instead, I cleared my throat and ripped off the rest of the Band-Aid. "Lindsay Greene said she'd like us in there on Monday afternoon to sign some papers. I agreed, but said I'd check with you about the timing. Okay?"

"Guess it'll have to be, won't it?"

I stifled a sigh. "If there's a better day for you—"

"There's no better day. It needs to be settled as soon as possible." Diesel picked at a fray on the leg of his shorts.

"Besides, I'm very grateful to you and your uncle Beau for helping me out."

I ground my back teeth together in annoyance. I knew it had been a crazy day after a long, crazy week. Diesel was not at his best, and neither was I. But I couldn't lie—it drove me absolutely batshit crazy when he clammed up like this nearly every time the lawyers were mentioned. I'd told him a billion times we didn't have to use this firm if he didn't want to, and we didn't have to do anything he wasn't comfortable with. I wanted Diesel to feel in control. I wanted confident, teasing Diesel back.

Instead, he'd always mention how damn "grateful" he was.

"I don't want your gratitude, Diesel. I just want you to be happy. You and Marigold."

Diesel sighed. He glanced sideways at me again and then reached out to pull me in close to his side. "I'm happy. It's just... hard."

I wasn't sure what was hard—the week, the situation with Mari, the situation with me, his whole entire life? I wanted him to tell me more, to explain what was happening in his head, but I wasn't sure I deserved that explanation, not if I'd be out of his life soon. And besides, it wasn't like I was being entirely honest with him either. Not about my past. Not about my feelings. The only time things felt really solid and honest between us was when he was touching me, whether it was him reaching for me across the bed at night, or his hand in mine while we were walking through that engagement party this afternoon.

Normally, I was a party person—I liked meeting new people and learning about their lives; I liked making those connections—but today had been tough even for me, and I just hoped it hadn't shown. I'd really started to like all the crazy people in this town—people generous enough to throw a near stranger an engagement party after that stranger had corrupted their Pickin' with a strange new tradition—and it was weird lying to them. Harder, in a way, than lying to Beau, who I was pretty sure would forgive me and understand my motivations once the truth came out. I felt like I was burning bridges every time someone asked me when the wedding would be.

It was harder still, in a way, because it hadn't felt like lying. For a few blissful seconds here and there, it would feel like all my dreams had come true—Marigold in my arms, Diesel standing behind me—and then it would all come crashing down anytime a well-meaning townsperson asked us a question about the future.

After we'd gotten home, Diesel had taken Marigold out into the yard without a word, and I'd gone immediately to the kitchen, grateful for the chance to regroup. I felt a hundred times better now, but it didn't seem to have worked for Diesel, and I wasn't sure what to do about it.

Marigold gasped, and I turned my head to watch her watching a butterfly flit across the grass. She seemed fascinated.

"A pipevine swallowtail," I told Mari, leaning over Diesel's lap so I could speak softly in her ear. "Isn't it pretty? Those are my favorite." It felt kinda symbolic that one had appeared right now.

I took a deep breath, sat up straight, and summoned a teasing smile. "Hey, did you know that you have no meat in your house? Like, none. Not in the fridge, and not even a pack of bacon thrown in your freezer?"

Diesel scraped his teeth over his bottom lip. "Yeah, I know. The thing is..."

"You go through it like crazy," I guessed. "I'm not criticizing! You have plenty to keep on top of. Remind me to get some stuff tomorrow after we're done with the lawyers, okay? I can prep some stuff for the freezer."

Diesel took a deep breath, like he was getting ready to say something, but then let it out in a rush. "That's really sweet, babe. Thank you."

I smiled and rubbed his knee softly. "Of course. This is a stressful time. We need to take care of ourselves and each other. We're a team, right? Team Marigold?"

Diesel smiled. "Team Marigold."

"Right. And speaking of Her Highness..." I nodded at Miss Thing, who rubbed her eyes tiredly. "I think someone's ready for bed." I stood and dusted off the back of my shorts before picking her up.

"You'll take care of the girly while I take care of the girls?" Diesel said. "Deal."

It didn't take me long to get Mari in her favorite jammies—okay, fine, *my* favorite jammies for her, but I was pretty sure she'd say they were her favorite too, if she were capable of expressing a preference—and put her down with her chicken passie. She was tired enough that she drifted off without a fuss, and I made my way back out to the kitchen to find Diesel standing by the table. He'd gotten the rice out of the warmer and set it on the table.

He'd also gotten the candle out of the cabinet and lit it.

I swallowed. "Wow. Nice." It was the understatement of the century. One little candle should not make my heart gallop the way it did.

"Wind's whipping up," Diesel said gruffly, his eyes on a spot somewhere over my shoulder. "I figured, good to know where a candle is, just in case, right?"

"Ah." I nodded. "Spoken like a true Camper Scout."

"Which I was, back in the day. For a few years anyway."

He grinned. "Got my preparedness merit badge and everything."

"Sexy."

"Yep. That's primarily why I did it," Diesel said blandly. "Even at age seven, I knew someday my knot tying and planning skills would get me laid." He wiggled his eyebrows. "Now it's all finally coming to fruition. Wait until I tell you about my carpentry merit badge."

I giggled and my heart soared. I had no idea what had changed so suddenly, but seeing him look so much lighter and more confident made me feel lighter too.

I sat down at the little square table, and Diesel sat beside me. He actually *did* tell me about his carpentry badge as we ate and how he'd transferred those skills into making the Pullet Palace for the girls, which was really fun. We segued into talking about his tattoos too, which was *endlessly* fascinating to me. I would've happily sat there all night while he told me the story of each and every piece on his body.

"I'm boring you, aren't I?" Diesel said eventually, and I shook my head wildly. The man had no clue how badly I wanted him to open up to me.

"You couldn't possibly be boring *ever*. Tell me more. Which one was the first?"

"Uh. The one on my shoulder blade." He pointed over his shoulder. "The sunflower. That was for Beth. Sunflowers and marigolds were always her favorite when we were kids, so that was my way of remembering her." He shrugged. "I guess all of the tats are memories, in a way. Some happy, some cautionary tales. People don't stick around, but these guys are permanent." He patted the bird on his collarbone fondly, and his eyes found mine. "You know, Parrish, you and I—"

I leaned forward eagerly... and Marigold began crying.

I closed my eyes and sighed. "I'll go soothe her quickly," I said, standing up. "Don't move a muscle. For real. Two minutes."

But of course, Marigold's schedule was slightly different from mine. Two minutes became twenty and then forty. I held her and rocked her, and I even downloaded a white noise app on my phone, but every time I tried to put her down, she'd wake up and scream more frantically.

"You're fine, my love," I told her for the billionth time, rubbing her back softly. "We're right here. Your daddy and I aren't going anywhere, okay? Shh shhh shhh."

Diesel touched my shoulder. "Go relax, babe. Let me try."

I blew out a breath but nodded. I was probably so keyed up, my frustration was fueling poor Mari's.

Diesel kissed my forehead and tucked Mari against his shoulder with the confidence of a guy who'd done it a thousand times, a total change from a couple of weeks ago. I couldn't help but smile as I made my way out to the living room and shut the door gently behind me.

Then I saw the empty kitchen table and sighed. Diesel had already cleaned up our dishes and put the leftovers away. He'd blown out the candle and packed up the tablecloth. I tried very hard not to be overly dramatic or to see this as symbolic of our relationship, but I sort of wished Miss Sara was around to talk to.

At this point, either Miss Sara would've done.

Instead, I threw myself on the sofa and listened to Diesel singing "You Are My Sunshine" to the baby.

He'd finally figured out the words.

A second later, Diesel's lips were on mine, and I opened my eyes to find the house in full darkness. The sky outside was pale pink, lit occasionally by flashes of purple lightning and thunder rumbled menacingly directly overhead.

"Marigold?" I asked blearily.

"Asleep, finally." He rubbed his nose along mine. "I downloaded the same sleep app you have, and I hooked up an extra battery charger too. She went out like a light... around the same time the actual lights went out." He stood up and held out a hand to pull me up.

"Sorry I fell asleep." I rubbed at my eyes and yawned. "I guess I was more tired than I thought."

"You've slept about as much as I have the last couple nights. Which is to say, not a lot." He held me against him in the dark, and I noticed with sudden interest that he wasn't wearing a shirt. "Have I told you lately how much I appreciate all you do for me and Mari?"

I sighed. "Have I told you lately that I don't—"

"Want my gratitude, you just want me to be happy? Yeah, you have. And I appreciate that, too, in the moments when I can actually wrap my head around it." I felt him smile in the dark. "Come on."

He took my hand, and I stumbled after him.

"Wait. Bedroom's that way."

"Yup. But the storm's outside," he whispered.

He led me out the back door and onto the porch. The wind rushed over us, and over in the junkyard, something banged. Just beyond the deep overhang, rain poured down in buckets, but the porch itself was perfectly dry.

"Oh, wow," I breathed, rushing forward to brace myself on the railing and lift my face to the breeze. "This is amazing."

Diesel slotted himself in behind me, kissing his way down my neck from my ear to my shoulder. "No, Parrish, *you're* amazing," he whispered against my damp skin. I full-body shivered. "And I'm gonna show you how much."

He reached both hands around me to pull my T-shirt up all the way to my neck. His fingers plucked at my nipples while his tongue laved my neck, and I had to grab the railing because it was so good I felt like I was floating.

Diesel stepped back for half a second and, without a word, stripped my shirt off entirely. My heart rate tripled, and I reached one hand behind me to grip his hip and pull him against me again. His dick was already hard, and the feel of him against me made me moan.

"Fuck, yes," Diesel breathed. He pulled a bottle of lube and a condom from his pocket and set them on the railing where the wind couldn't get them. "Wanna be inside you so bad."

I nearly swallowed my tongue. "You planned this..."

"Oh yeah. I heard Camper Scout preparedness turns you on—" He rutted against me slightly.

"God, it really does," I said a little desperately.

"—so when I saw you sleeping on the sofa, missing the storm, I came up with a plan—"

"For me?"

"For you," he confirmed. "I'm gonna teach you a whole lot more questionable skills so you can turn them back on me later. You ready?"

I shivered again, as much from the "later" as the intent in his voice. Had I mentioned how much I liked confident, take-charge Diesel? Because I did. I so, so did. "Always."

He pulled me back from the railing slightly, then pivoted so he was standing in front of me.

The only thing better than the ozone and damp grass smell of Tennessee in a rainstorm was the clean sandalwood smell of Diesel Church. His skin was moon-pale in the dim light, and his beautiful tattoos stood out in sharp relief. He was so gorgeous, he should have been fictional, and despite everything we'd done together over the past few days, I still felt the need to pinch myself to prove that this was really happening. Instead, I lifted my hands to his neck to tug him down for a kiss, and he let me, just like he always did.

I sighed happily. But before I could deepen the kiss, he pulled back and gave me a smirk before sinking to his knees.

"I have plans, Mr. Partridge. Remember?"

"Oh."

"Never come between a Camper Scout and his plans."

Well, shit.

I stared down at him on his knees on the wooden deck and focused on keeping myself steady. Even though his face was shadowed, I could feel the intensity of his gaze on me. He splayed his hand over my chest, fingers wide, and it reminded me forcibly of our size difference—his spread fingers could almost touch both of my nipples. But once again, it was hard to care that I wasn't more built and muscly when Diesel seemed to appreciate the fuck out of the body I had.

He dragged his palm down the center of my chest and torso. I loved the feeling of him touching me... and I loved even more that I felt claimed by the gesture.

I was rock hard and panting already. I felt like the rolling clouds I'd seen earlier, coiled and tense. Waiting to unleash.

I didn't have to wait long. Diesel dragged my shorts down with both hands, and before I had time to do more than moan his name and anchor my hands in his hair, he'd sucked the tip of my dick into his mouth and pushed his tongue into the slit.

"Oh, sweet blessed corn niblets!" I yelled, like the most idiotic idiot to ever accidentally have sex.

I could feel Diesel's answering amusement against my dick, and my face flamed.

He popped off a second later to nuzzle his nose into the join of my hip. "You're so damn adorable, you know that? Shit. So damn pure and so damn perfect." He chuckled darkly. "Makes me wanna mess you right the fuck up, so you'll be no good to anybody but me. Makes me wanna own this body entirely. Tattoo something right here—" He stroked a thumb over my hip bone. "—so you never forget how good this was."

Fuck. A tattoo of Diesel? Hell, yes. But also…

Forget? Was he joking? This night would be seared in my memory banks for as long as I lived. Hell, *longer*. Centuries from now, when aliens found my bones, they'd see this night written right where my heart used to be. I opened my mouth to tell him so… but Diesel lifted his free hand to my mouth and tapped my bottom lip with two fingers.

"Suck," he commanded.

Wordlessly, I took his fingers into my mouth, running my tongue up and down each digit until they were slick with spit.

His eyes looked glazed over as he stared up at me. "So damn perfect," he repeated, and then he opened his mouth and sucked my dick all the way in, and I forgot everything else.

Point of fact: Diesel Church was a dick-sucking god. In my entire life, I'd never felt so utterly consumed, literally and figuratively, as I was at that moment, with his lips tight around me and his tongue playing against my shaft. His hands slid around my hips and gripped my ass cheeks with enough force to leave marks—marks I craved like the tattoo —before he moved to graze his wet fingertip over my hole.

"Dearly beloved—I don't—This was *not* in the Camper Scout manual!" I moaned as his mouth worked my cock and his finger teased my opening with such perfect coordination my knees started to give out.

I realized I was holding his hair in a grip that had to be painfully tight, but when I tried to loosen it, he growled around my dick and wrapped his hand around my hand, forcing me to yank harder.

Purple lightning filled the sky, and his eyes were fierce on mine. My stomach flipped end over end like a Slinky falling down the stairs, and thunder rolled in the distance.

"More," I whispered, pulling at his hair until he slid off with a pop. "I want you to fuck me. Please, Diesel? Please fuck me?"

"Yeah. Hell, yeah." His eyes were intense, and his breathing was ragged as he pushed to his feet and shucked his shorts with no finesse whatsoever. He held up his hands so I could see them tremble. "Look what you do to me. Shit. I need you so much, Parrish."

I exhaled a sharp breath. Those were not the three words I most wanted to hear Diesel say, but they were as close as I was going to get in this lifetime, and for tonight, they were enough.

They were *plenty*.

"Then take what you need. Right now. Hard and fast," I reminded him as he moved behind me and pushed me down so I was bent over slightly with my hands braced on the railing. "I'm not delicate."

But when Diesel grabbed the lube and drizzled it down my crack, he seemed to slow down somehow. I peeked over my shoulder to find him watching me, transfixed.

"Diesel? Please?" I whined. My cock was throbbing so hard I had to take one hand off the railing to give it a little relief.

He stepped closer to bat my hand away. "Patience, Butterfly Boy. I'm looking at this ass. This ass was made for fucking."

I let my chin hang to my chest and clutched the railing with both hands. "I really thought we agreed Butterfly Boy was a no," I whimpered.

He ran his fingers through the lube and pushed two inside me, since he'd already worked me open. "Oh, I think Butterfly Boy is a definite *yes*," he said, his voice a scratchy rumble. Then he leaned over me so he could sink his teeth into the tendon at the side of my neck.

I jumped at the sensation, and so did my cock.

"You're so damn responsive. I can feel how much you want this. How much you want *me*. It drives me crazy. And the noises you make, baby... Shit. I wanna bury myself in you until you can't tell where you end and I begin." His long fingers hooked inside of me, tagging my prostate.

"Oh, for the love of Cobb salad. This is torture," I said, my voice slurred. "This is... this is... a serious violation of... of..."

Diesel's fingers paused. "If you were gonna say the Camper Scout handbook, I'm going to slap your ass."

I clamped my lips shut, pretty sure that was exactly what I was going to say, but unsure if I should admit it. "I might have been?"

Diesel laughed softly and stroked my aching length with his free hand. "We're gonna talk about this another day, darlin'. You're so gorgeous, I can't hold out very much longer."

"You shouldn't hold out *any* much longer," I babbled. "Fuck me now. Now would be good... for the fucking."

He placed a laughing kiss on my shoulder blade and pulled back to cover himself with the condom and slick himself up with more lube. Seconds later, he spread his legs wide to get the angle right, pulled my ass cheeks apart, and poised himself at my entrance.

Holy fuck. When Diesel slid inside me, the sensation was so incredibly right, it brought tears to my eyes, and I bit my lip to keep from sobbing.

"Oh, Parrish. Baby. Goddamn, the way you feel," he breathed. He pressed sweet kisses against my shoulder blade. "You okay?"

I nodded fervently, still unable to speak.

"No 'Sweet candied okra!'?" he teased lightly. "No 'Holy pickled watermelon!'? No 'For the love of the blue swallowtail!'" He coasted warm hands over my stomach in circles like he knew I needed a minute to adjust, but it wasn't the physical invasion I needed to adjust from.

I wasn't sure how it was possible to feel more myself with someone else than I ever could on my own, but here I was. How was I supposed to go back to living without this in a matter of days or weeks? How was I supposed to go back to living without *him*?

How had this lie of a relationship become the realest, truest thing in my life?

Diesel slid partway out of me, then back in, and I couldn't hold back a moan.

"Candied okra is horrible," I managed, which was the world's worst code for "please fuck me now and make my brain stop," but Diesel got it. Of course he did. Just like he understood my humor and never made me feel small or stupid for the things I enjoyed. Just like he thought my silly sayings were adorable and my ass was made for fucking. He got me in a way no one else ever had... in a way no one else had ever wanted to.

I held the railing in a death grip, bracing against the powerful thrust of his hips as he moved inside me over and over, tagging my prostate with nearly every stroke.

"Parrish," he said as he ran a hand up my back to clasp the back of my neck. "Parrish," as he broke rhythm just long enough to lick a drop of sweat from my back. "Parrish," as he finally, finally reached for my cock.

I felt my orgasm barreling toward me, amped even higher by the incredible connection between us, and it was impossible in that moment to believe that he didn't feel it too. Something this instinctive and all-consuming couldn't be one-sided, right?

"I'm so close," I told him. "God, please don't stop."

"Not stopping. Not ever. Come on, baby."

Diesel gave me one last perfect stroke, and that was all it took. I came with a cry, and he did too, the sound washed away by the storm.

He pulled out and quickly removed the condom before gathering me in his arms and pulling me upright with his chest against my back. He peppered my neck and the side of my jaw with tiny, happy kisses that had me laughing even as I gasped like I'd run a marathon.

"Jesus, that was perfect," Diesel breathed, chuckling slightly. "But my knees are going to feel this for weeks. I hadn't considered the height thing. Next time I'm gonna get something for you to stand on." He lifted my hands to examine them and brought them one at a time to his lips to kiss. "And maybe a blanket to save your hands from the railing."

"What I hear you saying..." I turned in the shelter of his

arms and took a deep, steadying breath. "Is that you're not ready for your porch sex merit badge yet, Camper Scout Church."

He laughed out loud. "We can't all be as perfect as you, Camper Scout Partridge."

"Aww. Don't be sad. Think how much practice we needed just to get the believable kissing down."

He laughed again, and I decided I really loved that sound. Then he pushed me up against the railing and kissed me until I was breathless again. "Just look at us now, huh?"

"Just look at us now," I echoed, letting him pull me against him again, and I grinned, thinking that being with Diesel felt a lot like being in the center of a thunderstorm. Wildly exciting—thrilling—but safer than I'd ever been in my whole life.

It was only later, after he'd taken me by the hand and led me through the house, after we'd curled around each other in his bed, that I lay in the dark and listened to the silence... and remembered that thunderstorms didn't last.

Chapter Fourteen

Diesel

"Did you tell Ava about the strawberries?" I asked, fidgeting nervously with the silk noose around my neck.

"Yep." Parrish leaned forward and pressed the elevator button. It was Monday morning, and we were in Nashville to meet with the new attorneys. Needless to say, I was probably going to pass out and make a scene.

"It's just that if she has too many—"

His hand pressed against my lower back, nudging me through the open elevator door. "I know, babe. I told her."

"And if she bangs at her cheek—"

"Give her the teething pain relief. I told her." His voice was patient and didn't even border on patronizing. "She'll be fine. It's only for a few hours."

"But—"

The elevator doors opened again, and we were suddenly there. The sleek high-rise office of Merchant, Greene, and Chandler sparkled in minimalist perfection. I glanced down to make sure I didn't have my dirty boots on somehow by accident.

Parrish stood on his toes to brush his lips against my ear. "It's going to be okay. I promise."

I closed my eyes for a second and breathed in his familiar clean scent, nuzzling the top of his hair with my nose before leaning down to press a kiss to his lips. "I l-l-like being reassured," I finished lamely. I'd come this close to telling him I loved him, which was ridiculous. We'd known each other for a hot minute, and I had no business having strong feelings for a man so far out of my league.

But his sweet words of comfort—hell, his noticing I even needed comforting in the first place—were enough to make me feel all kinds of ways.

Now wasn't the time, though. We were here to get things squared away for Marigold and me, and if there was one thing I was willing to walk through all kinds of fire for— including wearing a suit and tie to a Nashville law firm—it was the future of that baby girl.

Parrish studied my face for a beat before plastering on his polite smile and approaching the reception counter. "Good morning, and how are you today, Kerrianne?"

The woman dropped her own polite smile and grinned wide. "Hey, Parrish. Doing fine, and you?"

"Good. How's Brady? And Hoss?"

"They're good. Brady started kindergarten already, and I about cried my eyes out on the day. Even Hoss had to wipe off a tear, not that he'd ever admit it."

I gritted my teeth against the small talk. Social niceties were one of the things I liked most about Parrish. He was attentive and kind, thoughtful like a true friend. But right now I wanted to get down to business. Parrish must have sensed my lack of patience because he leaned forward and whispered, "We're here for our ten o'clock, but is there any way of tracking down a Coke or something for this guy?

This is my fiancé, Diesel Church. Diesel, Kerrianne Timothy."

I smiled as best I could and nodded. "Nice to meet you."

"You too. I sure can get you something. Follow me."

She led us back to an all-glass conference room with views of the river leading northeast to Opryland. I walked over to take it all in while Parrish continued to chat with Kerrianne.

I remembered wanting to go to the Opryland theme park when I was really little. By the time I was old enough to ask for a visit for my birthday, the place had closed down. After that, it became a fancy hotel and convention center, not at all the kind of thing a kid gives a shit about.

But my parents had tried to make up for missing the theme park by taking us on a riverboat cruise. It had been boring as hell, but Beth had gotten a new camera for her birthday that year, and the two of us had taken a million pictures in crazy poses on the deck. I wondered what had happened to all of those photos. Did the Kensingtons have a box somewhere in their attic full of my family's memories?

"Babe?" I turned to see Parrish's forehead crinkled in concern. He handed me a cold glass of Coke poured over ice cubes.

"Yeah, thanks." I took it and swallowed down a big sip, letting the caffeine work its magic.

Parrish had known I wouldn't want coffee. I was already sweating in the suit despite the cool air-conditioning in the office, but the cold soda was perfect. I grabbed his hand and squeezed it. "Thank you," I said again, making sure he knew how much I appreciated his thoughtfulness. With him by my side, there was no reason to be nervous. We were going to be fine.

His face relaxed into a smile as he pulled out two chairs for us next to each other. "Anytime."

When the attorneys and their assistants began streaming into the room, I had a moment of panic at the sheer number of people attending the meeting. Parrish reached for my hand under the table and held it steady.

The whitest-haired man of the group took the lead. "You must be Edwin. I'm Ian Merchant."

Before I could react to being called a name I'd barely heard in the years since my parents died, Parrish leaned forward. "He goes by Diesel. It should be in your paperwork."

Instead of the sneer or judgment I was expecting, he looked truly sorry for the misstep. "Oh, I apologize, Diesel. I remember Antonia telling me that, and I completely let it slip out of my head. I do know we are here to talk about sweet Marigold. First of all, I'd like to tell you how truly sorry we are for the loss of your sister, Beth. According to everything we've discovered in preparing for your case, she was a wonderful woman with a big heart. Please accept our condolences, Diesel."

I nodded and swallowed. I hadn't been expecting that sincerity, but then again, Beau was a kind, sincere man himself. It stood to reason he'd select good people to give his business to.

They began with a summary of the situation to make sure they understood the case the way I understood it. Parrish helped clarify some details when my nervous grunts didn't seem to do the job.

"We understand you're engaged to be married," Ian said. "Congratulations. Having a solid, two-parent household will go a long way toward convincing the judge you can provide Marigold the family security she needs. In fact, we think this is such an important factor in your case, we've taken the liberty of drawing up some papers to get the ball rolling in the right direction, purely from a legal standpoint. Why delay, when acting quickly could save so many headaches down the line, right?"

I frowned but nodded again. Acting quickly sounded good.

"You'll also see we've drawn up preliminary last wills and testaments for both of you—well, Parrish, you already have one, but this will replace it, of course—as well as an education trust Beau directed us to initiate. He feels that having financial security already set aside in Marigold's name would help..."

The words began to get lost behind the loud rushing sound of blood in my ears. I felt light-headed and wrong-footed. While I knew intellectually this was the right move to help secure Marigold's future, I felt completely turned around, that all of this was not of my own making and was a complicated set of gears spinning out of my control.

Parrish's calm voice cut through all the noise. "Would you mind if we had a moment alone?"

I felt all of the eyes on me while I kept my gaze focused on a tiny scratch on the wooden conference table. That simple imperfection and Parrish's warm palm in mine were the only things anchoring me here while everything else spun around us.

"Of course. Take all the time you need."

After a minute, I felt Parrish's hands on my face. "Hey. Hey, look at me." I blinked up at him. "We can leave right now. We don't have to do any of this."

"I'm okay."

"You're most definitely not okay. Diesel... talk to me. You've been in your head about this for days, and I feel like… I feel like I don't know what you're thinking. Am I doing something wrong? Am I pressuring you? Because that's the last thing I want."

I swiveled our chairs toward each other so I could pull him in for a tight hug. "You're doing everything right. I don't know where I'd be without you right now. I'm just so scared of losing her, of letting Beth down. And I… I've never had anyone fighting this hard for me before. What if it's the wrong thing? What if I'm the wrong choice for her? And I don't want handouts, Parrish. I've worked really hard my whole life to not wind up beholden to someone else, and I can't imagine how much all of this is costing. I can't… I can't…" I wanted to say I couldn't thank his family enough, but the words failed me.

Parrish pressed a kiss into my neck. "We love Marigold. And we think you're the best choice, even if you don't. When you're not feeling strong enough to be the right choice for her, we'll be standing behind you making you stronger."

It was the first time he'd implied this wasn't just temporary—that he'd still be around to support me even if and when I got custody of her. Something about that assurance finally loosened the knots tied up in my gut.

"Promise?" I asked like a terrified child getting ready to jump into water not knowing how to swim.

Parrish pulled back until our foreheads were touching. "I'd pretty much promise you the moon if I had a way of grabbing it," he said softly. "You deserve love, Edwin Church. And you love that girl, and she loves you. I promise to help support both of you through this, okay?"

I nodded.

"And someday you're going to explain to me how your name became Diesel," he teased, holding my hands and stroking his thumbs over my knuckles in a way that was both distracting and soothing, "but that doesn't have to be today."

"Oh, that. Dumb story, really. Back when I worked with Stix, he tried teaching me about cars. He'd have me take them apart and put them back together. He taught me to drive. Used to let me gas up his truck, and the wrecker, and the Bobcat, and all the other equipment—"

"Oh, no," Parrish said, guessing where this was going.

"Oh, yes." I shook my head, remembering my own stupidity. "I went to fill the Bobcat with regular gas, and he stopped me just in time. I thought for sure he'd kick me out and tell me to never come back."

"But he didn't."

"Nah. He started calling me Diesel to remind me..." I cleared my throat. "To remind me he cared about me and trusted me."

Parrish smiled his gorgeous smile, and his eyes glistened. "Well, then. I'm glad to call you Diesel." He winked.

I took a deep breath and let it out slowly. Parrish Partridge was a miracle worker. He'd somehow brought things around and made it all okay.

I wished in that moment there was something I could give him, something that would mean to him even a fraction of what his help with Marigold meant to me. Maybe I could offer to tune up the Mustang or find out if his home in Nashville needed any handyman work.

I shook my head against those ridiculous ideas. Surely, the man had everything he needed already. I'd never be able to repay him.

"Thank you," I croaked. "I... thank you. You're a really good person, Parrish."

It sounded lame because it was the biggest understatement ever. But I knew now we were going to be fine.

And we were. For about an hour. Everyone came back into the room shortly after my freak-out, and we all got down to business. The attorneys had us sign reams of paperwork, and it got to a point I just signed whatever they put in front of me.

I trusted Parrish. I trusted Beau. More than that, I trusted the reputation of one of Nashville's biggest law firms. I had to, really. What else was I going to do?

We said our goodbyes and made our way back downstairs and out onto the city streets. Parrish chatted off and on about restaurants he liked nearby, Beau and Marnie's historic home in Belle Meade, the one-bedroom apartment he'd sublet when he'd moved down to the Thicket, and how strange it was to be back in the city after all those weeks away.

But as he talked, my brain caught up to what it had seen, and I finally began to process what had happened. Parrish led me to a restaurant nearby and got us seated while I began riffling through the papers in the folder they'd handed me. When I finally looked up, there was a Pabst Blue Ribbon in front of me and Parrish was looking through a menu while tapping his lips with his index finger.

"I'm thinking the Firehouse pizza. What are you going to get?"

I glanced through the menu long enough to spot a tomato pesto pie.

After the server took our orders and menus, I went back to idly leafing through the paperwork when one particular document stopped me cold. "Parrish? Is this... is this what I think it is?"

Surely I was wrong. I passed the paper across the table

to him and waited to see his reaction. He took a sip of his water and barely kept from choking on it when he noticed the wording at the top of the official-looking document.

"Marriage certificate?" he squawked. "What? *What?* What?" Parrish shook his head, presumably to get himself to stop repeating himself. "What in the Sam Frick is this?"

Two spots of red bloomed in his cheeks as he suddenly had some kind of thought. His eyes widened and he gawked at me. "I did not do this. I promise you, Diesel. I swear I didn't try to trick you into anything. I swear. We can march right back to Merchant, Greene, and Chandler right now and make them explain themselves. Better yet, they can come here. They can explain that this was all a-a mistake. Or something."

He was so adorably flustered, I couldn't help but let out a burble of a laugh. "I know, babe. I can't exactly see you trying to trick someone into marriage. Especially someone like me."

He shook his head violently. "I wouldn't. Ever. I swear on my... b-butterfly books." His teeth clacked together as if he wanted to stop himself from saying anything more.

I blew out a breath. "I remember them saying something about us needing to be married to make a strong case?"

"I remember them asking us what we planned to do for our vows." Parrish bit his lip. "But I thought it was all hypothetical. What else is in there?" He reached for the folder, and I handed it over.

While he riffled through the fat stack of documents, I took a minute to down several gulps of the cold beer.

He looked up at me with a frown. "What do you mean 'especially someone like me'? You're... you're the total package, Diesel. Anyone would be lucky to m-marry you."

His eyelashes fluttered as he looked back down at the

paper. "I'm... We're..." He looked back up at me. The red apples of his cheeks stood out even brighter than before. "You're my husband. I think."

Even though it was a mistake, or at least some kind of temporary legal step only meant to protect Marigold, it felt kind of nice for a moment to think of him as mine.

"My husband," I said, trying out the term. His eyelashes fluttered prettily as he looked away. I reached out and clasped his chin, gently turning him back to face me. With my other hand, I lifted up my beer bottle. "To my beautiful husband on the day of our wedding. I wish you nothing but love and happiness for the rest of our days."

It was half a joke, but the sentiment was real. He picked up his water glass and clinked his glass against the bottle. "Congratulations, Mr. Partridge," he said.

"You don't want to be Parrish Church?" I asked with a wink, and we both started laughing. I tried letting the shock melt away in his easy presence, but I couldn't shake the reality of what that paperwork revealed. We were actually legally married. Regardless of the reason, I would have to divorce this sweet man if I wanted to give him his life back.

As our pizzas came and we continued to sort through the papers while eating, reality set in. There was a prenup agreement protecting each of our assets. As if I had many assets. Still, it was nice to know the attorneys had been as careful to protect my house and the salvage yard from Parrish as they'd been to protect his big family money from me.

It wasn't until we were almost back to the parking garage that I came across the adoption petition. I froze in my tracks and didn't even notice the honking horns until Parrish yanked me off the street and onto the safety of the sidewalk.

"What the heck? You almost got smushed!"

I kept reading. "This... this says they're putting you on the adoption petition."

"Really? I mean, I guess it makes sense. If we're married and they think it would make a stronger petition..."

He nudged me toward the entrance to the garage. I scanned the papers manically. "This says you'd be an equal petitioner. That you'd have equal rights to Marigold..." I swallowed. "Marigold Partridge."

I started to feel light-headed. This had gotten way, way out of control. I didn't want Marigold Partridge. I wanted Marigold Church. Beth hadn't let the Kensingtons change her name, even after they'd adopted her. She'd claimed her name was her last connection to our parents and me. Now the lawyers were doing the same thing—making her a Partridge the same way the Kensingtons wanted to make her one of them.

Money always fucking won, didn't it? I wasn't good enough as plain old Diesel Church. I'd spent the whole day trying to trust the lawyers and trust the Partridge family, and now here I was getting ready to basically hand my baby from one rich family to another.

Why wasn't I good enough for her as just *me*?

I yanked open the passenger-side door and stopped feeling sorry for myself long enough to hand Parrish up into the truck before slamming the door closed and going to the driver's side.

When we got out of the garage and through the city streets to the interstate, I finally had to face facts. I'd gotten us into this mess, and now poor Parrish had gone down a road he'd never be able to erase from his personal history. He'd never be able to tell someone he'd never been married before.

Maybe it was a marriage only on paper, but it would forever be part of his legal history now. And if... if they gave custody of Marigold to both of us... the thought turned my stomach.

It wasn't that I didn't want him to be a part of her life. I *did*. But what if his family suddenly decided I wasn't good enough? Wouldn't they be able to help him get custody of her?

He would never take her from you.

I ground my back teeth together. How could I trust a man whose address I didn't even know? How stupid was I being right now?

"Pull over," Parrish said in a soft voice.

"'M fine."

"Pull. The fuck. Over."

I turned to find his fists clenched on his lap and his lips pursed in anger. His little nostrils flared, and I knew I was in for a tongue-lashing.

After pulling to the side of the country highway we'd turned onto, I threw the truck into Park. "What?"

Parrish lurched across the center console and grabbed the front of my dress shirt. "Talk to me! Yell at me! Tell me you don't want this. God, Diesel, please don't shut me out. You're practically levitating with tension, but you won't say a damned thing to me."

Part of me wanted to tell him I loved him, that half the reason I was so upset was because I was being handed a giant ice cream sundae but no spoon. He was everything I ever wanted. This, *this* was everything I ever wanted. But it wasn't real. It was a legal illusion meant to last only long enough for the custody hearing.

And what the hell was I supposed to do then? Just let him go? Divorce the sweetest, kindest man in the world and go back to being just friends? It was laughable. I'd never survive it.

"I'm grateful," I finally managed to say. "For everything you're doing. I can't—" My voice cracked. "I can't ever repay you, so I feel... I feel like..." I closed my mouth and shook my head.

"Don't you understand I would do anything for you? And, um... Marigold?" Parrish's voice was a whisper between us, a confession in the stillness of the clear September afternoon. Rows and rows of dried-out corn husks sat next to us in the field, baking under the sun's rays, and there wasn't even another car around as far as the eye could see.

I leaned forward and kissed him. I was sure he meant what he said, or thought he did, but there was no way I could let myself believe he meant staying with me and making this real. If I was going to get through this, I needed some space.

When I pulled back from the kiss, I gave him the best smile I could manage. "Forgive me for being in my head, okay? It's a lot."

Parrish nodded. "I know. But just talk to me, alright? I hate wondering what you're thinking. I'd rather you be mad than quiet."

I put the truck back in gear and shot him a small smile. "I can't really imagine being mad at you."

He chuckled. "You just haven't known me long enough. Give it time."

Maybe that was part of my problem. Maybe I was falling too hard and too fast for him because we'd practically been in each other's pockets since all of this started. I needed time and space to myself.

When I pulled into the lot behind the B&B, he turned

to me with a frown. "Why are we here? I packed a bag already, remember?"

I looked out the window and noticed a familiar face peering over the fence from the backyard of the bed-and-breakfast. I vaguely remembered Miss Sara from one of the aunts' book club meetings. She'd been around when I was a teen, but I hadn't given her—or any adult, really—the time of day.

"I know, but I..." I looked at him and came this close to caving, to pulling him into my arms and holding him as tightly as possible. "I need some time to think about all of this. I need some time alone with Marigold. It's not you, I promise."

His face fell and it almost broke my heart. "No, of course. Of course you do. I understand." Parrish tried to give me a smile as if everything was okay, but it so clearly wasn't. "See you... tomorrow? Or... or whatever."

"Parrish," I breathed, leaning in to kiss the tender spot under his ear. "Please understand it's not you. I'm just..."

He put a gentle hand to my chest and pushed me away. "Scared. I know." He cleared his throat and tried the fake smile again. "I'll see you when I see you."

After grabbing his bag from behind his seat, he hopped out of the truck and raced to the front door of the building.

When I looked back over to the back fence, Miss Sara wasn't there anymore. And I felt like the shitty good-for-nothing man everyone seemed to think I was.

I put the truck into gear and pulled away, heading to Ava's house to pick up my baby girl and hope like hell I could make it through the night without crying louder than she did.

Chapter Fifteen

Parrish

"Parrish, honey, hand me that trowel."

I turned away from my quiet contemplation of the clouds—there was one up there that looked exactly like Brenda the chicken, complete with giant feather crown, and it made me all kinds of sentimental—and twisted my head on the soft grass to blink up at Miss Sara, who knelt beside a raised planter box.

"The trowel," she repeated. "The little shovel with the red handle in the bucket over there." She tilted her chin toward the big metal pail in question since her two hands were busy holding a giant plant by the roots. "Come on now. You've been lying there sighing for nearly half an hour, and that's plenty of time for lallygagging. This bleeding heart isn't gonna transplant itself, so sit on up and help me out."

"Yes, ma'am." I sat up obligingly and did as she asked, but I felt Miss Sara's worried sideways glances even as I helped her loosen the soil and dig holes for the plants.

I guessed I should probably tell her not to worry, that I'd be fine in a day or two, but I was pretty sure that would be a lie, and I was heartily sick of lying. Besides, I'd decided the best way to handle the current destruction of my heart was to not think of Die—*anyone*—at all. This plan had worked fairly well for going on thirty whole minutes, which was kind of a new record for me.

"You know," Miss Sara said conversationally. "When I was troubled, my mama always had me pull weeds. Nothing like working in a garden to help you get your mind on the right path. And boy did I ever have a restless mind back in those days. Mama said busy hands helped you think more clearly."

I nodded politely as I patted the dirt into place around one of the root balls while Miss Sara supported the plant itself. Aunt Marnie had the same philosophy. It was one of the reasons I'd started restoring my Mustang back in the day. Probably one of the reasons I liked to pace when I was puzzling something out, even to this day.

"Eventually, once I'd pulled enough weeds my back was hurting, I'd've burned off enough energy to start talking about things," Miss Sara continued. "And that was when I could really see a problem clearly and find the solution, you know?"

She paused expectantly, so I gave her a small smile. "Er, yes, ma'am. Self-knowledge is important."

Miss Sara huffed out a breath impatiently, but when she spoke again, her voice was still light. "For example, when I was sixteen, I went steady with a young man I thought was the absolute *most*. Real nice guy. Smart too. And Lord above, was he a looker. Even my daddy liked him, and he didn't like anybody I brought home." Her mouth twisted up at one corner, and her eyes had a faraway look. "But Garvey had a whole life planned out for himself after school. His family was big in local politics, you see, and I was not cut out to be some rising politician's trophy wife, no sir. I wanted a career of my own. A college degree. Our relationship wasn't meant to be, no matter how much I wished it was, 'cause we wanted different things, so I broke up with him right after graduation. And Parrish, you'd better believe, there wasn't a weed that'd dare show its face in my mama's garden, or the neighbors' gardens either, that whole summer, I was that purely heartbroken."

My gut clenched, but I nodded. "Sure. Throwing yourself into work seems like a solid plan to get over it."

I wondered if maybe I should do that. Get back to the store and take care of any details that might have slipped when I was busy with Mari—*other things*—this past week. Heck, maybe it was time to pack up life in the Thicket entirely, since the store was going to open in just a couple of weeks. Heading back to Nashville would mean a clean break... or as clean as you could get when you were still legally married to a gorgeous, sweet, sexy, upstanding man who could never care about you the way you cared about him.

I sighed. Apparently thirty minutes was as long as I was capable of going without thinking about Diesel Church. This did not bode well for my future.

Miss Sara stabbed her trowel into the ground and dusted off her gardening gloves. "Right, then. That last sigh was gusty enough to do wind damage. What's going on, Parrish?"

"I told you—"

"Nope. You didn't." Miss Sara turned around so she was perched on the edge of the planter box, facing the spot where I was still kneeling. "You marched in here looking like your dog had died, and Diesel sat in his old truck and watched you walking like he wanted to reach out and snatch you back—"

"He did not."

"And then you tell me some cockamamie story about how you and Diesel are *married*—"

"We are! Technically."

"—but your details are scarcer than hen's teeth, and you're being all quiet and mopey, which is not the Parrish I know and love. So either you sit here and tell me what in the heckity is happening—*without* acting like you're sending a telegram and being charged by the word—or I'll call your uncle Beau to come and sort you out."

Whoa. Miss Sara could be a hard-ass. Who knew? Then the penny dropped about what she'd actually said, and I stared at her in horror. "You know Uncle Beau?"

"Yep. He stopped by here the other morning looking for you, and we had a lovely chat."

"Oh, right." I rubbed my forehead. Uncle Beau couldn't find out the truth. Not now. Not until the whole custody thing was finished. I didn't think he'd tell the judge on us or anything like that, but managing his hurt feelings and disappointment was gonna be hard. One crisis at a time.

"So?"

"So, it's just like I said. Uncle Beau's attorneys are handling our custody case, and we went to sign paperwork. And it turned out that we accidentally got married. And Diesel was so horrified, he dropped me off here and left to get Marigold." And go home.

To *his* home.

Which was not my home and never would be.

I shrugged.

"I can see I'm going to have to do this the hard way," Miss Sara muttered. "Let's work backward. You think

Diesel was horrified to find that you were married. Did he tell you that?"

"What? No! He's far too polite to say it out loud. He said..." I cast my memory back to our little toast at the Stillery and swallowed hard. "He said, 'I wish you nothing but love and happiness for the rest of our days.'"

She whistled. "Laws, I've never heard of anyone so appalled."

"Well, he was," I insisted. "Especially when he read the paper that said custody of Marigold would be given to both of us."

"Ahh, now we're getting down to it." Miss Sara made a face and narrowed her eyes. "Trust Merchant, Greene, and Chandler to make sure that got in there. Sneaky little so-and-so's."

"But it's not real," I insisted. "No more real than the marriage, I mean. It's just a piece of paper. It'll go away as soon as our marriage goes away."

"But does Diesel know that?"

"I don't *know* what Diesel knows," I snapped. "Because he won't talk to me about a darn thing."

I flopped back to sit and folded my legs up pretzel-style. A nice cool breeze blew through the yard, and I swore I could almost hear wind chimes jangle, though Miss Sara didn't have any wind chimes. "What do you s'pose Diesel and Marigold are doing right now? Bet they ate dinner."

"Getting close to sunset, so maybe so," she agreed.

"*I* was supposed to make dinner." I sounded petulant, like a kid whose toy had been taken away, except Diesel and Marigold weren't toys, they were... they were *everything*. "I was gonna make my chicken casserole again. It's his favorite."

"Diesel's?" Miss Sara frowned. "Really?"

"It's a very good casserole," I informed her. "It has cheddar bacon biscuits on top."

"Oh." She frowned harder. "But I thought Diesel—"

"He's probably giving her a bath by now. She sleeps so much better when she's had one." Another breeze blew through the yard. "Wonder if it's gonna storm again. He should probably put the white noise app on, just in case." I made a motion to grab my phone from my pocket so I could text him, but at the last minute, I remembered why I shouldn't.

"I'm sure Diesel knows what to do," Miss Sara soothed. "He seems like a great dad, from all you've said. I'm sure he can handle it."

"Of course he can! He always could. He never actually needed me. He just thought he did." And it had been nice to feel needed. And wanted. "I don't care what kind of idiot this judge is, there's no way he won't look at Diesel and see he's the best choice, even without my name on the marriage certificate."

Sara frowned again. "Yes, let's get back to that part now. How does one become accidentally married, Parrish? I know a thing or two about law, and I'm fairly certain that's not legal."

"Well." I'd spent a lot of time pondering that very question on the ride back to town. "I'm not a hundred percent sure. They put a bunch of forms in front of us—affidavits and petitions and whatnot—that were mostly a formality. I thought Diesel was paying attention to everything, 'cause he was sitting there frowning and nodding, so I just signed where he signed." I winced. "Uncle Beau would kill me if he knew that. First thing he ever taught me about business was not to sign anything I hadn't read."

Miss Sara shook her head and turned back to her gardening. "For good reason."

"Yeah, I know. I'm not usually this much of an idiot." Worry for Diesel had short-circuited my brain, that was all.

"Keep going," she prompted. "Get to the rest."

"You're not gonna like the rest." I ran both hands through my hair. "In my defense, I was a little distracted. See, the lawyers explained things—this form is about Marigold's education, this one is your prenup, this form simply confirms your intent to get married, and so on—and they asked me some questions, like, 'Do you enter into this contract willingly, Mr. Partridge?' And 'Do you understand this is a legally binding agreement?' And I said yes, because of course. And they asked if we'd be reciting our own vows, and I said heck, no, 'cause I couldn't imagine I'd ever wanna do that, even for a fake wedding that would never happen, and Diesel said, 'Just skip that whole part, please.'"

Miss Sara muttered something that sounded a lot like, "Oh, for fuck's sake," but couldn't have been, 'cause I'd never heard her cuss before.

"Pardon?"

"I said please hand me the rake. The... the little rake. In the bucket. I need to aerate the soil before I plant those tulips for next spring."

"Oh." I got her out the rake and handed it to her. "Anyway, Diesel kept getting more and more anxious. I thought —" My voice cracked and I cleared my throat. "I thought it was just about the lawyers, you know? He's been so prickly for days about that. And I figured he was worried they were Beau's people, not his own, and maybe he wasn't getting a fair shake. Every time they brought out another form, he'd sit up straighter and tug his collar a little harder. By the end, his eyes were glazed over, and all I could think was that I had to get him out of there, so I did." I hesitated, then added, "They congratulated us, when it was all said and done. But I thought they meant congratulations on finishing up all the paperwork." I wriggled my fingers in a tiny jazz-hands movement. "Yay!"

Miss Sara watched me with her mouth hanging open.

I shrugged sheepishly. "I mean, in retrospect it all seems a bit obvious, but at the time it was really overwhelming." I pulled at a clump of grass. "And then we went out for lunch, and even after we found our... our marriage certificate—" I had to bite my lip a little, because those words conjured up so much want inside me. "—we laughed it off. He teased me about becoming Parrish Church, and I said that was a ridiculous name, so he'd have to become Diesel Partridge, and it was fine, I thought. Back to the status quo. But then he found that adoption form, and he went all silent. It's a bad habit of his."

She snorted, but when I looked at her, she waved me off. "Finish your story, honey."

"That's mostly it. I told him I'd do anything for him and Marigold, and Diesel decided the best thing I could do for him would be to not be with him at all. He wanted me to give him *space*." I made air quotes. "Said it wasn't my fault, or whatever, he just needed to be alone with Marigold. 'Cause he's scared. So I told him I understood. What else could I do?"

"But you didn't understand."

"Oh, no, I did," I assured her. "I understand very well. Once he saw my name on that adoption form, it probably all got pretty real to him. Parrish Partridge is the best possible name to have on your paperwork, 'cause I'm such an upstanding citizen, and I'm pleasant enough to spend time with in the short term, but to actually be legally tied to me?"

I shook my head, and my stomach went cold. "Can you see a guy like Diesel Church introducing *me* as his husband? Nah. We've had fun, and I'm glad I could help him out, but I'm never gonna be the kind of guy a fascinating man like Diesel falls in love with. It's time I get that through my skull." I forced myself to smile just a little. "Too bad, though, since it turns out I'm the kind of man who fell in love with him real easily."

"Oh, Parrish. Honey—" Miss Sara reached out one gloved hand to pat my knee and shook her head.

"You know, the worst part is, I can't even be mad at him like I was with Payne? Diesel never lied to me. Not even once. He's been totally honest the whole time, Miss Sara," I said solemnly.

Shockingly, she laughed—first a little snort, then a deep chuckle that forced her to set down her gardening tool and press a hand to her stomach.

I tried not to be too offended by this.

"Oh, God. Oh, laws. Oh, mercy. Parrish," she sniffed. "I don't think the two of you have said a single honest word to yourselves or each other since this whole thing started. You're the lying-est pair of liars who ever lied."

"W-what?"

Miss Sara grabbed me by the shoulders. "Listen to me closely now. Diesel Church is not Payne Whatshisname. And you're not the same person you used to be either. You fell for Diesel because his feelings for you are genuine and always have been. He just hasn't told you that, the same way you haven't told him you have feelings for him. And the same way," she added in a disapproving tone, "that you haven't told him about Payne and the boys."

I blinked at her. "How'd you know I haven't told him?"

"Because if you had, he'd never have left you here to stew while he went off to clear his head."

Poor, deluded Miss Sara. Her advice was usually so spot-on, but I supposed everyone had an off day now and then.

"He asked for space," I reminded her. "From me."

"I know, honey. Because he's scared."

"I know he's scared! Heck, so am I, but you don't ask for space from someone you care about."

"Sure you do, if you're Diesel. Think about it. Diesel's parents died. His sister's passed. The man who left him the junkyard—"

"Stix Yancey," I supplied, frowning.

"Yes. He's gone too. And I'm guessing Diesel's dated once or twice, here or there, over the years?"

I shrugged. "I'd imagine so."

"And where are those guys, Parrish? How many of them stuck around?"

"Well, but—"

"And his friends? How many close friends are looking out for Diesel's best interests?"

"He's got Ava! And Paul. And Mal and Brooks."

"Sure, *now*. But that's only the last few months or so. You know I love the Thicket with my whole heart, but it's tough to find your place here when you weren't a Fighting Bovine in a letterman jacket like Brooks, or a talented artist like Mal, or a sweet, harmless boy like Paul, or a golden girl like Ava. Hard to find your place anywhere when you're tattooed to the gills and snarl meaner than a panther anytime someone gets close. And he did," she insisted, when I opened my mouth to argue. "Not with you, maybe, which just goes to show how special you are, Parrish, but that man was like a dog who's been kicked a time too many, craving love but not knowing how to get it, half-ready to run away, half-ready to bite the hand of anyone who came too close. I noticed it a long time ago, but I was never sure how to help him. Turned out, he didn't need my help." She smiled softly. "He needed you."

"No. That's... that's nonsense. Diesel is amazing. He's worth more than all the rest of them put together. He's overcome so much. He's *lived*. And every one of those tattoos is a story, a memory."

"I bet. And I'm glad you know it. But remember, when you say you're scared, you mean you're scared you'll lose your heart and feel like an idiot again. Diesel, on the other hand... Honey, he's lost everyone who's ever meant something to him. And then came you."

The idea of that—the *hope* of it—was terrifying.

"But it was all a lie," I whispered. "He can't want me."

"Why not? It started as a lie, but you want him," she pointed out with ruthless logic. "So be patient with him. Talk to the man without making assumptions. And don't give up." She clapped her gloved palms together once. "And now, for the love of Peter, Paul, and Ringo, come help me plant these last few bulbs before it's full dark out here."

"Yes, ma'am." I scrambled up and took the hand rake she offered me. "I see what you mean about the gardening being helpful. I do feel better. And for what it's worth, Garvey was an idiot if he picked some trophy wife instead of you."

"Oh." Miss Sara laughed again, and her cheeks turned pink in the twilight. "Well, as it happened, he didn't. See, I was so sure a man like Garvey could never be happy married to a woman like me that I never thought to ask *Garvey* what *he* wanted. Fortunately, Garvey wasn't the sort to entertain my bull puckey, so by the end of that summer, he'd wooed me back and showed me I was exactly the sort of person he'd be happy with. In fact, I was the *only* person he'd be happy with. And he was. For forty-two beautiful years."

"Wait, really?" I demanded. "But…"

"Get to planting, Parrish," she said with a nod. "Don't give up on Diesel. Things will work out if they're meant to."

I wasn't sure that they'd work out as happily for me as they had for her, but I'd meant what I told Diesel earlier. There was nothing I wouldn't do for him and Marigold. And if being patient was what he needed… I'd try.

Chapter Sixteen

Diesel

I FELT LIKE AN ASS. Parrish had looked so disappointed in me, but I'd known I was going to be terrible company. Even Marigold must have sensed my mood because as soon as I picked her up from Ava's, she'd been especially snuggly and clingy, which had suited me just fine. I'd put her in the front carrier and kept her close to me as I cooked and cleaned and basically kept myself busy with nonsense chores.

But I'd eventually put her to sleep in her portable crib and had to face the rest of the evening with only my company. And my company was for shit.

I had way too much time to think, and all of my thoughts centered around Parrish's fake smile as he tried to reassure me when I'd dropped him off at the bed-and-breakfast. That fake smile was like slapping my heart into a vise and then turning the crank.

Needless to say, I spent most of the night rubbing my chest. I thought about what a fucking coward I was. I wanted Parrish. I wanted this to be real, and I could tell he had some feelings too. But what if those feelings were temporary? What if he tried things on with me and then realized he wanted to go back to the right side of the tracks after all?

I wasn't sure I could bear another big loss in my life, especially if I didn't get custody of Marigold.

My sleep was fitful at best. The baby had mercy on me and made it through the whole night without a fuss which meant I woke up with a somewhat clearer head. I decided to take Marigold to the splash park meet-up since it was Tuesday and the weather was still plenty warm for it. If nothing else, Marigold would have a chance to see some non-scowling faces. Staying cooped up together at home was a recipe for a disappointing day.

After feeding us both breakfast and getting us dressed and ready, I had to take care of the chickens and help a few customers on the lot. When it was finally time to get going, I decided to make use of the stroller and walk to the park instead of driving.

Mari dozed with a face full of teething cookie crumbs. I stopped partway to apply the sunscreen I'd forgotten to take care of at home, and when we finally arrived at the park, most of the other parents and babies were already settled around on blankets and towels at the edges of the splash pad.

I found Ava sitting with several other parents. All of them were familiar, so I didn't feel as awkward joining them this time. Ward looked up from the bottle he was giving his baby. "Hey, there he is. Come sit by me. They're talking about boob shit, and I'm feeling increasingly irrelevant."

I huffed out a chuckle and parked the stroller before pulling out my backpack and Marigold. When I joined them on the ground, Mari practically threw herself at Ava with a happy squeal. Ava caught her and gave her big, exaggerated faces as she cooed a welcome.

"You look like poop," Ava said to me in cheerful baby talk. "Bad meeting yesterday?"

My face must have dropped even more because her big smile was replaced by a frown. She sat Mari in her lap facing outward and handed her a set of plastic loops from a pile of colorful toys on the blanket. Her son, Beau, was nearby slapping at a puddle of water on the soft, foam floor of the splash pad. I noticed Paul was watching him which probably meant he'd been able to duck out of work for his lunch break. I returned his silent wave.

"I mean," I began. "Not really? The firm definitely felt good about our chances, and they were... on top of things."

Ward's forehead creased between his eyebrows. "Then why do you look like someone took your pony away?"

Maureen's soft look of concern was touching, and Ginger reached out to squeeze my knee. These four new parents made me feel so much less alone in trying to figure things out with Marigold. After I'd first met them, Ava had insisted on including me in a group text, and the messages flew back and forth throughout the day—questions about developmental milestones and parent guilt, tips for quick snack ideas, and the best Spotify playlist for keeping a sleepy baby awake in the car. I'd only known them a very short time, but I already felt like I was beginning to have a crew of sorts.

I laughed at myself. Maybe at one point I'd imagined having a *biker* crew. I'd certainly never anticipated having a mommy crew.

"Parrish and I... um... got married," I said hesitantly. "Kind of... by accident?"

Four sets of eyes stared at me without blinking until Ava tilted her head. "Yeah, run that by us again?"

I pressed my lips together, second-guessing myself

about revealing this information. But I was messing every-thing up with Parrish, and I needed some help.

"So, like—" I cleared my throat. "The lawyers said our chances would be better if we went ahead and got married on paper even though..." I glanced around, reminding myself they all thought the Parrish engagement was real. "Even though we wouldn't normally have the, ah, the cere-mony until later."

Ava threw some attitude. "Damned right, you wouldn't. One needs time to plan certain things. And I had *plans* for that wedding."

I continued. "Right, so, we didn't really understand at first what was happening, and then afterward when we saw the marriage certificate—"

Maureen held up a hand. "We're going to need details about how one can be tricked into marriage by highbrow attorneys."

"We weren't tricked," I assured her. "We were just kind of not paying enough attention."

"Mpfh," she huffed, crossing her arms in front of her chest. "Continue."

I tried to think about how to ask them for advice without telling them the whole story. "I was upset, and I dropped him off at his place instead of bringing him home with me."

Ava's face dropped, and Wade let out a muffled "Uh-oh."

"I think I messed things up," I admitted before lowering my voice. "I just... I just don't know if someone like Parrish Partridge can really want to be with someone like me."

The slap to the back of my head came from Ginger. The otherwise sweet, unassuming woman glared at me. "Diesel, lemme ask you something," she said in her Southern drawl.

"Who changed Pastor Mitchell's flat tire the night his niece went to the hospital for appendicitis?"

"I was already out that way. Anyone would have done the same." I busied myself pulling out Marigold's water cup, but she kept going.

"And who made a million mini quiches for the senior center when their kitchen went on the fritz in April?"

I shot her a warning look. "That was supposed to be anonymous. Besides, I had extra eggs that needed cooking."

Maureen chimed in with a knowing smile. "And who donated a new washer and dryer set to the firehouse last year when theirs succumbed to the most ironic lint fire in history?"

"It was hardly new," I corrected. "And, again, anonymous..."

Maureen laughed. "Hard to sneak two big metal machines into the firehouse without someone noticing. And anyway, those guys are the worst gossips in—"

Wade interrupted, wrinkling his nose in dismay. "And who always volunteers to change poopy swim diapers at the splash park?"

"Nice try," I said.

Ava reached over to take my hand in hers. Her smooth, clear skin stood out in contrast against my ink. "Diesel, anyone with eyeballs can tell that sweet man is loopy for you. He's also the kind of human who has a huge heart. Do you agree?"

I nodded automatically.

"Right," she continued. "Does he seem like the kind of person who would reject someone over where they came from or how they live or what they look like or—"

"No!" I said harshly. "Never."

She smiled knowingly, and I realized I'd been had.

"What exactly do you think he wouldn't approve of? The fact you run your own business? The way you love your niece more than anything? The little anonymous things you do to better your community?"

"Apparently there's no such thing as anonymous in the Thicket," I muttered.

Ginger laughed. "Your lips to God's ears."

Paul stepped over and grabbed Marigold from Ava's lap so she could sit next to Beau and splash. I gave him a smile of thanks.

Ava pulled her knees up and wrapped her arms around them. "Maybe you should do something nice for him. Plan a surprise that will show him you're sorry and you love him."

I swallowed around the lump in my throat that had formed the moment she mentioned the "L-word."

My mind drew a blank. "Like what? Take him out to dinner or something?"

Maureen rolled her eyes. "Seriously? You're more romantic and creative than that. Besides, any ole guy can wine and dine Parrish. What can you do that will really show him you know him better than anyone?"

I fidgeted. I didn't know him better than anyone. How could I when we'd only known each other such a short time?

"What's his secret pleasure?" Wade asked, settling back down after a trip to the restrooms nearby and placing his baby on the blanket in front of us. I watched her roll to her front and try and get up on her hands and knees.

Cora's little butt was covered with a giant blue-and-yellow butterfly stitched into the cotton pants she wore.

Suddenly, I knew what to do. I looked up and grinned at everyone. "Thanks. That helps a ton."

After we finished hanging out with everyone and eating

the lunch we'd packed, I got home and put a happy but exhausted Mari down for a nap. Then I pulled out my phone and got to work.

———

I PULLED up to the Partridge Pit the following day and grabbed Marigold from her car seat. I'd dressed her in the butterfly romper Parrish had given her in hopes of helping sell him on my idea. Even if he could resist my bumbling efforts, I hoped he wouldn't be able to resist spending the day with her.

When I walked in, Gil Hammersmith was all up in Parrish's business with a flirty smile and his hand on Parrish's upper arm. Parrish's ears were pink, and his hands fidgeted nervously with a tablet and stylus. Petty jealousy rolled through me with a spike of heat and adrenaline.

The restaurant looked almost finished, and I wondered how much longer the contractor would need to be on-site.

Before I had a chance to call out to Parrish, Marigold spotted him and let out a happy shriek. Parrish's face immediately lit up, enough to make my heart thunder in my chest.

He spun to face us, automatically pulling out of Gil's grip. "There's my sweet girl!" He seemed to realize what he'd said because he began backpedaling. "I mean not *my* girl. Obviously. I just meant—"

I strode forward and thrust her in his arms before leaning in and pressing my cheek to his in a kind of weird side hug. I wanted—no, needed—to touch him, to hold him. But I didn't want to be too presumptuous after what had happened the other day.

"I missed you," I breathed into his skin. "I'm sorry."

I felt his entire body relax into mine, and his free arm came up to wrap around my waist. "I missed you too," he whispered before turning to bury his face in my neck. I felt the tiniest of kisses against the skin there.

We stood like that for several beats, simply breathing each other in and pressing the reset button. Or, at least, I hoped we were. I had a lot to make up for, and all I could ask for was the chance to spend enough time with him to explain myself.

Gil cleared his throat. "Diesel. I take it you and Parrish know each other?"

I narrowed my eyes at him. After my experience at the splash park, I had a hard time believing Gil hadn't heard about Parrish's engagement.

"We do." I tightened my arm around Parrish's waist when he tried pulling away. "Parrish and I are..."

I couldn't bring myself to say the word in case Parrish didn't want anyone knowing, so I was floored when Parrish turned in my arms and leaned his head on my shoulder before saying it. "Married."

Gil stared at us. "Married? To whom?"

Parrish smiled. "To each other. Diesel is my husband."

"But... but... really? You don't have a ring or anything."

Parrish pressed a kiss under my jaw and stepped free of my hold so he could flap his free hand in the air while he still held Marigold on the other hip. "Diesel doesn't wear one because of his work with machinery, and I left mine on the nightstand this morning. It got kind of..." If it was possible, he blushed a deeper pink. "Gunky last night."

I bit my tongue to keep from dropping my jaw.

"Anyway," Parrish said, moving across the space to grab his messenger bag, "We have a pediatrician appointment for Marigold today. She's always a little sniffly after her vaccines, so I probably won't be back in today. If you need anything, contact Debbie at the office."

He grabbed his bag and then led me outside. Once we got into the truck, he blew out a noisy breath. "I'm sorry about that. You can just drop me at the B&B."

"I came to ask you to spend the day with us," I said, buckling Mari into the car seat. "We planned an apology surprise for you."

"An apology surprise?"

"It's like an apology casserole but with 100 percent less cream of mushroom soup."

Parrish's face softened. "You don't need to apologize to me."

"Actually I do." I closed Marigold's door and climbed into the driver's seat before turning and reaching for Parrish's hand. "I shouldn't have left you the other night without at least a conversation first."

"Maybe not. But I understand why you did."

I nodded and started the truck. "I have some things I want to tell you, but I'd rather get out of here before Gil Hammersmith comes storming out of the Pit brandishing a nail gun at me."

Parrish chuckled. "Sorry about all that. He just won't take no for an answer. I hope you're not mad about... about the marriage thing."

I shook my head. "Not one bit. Especially not with that guy. How close is he to being done with the project?"

We spent the drive talking about what all was left before the restaurant would be ready for its grand opening. When we finally got to the Cherryville Butterfly Conservatory which was about forty-five minutes back toward Nashville, Parrish's eyes about popped out of his head.

"Really? I haven't been here since I was little. How did

you know about this place? I thought you grew up in Kentucky."

"I did. Just over the line in Bugtussle."

"No."

I laughed. "Not to be confused with Mud Lick or Flippin. It's only about an hour southwest of Bowling Green."

"That has to be a joke."

"Kind of. I grew up in the Bowling Green burbs, but those are all real places in Kentucky."

He grinned at me. "Now I'm disappointed. I wanted you to be from Bugtussle, Kentucky."

"My accent's not strong enough," I teased.

"True."

"The company my dad worked for was headquartered in Nashville, so he was real familiar with it. We came down there sometimes. I even saw the Titans play when they were still the Tennessee Oilers."

"Is that some kind of sports thing?"

I stared at him for a beat before he cracked a smile and continued. "Joking. I'm joking. Uncle Beau has a box at the stadium, but I admit I mostly go because the caterer he uses makes these amazing little veggie puff pastry things."

My ears perked up. "I make something like that. Maybe I can fix it for you sometime."

"Yeah? Does yours have cheese and onions in it?"

"Yep," I said, pulling into a parking spot. "And green peppers, but I can leave those out if you don't like them. I usually use whatever veggies I can grab from my garden."

"That sounds amazing."

Things felt more comfortable between us again, even though I hadn't really had a chance to talk to him yet. I grabbed the backpack and stroller out of the back of the truck while Parrish unbuckled Marigold and brought her around to put her in the stroller. I loved listening to his chatter with her.

"Did Daddy put you in this cute little outfit today on purpose? Do you think we'll see a brush-footed butterfly, hm? Maybe a glasswing?"

She held the front of his work shirt in her chubby fist and clung to his arm with her other hand. It was so sweet, I almost didn't want to remove her from his hold to put her in the stroller. But I also didn't want to wear him out with a heavy baby before we even got into the conservatory.

We crossed the parking lot and entered the gates by showing the tickets I'd pre-purchased online. Once we were inside the gates, it was like a giant, landscaped park in every direction with a large glass-topped building in the center. By unspoken agreement, we meandered through the park. Paved walkways twisted here and there between shrubbery and mature trees. Clusters of flowers were planted all over the place as natural butterfly magnets and the place was quietly alive with color.

Marigold didn't last long in the stroller before Parrish hauled her back onto his hip so he could get her closer to the flowers and point out the butterflies. "This is bee balm or monarda. It's actually in the mint family. See the pink spiky petals? Those attract the butterflies to the flower, but it's actually the center part here that holds the nectar butterflies eat."

He went on to explain about their curled proboscis and how it worked. Marigold stared up at him like he was nature's gift to budding entomologists even though she surely didn't follow a word he was saying.

I knew how she felt.

When he stood back up from his crouch, he turned a wide smile at me that nearly brought me to my knees. "She may not be saying it, but she's currently putting a butterfly habitat at the top of her birthday list."

I wanted to touch him, to cup his face and simply stare at it for several minutes to drink in every detail. Having him here all to myself was a gift, and I didn't want to waste a minute of it.

"Are you hungry? I brought a picnic," I said gruffly.

He nodded. "I think there's an area with tables unless you wanted to sit on the grass. Might be easier for Marigold if we sit on the ground."

We found a spot under a shade tree at the edge of the park and unfolded the thin blanket I'd packed. Once we distracted Marigold with a little bowl of ripe banana pieces that were probably going to end up more in her hair than her stomach, I pulled out the stuff I'd brought for us.

"This is an orzo salad with veggies and smoked gouda. There's a fresh baguette and butter too. I got it from the place you seemed to like when I saw you at the Lickin' Pickin' vendor stalls. If you don't like those options, I also brought..." I rummaged through the cooler to see what else I'd packed, but Parrish laid a hand on my arm.

"That sounds amazing. Thank you."

I nodded and busied myself fixing bowls for us while Parrish grabbed the slices of bread and slathered butter on a few. After pulling out a couple of water bottles to add to the spread, we dug in. It didn't take long before I couldn't hold back any longer.

"I like you. For real. Not pretend. Not fake. Not for the attorneys or for custody or anything like that. But because you're kind and thoughtful, helpful and so fucking sweet. You're smart and capable, funny and—"

I hadn't been looking at him when I'd said all those things, so I didn't see him lunge at me. His mouth hit mine with a warm smack as he laid one on me. I quickly reached my arms around him to keep us from toppling over. He kissed me like he was starving for it, like he'd run out of words and only had this kiss to tell me his own feelings. I cupped the back of his head with one hand and held him there, savoring his lips until both of us ran out of oxygen.

When he pulled back, he was dazed and glassy-eyed. His lips were wet and a shade of pink darker than his rosy cheeks.

"Me too," he said breathlessly. "Me too, so much."

I laughed and leaned in again, kissing him more gently this time and reveling in the relief I'd felt. "I'll do anything to deserve you," I whispered.

He pulled back and met my eyes. "You already deserve me. Why in the world would you think you wouldn't?"

I sighed and looked away. "I'm not the best choice for you, Parrish, and we both know it. But I'm too selfish to be the one to do anything about it."

His hand shot out and gripped my chin, turning me to face his now-furious expression. "Don't do that. First of all, you *are* the best choice for me. Secondly, I get to decide who's the best choice for me, not you. Third of all, I... care about you. A lot. Oodles, really. So it makes me angry as a hornet to hear you denigrate someone I... care about. Do you get that?"

He seemed so sure, like it was obvious I was the right choice for him and there was nothing wrong with me at all.

I swallowed and nodded. "Okay."

"Say you're good enough for me, Diesel," he said softly. "Say it out loud."

My teeth refused to unclench.

Parrish's hand moved until he was stroking the side of

my face with heart-wrenching tenderness. "Please," he whispered. "Say it."

"I will try my best to be good enough for you," I said, forcing the words out over gravel.

He smiled. "That's not the same thing, and you know it."

"I'm a work in progress."

He leaned in and kissed the edge of my lips. "That'll have to do. For now."

"I want to tell you why I'm... this way," I said, trying to be brave. For him. For us. "I want to tell you more about Beth and my parents."

Parrish turned back to me after putting eyes on Marigold to make sure she hadn't crawled off. She'd lain down on her back and was kicking her bare feet through the blades of grass at the edge of the blanket. I could tell she was almost ready to doze off.

Parrish's expression was sincere. "I'd love to hear more about them. Always."

I pulled out a crinkled envelope from my back pocket and handed it to him. "And maybe you can help me read this. It's a letter Beth's lawyer gave me when he read the will. I haven't..." I cleared my throat and continued. "I haven't had the balls to read it yet, but I think it's time."

He held the letter and looked from it to me in surprise. "You haven't read it?"

I shook my head. "Too scared," I admitted. "Once I read it, that's it. No more messages from Beth forever."

Parrish nodded and then handed me the letter back before turning to clean the mashed banana off Marigold. Once he had her cleaned up, he grabbed her and scooted back into the space between my legs. Once his back was against my front and Marigold was snuggled in his own lap, he reached back for the letter.

"Let's read it together," he said before carefully opening it. "Do you want me to read it out loud or do—"

"Yes," I said quickly. "Please."

I closed my eyes when I caught sight of her familiar handwriting. It was a good thing Parrish was the one reading it. I wouldn't be able to keep my composure enough to do it myself.

"Dear Eddie," he began. I snorted unexpectedly, and he paused.

"She always called me that because it pissed me off. Keep going."

Parrish snuggled back into me, and I wrapped my arms around him and Marigold. With my quasi little family in my arms, I felt like maybe I was strong enough to finally hear these final words from my sister.

"I know you're wondering why I chose to leave Mari with you. You're probably second-guessing yourself all over the place and thinking the worst. I at least hope you aren't regretting it. I hope you don't wish I hadn't left her with you."

"Never," I huffed under my breath.

"But you're the kindest, most loving person I know, and that's what I want for Marigold in case something happens to me. I want her to feel loved and secure the way we did growing up. I want her to feel comfortable in her own skin and free to be whatever and whoever she wants to be. The Kensingtons gave me a good life, and I don't regret it. Not at all. But they didn't give me what I needed most after Mom and Dad died. I needed love and affection. I needed someone to listen. Stella did that for me. She was the best friend I could have ever asked for, and I hope if you decide not to keep Marigold, you'll ask Stella first before considering other options. But, Diesel, I really want it to be you."

Parrish stopped for a minute to take a breath. He reached for my hand and squeezed it tightly. "You okay?" he asked, craning his head back to meet my eyes.

My own eyes were wet, but I was okay. I nodded and kissed his forehead.

He kept reading. "I want you to teach her how to change the oil in her car, how to throw a curveball pitch, and how to plant a garden."

The words surprised me since all of those were things I'd learned after moving to the Thicket. We'd talked over Facebook and email, but I guess I hadn't realized just how much of my life she'd picked up on.

"I want you to show her that love comes in many forms and that even when you fall down there are other people willing to help you up. I want her to watch you and know that despite the crappy hand you were dealt, you made a good life for yourself and never stopped being a good person."

Parrish's voice began to falter with emotion, so I took the page from his hand and continued in my own shaky voice.

"I'm proud of you, Diesel. And I will love you forever. I understand why you left, but I still regret missing out on all of those years with you. Marigold is only a week old right now, but all of the baby books advised making a will as soon as possible. Hopefully, you'll never have to read this letter, but you still deserve to know how much I love you. I'm going to call you right now to see if you want to come meet her. I want you to be a big part of her life no matter what, just like you have been for me."

I croaked out a harsh laugh. "She did call me. I drove

over and met her right after that. She was living in Memphis because she had a job in a rehab facility there. The drive was four and a half hours each way, so I only got back over there a few times before..."

Parrish scrambled around and hugged me tightly, holding Marigold to the side so she wouldn't be squashed. I cried silently into the side of his face and let myself mourn for the sister I'd lost so much time with. When I finally finished, I pressed a long kiss to the side of his face and whispered my thanks.

The rest of the letter was mostly just goodbye and a repetition of the hope I'd never need to read it. When I was done, I carefully folded it back up to save for Marigold one day.

Parrish wiped his own face with a baby wipe. "Did you know that some people think butterflies are messengers from the spirits of our deceased loved ones?"

He quickly added, "I mean, I'm not really into all that woo-woo stuff, but lots of people are, and I just thought..."

I cupped the back of his head and pulled him in for a kiss, a *real* kiss. He made a muffled *mhmm* noise and let me invade his mouth with my tongue. I wanted to tell him how deep my feelings were for him, but I was feeling too raw right now to say the words.

Instead, I let my touch and my kiss tell him, and when his eyes rolled back in his head, I thought maybe the message had been received loud and clear.

Chapter Seventeen

Parrish

By the time Diesel Church stopped kissing me, my vision had blacked out, my heart was racing, my breathing had gone all hitched and wheezy, and I wasn't sure if all my fingers and toes were still attached.

I'd never felt better in my whole life.

In fact, I'd never have moved from that spot, if I could have helped it. The Conservatory could've sold tickets to see me and Diesel all wrapped up in each other for the next fifty years or so, and I'd have considered it a life well lived...

But Miss Marigold had other ideas.

"Baabaabaa!" She patted my face determinedly, trying to wriggle off my lap. "Baa!"

I pulled back from Diesel just enough to see him smile, his eyes warm on mine. "I feel like Miss Thing is ready to go see more butterflies."

"Miss Thing has no concept of timing," I sighed. I reached up to push his floppy dark-gold hair out of his eyes and felt suddenly giddy that I had the *right* to touch him in that small way.

"This is our life now," Diesel said wryly. "We'll have to get used to it."

I grinned hugely. Just hearing him say those words was like having Christmas come in September. "We will," I confirmed.

Diesel scrambled to his feet and reached out a hand to help me up while I held Marigold. He packed up the last few things in the carriage, while I swung the baby high and listened to her giggle. It felt like a lot longer than forty-eight hours since I'd seen her, and my heart soared at the idea that I'd never have to go that long without seeing her again. There was no way we'd lose the custody case—not when Diesel and I stood together as a united front, with Uncle Beau's wonderfully sharky lawyers at our back.

I carried Marigold in my arms as we trudged up the grassy incline to the temperature-controlled glass building where the majority of the Conservatory's tropical specimens lived. Diesel walked beside me, pushing the empty carriage one-handed while keeping one hand tucked firmly at the center of my back. Along the way, we talked about everything and nothing—butterflies, and the weirdly colored egg Miss Sara (the pullet) laid, and whether Gil or Ava would inform the town about our marriage first (we decided it would be Ava), and whether we should call Miss Sara (the not-pullet) to tell her I'd be moving out sooner than later, and how to make sure Gil got the message that I was Not Interested At All.

Just like earlier in the truck, I loved that we could talk about everything and nothing together. I loved that with his hand on my back, the boring minutiae of our lives seemed really fun and exciting, and the anxiety-inducing parts didn't seem so bad at all. I'd never felt like part of a team before, not even when I was with...

I paused just outside the front door and bit my lip.

"Baby?" Diesel asked, a quizzical smile on his face. "You good?"

I gave him a little nod, and he frowned.

"You sure? You're not—" He hesitated. "You're not having second thoughts?"

"Never," I whispered. I reached out my free hand to wrap around his waist and pull him against me. Diesel seemed to like my claiming touches as much as I liked giving them. "Not *ever*. Just... taking it all in. You know? Committing it to memory."

"Oh, yeah." Diesel grinned and his voice was soft. He reached out a hand to cup my jaw. "Yeah, I know."

God, Diesel made me feel so cherished. The idea that he could doubt himself—doubt *us*—for even one second because of my hesitation killed me. I'd let Payne Geller take enough happy days from my life, and I would not let him claim one more.

So, after a smiling attendant ushered us inside the warm, muggy exhibit, and we'd walked a little way down a stone path, I pulled Diesel over to a low stone bench where we could have a little privacy while Marigold sat in the carriage nearby, watching the butterflies stopping to sample the fruits laid out for them and babbling happily.

"I'd like to, um... to tell you a story." I swallowed. "I mean, not a big deal, exactly. Just... you shared about Beth, and it meant so much to me that you did, so I... wanted to tell you a little bit more about me. About my past. If you wanted to know."

Diesel blinked. "Is that a trick question? Parrish, I always want to know about you, I just never felt like I could ask."

I laughed a little. "Well, you can. You can ask me

anything, anytime. But, um." I rubbed my hands together in my lap. "Gosh, I don't know where to begin, exactly."

Diesel laid one large, tattooed hand over mine. "Anywhere you like is fine. There's no rush."

I nodded. God, life was so much better with this man by my side. "I dated someone pretty seriously a couple of years ago," I blurted. "We were engaged, actually."

"Okay. Wow." Diesel frowned. "Since it didn't happen, I'll automatically assume that he's an idiot."

I laughed again. "No. I mean, yes. I mean, he's an attorney, so he's very intelligent and driven. Maybe a little too driven. We met at an event for Clover House, one of my aunt Marnie's favorite kids' charities back in Nashville, which puts on a kinda carnival with pony rides, and animals to pet, and face painting, and a couple of athletes who sign autographs and take pictures, that kind of thing. He was cute, in a way. Very buttoned-up. Very status conscious."

"Really? He doesn't sound like your type at all."

My mouth lifted up in a half-smile, and I pressed my lips to Diesel's jaw. "He wasn't."

In fact, looking at the man in front of me now, I couldn't imagine how I'd ever found Payne even remotely attractive, either in appearance or personality. It was like I'd looked at a moth and thought he was a butterfly... until the real thing came along, a hundred times rarer and more special.

"Anyway, Payne had been married before, to a woman he claimed was a terrible selfish cow. They had two boys together, and the youngest was just an infant. He was trying hard to get primary custody of his sons, but his ex was making it impossible because Natasha had money and connections Payne didn't have. He didn't want his kids to grow up in a loveless home. So a couple months after we started dating... he asked me to help him get custody."

"Oh, baby, no." Diesel's voice was filled with dread, like he could predict what was coming. Probably because he could, sort of.

"Oh, yes." I cleared my throat. "He knew it was rushing things for us to get engaged, he said, but he loved me. He wanted us to be together—to raise the boys as a family—and he knew he'd have a much stronger case if I were on his side. My character was unassailable, right? So boring and basic, I didn't even have a parking ticket to my name."

Diesel groaned, and I pulled my hands from his so I could rub my damp palms against my thighs.

"Even after just a few weeks, I loved those boys so much, of course I said yes… even though I had some misgivings. Even though I knew it was moving too fast. Even though I wasn't sure I really loved Payne. And at first, it was great. Family picnics. Even a trip to Gatlinburg to see the Stampede with Beau and Marnie once. He wanted me to buy us a house—in his name, of course, to strengthen his case—but even I couldn't make myself go that far."

"Parrish, I can't believe—"

"That I was such an idiot?" I smiled ruefully. "Me neither, but I was. I jumped in with two feet *and* two arms. I'd always wanted a family, you know? So when diapers needed changing, I changed them. Heck, I researched the best variety for the baby's sensitive skin and bought them in bulk. I felt so privileged to get to be a part of the boys' lives, that when Payne asked me to start handling the preschool drop-offs in the mornings, of course I said yes. It just made sense, because it was on my way to work. And when I had to pick them up in the evenings, that made sense too, because Payne's schedule wasn't nearly as flexible as mine. And when he had to work late and needed someone to put the boys to bed… of course I didn't mind. I mean, this was my family, right? It's not babysitting when they're your—" My voice cracked a little, and I forced myself to continue "—your own kids."

"Listen to me," Diesel said in a rush, grabbing my hands back in both of his. "Whatever you think this says about you, Parrish Partridge, you're wrong. You're not an idiot, you're the—"

"You haven't heard the end of the story yet," I interrupted bleakly. "Months passed. The custody case progressed. Slowly, though. Aunt Marnie never liked Payne, and Uncle Beau loathed him, so even though they doted on the boys, you'd better believe there was no Merchant, Greene, and Chandler involved. When the boys were sick, I called in to work. When there was an awards night at school, I was there. Payne and I... we hardly saw each other anymore, but hey, that's what happens when you put the kids first, right? When Payne's job meant he could provide for them? And he was clearly not happy with me. Everything I did was juvenile or basic, from the foods I made to the clothes I wore. He would *not* have enjoyed my chicken casserole."

Diesel's grip on my hands tightened. "Parrish, I—"

"Anyway, long story long, all those evening meetings were not meetings. I mean, obviously." I rolled my eyes. "There was another woman—an associate at his firm, because he's a walking, talking cliché. And I didn't find out dramatically or anything. He explained it all to me very calmly and rationally the night before the custody hearing. He thought it would make a better case if he went into the hearing with his new girlfriend, but he still wanted me there for moral support and as a character witness."

Diesel jumped up from the bench. "I'm going to kill him," he announced.

"No, you are not." I grabbed his hand and pulled him back down to sit. "He's not worth it. Not even a little bit. He's *gone*. History. Besides, his whole plan backfired spectacularly. I absolutely refused to appear as his character witness under the circumstances." And it had been kinda lowering to see just how shocked Payne had been by that. "That set his whole case back by months. And just before I moved down here, I saw on Facebook that Natasha ended up winning primary custody. Payne was not happy about it at *all*, and he sent me some pretty vile messages blaming me, but it was probably for the best. The boys adored her. I think he lied to me about what kind of mother she was."

"Because he's a piece of trash, lying cheater who used you, and you're an amazing, loving—"

"Shush," I soothed, stroking his arm and the side of his face, but I'd be lying if I said it didn't make me feel incredible that he was ready to stand up and fight for me. "I didn't tell you to upset you, I just needed you to know why maybe I've been skittish or hesitant. It's not that I didn't care about you or think for one minute that you weren't good enough. I was just scared that I was falling too hard and fast. I needed a minute to make sure it was real."

Diesel shook his head. "I don't know how you ever agreed to this, baby. God, if I'd known you had all this in your past, I never would have asked you—"

"I know." I summoned a smile. "I know. So I guess I'm glad you didn't know, because if you hadn't asked me to lie, I would have missed out on having a *real* relationship with the kindest, most honest man I've ever met." I grabbed his face with both hands and forced him to look at me, because it was so important that he believed me. "You are the best man for me, Diesel. Don't ever doubt it."

He nodded, his eyes shiny. "Parrish, I—" he began. I

leaned toward him to catch every word, and he blurted, "I'm a vegetarian."

"You... What?" I stared at him, stunned. "But, but... What?"

"I'm sorry. I lied. I couldn't tell you. You brought me that apology casserole, and I wanted you so much, Parrish—not just for the custody arrangement, I swear, and I'll work as hard as I can to prove that to you, but because you're gorgeous, and funny, and loving, and—"

"Get back to the chicken," I interrupted.

"Right, well." He licked his lips and darted a look at me, like he worried that I'd be furious, which was kind of adorable—okay, maybe more than *kind of*—but even though I tried hard to summon some outrage, I couldn't seem to.

"You know I got Talia first, right? But then I got Brenda —she's the silkie with the huge hairdo—"

"I know which one Brenda is," I scoffed. "Obviously."

Diesel smiled at me dopily for half a minute, then pulled me in for a quick kiss. "Yeah. I guess you do."

"The chicken?" I repeated.

"Right, well, Brenda has this totally bitchy attitude, which is why I named her that, so when she first came, I had to spend a ton of time with the girls making sure she didn't peck anyone to death, and... I dunno. I got to talking to them." He shot me a sheepish look. "I bet you think that's crazy."

I tried hard not to laugh. "Not nearly as crazy as you might think."

"Anyway, once I got to know them, I couldn't bring myself to *eat* them. It seemed inconsiderate."

I did laugh then. "I can see that. But you're telling me that our whole relationship was a lie, based on an apology casserole you never even ate?"

"It maybe started out as a lie, but you said it yourself a minute ago: this is real," he promised, leaning in to taste my lips again. "And I'm gonna take you home and prove just how real, once you're done watching the butterflies."

I bounced to my feet in front of him. "I'm ready."

"But..." He frowned. "Baby, we have all the time in the world. Enjoy your surprise."

"I will," I said, looking down into the eyes of the biggest and best surprise I'd ever gotten. "We can come back another time. Heck, we can bring Mari here every week. But if you study butterflies long enough, you learn that they don't live very long in the human scheme of things. When you find beauty you have to enjoy it while it lasts, with no hesitation." I pulled him to his feet and told him solemnly. "I'm so happy I found you."

"Me too. I knew that day in the courthouse that my life was going to change, but I had no idea how good it could be. And finding out I was *really* married to you was a shock, but it was also the best thing that ever happened to me."

I sighed, because for once when he said those things, I found it in myself to believe it. He might not be in love with me—it was way too soon for that, no matter what my heart said—but he cared about me. He *wanted* me. Maybe almost as much as I wanted him.

"So, home?" I asked with a hopeful smile.

"*Our* home," he said a little shyly but happily, making my heart flit around like the fiery skipper on a nearby bush. "Such as it is. We might need to add on a room for Marigold at some point."

Diesel deserved so much more than trying to squeeze the three of us into a house Stix had built for a single man. I wanted to give him the world, and I had a few ideas about where to start.

Chapter Eighteen

Diesel

AFTER HEARING Parrish's story about Payne, I was floored. How was it possible for the man to end up in two such similar situations? And more than that, how was it possible he'd gone along with my crazy scheme after being thrown over so horribly by that fucker?

"Why'd you say yes when I asked you to pretend to be my fiancé?" I asked later that night. We'd already put Marigold down and had just finished devouring the grilled veggie wraps I'd thrown together for dinner. Parrish hadn't been able to stop teasing me about the "big vegetarian surprise" as he called it, and I was pretty sure I'd heard every vegetable pun in the English language.

Parrish stood up to take his dish to the sink. "I didn't. If you recall, I left a Parrish-shaped smoke outline on your front porch as gravel shot out behind my tires."

"But you came back," I reminded him, following him with my own dish. "With a Parrish-shaped gift basket full of thoughtful baby stuff and an offer of marriage."

He tried to hold back a snicker and failed. "Not exactly. The baby stuff was part of my apology for *not* agreeing to help you. But then you were all adorable and helpless and... I guess I'm a sucker for the helplessly adorable."

I slid an arm around his waist and pulled him toward me. "Tell me why. Why, after your awful experience with Payne-in-the-ass, would you ever agree to help another useless idiot get custody of a child?"

Parrish's hands landed on my chest and smoothed upward. His smile dropped as he thought before answering. "I honestly didn't do it for you, Diesel. I did it for that sweet girl in there who deserves to grow up loved. I had my parents and Uncle Beau and Aunt Marnie. There was never a moment when I didn't feel cherished and adored. I want Marigold to have that."

He stepped in closer, nudging my leg to the side so he could slide one of his between mine. Our hips brushed against each other, and I shuddered. Parrish's warm hands slid up my neck to my jaw. "Diesel, it took me about three seconds to see how much you cared about her. You can't fake the kind of panic you had when you realized she'd grabbed the coffee mug that day. Your first thought wasn't about how to downplay what had happened. You did the opposite. You blew it up into a huge example of how you weren't good enough for her. In other words, you thought she deserved the best. You wanted her in the safest hands, even if it wasn't yours. That's the kind of parent she needs."

My heart thumped in a combination rhythm of nerves at the memory of how close she'd come to getting hurt and also excitement at how much of Parrish's body was now pressed against mine.

"I can't think when you're touching me," I admitted breathlessly.

Parrish's fingertips moved lightly back down my neck,

making me feel drunk and slightly disoriented. "You fell into my trap, then. I don't want to talk."

I could have sworn we were discussing something serious. Something important.

"Ngh," I said when his hip rolled against my hard dick.

He caught his bottom lip with his top teeth and nearly caused me to toss him face-first onto the kitchen counter and tear open the back of his pants like an animal.

"And anyway," Parrish said in a teasing voice, "who cares why? As long as we're here together now. Does it really matter how it came to be?"

I shook my head and used my single remaining brain cell to reassure him I'd never be like Payne. "I promise I'll try to be worthy of you," I said in a rough croak.

His eyes widened for a split second before softening again. His smile was wide and sincere. "And that's how I know you're different."

He rolled that hip into me again, taking my breath away completely. I sucked in a curse.

I leaned down and pressed my lips to the thin skin behind his ear. I'd learned early on in our make-out sessions on the sofa that he always shivered when I brushed my lips across it.

"Not fair," he breathed. "Fighting dirty."

"Remember when you said you wanted to explore all of my tattoos with your tongue?" I suggested before sucking on his ear lobe.

"Yuh-huh."

"Well, I want to do the same to you." I pressed him back against the counter and lowered to my knees before reaching for the button on his pants.

"I don't have any ink," he said. His eyes were dazed, and

his hair was a little messy on one side from where my nose had nuzzled it into a puffy nest.

"Let's pretend," I suggested, slowly pushing his pants down to reveal another adorably bright pair of briefs. These were turquoise with orange stitching. His erection already tented the cotton pouch in the front enough to pull the elastic band out from his skin. I rubbed my cheek against it and enjoyed the ragged breath it drew from him.

I looked up and met his eyes. "I'm going to describe what I see, the imaginary tattoos on your pristine skin."

Parrish's chest rose and fell more quickly. "Can we..." He looked around, suddenly realizing the only bed in the place was in the room where the baby slept, and I realized I was going to have to get serious about building an addition on this place sooner than later.

For now, I scooped him up and brought him into the living room where I nudged the coffee table aside and threw down the sofa quilt before setting him down on it. "Better?"

He nodded and reached for me, but I pulled back so I could get undressed before touching him again. I knew if I began kissing and touching him again, I wouldn't be able to stop. Parrish watched me hungrily as I stripped down. He finally realized he still had some of his own clothes that needed removing, so he got to work pulling off his shirt. Thankfully, he left the sexy briefs on. He'd already learned how much I enjoyed removing them myself.

I started with the skin at the top of his foot. "Pholisora catullus," I murmured, dropping a light kiss. "A black one with white specks." I moved over to the delicate skin covering his ankle. "Lerodea eufala. They're nondescript but chill. I like them because they have a kind of shrug."

As I dropped kisses up the inside of his lower leg, I continued. "And right here, I'm imagining a Thorybes diversus or maybe Vanessa annabella." When I got to the meaty round shape of his calf, I met his eye. "For sure an Ornithoptera alexandrae right here. In a gorgeous bright blue."

He put his palm over his mouth, and that's when I noticed his eyes were bright with tears. I quickly moved up to find out what was wrong. After swiping my thumb under one eye to catch a rogue tear that had escaped, I asked if he was okay.

"You learned about butterflies."

I smiled down at him. "A little."

"For me," he added.

"They're important to you." I caressed the side of his face. "Which means they're important to me."

Never in my life had I felt such an intense need to make someone feel special, to make sure—without a shadow of a doubt—he knew he deserved respect and kindness. I wanted him to feel heard and desired, valued and adored. I didn't want him to experience one single moment of wondering whether or not he was cherished.

Parrish turned his face into my chest and muffled a sniff. "Sorry," he squeaked.

I ran a hand through his hair and lay back, pulling him onto my chest. "I didn't finish," I said lightly. "I was kind of looking forward to inking the inside of your thighs with my tongue."

Parrish shucked off his briefs and scrambled back until he was sprawled in the center of the quilt like a snow angel. "Continue."

I went back to kissing and nibbling my way up the inside of his legs until spending so much time on the upper part of his inner thigh, he started whimpering and begging. I nosed past his sac and licked the crease between his leg and his balls before moving to his hip and sucking up a pink bruise.

Parrish couldn't keep his legs still, and he'd finally let go of his manners and grabbed handfuls of my hair to yank my head up.

"Inside me. Want you inside me. Please."

I lunged up to kiss him on the mouth, to steal my way inside of his sweet kiss and taste him before seeking out some lube and a condom. Once I'd kissed both of us breathless, I raced across the small house like a naked intruder to grab what I needed from the bathroom.

When I got back, one hand was stroking his dick slowly and the other was reaching further down to brush fingertips against his hole. Part of me wanted to watch him play with himself, but a much stronger part of me wanted to be the one doing the playing.

I kissed him again before moving down and nudging his hands out of the way. After giving his dick a few good sucks, I moved down to kiss his hole, gently at first and then much more aggressively. Parrish made a little *meep* sound of surprise that quickly turned into a groan of pleasure. I sucked and licked and plunged my tongue into him until his body practically melted into the ground.

When I finally grabbed the lube, I glanced up at his face and almost laughed. He looked drunk. His face was flushed, and his eyes were unfocused. His lips made a little o shape, and there was a patch of beard burn on the tip of his nose.

"You're so fucking beautiful, sweetheart," I said reverently. "I can't believe I get to be here with you like this."

I thought about our new reality. For better or worse, we were *married*. Even if it was just on paper, it was a fact. Parrish Partridge was my husband.

Our eyes met and a million unspoken words passed

between us. When I finally couldn't wait any longer, I slid lubed fingers into him for a moment, rolled on the condom, and pressed inside him.

I couldn't hold back the groan of relief at being back inside of him, being back as close as possible to him both in body and spirit. I finally felt like I could be honest with him about my fears and my hopes. I finally felt like this was *real*.

"Parrish," I said, voice breaking with emotion.

"I'm here," he whispered back across the small space between us.

Our eyes locked and stayed that way as I began to stroke slowly in and out of him. He moved his hands up to clasp my shoulders, and I felt the little imprints of his fingernails as his grip tightened. I didn't want him to let go of me. Ever.

I wanted to push deeper and deeper inside of him until I settled there, safely locked in his care and gentle protection forever. He was fiercely protective when he wanted to be, and I'd felt every bit of it whenever he'd perceived a threat to me or Marigold.

Then there was the part of me that wanted to do the same to him—to lock him inside of me and protect him at all costs.

"Stay with me," I begged.

"Yes."

I wasn't sure if he realized I didn't just mean right now or even tonight. But it was enough.

I kissed him everywhere I could reach as I thrust in and out of his body. Our skin became slick where it pushed and slid together. The hair at his temples darkened as the red splotches on his neck and chest did the same.

"Want you to come," I grunted, reaching down to stroke his hard dick. I felt the precum in a slick streak down the tip and used it to smooth my hand as I pulled him toward his orgasm.

"Dee..." He threw his head back and sank his nails into my skin as his body arched up toward me. I slammed into him two or three more times as I watched him lose control and come all over himself.

"Fuck," I cried as my balls drew up. "Fuck, God, *fuck!*"

I buried my face in his damp neck as I tried to catch my breath. The heat of his body still held my dick, and I hated that I had to pull out of him. Maybe one day we could ditch the condoms and I could stay in him longer.

I pressed a kiss to his temple. "Incredible," I said softly under my breath. His head lolled to the side. He winced when I pulled out. When I got back from disposing of the condom, I snagged one of the packs of baby wipes we kept in a caddy under the sofa table.

"Handy," he said with a laugh, reaching for the package. I held it out of his reach and plucked out a few wipes to do the cleaning myself.

"I'm a full-service top," I teased.

He relaxed back onto the quilt. "Then I can be a pillow princess just this once."

"Not just this once. Always," I said as I cleaned him up gently. He watched me with an affectionate expression that made me feel good but also a little squirmy. I wasn't used to being noticed, and I wasn't comfortable with it, even though it was Parrish.

"What made you say yes?" His voice was soft and hesitant.

"Yes to what?"

"This. Me. Us."

I met his eyes and noticed how unsure he suddenly seemed. After stretching out on my side next to him, I reached out and took his hand in mine. "Saying yes to you is the easiest thing I've ever done, even if it's the most selfish too."

He searched my eyes. "No, I mean... why me? Why did you finally start letting me in? You've been so closed off in some ways, and I get the feeling you've probably been like that for a long time."

He wasn't wrong. I considered his words for a minute before answering. "I talked to Ava and the splash park crew about it. They helped remind me that you would never hurt me. You're a safe place, Parrish. And I haven't had a safe place outside of the aunts for a really long time."

I pulled his hand up and pressed a kiss to it. "And I couldn't take the chance of losing you before I really even had you. I knew you deserved better than someone who didn't at least try to be an equal partner. If I want to know all about you—which I *do*—then I have to be willing to share all about me."

My face felt like it was on fire, but I believed what I was saying. He deserved it.

Parrish smiled at me. "We're going to get custody of Marigold and live happily ever after, Diesel. I just know it."

I was glad he felt that way. I wanted to give him his happy ending more than anything in the world. But life had never worked out that way for me in the past, and I knew better than to expect it to now. All I could hope for was that when the judge declared me unfit to be Marigold's legal guardian, Parrish Partridge would be there to help pick up the pieces and put me back together.

Chapter Nineteen

Parrish

"I get it, girlie," I told Mari, wiping the last bits of oatmeal from her face and hair with a baby wipe. "You're an artist, and the world is your canvas. But here's the deal: oatmeal is not an art medium. The kitchen looks like part of a gluten-free crime scene, and so does my work shirt."

Mari grinned a drooling grin that showed off her four chiclet teeth and clapped her hands.

"Yes, you seem super remorseful. And while I know wearing clothes is seriously annoying, it's getting too chilly for Splash Park Tuesdays, so if you want Daddy to take you to see your friends at Crafty Tuesdays at the library later, you've gotta let me put your sweater on. Are we gonna do this the hard way or the easy way?"

Mari babbled out a protest and deliberately pushed her leggings onto the floor next to the changing table, then looked up at me expectantly.

I mock-gasped. "I *see*. Hard way it is, then, Missy! I'm gonna getcha!" I bent over to blow a giant raspberry on her stomach, and she giggled with delight. While she was distracted, I popped a cute sweater over her head, then repeated the move to get each of her arms in the sleeves. "Ta-da! And that's how that's done."

Out in the kitchen, I heard the back door slam as Diesel came in from feeding the animals.

"Parrish?"

"In here," I called, though honestly it was pretty self-explanatory where I was. Diesel's house was my home since it contained my two favorite people on the planet, but there was no denying it was cozy for the three of us.

A little too cozy.

Fortunately, I'd made a few calls about correcting that situation, and while nothing had panned out yet—the only house for sale in the neighborhood was the gorgeous old Victorian in back of the salvage yard that Diesel had said was way too expensive—Cameron, the same broker who'd helped us buy the Partridge Pit location was supposed to call me back that very afternoon with a lead on a couple of other houses in a lower price range.

I figured there was no rush. After all, with the final custody hearing coming up on Friday and the grand opening of the Partridge Pit flagship store the week after that, we both had bigger fish to fry.

"Hey." Diesel came up behind me, braced his hands on my waist, rested his chin on my shoulder, and grinned down at Mari, who was doing her best impression of Harry Houdini, trying to twist herself out of the sweater already. "I have a very, very important question to ask you. You ready?"

My lips wanted turn up in a smile, but I fought it valiantly. "No."

"Oh, I think you are, baby. I think you're ready."

I shook my head emphatically, and Diesel snickered like a little kid. Then he bit the side of my neck in the spot he knew would make me shiver, which was super unfair.

"Do you know, Gil Hammersmith has to force himself to make eye contact with me now because the look my giant, tattooed husband gave him the other day was *that* intimidating? If only he could see you now," I fake-complained. "Giggling at your own jokes."

I felt Diesel shake with silent laughter. "Come on. This is the last one, I promise."

"That was what you said last week. And yesterday. And earlier at breakfast." I heaved a mighty sigh, like I was not the luckiest idiot to ever be gifted a more beautiful future than he could possibly dream up, and grumbled, "Fine, then. Ask me."

"What did the chicken detective say when leaving the crime scene?"

I rolled my eyes and leaned my head back on his shoulder. "I don't know, my darling. What *did* the chicken detective say when leaving the crime scene?"

Diesel was already consumed with laughter—I could feel it in the ripple of his biceps and the puffs of air against my cheek—and his joy made me giddy. "He said... 'I suspect fowl play.'" He waited a beat. "Get it? Get it? *Fowl* play."

I couldn't help it. I gave in to the urge to laugh, not at the terrible joke, but at how freakin' great my life was. So great, it brought tears to my eyes I had to wipe away.

"In retrospect, Marigold, buying your Daddy *The Great Big Book of Dad Jokes* at Kinder-potamus was what we call a tactical error," I informed the baby, lifting her up and pressing a kiss to her cheek before she could fuss. "Wasn't it? Hmm?"

I was totally lying. The look on Diesel's face when I'd handed him the book in bed the other night and told him he'd need to work on his humor now that he was a *dad* had been worth all the many, many (who the hell knew there could be that many?) puns I'd heard since.

"I feel like Papa protests too much, doesn't he, baby girl?" Diesel brushed a hand over Marigold's riot of curls. "'Specially since we overheard him telling your uncle Beau one of those very jokes about a duck getting up at the quack of dawn."

"That... was done ironically," I sniffed. "Besides, everyone knows duck jokes are a superior form of humor to chicken jokes."

"Sure they are. Especially when you tell them. Your duck jokes are like... poultry in motion." Diesel pressed his smile to my shoulder.

"That doesn't even make *sense*," I groaned, leaning my head back against his broad chest. "No one should be allowed to be so sexy and so dorky at the same time."

"Oh, I don't know, Butterfly Boy," he said softly. "I personally think dorky guys are the sexiest. Take my husband for example."

What little bit of me hadn't already turned to goo melted into a puddle at his feet, and I turned around, keeping one hand braced on Marigold, to kiss Diesel Church just as thoroughly as he deserved.

He squeezed me tightly for a second before letting go. "You gotta get going, right?"

I nodded. "I wanna be in before nine. Colin's kiddo has a stomach bug, and if he has to stay home, I might have to drive out to the courthouse and coordinate with one of the building inspectors myself. The store opening is getting down to the crucial stages. What about you?"

"Jim Orson's coming by with his wrecker in..." Diesel flipped my wrist to look at my watch. "Twenty minutes.

Marigold and I will have to go down and let him in. You wanna duct-tape some pants on this girl before you go? Or de-oatmeal the kitchen?"

I looked down at myself in my sleeveless undershirt and slacks. "I pick the one that's less likely to ruin another work shirt."

"Yeah, you're gonna have to be more specific than that," Diesel teased, and I laughed out loud.

I wasn't sure I'd ever laughed as much as I had this week. Being with these two made me joyful and grateful every day, and I was nearly bursting with the need to tell Diesel I loved him.

Soon, I told myself.

"I pick dressing Marigold," I clarified. "So scoot. Don't forget to text me some pictures from Crafty Tuesday." As he left the room, I called out, "And let me know if you want me to pick anything up for dinner. Maybe some eggplant so we can make that veggie lasagna again."

"Sounds good."

I snagged the leggings from the floor and had just put Marigold down to finish dressing her when the doorbell rang, and I sighed. "So much for twenty minutes, huh?"

Marigold was as outraged as I was and showed this by drooling all over herself even more than she already had been.

"We've got it," I called to Diesel as I made my way to the door with the baby, clad in nothing but a diaper and half a sweater, propped on my hip. The living room was a bit of a disaster, with stacking rings strewn around the carpet from our morning playtime, and my cold coffee on the table behind the sofa where Mari couldn't reach. I kicked Diesel's boots out of the way and pulled open the door.

"Morning, Jim. You're earl—" The words died on my

lips as I spotted our caseworker. "Terry? What are you doing here?" I looked over his head at the older man and woman behind him on the little front porch. "What's going on?"

Terry hitched up his baggy pants and looked vaguely uncomfortable. He tapped the badge around his neck. "Sorry for the inconvenience, Parrish, but I'm here to do an unannounced home visit."

My jaw dropped. Was that a thing? "What the heck for?" I demanded.

"Well," he began.

The lady behind him stepped forward, elbowing him out of the way. Though she was small in stature, her stacked, blonde, call-the-manager haircut easily added another four inches to her height. "Because I will *not* allow my granddaughter to be a pawn in your charade any longer."

She pronounced "charade" in a put-on British way, despite the rest of her accent being pure East Tennessee, which predisposed me to not like her before my brain processed the rest of what she'd said.

Her granddaughter? Oh, crap. These were the Kensingtons? Here and now? While all three of us were half-dressed and Marigold was drowning in her own saliva?

I clutched the baby more firmly in my arm and held the doorknob with the opposite hand. "Diesel?" I called, slightly panicked. "Babe?"

Diesel came immediately and stood behind me, slinging a dish towel over his shoulder. "Hunt? Brenda? What's this about?" His deep, rumbling voice was as unwelcoming as I'd ever heard it.

I also finally understood how Brenda the pecky chicken had gotten her name.

Terry cleared his throat. "Mr. Church, it appears new information has come to light about your, ah... home situation."

"My home situation hasn't changed since the last time you were here," Diesel said. I felt him shift his weight behind me, and his arm wrapped around my waist. "And I was under the impression you didn't find any issues then."

"Well, no, that's true—" Terry began.

"So?" Diesel demanded.

"So that was before we found out that your boyfriend is a con man!" Brenda accused.

I felt the weight of four distinct gazes.

"Con man? Me?" I squeaked. "What?"

Diesel exhaled sharply. "You'd best watch your tongue, Ms. Kensington."

"I think you'd best watch yours, *Mr.* Church," the older gentleman said coldly. "My wife speaks the truth."

He stepped aside, and my jaw dropped at the literal, actual nightmare who appeared behind him.

"Long time, no see, Parrish."

"Payne?" I whispered, horrified. "What the..." I looked down at Marigold, who was watching me with wide eyes. "What the *flippity dippity* are you doing here?"

"Is that any way to greet your long-lost fiancé, baby?" Payne smiled his toothpaste-white smile and brushed a hand down his baby pink polo.

Diesel's hand tightened on my hip. "Parrish is not your fiancé," he growled possessively. "Or your baby."

Payne ignored him, the way he often ignored the truth. "You never responded to my Facebook message, Parrish. I have to admit, I was hurt."

"That was not a message," I whispered angrily. "It was a manifesto." I ran a soothing hand over Marigold's back and tried to control my temper. "Not sure how you expected me to respond to you spewing thousands of words about how I cost you custody of your sons when that wasn't true in the slightest."

"You don't think so?" His smile was oily and didn't reach his eyes. "I do. You manipulated me into an engagement, then withdrew your character reference when I got cold feet—"

"Me?" I squawked in protest at this bald-faced lie. "No way! You were the one who pushed for us to get engaged because you said it would help your chances of gaining custody! I just went along with it to help you."

It wasn't until a thick, tense silence fell, during which Terry winced and Payne grinned maliciously, that I realized what I'd inadvertently suggested.

"You see?" Brenda demanded. "A con man! A crook! A fiancé for hire!"

"No! Gah. That's not what I meant. I meant, I agreed to the engagement with Payne because I thought I was in love with him," I explained to Terry a little desperately. My breakfast oatmeal congealed in the center of my stomach at an alarming rate. "It wasn't fake, it was just... too fast. And ultimately wrong. But I was prepared to stick with it for the boys' sake, until he cheated on me."

Payne shook his head sadly. "I told you, Brenda, you can't believe a word he says! That's why I was so glad when you and Hunt came to see me and explained what was going on here. It seems Parrish is making a habit of interfering in good folks' custody arrangements."

I'd never been accused of anything so malicious and patently false in all my life, and where I usually couldn't keep quiet, I now found myself completely struck speechless. I stared at Payne and gaped like a fish.

I couldn't believe I'd ever found him good-looking. I couldn't believe I'd ever deluded myself into thinking I was in love with him or, even crazier, that he was in love with me. Most of all, I couldn't believe I'd wasted a single minute moping about the end of this relationship when I should have been celebrating. It was so obvious now that everything Payne did was to bolster his image—devoted single dad, loving boyfriend, savvy attorney—but there was nothing real beneath the surface. He'd only ever been selfish. He'd only ever wanted to take from me and give me nothing in return.

The man behind me was the exact opposite in every way. He'd shared his whole life with me. He'd given me love like I'd never known, even if he wasn't ready to say the words yet. And the idea that a skeleton from my past was trying to get revenge on me by jeopardizing this fine man's chances of gaining custody of Marigold made me want to cry... and possibly vomit.

Marigold pushed at my chest uncertainly, and I hefted her higher in my arms, inhaling the comforting scent of baby wipes and oatmeal as I tried not to cry.

"This is ridiculous." Diesel managed to sound bored to tears and ready to commit homicide at the same time. "I'm well aware of my husband's history, and there may be a couple facts that seem similar, but the cases are not the same at all."

"Husband?" Terry's head tilted to one side, and he looked back and forth between us. "Really?"

"As of eight days ago," Diesel confirmed, a note of pride in his voice. "You can check the records at city hall in Nashville."

"There was nothing about this in the paper." Hunt

Kensington made it sound like anything you couldn't find in *The Tennessean* couldn't be true.

"To be honest, we've been distracted by this custody case, and it felt wrong to be announcing our marriage when the rest of our family was in limbo." Diesel bent to press a kiss to Marigold's head. "We'll celebrate once we can announce our daughter's adoption at the same time. Parrish's aunt Marnie is planning some kind of thing—" Diesel poked me slightly. "What's it called, baby?"

"A Happily Ever After party," I supplied. I swallowed and forced myself out of my shocked stupor. "She and my mom created a Pinterest board of ideas, and Marnie's already working on the guest list." I gave Terry a smile and explained, "Marnie loves throwing parties, and Diesel and I are homebodies, so we told her to have at it."

Payne's eyes narrowed. "She never threw a party for our engagement."

"Duh." I rolled my eyes. "Because she never liked you." I told Terry, "To be fair, Marnie never said that at the time. It wasn't until after Payne cheated on me and broke up with me that Marnie let loose and said he was an arrogant, scheming son of a... gun, and that men like him always got their comeuppance in this life or the next. While we were together, she tried to be supportive."

"Ah," Terry said faintly. He cleared his throat again. "Well! None of this is going to be decided today, Mr. Church, and I am not the judge in this case anyway. Thank the good Lord," he added under his breath. "For right now, I have to do my due diligence and conduct a home inspection because of a complaint we received."

"From us," Brenda said unnecessarily.

Terry shot her a look, then turned back to Diesel with a sigh. "If I could come inside, it shouldn't take more than a few minutes. No one else needs to be allowed inside. In fact —" He gave Brenda another look. "No one was supposed to come with me today."

Brenda pursed her lips mulishly and folded her arms over her chest.

"Now's not a good time. Both of us have work," I protested. "And the house is messy. Diesel hasn't cleaned up from breakfast yet, and I haven't made the bed, and there's toys—"

"Oh, sweet Jesus, he admits my granddaughter is living in squalor!" Brenda exclaimed, throwing her hands up to the sky. "Hunt? Hunt, I will not allow them to steal custody of my beautiful Elizabeth's only child and let her grow up in filth."

"Beth," Diesel said quietly.

"Ex*cuse* me?" Brenda's voice was loud enough to make Marigold bury her face in my shirt.

"Not Elizabeth. Beth. Full stop. It was our grandmother's name, and Beth was proud of it. She kept it, even after she went to live with you. And I'm not stealing custody, Ms. Kensington. Beth asked me to raise her daughter, remember? She chose me. She trusted me. She wanted her baby raised the way our parents raised us, with lots of love and some dirty dishes in the sink. So if you loved Beth like you say you do, I wish you'd try to respect that choice. That way Marigold can have her grandparents in her life as well as me and Parrish." He set a hand on my shoulder.

For the first time all morning, Brenda Kensington looked uncertain. She blinked at Diesel, with his quiet dignity, then down at Marigold safe in my arms, and then she looked at me and her face firmed into resolve.

"I'm certain Beth would not want a person of dubious morals in her daughter's life."

I curled in on myself slightly at the sharp, sudden pain of those words. Suddenly, I was the dubious influence? I wasn't the slam-dunk, home-run, ace-in-the-hole, or any other sportsy analogy—I was the thing that could cost Diesel his family.

My family.

"I'm certain she wouldn't," Diesel agreed calmly. "Which is why I wish you'd thought twice before bringing Parrish's ex along with you, since he clearly has an axe to grind. No one will believe him."

Brenda frowned, but Terry didn't look convinced, and I didn't feel convinced either.

"My husband is loyal and generous," Diesel continued, "even to those who don't deserve him, and believe me when I tell you, that piece of trash right there did not deserve him." He nodded at Payne. "I'm sure if you get to know Parrish, you'll find that out for yourself."

The warmth that flooded me at Diesel's words was almost enough to burn off the cold fear that had gripped me for the last ten minutes... but not quite.

Diesel stepped back, pulling Mari and me with him, and threw the front door wide. "Come on in, Terry. Inspect as much as you like. Try not to get lost between the grand ballroom and the formal dining room."

"Oh, but—" I protested.

"Baby, we have nothing to hide," Diesel reminded me. "You're welcome to come in too, Hunt and Brenda," he told the Kensingtons. "Though you can keep your comments about my squalor to yourself. Not you," he said, stepping in front of Payne when he tried to pass the threshold. "You can go crawl back under your rock."

Payne straightened to his full height—which was, it must be said, half a foot shorter than Diesel's height. "You'll be sorry, mark my words. Parrish will turn on you when you least expect it. I *trusted* him, and he wasn't there when I needed him most." He shot me a sideways glance. "He ruined my life."

Diesel rolled his eyes. "You ruined your own life. Now get off my property—" He lowered his voice so only Payne and I could hear him. "—before I forget to set a good example for the baby."

"Where's Marigold's room?" I heard Brenda ask behind us.

"She doesn't have one. She's staying in a crib in the main bedroom temporarily," Terry told her as they moved in that direction. "It's definitely not ideal."

Shit. I turned to go after them to explain about our plans to move or renovate and—was there lube on the nightstand? Oh, Lord, what if we'd left the lube on the nightstand?—but Diesel stopped me with a hand on my arm. He waited until Payne had walked out to the driveway and propped himself against the door of a blue Mercedes, and then he spoke low but sure. "It's gonna be fine, Parrish. This changes nothing."

"But what if it's not fine?" I sucked in a deep breath and blew it out. "Maybe you should take my name off the adoption paperwork," I said in a rush. "It'll strengthen your case."

"It won't," he said stubbornly. "You and I are *married*."

"We could get a divorce," I blurted. "I have Merchant, Greene, and Chandler on speed dial. We could still be *together*, just not, you know legally—"

"Parrish," Diesel said firmly. "I need you to not freak out right now."

I shook my head. "Yes, no, I know. I'm not freaking out. Are you freaking out? I feel like you should be. I feel like one of us definitely should be."

"Nope," Diesel said. "I'm not freaking out at all. Do you know why?"

I shook my head again.

"Because for the first time in my life, someone showed me that there are people in the world willing to do the right thing, even when it risks their heart. Someone showed me that I was worth believing in and fighting for, and that I had what it took to raise this baby—"

I scowled. "Of course you do!"

"Uh-huh. And that amazing someone—*you*, Parrish—showed me there's every reason to believe that things will work out for the best." He winked and cupped my jaw so he could brush his thumb over my cheek. "So as long as you have faith in me—as long as you have faith in *us*—we can't lose. Team Marigold?" He ruffled the baby's hair.

"Yeah," I agreed, "Team Marigold. But what if—"

What if the judge buys Payne's story?

What if we lose custody 'cause I was an idiot who fell for Payne's lies?

How could you ever forgive me?

How could I ever forgive myself?

"No chasing 'ifs,' okay? Whatever happens, we'll deal with it, and—" A wrecker pulled down the gravel driveway and honked its horn, and Diesel rolled his eyes. "Ah, Jim's timing is impeccable as always. Can you hold the fort here for two minutes? If your ex moves his behind off his car, go open the chicken pen. I'd love to see what happens when Uncle gets at him."

"Yeah." I cracked a smile and felt my breath come a bit easier. I turned my face to press a kiss to his palm. "Good plan."

"Don't worry, baby." Diesel pulled me in to press a kiss

to my forehead, then further to press my cheek to his heart. "We've got this. You believe me?"

I nodded against his T-shirt. "I believe you."

And when he walked away, I really *did* believe that he meant every word he said—I believed that he cared about me, and I believed that he had confidence in our chances.

However, I was also determined that, as part of Team Marigold, I needed to do all I could to make up for the trouble my past had caused. I needed to make sure our team prevailed. So, I dug my phone out of my pocket and pulled up my contacts.

"Cameron," I said when the call connected. "Talk to me about that gorgeous Victorian. How fast can we move on it?"

Chapter Twenty

Diesel

I was trying not to panic. The custody hearing was supposed to start in fifteen minutes, and Parrish still wasn't here. Not only that, but I hadn't even heard from him since I'd awoken to find him gone this morning, and he hadn't answered any of my calls and texts.

When I'd stopped by the Partridge Pit, Colin told me he hadn't been in all morning, so I knew he wasn't at work either.

"Where the hell are you?" I muttered down at my silent phone.

"Bah!" Marigold called out to someone who walked past. The woman gave her a friendly smile and wave which made Mari wiggle and kick from her position in the front carrier on my chest. "Bah," she said again for good measure.

I needed Parrish here with me. I couldn't imagine where the heck he was, or what was keeping him, and I knew he had to be freaking out right now. He and I were solid, I knew that to my bones. But I was pretty sure we both also knew there was no way the judge was going to award custody to me without him, and when I heard the final decision, I needed him to help me pick up my broken pieces and make it back home. Hell, I was even worried about causing a big scene if they made me hand her over directly to the Kensingtons. Maybe I'd end up in jail. It wasn't that I had a bad temper, but how could I be expected to give this girl away to people who wouldn't love her like I did?

A fat ball of nerves lodged in my throat as I checked my phone for the millionth time and found nothing. Mari squirmed again, and I decided to do a last-minute diaper change before getting called into the courtroom. I couldn't take the risk of bringing her into the hearing in any less than perfectly cared-for conditions. Besides, I didn't want her poor butt getting a rash if by some chance she actually needed a change.

I made my way to the men's room and noticed there was no changing table. Typical. Single dads were supposed to, what? Change their babies on the nasty men's room floor? Nope. Not me. I pushed down my anger and stepped back out into the hallway where the woman who'd walked past us was coming back down the hallway from wherever she'd gone.

"'Scuse me, miss. Would you mind checking to see if the ladies' room is empty? I need a changing table, and there isn't one in the men's room."

She smiled and nodded before peeking in the ladies' room. "All clear. Want me to stand guard while you change her?"

I shook my head. "I'll be super quick, and you're the only person I've seen in the last fifteen minutes in this hallway. I'm sure it's fine."

She wished me luck and continued on her way as the restroom door closed softly. I got to work at the changing table, swinging Mari out of the carrier like a pro and pulling the needed supplies from the diaper backpack Brooks and Mal had given us at the engagement party. They'd filled it with beer bottles where the baby bottles were supposed to go, and lube and condoms had overflowed the diaper and wipes section. Parrish had opened it in front of his aunt Marnie, and his face had turned pink with embarrassment.

It was one of my favorite baby items now because it reminded me of his adorable blush.

"Don't hurl yourself off this time," I warned Marigold. "I'm onto your little tricks."

She yanked the chicken passie out of her mouth, made deliberate eye contact with me, and dropped it over the edge of the changing table. Suddenly, I flashed forward to a teenaged Marigold being rebellious and turning my hair gray prematurely. Lord help us all.

"Joke's on you, little miss. I have five more where that came from," I muttered, performing the diaper change like a NASCAR pit crew. Within seconds, she was freshly diapered, dressed, and back in the front carrier as I washed my hands in front of her. She tried reaching the flowing water, but I knew the exact angle to hold my body in order to keep her from creating our very own splash park.

"What the f-freak?" a woman's voice said as the door opened.

It was a familiar voice. Ava walked into the ladies' room with wide eyes. "Diesel?" She stepped back to check the sign on the door before crinkling her forehead at me. "I guess I never asked your pronouns, and I should have."

God love that woman. "He and him. There's just no changer in the men's. Sorry."

Her eyes narrowed. "Stupid fucking small-town bull-shit," she said with more vitriol than I would have expected.

"Don't worry. We'll change that. The parent group already got one put in at the Tavern and in the bathroom at the rec center."

"It's okay, really," I said. "All done. It was more a way to keep myself distracted than anything. What are you doing here?"

I assumed she had business at the courthouse. Maybe something to do with the Beautification Corps or something.

"We're here for you, silly man."

I blinked at her. "What do you mean?"

"Your custody hearing. You didn't think we were going to let you come alone, did you?" She grinned at me. "Now, scoot. I need to pee."

Her words repeated themselves in my head as I walked out in a daze to find the previously empty hallway overflowing with familiar faces. Brooks, Mal, Paul, Ginger, Wade, Maureen, Latonya, and even Brooks's parents were there. Mrs. Johnson seemed to be handing out muffins or something from a cloth-lined basket. My aunt Dot sat on a bench crocheting calmly and gave me a happy wave when I looked at her, while Aunt Birdie looked ready to storm the courtroom herself if things didn't go my way. Even Crow and several of the Devoted Dogs MC were there, chatting happily with Wade and flirting with Ginger.

"What's going on?" I asked to the group in general.

Mal grinned wide. "It's Daughter Day. We couldn't let you celebrate on your own."

The lump in my throat threatened to suffocate me. "I'm not going to get custody," I croaked out. "She's not going to be mine."

Wade broke off from the little circle of people he was talking to and came over to squeeze my shoulder. "That's not true. You're a good father to her, and we're all here to tell that to the judge."

I gave some kind of combo head nod and grunt that was supposed to express gratitude. It must not have worked. Wade looked concerned.

"Where's Parrish?" he asked.

I shook my head but couldn't get the words out. Brooks and Mal noticed the interaction and stepped closer. "He's not here?" Brooks asked. "Where is he?"

I shrugged and glanced over to the courtroom door. Even my attorneys weren't here yet. I started to feel light-headed. "Can you call Stewie?" I said in a rough voice, handing Mal my phone. "The number's in there."

Marigold must have sensed my distress because she started trying to turn around in the carrier to face me. I unbuckled her and held her in a hug. "Shh, it's okay, baby girl. Papa's coming." But he wouldn't be Papa for long. What would I tell Parrish if I lost Marigold? That his dreams of becoming a parent had been dashed again?

I felt my face begin to tingle and my hands start to shake. Suddenly, cool fingers clasped my neck. I turned to see Ava with a concerned expression. "You okay?" she asked softly.

After shaking my head once again, I busied myself checking through the backpack for my folder. The least I could do was make sure I had all of the necessary items for the judge.

Ava brushed some lint off my jacket shoulder. "Oh, by the way, I saw a bunch of fancy lawyers at the coffee cart outside. They should be here any... oh look. There they are."

I glanced up and saw four familiar attorneys approaching. Ian Merchant was carrying a drinks carrier with an extra cup. When they approached with all smiles, Ian offered it to me. "Diesel, we heard from the clerk that they're running a few minutes behind. When we tried calling you, it went straight to voicemail."

I checked my phone again and discovered the ringer volume was all the way down. Mari had been grabbing for it earlier, so I shouldn't have been surprised. I desperately clicked through to see if I'd missed any calls from Parrish, but there was still nothing.

I tried him again. No answer.

"I don't think he's coming," I said hoarsely. "Something must have happened."

I heard a snicker from behind me and turned to see the Kensingtons' attorney. The last time I'd seen him, he'd been a smarmy jackass, trying everything to make me look like a loser if not a criminal.

I tried ignoring him.

"C'mon," the guy said. "We all knew this was going to happen. It's exactly what he did with his previous—"

I stepped forward to get in his face before remembering I was holding Marigold. Thankfully, Ian stepped between us and held out his hand to the man. "Darren, nice to see you again. I heard about Moffie's fall. I was sorry to hear about her hip. How's she doing?"

The opposing attorney looked surprised when he caught sight of Ian. "Oh, ah, fine. She'll be back racing in no time. How's Kana?"

They spoke about their wives for several minutes while one of Ian's associates tried to distract me by saying hello to Marigold. Her little forehead crinkled in confusion when he played peek-a-boo with his necktie. I appreciated the effort, but I agreed with the baby. He looked silly.

"Do you know their wives?" I asked.

The associate straightened. "Wives? Oh! No, Moffie and Kana are horses. Two-year-olds. They race on the same circuit as the Kensingtons." He lowered his voice. "Darren's been married like four times, and the last one cut out six months ago. Moffie's lasted longer than she did."

Jeez. Like I needed more reason to worry about Marigold living with these people.

"Diesel."

I turned and looked down at my aunt, whose gray head barely reached my shoulder. "Hey, Aunt Birdie. I was gonna come over and say hi. I didn't expect to see you two here today! Thought you still had a couple more days touring... Helsinki, was it? On your great European tour?"

"It was Zagreb. Helsinki was before that. And we cut our trip short soon as Ava messaged Dotty about Marigold's custody hearing today." She scowled. "Poor Dotty thought Ava must've lost her mind. 'Custody?' she said. 'Not our Diesel! No way. Surely if he were fighting for *custody* of a *baby*, we'd know about it.' But sure enough, Ava ain't the crazy one." She set her hands on her hips. "What is wrong with you, Edwin Church?"

Hearing that name, my *real* name, in a tone of voice that implied I was crazy brought me up short. Did Aunt Birdie doubt my ability to parent a child too?

"Well, I—" I cuddled Marigold closer. "I wasn't sure what else to do. Beth left her to me, and at first I took care of her for Beth's sake, but now I love her more than life, just for her own sake. She's a great kid—smart, funny, adorable."

"Bah," Marigold agreed, reaching for Birdie's hair. Birdie's face softened, and she kissed Mari's palm before scowling again.

"I'm learning to take care of her, with Parrish's help," I

assured her. "I know I don't know anything about taking care of a baby, but—"

"Uh-huh. *Parrish*," Birdie repeated. "Who, according to Ava, is somehow your *husband*?"

"Well." I winced. "Yes."

"Sweet butter biscuits, Diesel, when were you going to tell us that any of this was happening?"

"When you got back?" I shrugged. "I didn't want to ruin your vacation. It's a once-in-a-lifetime trip, after all, and—"

"And you didn't think we'd be a little more concerned about *you* than about some old, drafty cathedrals?"

Aunt Dot came scurrying over with a large rectangle of pink material she'd crocheted and held it up to Mari's back. "There we go. Sized it perfectly on the first go! I'll have this worked up for my baby in a jiffy, won't I, sweet girl?" She ran a hand over Marigold's head. "I won't upset you by holding you right now, angel, since you don't know me yet, but we're gonna have so much fun together, and—"

"Dorothy Ann," Birdie interrupted pointedly. "I was telling Diesel off for keeping us in the dark, and you're stealing my thunder, honey."

"Oh. Did you get to the part with the drafty, old cathedrals?"

"Yes."

"And the bit where we think of him as the son we never had? And how proud we are of the man he's become? And how lucky Parrish is to have him? And how we can't wait to see them kick butt at raising this baby? And how we want to support them in whatever way we can?"

Aunt Birdie sighed. "No, I hadn't gotten there yet."

"Oh." Dot shrugged and smiled saucily. "Well, it's not my fault you can't cut to the chase." She gave me a loving look. "But really, Diesel. We love you. We're family. And family's not just for barbecues and gift-giving occasions, okay? You should've told us. You should've let us support you. You aren't alone."

It was hard to speak around the giant lump in my throat, so I nodded. "Okay."

"All parties in the case of Marigold Church, please step forward," the bailiff called.

The aunts hugged me quickly, and I stepped forward to take my place, even though my nerves were eating at me. "I can't do this," I whispered to no one in particular. "I need Parrish."

Ava stepped in front of me and put her hands on my cheeks. "I'm sure Parrish will be here any minute, but you don't need him to win this case. You never did, do you hear me? You were always good enough for that little girl, with or without your husband. You're a hard worker, a business owner, a generous member of your community. You are strong and loving, and you have all the support you need to bring Marigold up to be the same. We are your family, do you understand? All of us." She gestured to the packed hallway where more of the Thicket citizens had gathered while I'd been busy wallowing in my pity party. I saw Tucker Wright and Dunn Johnson, Amos Nutter and Emmaline Proud. People I'd given eggs to, sold parts to, or somehow met or interacted with during the decade I'd lived in the Thicket.

It was overwhelming. I'd still thought of myself as the troublemaker, the scared and angry teen who'd hitched a ride to Stix's salvage yard, the loner who tried not to be noticed as much as possible. But now here they all were.

For me.

Somehow along the way, I'd become a true Thicketeer without realizing it.

Mal and Brooks came up behind Ava. "You got this," Mal said.

"Give 'em hell," Brooks added gruffly.

Ian shot me a calm, reassuring smile. "You have a strong case, Diesel. Let's go convince the judge you're Marigold's future."

I nodded and strode forward into the courtroom, almost believing his words. He was smarter and more experienced than I was, so maybe he knew more than I did about my chances.

But as soon as I looked at the raised dais where the judge sat, my stomach fell. Ian shuffled me to our table as reality came crashing down.

The bailiff stood forward to speak. "All rise. The Honorable Sarabeth Kelly presiding."

I stared at Miss Sara in the somber black robes of a family court judge.

Miss Sara, as in Parrish's landlady? The woman who knew *everything*? The woman Parrish had confided in about the sham engagement agreement, the marriage on paper only, and the horrible way I'd treated him when I'd gotten scared? God, she even knew his past with Payne's own custody situation had been real.

"Miss Sara is a judge?" I managed to squeak out under my breath.

Ian turned a concerned look at me. "Don't worry. She's more than fair. She taught my torts class at Vanderbilt years ago before she took the bench."

"But... but she runs a B&B..."

He chuckled. "That was her husband's pet project. I think she keeps it going to honor his memory, although how she manages to run it while she's also working the family court circuit, I have no idea."

I tried one more time. "She wasn't our judge at the first hearing."

He shook his head. "The judges rotate between here and a couple of other courthouses around the county. It's the luck of the draw on who's presiding on any given day."

All the blood had left my face, and my body felt completely numb. The luck of the draw had just lost me my most precious girl, the only family I had left on this earth.

"Oh," I said stupidly.

Chapter Twenty-One

Parrish

I'D HAD it all planned out. It was going to be perfect. *Perfect.* Uncle Beau had discovered the holding company that owned the old Victorian behind Diesel's place was actually owned by his friend Sammy Frye. I'd met Mr. Frye on several occasions at Beau's country club when Uncle Beau had dragged me along and forced me to pretend to know how to golf.

"We just need to drive down there and convince him to sell it to us," Beau had said to me over the phone. "We'll zip down there, take him to breakfast, and then get you back to the Thicket in plenty of time for the hearing. Just think! You'll ride in on your proverbial white horse with a brand-new home for your brand-new family. Why, it'll be fan-spankin'-tastic."

But I'd forgotten the most annoying thing about Sammy Frye.

Mrs. Frye and her "just perfect for you!" granddaughter Ophie, both of whom joined us for brunch. Ophie blushed and tittered at me, bless her heart, and Aunt Marnie asked me at full volume how my husband was. None of it mattered—Mrs. Frye spent the entire hour and a half trying to matchmake us, and Mr. Frye spent the entire hour and a half trying to get me to agree to a round of golf before discussing the house purchase.

I finally laid all my cards on the table. "Mr. Frye, I'm real sorry about this, but I have a very important court hearing to get to back in the Thicket. Would it be possible to meet you for that golf game another day? And maybe we could talk about the house then too?"

He flapped his hand and smiled. "Naw. I brought the paperwork for the house, so we can go ahead and get that out of the way as long as you're willing to pay the appraisal amount. But I'll hold you to the golf game, son. Don't you worry about that. Then maybe after that, you and Ophie can go for a sandwich over at the soda fountain."

He wasn't kidding. Elliston Place Soda Shop had been restored to its former glory, and Mr. Frye's dream of having his granddaughter meet up at the same place he'd most likely taken Mrs. Frye once upon a time was probably too good to pass up.

"Yes, sir," I said, shooting Ophie an apologetic look even though she'd seemed as oblivious as her grandparents had been. "Maybe I can bring my husband and... our daughter too."

The words were more of a wish than a reality, but I used them anyway. Aunt Marnie let out a sigh of happiness, and Uncle Beau had clapped me on the shoulder in support.

And then I signed the papers for the house right there on the restaurant table and lit out of there like my ass was on fire. There was no way I'd make it back in time unless I drove flat out.

I really wished I had my Mustang. People could say

what they liked about her, but she drove like a dream, and she was fast too.

"Take my car, sweetie," Aunt Marnie had said, handing me the keys. "You'll get there much faster than in Beau's Caddy. Besides, I just filled her up."

I sped back toward Licking Thicket in the sleek Mercedes roadster as fast as I could when suddenly the rain started chucking down in thick sheets. Within seconds, the car in front of me hit a slick patch and went sideways. I was already pumping the brakes to give myself some extra breathing room when the truck behind me plowed into me, sending Marnie's brand-new convertible into the guardrail with a sickening metal crunch.

I sat there for a few beats before scrambling for my phone to call emergency services. There was no phone. I kept looking for it frantically before remembering I'd left it in Beau's car so I wouldn't be tempted to check it while having breakfast with the Fryes. "Oh God," I breathed. "Oh God."

The image of Diesel and Marigold flashed through my mind, bringing tears to my eyes. I could have lost them. Just like that, I might not have come home to them again.

What if someone was hurt? A smooth voice came from a speaker in the vehicle. "Emergency Response. A sudden impact was detected. Do you require medical attention, Mrs. Partridge?"

"Send an ambulance," I managed to say through clattering teeth. "Someone might be hurt. At least three cars. I think... I think I'm okay, but one of them might not be." I moved to unbuckle my seat belt and get out of the car.

The rain was coming down so hard, it spattered mud everywhere as it landed. I stepped directly into a deep mud puddle and immediately lost my shoe to the muck in the ditch. I raced over to the car ahead of me that had originally hydroplaned. A woman and a preteen girl looked dazed but lucid. I helped as much as I could but was relieved when I heard the sirens.

It took ages before I finally managed to catch a ride with the tow truck. I offered the driver an obscene amount of money to drive me all the way to Licking Thicket. He couldn't, but one of his mechanics could. We had to go back toward Nashville before I could get the ride. I managed to convince the woman driving me to let me use her phone, but I couldn't get a single person on the line. I didn't know Diesel's cell number by heart, and when I finally got through to the law firm, they said the attorneys were unavailable, most likely due to being in court.

I was at the absolute end of my rope. I was covered in mud, roadside debris, some snot from the poor preteen girl who'd been scared out of her mind, and even some blood from where I'd accidentally bitten my tongue during the impact.

All I could think was, "How could I have messed up so badly?"

I'd been so focused on getting this house, like all our chances hung on this one piece of real estate, that in the end, I wasn't going to be there to fight for our girl. Stupid Payne's parting words from the other day played in my head —"Parrish will turn on you when you least expect it. I *trusted* him, and he wasn't there when I needed him most." — and I tormented myself with the idea that Diesel might think I'd abandoned him.

He'd begged me to have faith in him, in us, but I'd wanted this house as an insurance policy. I prayed that Diesel's faith in us was stronger than mine had been.

The sob came out despite all my attempts to hold it in.

"You okay, darlin'?" the mechanic asked. She was a woman about fifty years old who looked right at home in gray overalls and a rolled-up red bandana headband.

I sniffled. "I... I was supposed to do something for someone, and I messed up. I let him down."

She studied me for a minute before looking back out the windshield of the rusty old truck she drove. "Messed up by gettin' your ass kicked by a summer storm, you mean?"

"I guess. It was really important, and I missed it." I couldn't stop the tears from coming. "He deserved better than me going off on a lark to Nashville on the most important day of his life."

She looked over at me again. "You miss somebody's wedding or something?"

I shook my head and looked out the side window. "My boyfr... my *husband* is in court today trying to get custody of his niece. I was supposed to be there to help."

"Does he need the help?"

Her question stopped me in my tracks. Did he?

As she took the turn off the highway to town, I thought about Diesel's case, about everything he had to offer and how well respected he was in town and by his customers.

"Maybe not," I admitted. "But I never want him to feel alone. Ever again."

She smiled without looking over at me. "Sounds like a lucky man."

"I am," I said with a pitiful sniff. "So lucky."

She pulled up to the curb outside of the courthouse and turned to me with the same smile. "I meant *him*, darlin'. Go in there and squeeze your little family. I'm sure they'll be gladder than glad you made it home safely even if you missed the court thing."

I handed her a stack of bills from my wallet, but she

waved me off. When I hopped out, I placed the money on the seat and shot her a wink. "He'd want me to thank you for getting me here safely," I said, calling her on her earlier words. "And make sure you take care of yourself too. See you soon about the Mercedes. Thanks again."

I knew Aunt Marnie would be ten times more grateful for my safety than her car, but I still felt a gut punch of remorse that I'd been in her vehicle when the accident happened.

After waving her goodbye, I turned and ran, ignoring the loss of one of my shoes and the damp, mud-caked suit I had on. Grease and dirt lined my face, my shirt was half-untucked, and my jacket pocket had been ripped off somewhere along the way.

But I was here. Come what may, I was here to take my family home.

Chapter Twenty-Two

Diesel

THERE's something to be said about knowing the outcome of an event before it happens. You can sit back and take it all in, knowing without a shadow of a doubt that nothing you do will change anything.

"You may be seated," the bailiff said in a deep voice.

We sat. I held Marigold on my lap like a security blanket while she watched the proceedings with big eyes. Ava had volunteered to hold her for me if needed, but right now I just wanted to enjoy my final moments before having to tell her goodbye.

The blood rushed loudly in my ears, and I tried blocking out the words the attorneys were saying. It wasn't until Ian nudged me and tilted his head at Miss Sara—Judge Kelly—that I tuned back in.

"I'm sorry," I said, clearing my throat. "Can you please repeat the question?"

Her face was softer than I'd imagined. Kinder. I was sure it was never easy making a decision in a custody case, no matter how clear-cut it was.

"Mr. Church, in custody cases like these, we try to take

the biological parents' wishes into consideration. Mr. Merchant has provided us a copy of your sister's will, but he mentioned you have a letter too?"

I nodded and reached for the folder I'd brought while the Kensingtons' attorney blustered about wishes not meaning anything about the suitability of a proper legal guardian. The judge politely reminded them that they would get the opportunity to raise questions in a little while.

After I handed Beth's letter to Ian, he took it to the bailiff to hand to the judge. In the silence that followed, I heard whispers behind me. I turned to see the courtroom absolutely full of my friends and neighbors. Tucker shot me a double thumbs-up. Ryder from the Devoted Dogs MC, who was sitting next to Parrish's friend Colin, gave me a stoic nod. Even Mrs. Snowdon next door, who complained about Lloyd crowing at all hours, gave me a smile and patted her chest over her heart. I turned back to face forward before I lost my shit completely.

When they decided in the Kensingtons' favor, everyone I knew was going to be here to witness it. I couldn't decide if that was a good thing or bad thing. Maybe they'd all help keep me from doing something I'd regret.

I turned again and glanced at the door to the hallway. Still no Parrish. Something had happened to him, and I knew it had to be something big to keep him from Mari's custody hearing, so my stomach churned with nerves for him on top of the ones I already had about Marigold.

Judge Kelly put the letter down and pulled off her glasses before shooting me an empathetic glance. "I'm sorry for your loss. Regardless of what happens here today, it is clear that this sweet child and all of you have lost something important she'll never get back. Our job today is to make sure we come as close as possible to giving her the kind of life she'd lead with her biological parent."

I bit back a sigh. That sure as hell wasn't me. Her life had been money and private school, brand names and opportunity. Mine wasn't like that at all.

Sure enough, the judge began to go through everything, hearing evidence put forward by my attorneys about why I was the right choice and hearing evidence by the Kensingtons' attorney why they were the ones who should get custody. It was brutal—ten times harder than I'd anticipated—and all I wanted was the warm grip of Parrish's hand in mine reassuring me that I'd survive this. That even if I lost Mari, I wouldn't lose him too.

Judge Kelly asked me a million questions and then asked the Kensingtons just as many. My head spun with thoughts of Mari's future, my future, Parrish's future. When she finally announced she'd made a decision, I was almost grateful. It was a bit like ripping off the Band-Aid. Sure, it was going to hurt like a bitch, but it had to happen at some point, right?

I inhaled Marigold's baby shampoo smell and murmured words of love in her ear.

"I may not be your daddy the way I planned, and Parrish might not be your papa, but I will always be your uncle Diesel, you got me? And Parrish will be your uncle Parrish. Wherever you are, whenever you need us, say the word, baby girl. We will drop everything and come running, you hear me? I love you more than anything." My voice broke and the tears began to slip down. I tried blinking them away.

"I am awarding full custody of Marigold Estelle Church to Mr. Edwin Montgomery Church. Diesel, it's clear to this court that Beth's wishes were made with clear consideration as to your ability to care for her child. You have been running a profitable business for over eight years, and you have put down obvious roots in your community as evidenced by..." She riffled through a stack of papers in front of her with a smile. "These twenty-five plus character recommendations from community members and leaders. I also personally know you to be generous, dependable, and kind. You have a healthy support system that will serve you well in the years to come, parent friends who have all volunteered to help with babysitting needs, and an adequate living situation in which to raise your niece. Further, it is the court's decision that you may fully adopt Marigold at this time."

The words didn't make any sense. I tried to listen more carefully, but my brain was on the fritz.

"Diesel? One last thing." Miss Sara peered over the bench at me, her eyes calm but intent. "I'm also in receipt of these forms requesting your last name be changed to Partridge, in light of your recent marriage to Parrish Partridge? And, pursuant to that, you wish Mr. Partridge to be added to the adoption petition, and for Marigold's adoptive surname to be Partridge, as well?"

Oh. This part I understood. "Yeah. Uh... I mean... yes, Your Honor. That's correct."

Miss Sara—Judge Kelly—smiled. "I just want to be clear, you can choose to file this paperwork now, or you can wait until later." Her eyes traveled around the room hesitantly, like she was just as surprised as I was that Parrish wasn't there. "Frankly, you need never file it at all, if you'd prefer. Your qualification for adoption is not predicated on your marriage. Do you understand? You could parent Marigold all by yourself."

I nodded, because I understood the words she was

saying, even if I could barely make myself believe them. I'd won on my own. I was good enough on my own, not because of Parrish's money or his last name. I could choose whether I wanted to take this step or not.

But I'd made that choice weeks and weeks ago, back in the men's room just down the hall, even if I hadn't known it at the time.

"I could, ma'am, but I wouldn't want to. Both our lives are better with Parrish in them."

"Alright, then. So be it. Congratulations, Mr. Partridge." Judge Kelly turned to the Kensingtons. "Mr. and Mrs. Kensington. It is clear to me that you have done an admirable job in providing a secure childhood for a girl who so desperately needed it. The court thanks you for taking Beth in and raising her as your own. Hopefully you understand that it is the court's position that when possible, placement with a blood relative is preferable unless there is sufficient cause to doubt that placement. In this case, there is not. However, I do hope for everyone's sake, especially Marigold's, that you and Diesel can work out some kind of visitation agreement in order to give Marigold as many people in her life who love and care for her."

Ian Merchant's hand squeezed my forearm, and I looked over at him. His face held a guarded smile, like he was almost as shocked as I was.

"You did it," he said under his breath. "Congratulations, Daddy."

Daddy.

I put my face in Mari's hot neck and let more tears come. Could this be right? And where the hell was Parrish?

Ava's cool hand landed on the back of my neck again and squeezed. "I'm so freaking happy for you." Her voice was choked with emotion.

Brooks and Mal came up to clap me softly on the shoulder. "Miss Sara made the right decision."

I glanced over at Judge Kelly, wondering why she hadn't said anything about all of the fake plans we'd had, all the lies we'd told. She came out from around the dais and murmured something to the Kensingtons before approaching me.

"Before you ask, there was no conflict of interest for me, just because I knew Parrish. In cases like these, the goal is to place the child in the right home, and because you're Marigold's blood relative, that was always going to be you unless we'd found a compelling reason to nullify Beth's will." She smiled. "There wasn't ever a question in my mind you were the right choice for Marigold, Diesel. Reading Beth's letter cemented it for me. I've watched you since you were an angry teen who'd gotten a crappy deal. You worked hard to make something of yourself, and you never, ever stopped thinking of others along the way. Marigold is lucky to have you." She met my eye. "And so is Parrish," she added with a wink. "Speaking of which, bring yourselves by the bed-and-breakfast tomorrow. I've got butter cake with frosting and nobody to eat it. Besides, I got awful fond of the way that boy talks.

"Now," she said a little louder. "I think it would be nice to give the Kensingtons a few minutes to say goodbye to Marigold, and hopefully you can exchange contact information and set up some visits. Keep in mind, however, it's not mandatory. Just a suggestion."

"Thank you," I croaked. "Thank you so much."

She reached out to smooth a hand over Mari's dark curls. "You will come to me when you need help, do you understand? You are not in this alone."

I swallowed around a huge lump in my throat. "Yes, ma'am."

After she stepped to the side to catch up with Ian, I made my way over to the Kensingtons. "I'm sorry," I said, mostly because I wasn't sure what else to say. "Do you want to hold her for a minute?"

I could tell neither one of them wanted to say a damned word to me, but they also didn't want to give up a chance to get their hands on Mari. Right when I handed her to Brenda, the courtroom doors clattered open noisily.

"Here! I'm here! Oh my God, I'm so sorry, I—" Parrish's shout was followed by the loud clopping sound of dress shoes as two uniformed security guards chased his ass down the aisle toward me.

He stopped as he saw me handing over the baby.

"No," he whimpered. "No, please. No."

His eyes filled and he looked at me in desperation. He was covered head to toe in grime, and his hair stood out in messy chunks. His suit looked like it had been half mauled off his body, and he was missing a shoe.

"They decided," Wade said helpfully. "Miss Sara from the bed-and-breakfast was the judge. Can you believe it?"

He had no idea what he'd just done. Parrish met my eyes, and in that split second, I saw all of the horrible devastation that I'd been feeling earlier pass across his face.

"Oh God," he breathed. "I ruined everything."

I finished giving Mari to Brenda and reached for Parrish. "You ruined nothing. She's ours. Marigold's ours, baby."

"What?" He looked at me with a pale, shocked face. "What? How? What?"

I cupped his cheeks. "Are you okay? What happened?"

He shook his head. "No, you. You, what happened?"

Poor, sweet Parrish was out of it. Someone had called off the security guards, but they were still eyeing him suspiciously. I could hardly blame them. He looked like an escaped convict from a chain gang.

"We won," I said, leaning in to press my forehead to his. "We're taking home our daughter today."

"But how? Miss Sara…"

I shook my head. There was plenty of time for me to explain everything he'd missed, but I had something to say that couldn't wait a minute longer. I leaned in and pressed a long kiss to his lips. "I love you," I said against his soft mouth. "I love you so much."

When I pulled back, he looked dazed. "You do?"

I nodded. "When I didn't hear from you, I assumed the worst—"

He opened his mouth to explain, but I shut it with a finger.

I continued. "And my first thought in that moment was that you might be hurt somewhere and not know how much I loved you."

He pulled my hand down so he could speak. "Oh, God. I love you too. So much. And I…" His voice broke. "I was so afraid you'd think I'd bailed on you and Marigold."

I grinned at him. "Never. Never for one second did I think that. I knew if you weren't here, it was because you'd been in a car accident, kidnapped by bandits, or abducted by aliens."

"The first one," he admitted. "But I'm here now."

I searched his face and body for injuries. "And you're okay? Are you sure?"

A laugh burbled out of him. "Are you kidding? I have you? And you have Marigold? I'm the best I could ever be."

"Where'd you go this morning?"

He sighed and shook his head before burying his face in my chest. "Never mind. Worst decision ever."

I pulled out a nearby chair and sat down in it before pulling him onto my lap. "Tell me," I said, pushing the crazy hair out of his face.

His eyes filled again. "I bought us a house. I'm sorry."

Now it was my turn to laugh. I laughed so hard, Parrish jumped and Ava whipped her head around to see what was going on.

"You're sorry you bought us a *house?*"

"Don't wanna talk about it," he muffled into my shirt. "Stupid. I prioritized the wrong thing. I'd make a terrible parent."

I held him tightly against me while our daughter got her final hugs from my sister's adoptive parents.

"Do you know," I began, relishing in the feel of him despite the slight stench of highway and mud puddles emanating from his clothing, "someone wise once told me that you just have to decide your kid deserves the best of everything, and not be too proud to try, even if you mess up. End of."

Parrish lifted his head and glared at me. "That's different. I was talking about you when I said that."

I laughed again, and this time the edge of Parrish's mouth turned up. "Well, babe," I said, "you're officially her parent now whether you're terrible or not, so I guess we'd better keep trying."

"Wait, I am?" Parrish blinked in confusion. "*Officially* officially? You had Miss Sara put my name through, as well?"

"Of course. She even banged her gavel about it," I confirmed with a wink. "And I think that buying your child a house to grow up in is a pretty damned good way of deciding that your kid deserves the best of everything. What do you think?"

The Kensingtons interrupted us to pass Marigold back over to us. I handed her immediately to Parrish, who needed some Marigold cuddles almost as much as he needed a shower and change of clothes.

I turned back to the Kensingtons. "Thank you for everything you did for Beth. Judge Kelly was right."

Brenda's nostrils flared and her eyes refused to land on mine. "She was a good girl. We were happy to do it."

Her words surprised me, but Hunt's surprised me even more. They were filled with emotion. "Please let us be a part of her life. We don't want to lose our connection to the girls, and Marigold is all we have left."

I wanted to remind them that they still had a daughter somewhere in the world who probably wanted their love more than anything, but I didn't. That was Stella's canyon to bridge, not mine. "I will." I pulled out a business card and handed it to them. "All my info is on there."

Hunt nodded and slipped it into his wallet before they both made their way out of the courtroom. I turned back to Parrish.

"Ready to take our baby home?" I asked.

He pressed a long kiss to her curls and stood up to wrap his free arm around me. "Ready. I'd go anywhere with you, Diesel Church."

"Church?" I frowned in mock confusion. "I'm afraid you've got the wrong guy. My name is Diesel Partridge, and this is our daughter, Marigold Estelle Partridge."

Parrish's eyes widened, and I think that was the moment when it all truly hit him.

I was his. He was mine.

Marigold was ours. Forever.

He squeezed his eyes shut and pressed his forehead to my chest. "I won't forget again," he whispered.

I hugged both of them for a long time before leaning in to kiss Parrish. "I'm expecting an epic apology casserole, you know."

His eyes widened. "Apology? For being late?"

I grabbed our things and reached for his hand. "No. For telling the judge on my case that you only married me for—"

He slapped a hand over my mouth before I could say the words. "Are you frickin' crazy?" he hissed.

"My cock," I finished against his palm.

Parrish's face flushed pink.

"I'm referring to Lloyd and his fancy foot feathers," I added. "What did you think I meant?"

Epilogue

Parrish

"I KNOW we're already running late for the Gobblin', so I don't expect an answer right away, baby, I'm just saying... consider it. Okay?"

I plopped down on our bed and purposely bent over to tie my boot because Diesel was standing in front of me, all warm, and strong, and twice as sexy as any man had a right to be—especially any man wearing the ridiculous outfit he was currently wearing—and I could *feel* his big brown eyes pleading with me... which was why I refused to look up at him. Those eyes were deadly weapons—the kind that caused me to set aside all my caution and good sense—and I would not fall for them again.

Or at least not *today*.

"Parrish," Diesel had said a few weeks ago, the morning after our custody win, when we'd gone to poke around inside our rambling Victorian and found that it was not quite as move-in ready as Cameron the Realtor had suggested it was. "What if I renovated the kitchen myself so we could do everything to our own specifications? Just consider it, okay?"

He'd shown me those eyes, and my stomach had flipped, and I'd agreed enthusiastically. Anything to make my husband happy and to help him feel like this house was *ours*.

"Hey, Parrish," he'd said a week after that, when our new kitchen was in the throes of demolition and the Partridge Pit flagship location's grand opening had been a resounding success, "I'm thinking you're right about us moving the girls up to a bigger pen at the new house, but what if we put an addition on the Pullet Palace so we could handle a couple more birds? Sid Tinson, one of my customers, was telling me about these rescue chickens and... Just consider it, okay?"

But one look in those eyes and I hadn't needed to think twice. What bother was an extra chicken or two?

"Baby," he'd said the following week, when the hardwood floors had been laid in the kitchen, construction of the Chicken Chateau—complete with a nest box turret—was underway, and Marigold had started cruising around the living room in a way that suggested she'd be walking in no time, Lord help us, "what if we get a dog to kinda guard the place? One that could grow up with Mari? Jim Orson was telling me his sister's having trouble finding a home for the runt of her last litter. Just consider it, okay?"

Heck, what was there to consider when Diesel's brown eyes were so imploring and when a guard dog would be useful anyway?

Three weeks ago, when the kitchen cabinets were in, the Chicken Chateau had been wired for light, heat, and cable television—kidding, but barely—and Marigold had taken to toddling around led by Biscuit, our new three-legged beagle/Bernese mountain dog mix, Diesel had done it again. "Parrish, since we've already broken the seal on getting a pet... do you think we could get another? I wouldn't suggest it, but someone abandoned a mama cat and her kittens in a cardboard box by the splash park, and the no-kill shelter is full. Just consider it, okay?"

Poor Diesel had looked so outraged on behalf of the mama cat and her poor babies that only a heartless man could have said no, and I was not a heartless man. Especially not since Diesel Chur—that was to say, *Diesel C. Partridge*—had come into my life and shown me what it felt like to be truly loved and wanted for who I was.

Two weeks ago, when the countertops were in place and the kitchen was painted, when the Chicken Chateau had been outfitted with fresh straw bedding for the girls, and Marigold, Biscuit, and Drumstick—a brown-and-white tabby with the biggest ears and longest legs any of us had ever seen on a feline—were doing their nightly parade around the tiny living room back at the little house, my husband had come to me once more. "Parrish, I have the best costume idea for us to wear for trick-or-treat this week. Something the whole family can get into. Just consider it, okay?"

And though it had been on the tip of my tongue to say no—costumes were not my thing and never would be—when I'd seen the genuine excitement in his eyes as he said the word "family," I'd caved like a cheap card table.

Then last week, after we'd finally moved into the Victorian, gotten all Diesel's girls—including *fourteen* rescue chickens, which seemed excessive—comfortably ensconced in their chateau, and put Marigold and her fur babies to sleep in her sunshine-yellow bedroom down the hall for the first time, Diesel had caught me in a very satisfied, very breathless moment to ask me about hosting Thanksgiving in our new home with Marnie, Beau, Birdie, and Dot, his single-dad pal Wade, and Wade's baby Cora, Miss Sara, Colin from the store, Colin's husband and kid, and "a couple other folks" who wouldn't be able to travel for the holiday. "I know it's a lot, but they'd all be cool with eating tofurky, and we can make it like a potluck, so just consider it, okay?"

That time, I actually *had* stopped to consider it, because even the power of those eyes was not enough to make me impetuously agree to hosting a holiday dinner for an unknown number of people. In the end, though, I'd said yes to that too, because it turned out that the big, hulking, tattooed badass I'd married was a collector of strays. And I kinda liked that about him.

In fact, I kinda loved it.

A lot.

Still, I had my limits, and today's ask was one of them.

I finished tying my laces and stood, brushing my chest against Diesel's. Instinctively, his arms went around to steady me, and no matter how dangerous my proximity to those killer eyes was, I couldn't *not* kiss the man when he was so damn sweet.

"Diesel. Baby," I said when he finally let me go. "You know I love you."

Diesel grinned and his golden-brown hair flopped over one eye. "I do. And I love you too."

I nodded, believing it to my very core. "And you know I truly want to support you in all your endeavors—"

"I know." His breath hitched. "So, wait, does that mean we can..."

"No. It means *no*, I would not like to adopt a homeless turkey at this juncture. Maybe sometime down the line."

"Oh," he said, that one tiny syllable filled with sadness. "Ah, well... I suppose it is a lot all at once."

"It is," I agreed, relieved. "It definitely is. Remember, turkeys aren't at all like chickens. For one thing, they fly—"

"Did I not mention this one had one of his wings clipped?" Diesel grimaced. "His last owner messed up the job too, so it's permanent. He can only fly in a sad little circle."

"Oh." I blinked, then steadied my resolve. "But turkeys are annoying. I'd hate for it to chase after the girls—"

"I guess I forgot to mention he weighs seventy-four pounds, didn't I?" Diesel shook his head sadly. "Poor Wattle just... well, waddles."

The turkey was named Wattle? Of course he was.

I felt myself weakening.

"But it's probably for the best." Diesel nodded firmly and ran his hands up and down my flannel-covered arms. "After all, you might have to start traveling for work—"

"I meannnn... not really. I told you, Beau said he was perfectly happy to have me operate from the Thicket permanently, and my cousin Shelby wants the chance to do more traveling, so I'd only ever be away for a night at a time."

"—and maybe we've taken on enough projects, what with the kitchen renovation—" Diesel twisted his mouth to one side. "We're busy people."

"But the kitchen's already finished," honesty compelled me to interject. "And you did a kick-ass job of it, with help from Colin's husband and the other Devoted Dogs."

"Plus, I'm sure you're wise to remember that Thanksgiving is in two weeks," Diesel continued, "with Christmas coming just four weeks after, and our family'll get even busier. Too busy to worry about a turkey adjusting to life in the chateau."

"Yes. Exactly." I frowned. "But wait. What'll happen to the bird when the weather gets colder?"

Diesel bit his lip and shrugged, and my gaze flew to his. *Gah.*

"Okay, I changed my mind," I said to the ceiling. "Yes, we can adopt the obese, homeless, flightless turkey."

"You think?" Diesel's smile was magic—addictive, beautiful magic. "I seriously don't want to pressure you."

I knew he meant that as well as I knew anything in life. But still, I said, "I insist," because I was starting to understand that saying yes to Diesel, even when the things he suggested were crazy—heck, *especially* when the things he suggested were crazy—didn't just make *him* happy, they'd made me happier than I'd ever been in my life too.

Diesel spun me around in a circle and pressed another quick kiss to my lips. "Thanks, baby." He adjusted the straps on my overalls, then patted my chest and tossed me a wink as he walked out the bedroom door. "I'll grab Biscuit and make sure he's had his walk before we get in the car. You got Marigold?"

"Absolutely. Diaper bag is packed, and I've got her costume ready to go," I assured him. "Be down in two minutes."

But after Diesel left, I took a second to look around the quiet room before I followed him down the hall. Early afternoon sunlight poured through the double windows, turning all the trees flame colored, and beyond the tall fence that ringed our enormous yard, I could just make out the roofline of the little house by the junkyard where we used to live, which Diesel was repurposing as an office. In front of the window sat the giant wrought-iron bedframe Diesel had rescued from his own salvage yard and refurbished to fit a king-sized mattress, and on top of that was the double wedding-knot quilt his aunt Dot had sewn just for us.

Taking it all in, I smiled. The room was a perfect representation of Diesel and me. A little bit who we had been, a whole lot of who we were now. A little bit of junk other people had thrown away because they hadn't seen its value, and a whole lot of beauty stitched together by our family and friends... not to mention, the friends who'd become family.

I grabbed my straw hat off the bedpost, grinned at my own dopey reflection in the mirror, and went to find my daughter.

As I walked down the hall, I could hear her talking to her stuffed animals, which was her usual habit after waking up from her morning nap. It was safe to say Marigold had adjusted better to her being in her own room than Diesel or I had. There were still occasional nights when I felt Diesel get out of bed just so he could check on her, and even more nights when I did the same.

"Hey, girlie!" I said, pushing open her door to find her standing in her crib with her hands on the front rail.

"Pa!" she said delightedly, tiny genius that she was, and she held out her arms for me to grab her.

"'Kay, no fussing now, 'cause we're on a schedule," I said seriously, nevertheless taking a moment to inhale the sweet baby smell of her and press a dozen little kisses to her neck. "We've gotta get your pretty outfit on, so you can see Uncle Beau, okay, little chickie?"

Marigold Partridge, future Oscar nominee, had learned the importance of looking her best for her public and stayed perfectly still while I changed her diaper and put her Halloween costume on her—for the second time in two weeks.

"Only in this town," I said, picking her up and sliding the diaper bag on my shoulder, "would they have a second costume holiday halfway between Halloween and Thanksgiving. They're crazy, but we love them."

Especially because, as Red Johnson had explained to me a few weeks ago when I thought he was kidding, the whole point of the costume parade at the Gobblin' was because the kids got so disappointed when Halloween was over.

"Why only have Halloween once a year?" he'd asked me, like this was a perfectly reasonable question, and I supposed in a town where people wagered money on how fast they could run through the woods with a milk pail, it kind of was. "That's why it's called the Gobblin'. 'Cause there's goblins, like the scary things from Halloween, but also gobble gobble, like what turkeys do, *and* gobblin' like we'll all do with all the pecan pie and corn pudding and pumpkin bread the town'll cook up!" He'd rocked back and forth on his feet, clearly proud of his forebearers' ingenuity. "That there's what they call a triple entendre, Parrish."

"Wow," I'd said. "That's..."

"Sophisticated? I know," he'd said modestly. He'd patted me on the shoulder. "And just think, you're one of us now!"

The fact that this didn't trouble me in the slightest meant that I'd gone all in on this town, probably around the time I'd fallen in love with my husband.

Diesel had already gotten Biscuit in the truck by the time we got down there, so after popping Mari in her car seat, it was only five minutes until we'd parked over at the fairgrounds, gotten her decorated stroller out of the bed of Diesel's truck, put Biscuit on his leash, and entered the madness.

On one side of the entrance, a really talented band played some peppy country-pop tunes in a gazebo, while Amos Nutter and Emmaline Proud did a line dance I'd never seen before, possibly because they were making it up as they went along. Along the other side of the entrance was a seven-foot-tall wall of hay bales, and a sign draped over a gap between the bales proclaimed, "Licking Thicket Hay Maze! Enter Here. Lose yourself and find yourself again!" which was about as good a slogan for this town as any I'd ever heard. The air smelled like pumpkin and crisp fall leaves, and I felt as weightless as I'd ever felt in my life.

"You're here!" Ava rushed up in a blue-and-white-checked gingham dress. "Oh my God, those costumes get better every time I see them, I swear." She pressed a kiss to my cheek. "Farmer Parrish." She motioned for Diesel to bend down so she could kiss him too. "Diesel the cow." She knelt by Mari's carriage, and her smile widened as she ruffled the yellow feathers of Mari's chicken costume. "And my favorite Pullet Princess. Have you been keeping your daddies out of trouble?"

Paul, dressed as the Cowardly Lion to her Dorothy, came strolling up behind her, with baby Beau dressed as a scarecrow propped on his hip. "I'm so glad I'm not the only one who got conned—I mean, *convinced*," he corrected when Ava shot him a look, "to wear a costume." He smiled at me, in my overalls and plaid shirt. "You got off relatively easy, Parrish." He gave Diesel an up-and-down and shook his head. "Where the heck did you find a cow-print onesie in your size?"

"Special order," Diesel mumbled.

Paul nodded solemnly. "Nice udders."

Mal and Brooks strolled over to say hello, and Ava straightened.

"I tried to get this guy to join our costume group, but he wouldn't," she pouted, locking arms with Mal. "Mal being the Tin Man would have made the whole thing perfect. He could've even soldered his own costume!"

"Uh-huh, and I *totally* would have, Ava, honey, you know that," Mal said. "But I couldn't leave my fiancé out." He fluttered his eyelashes at Brooks adoringly, and Brooks snorted.

"You're lucky to have such a loyal future husband," Mal informed him.

Brooks grinned and draped an arm over Mal's shoulders. "I really am."

"Hey, guys." Dunn hip-checked his brother in greeting. "How's it going? Have any of you seen Tucker?"

Diesel and I exchanged a glance and shook our heads. "The three of us literally just got here."

"The five of us have been going through the maze," Ava said with a shrug. "He wasn't there."

Dunn shook his head and sighed. "Honestly. He promised me he'd come today, but I haven't seen him and he didn't answer my text. I don't know what's up with him lately."

"I saw him in his office the other day when Mari had the sniffles," I volunteered. "He seemed fine."

"Oh, sure, at *work*," Dunn said darkly. "But outside of work, he's all... weird. Do you know, he hasn't gone fishing but once in the last month?"

I looked at Diesel, who shrugged. Once sounded like more than enough for a lifetime, but I had no idea what a respectable amount of fishing was for a man like Tucker Wright.

"I think he's all doom and gloom because he's been

unlucky in love. Last guy who caught his eye was you, Parrish, and look how that turned out."

I frowned. "Well, I—"

"No, no, don't apologize." Dunn waved a hand absently. "You weren't right for him anyway."

Mal shook his head and fought a smile.

"Anyway, I think he needs a date—"

"Who needs a date, handsome?" Jenn asked, wrapping her arms around Dunn's waist from behind. "You?"

He stiffened slightly. "No. And no one. What's going on?"

"I came to see if you wanted to come walk through the carving tent with me before the judging starts." The woman somehow made this sound like a sexual invitation. "My brother Josh did a butternut squash that looks exactly like Munch's *The Scream*."

"Yeah?" Dunn widened his eyes and opened his mouth, just like the painting. "Oh my gourd!"

Diesel, Paul, Mal and I laughed out loud. Brooks and Ava shook their heads and grinned.

Jenn, however, looked annoyed. "Never mind. Honestly, Dunn Johnson, you're such an idiot."

Dunn snickered as she walked away. "It's hard to find a woman who appreciates my sense of humor in this town." He sighed. "I swear, that's why I spend so much time with—"

"Tucker," Paul said.

Dunn nodded. "Exactly."

"No, Dunn, I mean... *Tucker*." He nodded over Dunn's shoulder, and all of us turned as a unit to see Tucker Wright kissing a cute guy in skinny jeans, thick black glasses, and a heavy cardigan.

"Well, now. Looks like he's doing just fine in the dating department, Dunn," Brooks remarked.

Dunn blinked at Tucker, lip-locked with the hipster, like they were a math problem he'd gotten wrong. "Tucker! Hey, Tuck! Come over here."

Tucker's cheeks went red when he saw all of us watching him, but he gamely led the man over to our group. "Hey. How's it going. Um. Cyril Larson, these are my friends Diesel and Parrish, Ava and Paul, Mal and Brooks, and uh... Dunn."

I wasn't sure if Tucker noticed Dunn's discomfort at being a footnote at the end of the sentence.

"I've been looking for you," Dunn said abruptly. "Did you see Bernadette yet? She was a little nervous earlier, so I gave her a pep talk, but I know it would mean a lot if you gave her one too."

"Bernadette?" I mouthed at Brooks.

Brooks rolled his eyes. "Bernadette is Dunn's pet pig."

"She's not a pet," Dunn said hotly. "She's livestock, Brooks, Jesus. She just... happens to have a name."

"And her own shed, away from the other pigs," Brooks retorted. "And you named me and Tuck her guardians if anything should happen to you."

Dunn's face flushed. "As any good livestock owner would, yes."

"No," Tucker interrupted, taking the heat off Dunn. "I haven't gotten over to the pig display yet. I'm afraid Cyril isn't a fan of animals."

"Not a fan of animals," Diesel repeated slowly, like he couldn't imagine such a thing. "Really?"

"Nor of jamborees. Nor hoedowns. Nor..." Cyril darted a glance at Amos Nutter, twerking to the band's cover of "Sweet Home Alabama." "Whatever you call this."

Tucker looked crestfallen. "I'm so sorry. I thought you said you liked festivals."

"*Festivals*, Tucker. Where one can appreciate music and culture. Something more refined." Across the way, Emmaline Proud yelled, "Yee haw!" and Cyril shuddered. "Something that's *in any way* refined."

Dunn narrowed his eyes. "Hey, we are *plenty* refined! Why, not thirty feet from where you now stand, one of our local artists has carved a squash into a replica of Edvard Munch's *The Scream*."

"Really?" Tucker's eyes widened. "Oh my gourd!"

Dunn snickered, then burst into laughter. "That's *exactly* what I said!" He and Tucker shared a grin... and the rest of us grinned at the two of them grinning.

Cyril huffed. "Well. Fun as this has been, I'm afraid I have a sudden, devastating headache. I'm going to get going." He motioned toward the parking lot.

"But." Tucker shook his head and turned away from Dunn. "I could get you something. I'm a doctor, after all."

"Ah, no." Cyril shook his head. "Thank you. I think I'll feel better once I get... home."

The charged silence that fell after Cyril gave us all a final nod and walked off was broken only when Dunn forced a laugh and walked behind me to grab Tucker by the back of the neck and shake him a little. "God, what a jerk, huh? Good *riddance*, Cyril. Honestly. What kind of a name is Cyril, anyway?"

When Tucker didn't reply, he soldiered on, "What do you wanna do first, Tuck? We can see the squash. We can find ourselves in the maze. We could go sample a Haunted Pilgrim over at the Tavern's booth? It's made with pumpkin and bourbon and guaranteed to make you see ghosts! Whaddya say?"

Tucker shook his head and rubbed his forehead with the heel of his hand. "Actually," he said, pulling away from Dunn, "I think whatever Cyril had might have gotten to me too. I'm gonna go home. Y'all have a good night."

Dunn shook his head as Tucker walked off. "That poor guy. You know, he's my best friend, but he's kind of odd. I've never known him to have a crush on anyone."

Diesel frowned and opened his mouth to state the obvious, but Brooks shook his head once in the negative, and Diesel closed his mouth again.

"I don't see *you* cashing in with the ladies, Dunn Johnson," Ava said. "You've got no room to talk."

"Meh. Me and Jen are doing a mating dance, that's all. We're on again, off again, but I like her just fine. Someday we'll prob'ly get married, just like you fine folks."

Mal, Brooks, Ava, Paul, Diesel, and I exchanged mutual ping-ponging looks of disbelief at this assertion but kept quiet.

"It's different with Tuck," Dunn continued. "He wants to find a special someone, but he seems to keep striking out. He needs a batting coach, like I did in high sch—" Dunn gasped. "Oh my God! He needs a coach. *I* could be his coach."

"You?" Mal demanded.

"Well, sure. Who better? No one knows Tuck like I do."

"Yeah, but..." I began, but Brooks shook his head once again, so I shut my mouth.

"Tucker Wright is the best friend I've ever had, you know? He's kind, and funny. And he makes the best jig and pig I've ever seen. Plus, he's a good doctor too, if you're into that sort of thing. He deserves better." Dunn set his jaw determinedly. "And I'm gonna see that he gets it. Operation Get Tuck Fuc—er... you know—is gonna begin now."

He marched down the path to the parking area after Tucker.

Mal elbowed Brooks in the side. "Why didn't you stop him? Why didn't you let *us* stop him?"

"I've known Dunn since he was born," Brooks said, still watching his brother stomp away. "He's the smartest fool you'll ever meet, and he's more stubborn than a field of goats. He needs to figure this one out on his own, trust me." He wrapped his arm around Mal's waist. "Now come on, baby. I'm starving, and I'll buy you some tater tots."

Ava laughed, and she and Paul sauntered away after them.

I looked up at Diesel. "Are tater tots symbolic?" I demanded. "Like, red roses mean love, shredded potatoes mean fidelity... How's that work?"

"Around here? Oh yeah." Diesel nodded. "French fries are for first dates, but if you spring for tots, that's a sign you're *committed*." He winked. "You want me to buy you some tater tots, baby?"

"Wow." I whistled. "You sure we're ready to take it to that level?"

"I'm sure." Diesel kissed me softly. "In fact, you're the thing in this world I'm most sure of."

I grinned. "Then lead the way."

We strolled down the pathway to the Partridge Pit booth, where Uncle Beau and Aunt Marnie stood chatting with straightlaced interior designer Colin and his biker husband, Ryder—arguably the Thicket's weirdest pairing, even more so than my own—and their sweet kidlet, while a couple of our line chefs and servers prepped orders.

When Beau saw the three of us coming, he grabbed a platter of barbecue off the counter and rushed out to meet us.

"Diesel—" he began proudly.

"Hey, Uncle Beau. How are you?" Diesel asked. "Any luck replacing the convertible yet?"

Beau waved his free hand. "Not a worry. Marnie got her heart set on one of them electric luxury cars. It's on order."

"Bah!" Marigold said happily. "Bah!"

"Would you listen to that? She said Beau!" Beau grinned. "She knows me!"

"Yes, sir," Diesel agreed, like the baby hadn't been making that noise for over a month. "She sure does."

I snorted and bent down to release Mari from the carriage.

"I have a treat for you, Diesel." Beau thrust the platter at Diesel with both hands. "Try this while I hold my baby."

Diesel accepted the platter instinctively but stared down at the barbecue in dismay. "Sir, I..." He glanced at me, and I shrugged innocently. "I don't eat meat."

"'Course you don't!" Uncle Beau's mustache twitched, and he looked proud enough to bust the buttons off his suit. "That's why this here is Miracle Meat, a plant-based meat substitute, covered in Partridge Pit's all-new *vegan* sauce." He grinned. "Inspired by my nephew-in-law and added to all Partridge Pit menus as of this very weekend."

"Really?" Diesel blinked. "You did this for *me*?"

It killed me that no matter how many times I told my amazing husband he was worthy, he still found it in him to be surprised when someone else thought so too.

"Who else?" Beau demanded. He seemed confused that Diesel would ever doubt that. "Sign out front of that booth says *Partridge* Pit, doesn't it?"

"Well, yes," Diesel admitted.

"And you're a Partridge." He shrugged like it was as simple as that... because to him, it was.

Diesel swallowed hard, then nodded and popped a morsel of the barbecue in his mouth. He grinned. "It's delicious."

Uncle Beau beamed. "You're not blowin' smoke, are you? It's really good?"

"Best ever, sir," Diesel said. "I promise." Then my big, strong, tattooed husband wrapped his free arm around Uncle Beau and hugged him.

In the end, I can't tell you if Diesel meant what he said about the barbecue or if, like with Marigold saying "Beau," it was a polite fiction. In the end, it hardly mattered. When Diesel said those words, what he meant was "Thank you" and "I love you," and if Diesel Partridge and I had learned anything together, it was that sometimes a lie was the biggest truth of all.

———

Want more Licking Thicket romance? Check out more hilarious reads set in the punniest small-town in America...
Flakes (Colin and Ryder)
Fakers (Brooks and Mal)
Fools (Dunn and Tucker's story)
Turkeys (Charlton and Hunter)
Peacocks (Lane and Jay)

Letter from Lucy & May

Dear Reader,

Thank you so much for reading *Liars*! If this is your first book by one of us and you'd like to read more, we suggest you start with *Fakers*, book one in the Licking Thicket series, or Lucy's *Borrowing Blue* and May's *The Date*.

We would love it if you would take a few minutes to review *Liars* on Amazon, Goodreads, or BookBub. Reader reviews really do make a difference and we appreciate every single one of them.

We've been friends and fans of each other's work for a couple of years, so we weren't surprised when writing our first collaboration went so smoothly. We were surprised, however, that it didn't end up being a standalone novel like we planned. The town of Licking Thicket stole our hearts and now we've turned a standalone into a series! Check out the rest of the Licking Thicket series on Amazon → http://www.lucylennox.com/l/1444576

Our most recent cowritten series is set in another delightful small town and you can go here → https://readerlinks.com/l/3077980 to check out all the shenanigans in Honeybridge, Maine. And if you like to stay in the Thicket a little longer, check out our spin-off series, Champion Security here → https://readerlinks.com/l/4189908

Be sure to follow both of us on your favorite retailer site to be notified of new releases, and look for us on Facebook for sneak peeks of upcoming stories. You can also join both of us on Patreon for exclusive content and behind-the-scenes glimpses. Find Lucy here → https://readerlinks.com/l/4255454 and May here → https://readerlinks.com/l/4255455!

Feel free to sign up for our newsletters, stop by www.Lucy-Lennox.com, www.MayArcher.com, or visit Lucy's Lair and Club May on Facebook to stay in touch.

To see fun inspiration photos for this book, check out the Pinterest page for Liars.

Happy reading!
Lucy & May

More From Lucy and May

Licking Thicket

Flakes

Fakers

Liars

Fools

Turkeys

Peacocks

Champion Security

Hijacked

Hitched

Hacked

Honeybridge

Firecracker

Mr. Important

About Lucy Lennox

Lucy Lennox is the USA Today bestselling author of over fifty gay romance titles including the GoodReads Hall of Fame winner Wilde Love. Born and raised in the southeast USA, she is finally putting good use to that English Lit degree she earned before the turn of the century.

Lucy enjoys naps, pizza, and procrastinating. She stays up way too late each night reading romance because it's simply the best.

For more information and to stay updated about future releases, sales and audio news and to grab some free and bonus reads, please sign up for Lucy's author newsletter on her website at LucyLennox.com or to stay in the know, join her exciting reader group, Lucy's Lair on Facebook.

facebook.com/lucylennoxmm

instagram.com/lucylennoxmm

amazon.com/Lucy-Lennox/e/B01N0IOYPT

bookbub.com/authors/lucy-lennox

patreon.com/lucylennox

pinterest.com/lucy_lennox

Also by Lucy Lennox

Find me online → https://linktr.ee/LucyLennox

Read my books:

Made Marian Series

Forever Wilde Series

Aster Valley Series

The Billionaire Brotherhood Series

After Oscar Series (with Molly Maddox)

Twist of Fate Series (with Sloane Kennedy)

Licking Thicket Series (with May Archer)

Champion Security Series (with May Archer)

Honeybridge Series (with May Archer)

Find a complete list of my stand alone romances and novellas at www.LucyLennox.com along with audio samples, freebies, suggested reading order, and more!

About May Archer

May is an M/M author who lives in Boston. She spends her days planning vacations, mainlining diet soda, avoiding the gym, reading M/M romance, and when all other forms of procrastination fail, writing it.

Visit her website at mayarcher.com to sign up for her newsletter to hear about sales and upcoming releases, freebies and behind the scenes info and more! Or join her Facebook group, Club May!

facebook.com/may.archer.author

instagram.com/mayarcherauthor

amazon.com/May-Archer/e/B075JQVGLX

patreon.com/MayArcherRomance

bookbub.com/authors/may-archer

Also by May Archer

Find me online → https://linktr.ee/mayarcherauthor

Love in O'Leary Series

Whispering Key Series

The Sunday Brothers Series

Copper County Series

The Way Home Series

Licking Thicket Series

(cowritten with Lucy Lennox)

Champion Security Series

(cowritten with Lucy Lennox)

Honeybridge Series

(cowritten with Lucy Lennox)

For a comprehensive list of titles, audio samples, freebies, suggested reading order, and more, visit my website at www. MayArcher.com!

www.ingramcontent.com/pod-product-compliance
Lightning Source LLC
Chambersburg PA
CBHW060647190726
48289CB00002B/306